D0093441

DEAD AND BURIED

The Benjamin January Series from Barbara Hambly

A FREE MAN OF COLOR
FEVER SEASON
GRAVEYARD DUST
SOLD DOWN THE RIVER
DIE UPON A KISS
WET GRAVE
DAYS OF THE DEAD
DEAD WATER
DEAD AND BURIED *

* *available from Severn House*

DEAD AND BURIED

A Benjamin January Mystery

Barbara Hambly

This first world edition published 2010
in Great Britain and in the USA by
SEVERN HOUSE PUBLISHERS LTD of
9–15 High Street, Sutton, Surrey, England, SM1 1DF.
Trade paperback edition published
in Great Britain and the USA 2010 by
SEVERN HOUSE PUBLISHERS LTD

Copyright © 2010 by Barbara Hambly.

All rights reserved.
The moral right of the author has been asserted.

British Library Cataloguing in Publication Data

Hambly, Barbara.
Dead and Buried. – (A Benjamin January novel)
1. January, Benjamin (Fictitious character)–Fiction.
2. Free African Americans–Fiction. 3. Private
investigators–Louisiana–New Orleans–Fiction.
4. Nobility–Great Britain–Fiction. 5. New Orleans
(La.)–Social conditions–19th century–Fiction.
6. Detective and mystery stories.
I. Title II. Series
813.5'4-dc22

ISBN-13: 978-0-7278-6867-1 (cased)
ISBN-13: 978-1-84751-225-3 (trade paper)

Except where actual historical events and characters are being described for the storyline of this novel, all situations in this publication are fictitious and any resemblance to living persons is purely coincidental.

All Severn House titles are printed on acid-free paper.

Severn House Publishers support The Forest Stewardship Council [FSC], the leading international forest certification organisation. All our titles that are printed on Greenpeace-approved FSC-certified paper carry the FSC logo.

Typeset by Palimpsest Book Production Ltd.,
Grangemouth, Stirlingshire, Scotland.
Printed and bound in Great Britain by
MPG Books Ltd., Bodmin, Cornwall.

For Jack Stocker

ONE

The rule was, you played them into the cemetery with sadness, but you left grief at the side of the grave.

You'd remember them – brother or son, or just a man whose flute could follow a *chaine anglaise* . . . But the pain would go into the tomb with the coffin, dead and buried. When the funeral procession emerged from the gates of the St Louis Cemetery and crossed Rue des Ramparts to make its way back to the dead man's home, the music would be the strut of joy and pride, a gesture of happy defiance waved under Death's pinched nose.

You might have snatched our friend from out of our midst, but all you got was dirt and bones. God's got his soul, and we have the memory of his laugh.

Benjamin January had not been an intimate friend of Rameses Ramilles, but he had known the man, literally, all of Ramilles's life. Rameses's mother lived next door to the house that St-Denis Janvier had bought for Benjamin's mother when he had purchased her – a beautiful mulatto house-slave of twenty-five – from a sugar-planter with whom he did business. One of January's earliest memories in that pink-washed cottage had been his mother going to help Nannette Ramilles with the birth of her first child. She'd taken along January's younger sister Olympe to help out, though the girl was only six, and when he himself had visited – remembering to go in by way of the back yard, and thence through the French door into Albert Ramilles's bedroom, as his mother said was proper for *gens du couleur libre* now they lived in New Orleans – he hadn't been allowed to hold the squirmy bundle that was his family's newest neighbor. 'You'll just drop him,' Olympe had said smugly, and Benjamin, delivering her the sharp kick in the shin that would have been perfectly acceptable a few months before when they were both just members of the hogmeat gang on Bellefleur Plantation, had been sent home with a slap.

Now, thirty-four years later, that tiny baby was dead.

The summer of 1836 had been a hard one. Though it was now the seventh of October, heat still lay heavy over New Orleans, and as the hearse with its four black horses drew up outside the gates of the old cemetery, the stench of the tombs made Rameses's wife Liselle gag. Yesterday's rains – they sailed in from the Gulf every afternoon with clockwork regularity – had left puddles among the whitewashed brick tombs, and where this morning's shortening shadows lay, mosquitoes whined like ash whirled up in smoke.

'It's all very well for M'sieu Quennell to provide gloves and rings and armbands,' murmured Hannibal Sefton, as Rameses's professional colleagues held their instruments aside to let the pall-bearers pass. 'Not to speak of plumes on the coffin as well as on the horses, which I'm sure is a great comfort to poor Liselle . . .'

'To her mother, it is.' January's voice was dry as he adjusted the tuning of his Spanish guitar. He had never liked Rameses's mother-in-law.

'Maybe someone could suggest something extra for the musicians – Medico della Pesta masks, perhaps? Those long-nosed Venetian things? One can stuff an astonishing amount of vinegar-soaked cotton in the probosci—'

'Would you really want to see what Liselle's mother would come up with, trying to out-do Rameses's mother in that department?'

Hannibal shuddered. 'A palpable hit, *amicus meus*,' he conceded. 'The competition for Most Lugubrious Veil is already pretty frightening.' He nodded in the direction of Nannette Ramilles and her lifetime rival Denise Glasson, each swathed in enough black tulle to suffocate an army. 'Two bits says Madame Glasson faints first.'

'And take her eyes off her son?' January nodded back toward the hearse, where Felix Glasson was loudly objecting to the insistence of Beauvais Quennell, the undertaker, that he bear the center of the coffin rather than one of its forward corners. 'Never.'

'M' bes' frien', damn you!' the five-foot-two Glasson was crying, in an agony of inebriated grief. 'Bes' frien' in th' world! You jus' want to hide me – put me where nobody can see me—!'

'Would that we might.' January glanced in the direction of

Madame Glasson, who chose that moment to burst into ostentatious sobs on the shoulder of her latest husband.

Beauvais Quennell, who prided himself on the elegance of his funerals, looked about to do the same from sheer vexation. All the other pall-bearers were six-foot tall.

January played a gentle riff, huge hands that could span an octave on the piano fashioning the guitar's softer voice into a wordless commentary of regret. Hannibal's violin joined its music to the guitar's, and they moved into the cemetery, the rest of the musicians taking up the sadness of Vivaldi's concerto for the lute. The music was hardly perfect, but perfection was not the object at a funeral – unless, of course, you were Beauvais Quennell. Rather, that every man who had played with Rameses at countless Carnival balls, opera performances, subscription dances and private entertainments black and white – on fiddle, cornet, clarionette and guitar – should play one more time, their music bidding farewell to the light notes of his flute.

The Free Colored Militia and Burial Society of the Faubourg Tremé – the 'back of town' where the *gens du couleur libres* lived – gathered to see off its own.

As they paced along the cemetery wall toward the rear section where the tombs of the free colored were relegated, January glanced back along the line of mourners. They filed among the close-crowded tombs like a sable river: the Faubourg Tremé Free Colored Militia and Burial Society was one of the largest of the free colored burial societies in New Orleans. Its balls and parties were among the best attended by the town's *sang mêlées*: though Rameses and his young wife had lived in a single rented room behind LaForge's Grocery, everyone in the back of the French Town had known him. The lovely *placées*, whose cottages lined Rue des Ramparts and the streets nearby, had danced to his music a thousand times, first as girls in dancing classes and then at the Blue Ribbon Balls with their wealthy white protectors. The clerks and artisans, many of whom were the offspring of such left-handed matches a generation or two before, had grown up with him, either shaking their heads at his decision to disobey his tailor father and become a musician, or secretly wishing they shared his courage. Even those *libres* who, like January's mother, had invested in property or slaves and grown wealthy, had had a smile for the young musician when they'd encountered him in the French Town's narrow streets, and had grieved to hear of the fever that had struck him down.

This same community – as close-knit and snobbish as their white cousins and half-siblings among the pure-blooded Creole French – had welcomed January, when he had returned after sixteen years in Paris, though when he'd been an overgrown boy they'd mocked his African blackness and the fact that his father had been a slave. But he was a part of them, as Rameses had been a part.

Pere Eugenius waited for them beside the handsome brick FTFCMBS tomb: the only white face, other than Hannibal's, to be seen. Family tombs crowded on all sides. In his years in France January had never quite gotten used to the sight of village churchyards, where the dead were let down into the earth itself. In New Orleans, three spade-strokes would hit water. It didn't take much to wash a body out of a grave. Some of his eeriest childhood memories were of crouching on the gallery of the kitchen building behind his mother's house during the Mississippi's floods, watching long-decayed corpses bob past in the yellow water that flowed through the streets.

Madame Ramilles and Madame Glasson had practically run a race to be the first to stand next to the priest when the coffin arrived at the tomb. January was hard put not to grin when he saw how their knee-length black veils puffed in and out with their panting. Even in grief, people remained what they were . . . Maybe especially in grief. Felix Glasson, he observed, had had his way and carried the right front corner of the coffin, which was lurching like a dinghy in a gale with the mismatched heights and the rum that the young man had imbibed.

January picked out his wife from among the wives and sisters who clustered around the widow: his beautiful, bespectacled Rose. His sisters were there, too – the exquisite Dominique, daughter of his mother's protector, St-Denis Janvier, and Olympe, his full sister by that African cane-hand of whom his mother never spoke. Their mother was further back in the procession among her own particular cronies of the free colored demi-monde, clothed in the elaborate mourning she'd worn for Janvier and for her subsequent husband, the briefly-tenured Christophe Levesque. As she came into view, Hannibal whispered, 'Think she'll manage to never be in the same room as Olympe at the wake? The place will be crammed.'

'My mother is a mistress of the art of avoiding people she doesn't wish to see.'

'Two cents says she can't.'

'I wouldn't embarrass you by making you borrow it from Rose.'

Hannibal seldom had a dime. Even his recent efforts to give up drinking and to reduce his intake of opium hadn't improved his poverty much. The fiddler was currently playing for tips at the dockside taverns and the barrel-houses of the Swamp, the district around the turning-basin where American flatboatmen caroused. Many of the musicians who made up the funeral band weren't even getting that much work.

Rose and January had more than once offered their friend a room in the attic of the old house they'd bought on Rue Esplanade, but Hannibal always refused. He tutored Latin and Greek at the school Rose had opened for free colored girls, but he recognized the school wouldn't survive the rumor that he was living under its roof. The whites in town regarded Hannibal as slightly degenerate for playing as he did among the free colored musicians; though the free colored accepted him, he knew himself to be, at the end of the day, an outsider, a *blankitte*.

Today he did not, January reflected, look well. Always cadaverously thin, when they stopped playing and stood aside to let the coffin pass, his long, thin hands shook a little, and there was a faint wheeziness in the draw of his breath. For nearly a year, Hannibal had been free of the symptoms of the consumption that had stalked him like the shadow of death. But sixteen years as a surgeon in Paris had taught January that 'cures' of that disease were never reliable. At best it slept. Today was the first time January had seen his friend completely sober at the funeral of a fellow musician, but the graveyard stink, the muffled weeping, the black veils, and the nodding plumes on coffin and hearse could not have been comforting.

'*Non intres in judicio cum servo tuo, Dominie*.' Pere Eugenius's voice rang clear and hard against the walls of the surrounding tombs.

'*Libera me, Dominie, de morte aeterna in die illa tremenda, quando caeli movendi sunt et terra* . . .' From the cracks of a tomb nearby, a crawfish nearly as big as January's hand crept out and dropped into a puddle; in the dense shadows at the rear of the open slot in the FTFCMBS tomb, he could see furtive movement among the scraped tangle of a previous occupant's hair and bones.

'He was m' only frien'!' Felix Glasson's voice raised in a self-pitying wail. 'Only one who cared 'bout me!'

'Remind me to give up liquor entirely,' Hannibal whispered.

'Lord have mercy on us . . . Christ have mercy on us . . . From the gate of hell, deliver his soul . . .'

Deliver Rameses's soul, thought January, who had always had more imagination than was good for a man. *After having his body pass through the obscene indignities of death by fever, his soul deserves deliverance*. Nannette Ramilles buried her face in her hands and gave herself up to sobs; after a quick glance at her, Denise Glasson wailed, 'Help me! I am faint!' and sagged into Quennell the undertaker's arms. On the other side of the coffin, Liselle pressed her hands to her veiled lips and turned to cling to her friends. Their sons were seven and two. After the death of Albert Ramilles, six years ago, Rameses's mother, Nannette, had sold the cottage on Rue Burgundy and gone to live with her mother's family down on Bayou LaFourche. Rather than put herself under obligation to her own mother, Liselle had chosen to have her husband's body laid out for viewing in the back parlor of Beauvais Quennell's coffin-shop on Rue Douane, where strangers and sojourners spent their final night.

'*Requiem aeternam dona eis, Dominie, et lux perpetua luceat eis. Amen*.'

The pall-bearers bent, lifted the coffin to slide it into the tomb, and Felix – who had spent the interval alternately sobbing and reviving his spirits from a silver flask – staggered in the slicked mud, failed to catch his balance, and – to everyone's horror – fell headlong, still clinging stubbornly to his corner of the coffin.

It struck the wall of the Delacroix family tomb with the force of a battering-ram. The polished cherrywood split from end to end and precipitated to the muddy ground not the body of Rameses Ramilles, but the corpse of a white man with close-cropped graying red curls, a ruffled white shirt, and a bright-green silk vest that was covered with dark, dried blood.

Liselle and several others – not all of them ladies – screamed. Madame Glasson, evidently forgetting that she'd been fainting with grief moments before, seized the undertaker by the arm, jabbed a finger at the corpse, and yelled at the top of her lungs, 'Who the hell is *that*?'

Into the momentary silence that followed Hannibal said, quite quietly, 'It's Patrick Derryhick.' He stood looking down at the face of the man in the mud and weeds at his feet, his own face chalk-white as if he were a corpse himself. 'He was up at Oxford with me.'

TWO

'Well!' declared Madame Glasson, 'I *trust* the Society isn't going to pay for *any* of this, considering poor Rameses wasn't even *in* that coffin!'

M'sieu Quennell – who was on the Board of Directors of the Faubourg Tremé Free Colored Militia and Burial Society – bowed. 'The matter will be discussed at the next meeting, Madame. Now perhaps Madame would care to see to her son? He does not seem to be well.' Felix Glasson, after a bout of drunken hysteria, had retreated behind the Metoyer family tomb to be sick.

January, meanwhile, helped Hannibal lift the stranger's body on to the flat top of a nearby bench-tomb, then turned to intercept Nannette Ramilles – who looked ready to yank her long-time rival Glasson's lavishly-feathered black turban off and pull her hair. M'sieu Glasson and Granpere Ramilles were arguing in the strained low voices of men who have disagreed all their lives and are about to start shouting at the top of their lungs. 'The Watch should be here any minute,' said January quietly. He'd sent his nephew Gabriel dashing for the Cabildo within minutes of Derryhick's body hitting the mud. 'We can't all wait here. It shows no respect— '

'Respect?' hissed Nannette Ramilles. 'It is *she* –' her gesture at Denise Glasson was like hurling garbage – 'who hasn't the slightest respect for my son, for all her crocodile tears— '

'How *can* you?' Madame Glasson sagged into the arms of the nearest member of the Board of Directors as if she had been shot. 'How *can* you, after all I have been through— ?'

'All *you* have been through?'

'Mesdames, please . . .' January's wife Rose stepped between them, something January wasn't sure he'd have had the courage to do. 'Before all else, we need to consider Liselle.' She took the young widow's hand, put an arm around her shoulders. Tall, slim, and with a curious air of awkward gracefulness to her movements, Rose had begun to acquire a position of her own in the *libre* community when she'd opened her school. Though many of the wives of the free colored artisans – and many of the quadroon and octoroon demi-monde – regarded her determination to teach free girls of color the same curriculum available to boys as quixotic ('*There's* a recipe for a life of poverty,' January's mother had sneered), her good sense and dedication had won respect.

She went on, 'As the wake was to be at my house – and all the food is there already – I'm sure poor Liselle would be much more comfortable out of this sun. If you, Madame –' she nodded to Nannette Ramilles – 'and you, Madame –' to La Glasson – 'would let it be known that is where you're going, you know everyone will follow.'

She gave Liselle a gentle hug and said in a quieter voice – but not so quiet that the two mothers couldn't hear, 'You must be suffocating under that veil, darling. And there's nothing you or I can accomplish here . . .'

Liselle whispered, 'Rameses,' but allowed herself to be led away among the tombs. They were joined by Olympe, whose husband had been left behind at the January residence to look after the children and greet returning guests. For a moment it was touch and go whether anyone would follow. Everybody present seemed determined to present their version of events to the Watch and to be in on the drama first-hand.

But in truth, the cemetery was blisteringly hot and smelled as only a New Orleans cemetery can smell on a blisteringly hot October day. The promise of shade, chairs, and lemonade won out. Uncle Bichet – tiny, bespectacled, and, like January, marching with a guitar instead of his usual bull fiddle – began to play a Rossini march with an odd little African twist to it, and the other musicians took it up. With luck, reflected January, they'd get all the people out of there before the Lieutenant of the City Guard appeared.

By the time he himself returned to his house – the largest of those owned by the members of the Board – the place would be, as Hannibal had predicted, crammed to the rafters, not only with those who had been to the funeral, but also with every other member of the free colored community as well.

And all of them talking at the top of their lungs, oh joy.

He moved through the crowd, picking out those he knew the Watch would want to speak to: Beauvais Quennell, the undertaker; Medard Regnier, who was the manager of the hotel that backed on to Quennell's yard. He sent one of the older children after his sister; as a voodooienne, she knew secrets that even the insatiable gossip of the French Town couldn't fathom, but he guessed she would be of more use at the house.

Then he went out to the hearse and fetched the sheet that Quennell used to cover the coffin, to keep the expensive velvet pall clean from funeral to funeral. This he carried back to the low bench-tomb where Hannibal sat beside the body of his friend.

'Are you all right?'

The fiddler considered the question for a long moment, as if translating it from a language half-forgotten. 'I'd thought . . .' he began, then fell silent.

'Help me with this.' January spread out the sheet. Hannibal took two corners. Together they covered the corpse.

'They're going to want to know what you can tell them about him.'

Hannibal drew a deep breath, a hoarse wheeze in his scarred lungs, and let it out. 'They can jolly well write to his family for the information.' He glanced up at January, the pain in his eyes almost physical, like a man who has been beaten. 'The address is Princeton Row in Dublin.' He picked up his violin, tucked it under his arm, and followed the moving mass of mourners away toward the cemetery gate, the long crape veil on his hat floating behind him like Death's shadow in the sickly light.

'I seen folks squoze theirselves into weddins,' drawled a voice from behind the nearest tomb. 'An' I won't say I didn't invite myself to the inauguration of Andrew Jackson *and* sleep that night on the floor of the White House – leastwise that's where I woke up –' Lieutenant Abishag Shaw of the New Orleans City Watch stepped into sight and spat a line of tobacco at a cockroach the size of a mouse, which was climbing up the broken remains of the casket – 'but this's the first time I seen a man stow away for a ride in somebody else's coffin. This our friend?'

With surprising gentleness he turned back the sheet, stood looking down at the square face with its pug nose and round chin.

'According to Hannibal, his name is Patrick Derryhick.'

January moved the sable linen further back, to let Shaw take the dead man's wrist and try to move the folded arms. Having raised the body like a dropped plank from the ruined coffin to the low top of the bench-tomb, he knew already Shaw wouldn't be able to do it. 'There's still a little flex in his ankles,' he added, as Shaw reached down to feel the rigid thighs and calves.

The Lieutenant of the City Guard, an unshaven, straggly-haired back-hills Kentuckian, didn't look capable of understanding the average newspaper, but he nodded and pushed back one of the dead man's eyelids. 'Can't have been put to bed much after midnight, then. I'm assumin' the feller who paid for the box was sleepin' at the overcoat-maker's last night, rather 'n in his own parlor?'

January nodded. 'Rameses Ramilles and his wife had a single room in Marigny, behind LaForge's Grocery on Rue Burgundy. His mother lives out of town. They have two sons. M'sieu Quennell—' He bowed as the undertaker approached, and Shaw held out his hand.

'M'sieu Shaw, is it not?' The undertaker's tinted spectacles glinted like demon eyes as he inclined his head. He spoke hesitant English; the Americans who dwelled on the other side of Canal Street generally took their dead to American undertakers, and in any case they wouldn't have used the services of a black man, no matter how fair his complexion. 'We have met, sir.'

'Over that feller whose son claimed he'd been poisoned an' wanted him resurrected an' looked at, yeah.' Shaw shook Quennell's hand. 'Can't say it's a pleasure, sir, but I will say it's damn unexpected.' He turned to consider the body. 'As I recollect it, you got a little room at the back of your shop, fixed up for them as slings their hooks whilst away from home.' His rather hard gray eyes narrowed. 'Left side as you goes in through the shop—'

'You are observant, sir. That's quite true. Yes, in a port city it is often that a man will die away from his home. For that reason I keep a supply of coffins ready-made and have fitted up the room at the back with chairs and a bier draped in velvet. This I placed at the disposal of the young Madame Ramilles. There are doors behind the draperies which open into the yard, where the coffin might be put easily into the hearse.'

'Any sign them doors was broke into?'

'*En effet*, M'sieu, I did not check, though it is true that the latch is a simple one. Had I had the smallest idea— '

'Oh, Lord, yes.' Shaw spat at a crawdad that had emerged from a puddle, missing it by feet. The arthropod continued its investigatory way toward the corpse. January had already covered the body against what seemed like every fly in the state of Louisiana, but he knew it would be only minutes before ants discovered the place as well. 'That your hearse out front? There a chance we can take the dear departed back to your establishment so's the maestro here an' I –' he nodded at January – 'can have a better look at him?'

'We will not pay for it.' One of the FTFCMBS Board of Directors – a stout little coffee-seller named Gérard – bustled over, like a man who fears he is about to be swindled. 'Nor can Madame Glasson or the Ramilles family be asked to do so. I had no objection, none, when Madame Glasson insisted that poor Ramilles should have four horses, and the extra plumes, but at *ten dollars*— '

'*And* I will not pay for the gloves,' thrust in Madame Glasson, who had evidently doubled back on her tracks. 'Nor the scarves for the mourners! They were for Rameses's funeral, and now, *if* his body can be found –' she glared at Shaw as if she suspected he had stuffed Rameses's corpse into one of his pockets to spite her – 'they will be all to purchase again. How can we make the gloves, and the scarves, and the plumes, and the mourning-rings given out for this . . . this *interloper*! – how can we make those do a second time? It is ridiculous! No more could a woman wear a white gown to her second wedding.'

'If'n there's a problem with the expense of four horses,' said Shaw patiently – in English, but he'd clearly followed Madame Glasson's Gallic tirade, 'can we maybe unhitch two of 'em, to drag the poor feller back to the shop? We purely can't leave him here.'

To judge by her expression, Madame Glasson saw no reason why not, but Medard Regnier – the manager of the Hotel d'Iberville – just then broke in with, 'But I know this man.'

All heads turned. Regnier rather self-consciously lowered the sheet back into place.

'He is at the Iberville, with a party of English travelers.

It is he who came in late last night in so great a rage; who ascended the stair crying, *I will kill him, the bastard*. The servants all say that the shouting could be heard everywhere, coming from their suite.'

'What suite?' January asked.

'The Blue Suite at the back, M'sieu, which overlooks M'sieu Quennell's yard. The whole suite is rented by the young Irish Lordship, the Vicomte Foxford. But it is – *was* – M'sieu Derryhick –' he nodded respectfully down to the covered form on the tomb – 'who pays the bills.'

'Will he keep?' Shaw asked, when he and January followed Regnier out of the Quennell establishment on to Rue Douane some thirty minutes later.

January glanced at the glaring noon sky. 'Long enough.'

Only minutes had served for the chairs, candlesticks, crucifix, and plume-bedecked corner-posts to be swept away from the plain trestle-table bier in the shop's back room and for Patrick Derryhick's body to be laid out and covered with clean sheets. In this task they were assisted by old Madame Quennell – the undertaker's placée mother, who had taken her white protector's name many years ago – and Young Madame, the undertaker's stout, gentle wife. Even Martin Quennell, the young white clerk, had been called down from his tiny office upstairs to lend a grudging hand.

As the son of that long-dead white protector by, presumably, his legal wife, Martin had borne himself with an air of martyred noblesse oblige, and had vanished upstairs again the moment he could.

Understandable, reflected January, as he, Shaw, and Regnier turned the corner on to Rue Royale. Young Martin's position was a complete reversal of the usual French Town pattern wherein the white protector used his connections to assist his second family 'on the shady side of the street'. When the private bank of Quennell and Larouche had collapsed, it was Martin – who could have been expected to follow in his father's footsteps – who'd had to become a clerk in some other man's bank, while Beauvais, whom their father had apprenticed out to a trade, had a thriving business of his own.

If the young clerk was aware that January's gaze followed

him back up the stairs he didn't show it, and January was careful to conceal his interest.

You don't even recognize me, do you?

Now Shaw's voice called January's thoughts back from the ramifications of the Quennell family's history. 'You got a look at his hands . . .'

Two nails had been broken, as if the man had clawed futilely at something – a pillow, a cushion, a sleeved arm – in his last moments on earth.

January nodded. 'He put up a fight, all right.'

Shaw left January and Regnier at the side door of the Iberville Hotel and went around to the main entrance on Canal Street. As he followed the manager into the Iberville's service quarters, January tried to push from his heart the anger that always grated on him in situations like this. Push it away, or at least turn it into something smaller and less corrosive: vexation or bemusement. As a surgeon at the Hôtel Dieu in Paris – and later, as a musician who played for the Paris Opera and at innumerable balls in the days of the restored Bourbon kings – January had been able to walk in through the front door of any hotel in France. People might look at him twice – powerfully proportioned at six foot three, he was used to that – but certainly no one would go over to him and say, 'This's an establishment for white folks, boy.'

An establishment for white folks where all the servants were black.

'Tell me about Foxford and Derryhick,' he asked, as he and the manager wound past offices and linen-rooms toward the lobby.

'Not a great deal to tell,' replied Regnier. 'There are four in the party: the young Lord Foxford, Germanicus Stuart; Foxford's uncle, M'sieu Diogenes Stuart, who I understand is in the British Foreign Service in India; the late M'sieu Derryhick, a relation of the Stuarts, who held the purse strings; and M'sieu Droudge, the Stuart family's business manager. He it was, who would have had the entire party lodged less expensively on the fourth floor, but M'sieu Derryhick insisted on the Blue Suite, the quietest and most handsome in the hotel.'

'Servants?'

'His Lordship's valet, M'sieu Reeve, and M'sieu Diogenes

Stuart's foreign manservant.' The distaste in the manager's voice would have chilled wine at ten paces. The Regniers had owned a small sugar-plantation on San Domingue, from which they'd been driven by the great slave-revolt of '91. Medard Regnier's complexion might be the identical hue of a Hindu manservant's, but the gulf between civilized and savage echoed in his voice.

They emerged into the lobby, an immense cavern decorated in the garish American style. A yellow-painted arch opened into the gambling room, which was operating full-cock even in the dead of a hot afternoon: January had yet to encounter a situation, including a double epidemic of yellow fever and cholera, that would slow down the gambling-rooms of New Orleans. An elderly clerk was extricating himself from an irate customer's harangue about the quality of food in the dining room at one end of the counter while Shaw waited, chewing contentedly as an ox, at the other. Before the clerk could address him, however, the god Apollo entered from the street, strode to the counter, and said, 'I'm frightfully sorry to keep on at you this way, Mr Klein – it is Mr Klein, isn't it? – but has there yet been no word of Mr Derryhick?'

Not the god Apollo, January amended, regarding that straight, short nose, those beautifully shaped lips, and the shining mane of hair. *A god is never that young*.

'My dear Gerry.' An older man sidled in at his heels: tall, obese, grizzled. Deep lines gouged a face both sun-darkened and slightly yellow with the chronic jaundice of white men who have lived too long in the tropics. Sunk in puffy pillows of flesh, the black-coffee eyes had an expression both wicked and weary, a sinner grown bored of sin. 'We're in the Babylon of the Western Hemisphere, for Heaven's sake. Let the man wallow a bit in its fleshpots and spend your Aunt Elodie's money. It's what he's good at, God knows.'

His Dear Gerry opened his mouth to retort, but Lieutenant Shaw loafed over to them, spat at, and missed, the cuspidor, and pushed his sorry hat back on his straggly mane of greasy ditchwater hair. 'Beggin' your pardon, sir,' he addressed the young man. 'You wouldn't be Viscount Foxford, now, would you?'

The fat man produced a quizzing-glass from the pocket of the outermost of his several stylish waistcoats and held it up, blinking at Shaw through it with feigned amazement. 'Good Lord, it's an actual keelboatman! A bona fide Salt River Roarer . . . You must permit me to shake your hand, sir. I have seen your spiritual brethren in a dozen saloons since our arrival in this astonishing town and I confess I have been far too fearful of violence to beg the favor—'

The young man stepped quickly forward. 'Please, sir, don't pay any heed to my uncle. He doesn't mean to give offense.'

'None taken.' Shaw extended his hand. ''T'ain't often a feller can gratify the honest wishes of a fellow-creature with so little trouble. Though I do doubt,' he added, catching the older man's dark eyes with his pale ones, 'when it comes down to it, there's much *you're* too fearful of violence to go after. My name is Abishag Shaw, sir, of the New Orleans City Guard. I trust I have the pleasure of shakin' the hand of Mr Diogenes Stuart, of His Majesty's Foreign Service?'

Stuart widened his eyes in a comical double-take, but the young man Gerry said quickly, 'The City Guard? Have you heard from our friend Mr Derryhick?'

'I have,' said Shaw. 'Maybe we best go sit someplace less public? The news ain't good.'

THREE

Every window in the Blue Suite had been thrown open in a vain – and ill-advised – attempt to mitigate the tropical heat. It was a mistake Europeans generally only made once. Lord Foxford said, 'Faugh!' as he opened the door of the parlor, closely followed by Diogenes Stuart, and strode across the room to close them; the lean man hunched over papers at the parlor's desk warned peevishly, 'You'll find the heat beyond endurance if you do that, My Lord.'

'I find the stench beyond endurance.' Foxford tried to thrust aside the long, gauzy shams and became entangled in them; his struggles liberated a couple of enormous horseflies, which the lightweight veils had so far blocked from the parlor, and the insects roared in, banging noisily at the ceiling.

'Now see what you've done!' The man rose from the desk, long-limbed, stooped and elderly in a rusty black cutaway and a neck-cloth that wouldn't have looked out of place in a portrait of America's Founding Fathers. 'I've spoken to the management and sent a note complaining to the owner of that pestilential establishment.' He jerked a hand toward the window. 'No wonder people die in this city . . . Well, don't just stand there, boy,' he added, catching sight of January. 'Do something about those damnable flies! And you, Regnier –' he pronounced the Assistant Manager's name Reg-ner, as if the French invented their pronunciations out of a malicious desire to trip up English tongues – 'did I not request that we weren't to be troubled by employees of the hotel? As long as we're paying first-class prices— '

'Mr Droudge –' the Viscount extricated himself from the curtain – 'this is Lieutenant Shaw, of the New Orleans City Guard, and Mr January. They say they have news of Patrick.'

January remained in the parlor doorway when Shaw broke the news of Patrick Derryhick's death. He kept his eyes on the elder Stuart's face, and noted the flattening of the lips, the way the chin came forward and the eyes narrowed for one instant before the man put on a more appropriate expression of shock to match Lord Foxford's anguished cry of 'Good God!'. Foxford pressed a hand to his mouth.

Stuart tilted his head, asked, 'Are you sure it's he?'

'Fairly.' Shaw brought from the pockets of his frayed and greasy coat the things they'd removed from the body: silver card-case, hip flask, penknife. A duelling pistol – Manton's, the best in England, and loaded. A woman's pink silk garter. A memorandum-book bound in expensive Morocco-leather, and a handful of gambling vowels. These he laid on the gold-mounted black marble of the parlor tabletop, and with a repetitive deliberation very unlike him, he began to take all three men through discursive explanations and queries, while January and the hotel manager stepped very quietly back through the parlor door and into the hall.

'Which room first?' Regnier held out his keys. All four chambers communicated not only within the suite, but with the corridor alongside.

'Stuart's. Then Droudge's.'

January knew Shaw capable of spinning out explanations and reiterations until doomsday, particularly with men who considered themselves smarter than he was. Had it not been for Hannibal's silent grief at seeing the face of his old friend, the matter would have been of only academic interest to him: he could not demand of one of the trio of Englishmen what had been done with Rameses Ramilles's body until he knew which to accuse of the greater crime. Beyond that, he really did not care.

But in the four years he had known the fiddler, he had never heard Hannibal speak of the friends he had left behind. He knew he had had them: for all his wastrel ways, Hannibal was a loyal friend and had saved January's life more than once, at the risk of his own.

According to Rose, the fiddler had begun playing in the saloons and ballrooms of New Orleans some five years ago, while he – January – was still in Paris, still married to the beautiful Berber woman whose death of the cholera had driven him back to the city of his childhood – the city he had hoped never to live in again. Hannibal himself never mentioned home or family, or how he had arrived in New Orleans, though when he was drunk his speech would become very Irish. He played like an opium-soused angel, and January knew enough about music to recognize where his violin had come from and the probable cost of such an instrument. His boots, too, scarred and stained with the gutter-mud of God knew which cities, had been made by Hoby of St James.

And Patrick Derryhick had been his friend.

So he searched Diogenes Stuart's room with efficient thoroughness, noting the ceremonial dagger and the large collection of pocket flasks wrought in the gold-work of India, Turkey, and Persia. Volumes of feverish pornography were tucked away beneath his shirts and drawers in the armoire; the garments gave off the characteristic spicy reek of the Orient, even after months of travel. On the desk, a locked silver box, shaken, gave off the dry rattle of papers inside.

The room of the business manager, Caius Droudge – separated from the rest of the suite by Diogenes Stuart's trunk-crammed dressing-room – was even less communicative: the chamber of a man who prides himself on the smallness of his life. The shipping news lay folded on the bureau, along with a Bible and an almanac. Ink pot, seal, stationery, pens. A businesslike portable strongbox beneath the bed, iron and manufactured in London. A memorandum-book containing long columns of numbers in the back, lists in the front: the number of trunks and portmanteaux; the date of departure from Queenstown, of arrival – Monday, 3 October – in New Orleans. Furious calculations of the cost of the less expensive chambers upstairs covered pages, as did the relative rates of dollars to pounds from the different banks in the city, and of dollars to dollars between the various private banks. Comparison of dinner prices at the hotel, at the Verrandah Hotel nearby, and at several cafés along Rue Royale. A meticulous tallying-up of how many shirts comprised his own meagre luggage, and the difference in cost between the hotel's laundress and Lucille Chabot, whom January knew did his mother's laundry.

A half-written letter to Mayor Prieur demanded to know why an establishment where deceased and rotting bodies were stored was permitted to continue within fifty feet of a respectable hotel.

Nothing seemed out of place.

The first thing that caught January's attention when he softly entered the Viscount Foxford's room was that the rug was missing. In the former two chambers, finely-woven straw-mats had made ovals of pale yellow beside the beds, smooth to the feet in the mornings and bright against the scrubbed reddish cypress-wood of the floors. In this, the handsomest room of the four, one would expect accommodation at least as good, in keeping with the gilt on the mirror-frame and the size of the armoire . . .

Yet there was none. Turning back the counterpane, January noted that one of the bed pillows was fresh, the sham rigid with starch, the other nearly so. The sheets also bore the appearance of having been slept in only once, and that briefly, the folds in most places still bright. Yet – he had heard his mother lecture her servant on the subject – beneath the counterpane, the bed had been clumsily made, with nothing of the taut care with which the chambermaids had renewed those in the other rooms. The dressing table contained a set of sterling silver 'gentlemen's furnishings' – brush, comb, toothbrush and powder, clothes brushes, and another bejewelled ceremonial dagger.

He tiptoed to the door that communicated with the parlor. Shaw was saying, 'Now, are you tellin' me this Aunt Elodie wa'n't allowed to leave her money where she chose?'

'My dear Abishag – may I call you Abishag? Such an *American* name! – when one reaches the more elevated levels of good society – in Britain, at least – the disposal of one's own property, however acquired, becomes very much the business of The Family . . .'

They sounded settled for some time yet. Soft-footed for so large a man, January knelt to look beneath the bed. As he put his face close to the floor he smelled, in the still pocket of air trapped by the hanging counterpane, the whiff of blood, a smell unmistakable after years of working in the night clinic of Paris's Hôtel Dieu. There was something under there that looked like a man's watch, but he knew Shaw would find it. Knew, too, that the item's position would communicate information to the policeman if left *in situ*. So, curious though he was, he lowered the counterpane again and crossed the bedroom to the door that opened into another dressing-room, and thence into the room of the murdered man.

As January passed between the neat shelves and piled luggage, he wondered how the travelers had come to the arrangement that they had. The two bedrooms adjoining the parlor were the handsome ones, clearly intended for the more important members of the party. Those on either end of the suite, though nearly as elegant in their appointments, were smaller and distinctly poky.

Had young Foxford requested Derryhick – who was, after all, paying for the suite – as a neighbor? Had Derryhick loathed – or mistrusted – both Droudge and Stuart to the extent that he'd choose to take a smaller room rather than lodge in one that either had access to?

Curious.

Derryhick's room boasted the same oval of braided straw beside the bed that had graced Droudge's and Stuart's. His pillows and sheets, like theirs, though clearly smoothed and readjusted by expert chambermaids, had been slept on several nights. Along with the usual brushes and toiletries there was another Indian dagger on the bureau, and a third tucked in the handkerchief drawer, beside a box of bullets for a pistol.

A curiously well-armed company. On the other hand, when January had lived in France, every single one of his friends there had been convinced that America was a place where one had to fight Indians every morning just to get to the outhouse.

He crossed back through the dressing room and the Viscount's room and out to where Regnier waited in the hall. 'Servants?'

'Separate chambers on the fourth floor,' the manager replied. January guessed that 'fourth floor' was the polite way of saying 'attic'. 'M'sieu Reeve refused to share a room with "Jones", as they call him, and who can blame the man? M'sieu Droudge,' he added drily, 'was all for dismissing Reeve for his refusal, which would cost the party an extra fifty cents per day, or alternately taking the extra room charge from his salary, but M'sieu Derryhick insisted on paying. M'sieu Reeve looked after him as well as His Lordship.'

'Do you happen to know where they were last night?'

'I'll find out,' said Regnier. 'I expect they were in the day room up there, playing cards. It's where the bells ring for the rooms.'

Up under the roof must be a jolly place to be stationed, at the end of a suffocating day. 'Who heard the quarrel?'

'Brun – the night-porter – and a woman named Liffard, a maid in one of the rooms above this one. Brun was on this floor but not close enough to hear more than the sound of shouting; the Liffard girl also heard only the raised voices. I myself was in the lobby when Mr Derryhick came through and went up the stairs two at a time. He was clearly beside himself with anger.'

'Any idea where he'd been?'

Regnier shook his head. 'He and M'sieu le Vicomte had been out together earlier that evening, at the gambling-halls along Rue Royale: Davis's, Hoban's, Lafrènniére's. I understand that M'sieu Derryhick could also be found on occasion at Madame Cléopâtre's on the Court of the Tritons –' he named one of the most elegant whorehouses in the American section of town – 'or the Countess Mazzini's on Prytania Street.'

'Could he indeed?' January walked back into the Viscount's room. From the parlor he heard the business-manager's sharp, nasal tones, complaining about something, broken now and then by Shaw, expertly leading him on.

'And was M'sieu le Vicomte in the hotel when M'sieu Derryhick returned in such a rage?'

'Of a certainty. At least his key was gone from the board, as was that of M'sieu Droudge. The uncle was out, I believe . . .'

'But the rooms connect,' said January. 'And the keys are all the same, are they not?'

'Oh, quite. Any one of them could have borrowed another's key. One can only guess, at a hotel.'

While at Quennell's shop, January had ascertained the dimensions of the courtyard that lay behind the back parlor and the fact that all nine of the Blue Suite's windows overlooked the roof of the stable where the undertaker's four black carriage-horses were housed. Looking up from the undertaker's yard – the gate of which bolted from the inside, but bore no lock – he had thought that there might have been an alley between the hotel's rear wall and the wall of the stable, but looking down from the window he saw that this was not the case. The stable backed directly against the hotel. A body lowered from the window of any of the Blue Suite's rooms via a sheet would come to rest directly on the sloping roof, and even the most casual glance through the windows would serve to show the location of the undertaker's handcart at one side of the yard.

When January stepped unobtrusively back into the parlor, the vulturine Mr Droudge was still carping. 'I can't say I'm the slightest bit surprised. Since our arrival at the beginning of the week the man has been forever in and out of gaming parlors. Of a piece with his behavior all of his life, of course: pitched out of one college for God knows what excesses, and bringing ruin upon everything he touched. *And* drawing others into his way of life.' He shook a skinny finger at Shaw, but his glance cut sidelong at the Viscount, standing again beside the windows, gazing out into the feverish sunlight.

Impatiently, Foxford said, 'Sir, Patrick never—'

'Are you saying your cousin couldn't wait to turn libertine on his own?' demanded Mr Stuart mournfully. 'Thank you, dear boy, thank you very much.'

'Uncle, you know I didn't mean that—'

'What happened to my son was Derryhick's doing.' The elderly diplomat's eyes glittered dangerously. 'Left to his own devices, Theo would never have come to the end that he did. Nor would—'

'Is he over there now, Mr Shaw?' Foxford broke in deliberately on his uncle's words. 'That is – you said he had been taken to an undertaker's . . .'

'He's over there.' Shaw glanced at January, then began to gather up the small impedimenta from the table with swift deftness that belied his earlier deliberation. 'Mr Quennell lays 'em out right pretty, an' for a fair price.'

'That remains to be seen.' Droudge sniffed and rose to fetch his extremely old-fashioned hat. 'My understanding has been that everything in the French Town costs between ten and forty percent more than the identical goods and services available in the American sector – *identical* – simply for the "cach-et", as they call it –' he mispronounced 'cachet' – 'of being French! And this Mr Quennell had better not believe that, just because you deposited his body there temporarily, I will not have Mr Derryhick's remains moved to another establishment if I find one less exorbitant. If you'll excuse me, gentlemen – though I suppose it's too much to expect that Mr Derryhick will have left so much as twenty shillings in the desk . . .'

''Scuse *me*,' said Shaw, intercepting the business manager on his way to the connecting door without the slightest appearance of hurry. 'But 'fore we goes, the Maestro here –' he nodded to January – 'an' I would like to have a look at Mr Derryhick's room.'

'Whatever for?' Stuart made a move as if to place himself in the doorway that opened from the parlor into his chamber, then stopped himself. 'It's clear as daylight what happened. Poor Patrick returned to his room and encountered a thief there.'

'Nonsense,' snapped Droudge. 'He quarreled with the man – I heard him. At least, I heard someone on the floor shouting—'

'An' you was here?'

'I was in my room – *trying* to get some sleep.' Droudge glared at the other two with weak, pale-blue eyes. 'I sleep most poorly, Lieutenant, and I must admit that with cotton wool stuffed into my ears – an habitual precaution in places of public resort – it wasn't easy to tell who was making such a ruckus, or where.'

'Patrick would quarrel with any stranger he found in his room!' added Stuart peevishly. 'He was a damned shanty Irishman and would quarrel with anyone when in his cups.'

'Uncle, that isn't tr—'

'Don't you contradict me, Gerry, you know it is. And furthermore, you know it's he who spoiled my poor son's temper with drink and God knows what else, until he'd react to the smallest provocation in the same way.'

'That's as may be,' remarked Shaw. ''Ceptin' that wouldn't explain why he went dashin' up the stairs yelling "I'm gonna kill that bastard".'

'Good Lord, I assume he'd just learned about another of old Droudge's damned "economies," like his attempt to sell my poor valet—!'

'Really, sir!' protested the business manager. 'A good Negro brings fifteen hundred dollars in this town, and I resent your implication that Mr Derryhick would use such language to me.'

'So he comes up here half-drunk, in a deuce of a temper, finds old Droudge asleep and some total stranger in his room . . .'

'Then if'n that stranger left his callin' card on the floor, accidental like, now's the time to find it.'

Droudge led Shaw to the connecting door of the Viscount's

room, glancing at him sidelong as if he fully expected him to scoop up any loose money or stray gold stickpins in the process. As they passed through into Derryhick's room, January heard him say, 'I trust you will give me a proper receipt . . .'

Behind him in the parlor, January heard the almost soundless rustle of Mr Stuart stepping back – light-moving for all his bulk – to catch the Viscount by the arm. Droudge's exclamation, 'Good Lord! What on earth—?' covered whatever soft-voiced words passed between uncle and nephew, but the Viscount cried, 'Stop it, for God's sake! Is that all you can think about?'

'It's what you should be thinking about, my dear boy. And it's no more than justice. He killed your father, and he killed my son, not to speak of robbing you into the bargain for all these years. So I think he owed us something.'

The young man said quietly, 'You are despicable,' and the next moment the corridor door slammed.

FOUR

Rose asked, 'What are they doing in New Orleans in the first place?'

January handed her a cup of tafia – cheap rum cut with lemonade – and perched on the gallery railing of what had once been cook's quarters above the kitchen. The two rooms that opened off the gallery behind them – one of them Rose's chemical laboratory, the other scoured and fitted with makeshift chairs and school desks – were the only two in the house not currently crowded with neighbors, friends, and semi-strangers, talking quietly, uneasily, angrily.

Hannibal had been quite right to wonder if two women who detested each other as did January's mother and sister Olympe could manage to avoid one another at the wake until morning.

At least the food was plentiful and good.

'It's a thought that's crossed my mind as well, my nightingale. Why would anyone in their right mind come to New Orleans at this time of year?'

After the burial, under ordinary circumstances the procession would return – joyful, dancing, waving handkerchiefs and scarves like flags – to the home of the dead man's family, or in this case to the home of the friend best able to host the night-long wake. Death was not invited to the party. January frequently suspected that his recent election as the newest member of the FTFCMBS board had as much to do with the size of the ramshackle Spanish house he and Rose had bought on the Rue Esplanade as with his willingness to be of service.

The house had sprung from Rose's ambition – realized last winter – to re-establish her school, which had been destroyed a few years previously by a combination of the cholera epidemic and the enmity of a socially prominent French Creole matron.* But in this slack infernal tail-end of the hot season, before the heat broke and the wealthy returned to town, January was glad

* *Fever Season*

he could open his doors for those who lived in rooms, for those whose families had been destroyed in the cholera or had left the town for good . . . for friends who otherwise might have had no one to give, on their behalf, a final party whose guest of honor could not attend.

There had been a time – not long ago – when he had numbered himself among them. In those days it had been good to know that he could count on his friends to see him remembered and wept for, one last time.

His mother certainly wouldn't have invited that many people into *her* house.

'According to Shaw,' January went on, his eyes on the crowded house gallery opposite, 'Patrick Derryhick intended to invest in cotton plantations upriver, in partnership with the young Viscount Foxford. Derryhick was a second-cousin of the family, completely impoverished until the wealthy aunt, whose private fortune the Stuarts had been counting on to retrieve the family acres from mortgage, left her money *not* to Germanicus Stuart, the twelfth Viscount Foxford, but to Derryhick instead.'

'Ouch.'

'I'm sure that's what the entire senior branch of the family said after the reading of Aunt Elodie's will. The Foxford lands in County Mayo cannot be sold because of the entail, but for three generations there has been virtually nothing to support them with.'

In the yard below them, children chased each other wildly in sticky-handed excitement. Thunder grumbled, and wind pushed a breath of gray coolness down on them from sullenly gathering clouds.

'And *had* Derryhick in fact murdered Foxford's father? Not to mention Uncle Diogenes's son?'

'There are two schools of thought on that.'

Bernadette Metoyer – a handsome woman in her forties whose tignon flashed with a sable firestorm of jet fringe – interrupted them, climbing the stair halfway and demanding, 'What have the City Guards found out about Rameses's body? Not that they will inquire, of course, the corrupt, lazy, *blankitte* pigs.'

It was a question January had answered twenty times between the time he'd entered the house and the time he'd located Rose in the crowd, but he replied, again, that it looked to be one of three men, but the Guards needed more proof before they made an accusation, and he descended to take the handsome chocolatiere's arm.

'And what proof do they need, to start searching the swamp?' Madame Metoyer sniffed. 'That's where they'll have thrown him.'

'Probably,' January agreed. In a week, in this weather, the body of an unidentifiable black man would raise no great fuss, unlike that of a white man traveling with those who seemed to have good reason to wish him dead.

He guided her up the back steps, across the crowded gallery, and into the dimness of the house. Under ordinary circumstances, the wake for a member of the FTFCMBS – or indeed for anyone in the tight-knit community of the *libres* at the back of town – would have involved wailing grief in one room, and lively music, jokes, dancing, and great quantities of food and tafia in the other, as people came to pay their respects and offer the family their support. But the circumstances were not ordinary. So there was neither the gay music nor the howling lamentation that the *blankittes* – the whites – found so disconcerting at such events.

Men and women gathered in the long central dining-room and parlor, in bedrooms and dressing-rooms and *cabinets*, hashing over the unfinished, and consuming the food that everyone had brought for the wake. In the parlor, Mohammed LePas, the blacksmith, was quietly organizing where the men would meet in the morning, to search the swamps that lay at the back of town. In the swamp-side bedroom – as such things were reckoned in Creole houses – the buzz of gossip among the women was like the throb of a bee tree. January picked out his sisters in the group: Olympe in her best dark Sunday Church-dress, like a market-woman save for the shape of her tignon, which announced to anyone who didn't already know it that she was one of the town's voodoo-queens; and the lovely Dominique, in sober spinach-green silk with touches of black where they wouldn't wash out her café-crème complexion. 'Liselle is in the *cabinet*.' Dominique nodded toward the smaller chamber, set up as Rose's office. 'Claire and Iphigènie are with her.' She named the girl's closest friends.

'Good,' said January. 'Best she's not alone right now.' Half a dozen infants were laid down on the bed, tiny faces like a box of bonbons. Dominique's year-old daughter Charmian slept among them, perfect as a furled rosebud. The French doors were open on to the front gallery that overlooked Rue Esplanade, and the older children dashed in and out, while mothers gauged the day's clouded darkness against how quickly they could get home before rain began.

Rain was beginning to patter as January returned to Rose. 'You were about to tell me how Patrick Derryhick had murdered the previous Viscount Foxford,' she said.

'Actually, the eleventh Viscount succumbed to perfectly natural causes at the age of threescore and two.' January divided with her the piece of Hèlaine Passebon's excellent peach tart that he'd picked up in the dining room and settled in the chair she'd brought out for him. 'Patrick Derryhick, in addition to being extremely charming where wealthy old aunts were concerned, was apparently what the English call a complete bad hat. He drank and whored his way through Trinity College, Dublin, and then Oxford, gambled his modest patrimony to perdition, and – at least according to Uncle Diogenes – had the unpleasant trick of drawing others, less resilient than he, into his way of life. His "merry band", as they called themselves, included the son of the eleventh Viscount Foxford, who drank himself to death on a bet in Paris at the age of thirty, leaving behind a much-relieved wife and a five-year-old son.'

'The current twelfth Viscount.'

'Germanicus Stuart.'

'Who suddenly decides to go into the cotton-growing business with Derryhick and crosses the ocean in his company? A thing possible and yet improbable, as Aristotle says. How *impossible* would it have been for that young man to have murdered Derryhick and sneaked his body into someone else's coffin?'

'Not impossible at all.' January edged his chair back from the gallery rail as the rain poured down in earnest. 'Beauvais Quennell, his wife, and his mother all sleep in upstairs rooms looking over Rue Douane – not surprisingly, nobody wants to sleep over that back-parlor. With a large hotel behind them, they must be used to noises in the night. Any man of normal strength could have lowered Derryhick's body on to the stable roof and thence to the ground, to be switched into the coffin, and from there it's only a few hundred yards to the river, with poor Rameses in the handcart.'

'The Swamp would be safer.'

'If you were familiar with New Orleans you'd know that. I doubt a foreigner would even be sure exactly where it lies, though Uncle Diogenes at least appears to have heard of it. There's a little more danger of being seen on the waterfront, but not a great deal at three in the morning at this time of year.'

'Hmph.' Her mouth took on the expression it did when one of her pupils was explaining that she hadn't the slightest idea who might have taken another girl's coral ring. 'And where do Uncle Diogenes and M'sieu le Vicomte claim they were while all this was going on?'

'Uncle Diogenes was gambling somewhere on Rue Royale – he says. You know how many gaming establishments there are within a two-minute walk of the Iberville. He returned to the hotel at three in the morning and found Droudge and Foxford both asleep. Foxford's key was gone from the desk, as if he were in his room all evening, but one of the porters saw him come in through the side entrance at a little after two thirty. He claims he had gone out for a walk and forgot to turn it in.'

'People do, of course.'

'He claims he left the hotel at nine thirty – he had been out earlier with Derryhick – but no one saw him go. The man who cleans the patrons' boots says that his were only barely splashed.'

'And is M'sieu Quennell's yard paved?'

January grinned. Rose never missed a trick. 'Bricked.'

'Hmm. Like the banquettes of the French Town between Rue Douane and the levee.'

'As you say. The sheets on his bed had been changed for fresh – only slept on for part of one night, by the look of them – and there were marks on the roof of Quennell's stable beneath the windows of the Viscount's room. Derryhick's watch, with blood smeared on its case, was found beneath his bed.'

Rose's eyes narrowed behind her spectacle lenses; January could almost hear the clicking of her thoughts. 'It would have been fobbed, surely? It's not that easy for a watch to come out of a vest-pocket.'

'He struggled with his killer.'

'I suppose.' She frowned into the distance, picturing it. 'Was the chain broken? Or the buttonhole of his vest torn?'

January shook his head. It was an old game they played, inventing possibilities and impossibilities – sometimes purely for each other's entertainment, the same way they would tell each other tales about strangers seen in the audience at the opera: *that one looks as if she has a secret lover; that one surely must have a collection of fifty thousand waistcoats . . .*

After a time, she asked, 'Would either of the traveling companions – Uncle Diogenes or Mr Droudge – have a reason for wanting poor Mr Derryhick dead?'

'Not to hear them tell it,' said January. 'I won't know until I've talked to Hannibal.' He got to his feet and stood for a moment, only breathing the cool benediction of the rain. On the back gallery of the house he could see his mother, still as slim and stylish as the young placées who made their appearance at the Blue Ribbon balls, deep in talk with her friends, most of them former placées like herself. Among them, Denise Glasson stood out like Mozart's Queen of the Night, veiled to her heels and topped, like the hearse, with a funereal confection of black ostrich-plumes, an advertisement for the depth of her sorrow.

Hannibal will lose his two cents. Not once had he seen his mother and Olympe in the same room.

In time, Rose said, 'I should go in. M'sieu Passebon –' she named the President of the FTFCMBS – 'has offered to see poor Liselle back to her room: I think Iphigènie is staying with her tonight, to look after the boys. What a – what a *horror*. And yet . . . how much worse it would have been for her, if when the coffin fell and split open, it *had* been Rameses inside. Someone should thrash that brother of hers.'

'Good heavens!' January widened his eyes in dazzled enlightenment. 'I didn't realize a drunkard's ways could be mended by thrashing,' and Rose thwacked him on the biceps with the back of her hand. But her sigh acknowledged his truth, and she stood.

'In any case, I'll need to be on hand when the crowd thins

out, to keep Madame Glasson from murdering, or being murdered by, Madame Ramilles . . .'

'Olympe promised me she'd keep them apart,' said January. 'On the subject of drunkards, I think I need to see Hannibal before I'm due at the Countess Mazzini's tonight. I suspect Liselle isn't the only one who shouldn't be alone this afternoon.'

Five more people asked January, as he edged through the dining room and parlor, what progress he and 'that American animal' (as the free colored community universally referred to Shaw) had made that morning toward finding poor Rameses's body. After he'd thanked Olympe's husband Paul for acting as host for the remainder of the night, clasped hands with Crowdie Passebon and Mohammed LePas in promise to join the morrow's search, and located his umbrella, he encountered two more queries as he stepped out through the French door of his study and descended to Rue Esplanade.

But as he paced the brick banquette under the steady torrent of the rain, his mind returned not to that squirming infant he'd held in his arms thirty-four years ago, but to the blunt-featured Irish face lying slack in the cemetery mud, and to Hannibal's hoarse light whisper: 'We were at Oxford together.' Sitting on the tomb at the dead man's side, he'd begun to say, 'I'd thought—' and had stopped himself.

Thought what?

Thought we'd all live forever, when we were young?

He knew what he'd find when he reached the Swamp.

Born a slave, raised first on a sugar plantation and then – free – in New Orleans, January had adapted himself to the almost-unthinking habit of making constant small adjustments in his behavior depending on where he was and who he was with: sniffing for danger, listening for sounds. Even the strongest black men took, perforce, their example from Compair Lapin, that wise and wily trickster rabbit of childhood tales, rather than from the defiant warrior heroes of the whites. For a slave, defiance was suicide, and suicide was the desertion of your friends and family to their unprotected fate.

You did what you must – paid whatever it cost – to survive. He'd learned early that there were places that were never safe to tread – like his former master's bedroom at Bellefleur

Plantation. That was good for a beating whatever the circumstances. Then there were places that were usually safe, and places that were likelier to be safer at certain times or under certain conditions.

The case in point today was the Swamp, that nebulous district that lay where Girod and Perdidio Streets petered out into muddy trails among the elephant-ear and stagnant pools upriver of the cemetery. Saloons patched together from tent canvas and broken-up flatboats strung along unpaved hog-wallow streets, offering games of chance, inexpensive coition and forty-rod whiskey for the benefit of ruffians, filibusters, and river-rats of all descriptions. At three o'clock in the afternoon, January knew most of the Swamp's inhabitants would be awake and stirring, but the rain would keep them indoors for awhile yet.

He also knew – although the knowledge operated at the wordless level of instinct – that he'd be safer approaching the Broadhorn Saloon across the wooded lots from behind, rather than by the more direct route up Perdidio Street itself, always provided he didn't trip over some drunk Kaintuck sleeping it off under a snaggle of hackberry bushes. If encountered singly, the worst a man of color usually got was threats and petty humiliation: piss stains and cigar burns. In groups, the encounter could be fatal. January moved with care.

The Broadhorn was a wooden house, a story and a half tall, L-shaped, unpainted, leaky, and squalid. Four dilapidated sheds at the edge of the trees behind it housed a collection of the most hardbitten women January had ever encountered in his life. It was a mystery to him how these two-legged she-wolves ever got customers, but they did. Two men were waiting, in the thinning rain, outside these 'cribs' when he emerged cautiously from the woods, and he stood out of sight for the five minutes it took for Fat Mary and the Glutton to finish previous bookings and admit them.

Once the yard was clear of possible observers, January climbed the rickety outside stair to the attic above the short end of the L.

The door at the top hung open in the spongy heat. Hannibal Sefton lay on the floor a foot or so back from the threshold, a square, brown whiskey-bottle empty on its side near his hand. A tin pitcher – the usual transport receptacle for the contents of the liquor barrel under the bar downstairs – lay empty, likewise, in a reeking pool of spilled brownish alcohol.

January checked his friend's breathing, more out of habit than anything else. He'd had plenty of experience over the past three and a half years of Hannibal's sprees. He'd brought a little powdered lobelia-root wrapped in a twist of clean paper, and this he mixed with water from one of the dozen tin catch-pans that stood about the attic beneath the ceiling leaks. He dragged his friend to a sitting position by the door and poured the mixture down his throat. Then he held Hannibal by the back of his coat and by his long hair while he vomited, and when he was finished, carried him to the bed.

Hannibal didn't open his eyes. 'You had to do that?' he whispered.

'I need you.' January walked back to the door – there was a sort of porch rail across the bottom half of the opening, but no actual porch – and looked out, in time to see one of the whores emerge from her shed and cross the yard toward the saloon proper, barefoot, scratching under her uncorseted breasts. 'Miss Margaret.' January called out her real name, though every man from Vicksburg to the mouths of the Mississippi knew her as Railspike. She stopped, stood in the faint final patters of occasional rain as he descended the ladder-like steps and crossed to her with the air of apologetic subservience that was the only thing that would lower the chances of his getting the tar beat out of him should any of the Broadhorn's customers emerge just then.

The honor of white womanhood must be protected at all costs.

'Miss Margaret, would you know if there's coffee in the kitchen?' He spoke English. This wasn't the part of town where whites spoke French. 'I'm afraid Hannibal's poorly.'

'What the hell happened?' Genuine concern shone in Railspike's usually hard eyes. January had seen her eviscerate a drunk sailor with a Bowie-knife and kick the dying man as she'd walked away, but she had a soft spot for Hannibal in whatever was left of her heart. 'He ain't got pukin' drunk in the daytime since I known him. An' he ain't *never* got so drunk he'd ask for liquor outa the bar barrel.'

'Friend of his died.'

'Oh, Jesus, Ben, I am sorry,' she said with complete sincerity and distress. 'You go on up, stay with him. I'll bring you up some coffee.'

'Miss Margaret, you are an angel.'

Coming back into the slant-roofed chamber, January thought Hannibal had passed out again, but when he sat on the end of the cot, the fiddler murmured, '*Wine is as good as life to a man . . . What life is then to a man that is without wine?*'

'*But a walking shadow*,' replied January gravely. '*A tale told by an idiot, full of sound and fury, signifying nothing*. But I need you sober.'

'God's teeth and toenails, Benjamin—' Hannibal pulled himself gingerly up so that his back might rest against the wall behind him, then suddenly turned a ghastly color and reached for the slop jar. After an agonizing time, his head and one long-fingered hand hanging over the edge of the bed, he whispered, 'Heaven pity the man who needs me sober.'

January went to fetch the dirty tin pot of coffee that Railspike had left on the floor just inside the door. He found a cup on one of the goods boxes that served Hannibal for shelves, filled it and held it out. 'Was he your friend?'

Hannibal nodded. It was as if the conversation begun that morning, sitting on the crumbling brick bench-tomb in St Louis Cemetery, continued uninterrupted.

'I take it you were part of his "merry band"?'

At the mention of that name the fiddler looked up, first sickened shock, then wariness fleeting across the back of his black-coffee eyes.

'He came to town with his relatives,' January went on, 'purportedly in quest of cotton plantations in which to invest the money that *should* have gone to them. By the look of the hotel rooms, and the evidence of the witnesses, he appears to have been knifed by the twelfth Viscount Foxford, but there's something about the business that makes my neck prickle. I wondered if you could tell me what that might be.'

FIVE

'The *twelfth* Viscount?' said Hannibal after a moment.
'Germanicus Stuart—'
'He's a child!'
'He's twenty-two,' January pointed out and noted with interest the look of aghast grief that crossed his friend's face. 'I take it you met him . . . longer ago than either of us would like to contemplate.'
'God.' Hannibal shook his head and raised the coffee to his lips with a hand that trembled. '*Òu sont les neiges d'antan?*'
'Did you know his father?'
'Not well.' He sighed. 'I think only Patrick knew him really well.'
'Then Derryhick didn't cause his death?'
'Patrick—!' For a moment Hannibal stared at him, open-mouthed. Then, in a different voice, 'Does the boy believe that?'
'It's what his uncle says.' January sat again on the end of the broken-down pallet.
'Uncle Diogenes? What's he doing on this side of the world? The man's been in Benares since Napoleon did his first rifle-drill. I understand he has a regular harem there that he's in no hurry to leave—'
'According to what Shaw learned while I was searching everyone's hotel-rooms,' said January, 'Uncle Diogenes came to Foxford Priory this spring, to wrap up the affairs of his son – another of Derryhick's "merry band". The boy had broken his neck while hunting. He was drunk, everyone said – apparently his usual condition, which Derryhick encouraged.'
'T'cha!' Hannibal turned and fumbled beneath his pillow in search of something that evidently wasn't there. 'Patrick never encouraged anyone to drink in his life . . . Well, not very hard. He was as happy drunk in sober company as he was among the befuddled – and, you should know, no drunkard ever needs anybody's "encouragement" to pick up a bottle.'
January fetched a second cup for himself, retrieving from

the floor on his way back a square black bottle that had once – to judge by the smell of it and the two barely-conscious cockroaches lying near its mouth – contained laudanum. This he handed Hannibal, who turned it upside down over his own cup in an effort to extract a final drop. But the only thing that slid out was a third, extremely befuddled, roach, which drowned without a struggle.

'*There is a willow grows aslant a brook*,' the fiddler said, quoting the death of Ophelia in *Hamlet*, '*that shows his hoar leaves in the glassy stream . . . Her clothes spread wide, and, mermaid-like, awhile they bore her up . . .*' With a sigh, he set the cup and its victim on the floor beside the bed. '*Too much of water hast thou, poor Ophelia, and therefore I forbid my tears* . . . That's why they think young Foxford killed him? Because Uncle Diogenes has been telling him for the past seventeen years that Patrick was responsible for his father's death? And you said they came here to buy a *cotton plantation*? With what? The family couldn't afford a parlor carpet.'

'With the money that a wealthy aunt had left to Derryhick instead of to the Viscount.'

Hannibal's raised eyebrows carried a whole ladder of wrinkles up his forehead. 'Not Aunt Elodie?'

'You know the story?'

'Lord yes; we all did. You can't drink and gamble with five other good-for-nothings without hearing everyone's life story, sometimes in several different versions . . . She left all her blunt to Patrick, did she? Good.' He grinned. 'Served the family right, for carrying on as if she'd married the village night-soil collector instead of a perfectly respectable India merchant. Patrick was the only one of the lot who treated her decently. I'm not saying he didn't have his eye on her East India Company stocks the way everyone else did, but at least he wasn't a hypocrite about it. *Look sweet, speak fair, become disloyalty* . . . And he did actually like her.'

His smile faded again, and he sat for a time gazing at the harsh block of the open doorway's light. With the rain's end the suffocating heat of the afternoon had returned, as usual made more unbearable by the steamy dampness of the puddles. In all the trees of the Swamp the metallic, whirring rattle of cicadas had started up. Below in the yard, a man whooped drunkenly and shouted, 'I am the first-cousin to the cholera, boys, an' I killed more men than the smallpox! Let me at that nigger!'

January flinched and glanced at the single other route of egress from the attic – a square hole in the building's gable end into which no one had ever gotten around to putting a window sash – but the hooting male voices down below retreated, so he deduced that it was some other nigger they had in mind.

'It isn't just because Foxford's father was a drunkard and the family believes Derryhick encouraged him,' he said after a time, and he related what he had told Rose, of the bed sheets, the watch, and the young nobleman's extremely long and surprisingly clean-footed 'walk' at the time of the murder. 'If it was me, I'd have used the blooded bedding to lower the body from the window to Quennell's stable roof, then packed it and the rug up to be shipped to general delivery in Natchez or Vicksburg, under another name: "left till called for".'

'I always thought you'd make a brilliant criminal if you weren't so damned honest.'

'Considering the average intelligence of the thugs you find hereabouts,' returned January, 'it's not difficult to appear brilliant. Uncle Diogenes claims to have been out yesterday evening as well. Did you know his son? The one who broke his neck?'

The fiddler shook his head. 'Frankly, from all Patrick told me about his uncle – well, his first cousin once removed, but everyone in that family called him Uncle – I'm surprised he married at all, much less fathered a child.'

January recalled the nature of some of the prints he'd found in Uncle Diogenes's hotel room. 'Shaw's checking his story, but, personally, my guess would be that he was at La Sirène's.' He named the owner of an extremely discreet house on the Bayou Road, where well-off gentlemen might avail themselves of entertainment 'of a specialized sort'.

Hannibal was silent for a time, twisting his long hair back from his face and fixing it with a woman's tortoiseshell comb into a knot on the back of his head. Then he said, 'There is, of course, the chance that the boy was at La Sirène's, or someplace like it. One doesn't have to be a dribbling old lecher to have unorthodox preferences.'

'I doubt it.' January cast his mind back for the chance

recollection that had eluded him earlier. 'I think we've seen the Viscount – I knew there was something familiar about his face. I'm not certain, but I think he was the blond boy who nearly called that Englishman out at Trulove's birthday ball Monday night.'

That had been in Milneburgh. The bustling little port on the lakeshore, some five miles behind New Orleans, was the summer residence of whoever in the town could afford to escape the airless heat and risk of fever. Most of the wealthy French Creoles – and a number of American planters as well – owned summer houses built on pilings along Lake Pontchartrain's swampy verges and would take up residence with their families in Milneburgh, or across the lake in Mandeville. Many bought or rented discreet little cottages in those towns for their mistresses as well, and for what the country Creoles sometimes referred to as their 'vulture eggs': children – like Dominique or Beauvais Quennell – acknowledged and looked after as part of the wider family. The balls and parties among those bucolic seekers after healthful air – white and *sang mêlée* alike – provided almost the only income that most musicians had in the summer season.

In New Orleans itself, it was rare for the French and Spanish Creoles to mingle with the American planters and businessmen. The two communities despised one another, to the extent that the Americans – frustrated at being shut out of city government – had that spring finally succeeded in having New Orleans divided into three separate 'municipalities': the Old French Town and its swamp-side suburb of Tremé; the new American suburb of St Mary; and Marigny, the downriver suburb where the poorer free colored, and those French and Spanish Creoles who couldn't afford the French town, lived side by side with immigrants from a Europe ravaged by twenty-five years of revolution and Napoleon.

In New Orleans itself, French Creole doctors, lawyers, and newspaper editors routinely challenged their American counterparts to duels, and both City Council meetings and criminal trials were still conducted, stubbornly, in French. But in Milneburgh there was enough of an atmosphere of being all fugitives together – albeit comfortably-housed fugitives whose breakfasts were served on time – that nobody had turned down an invitation to the enormous ball that British planter Fitzhugh Trulove had hosted at the Washington Hotel in honor of his wife's birthday at the beginning of that week. It went without saying, January realized, that the Englishman would have extended an invitation to an actual bona fide Viscount the moment he'd known the young man was in town.

'*A bawcock and a heart of gold*,' mused Hannibal. 'If I'd known who was involved I'd have bet more than two cents on the boy.'

As January recalled it – though owing to the crowd in the ballroom, and the fact that the whole incident took place in the middle of a lively quadrille, his view of the proceedings had been limited – young Foxford, impeccable in a London-tailored blue cutaway and fawn-hued inexpressibles, had taken exception to the attentions that a larger and gaudier English gentleman had been paying one of the small bevy of French Creole girls. Both men had been rendered argumentative by Mr Trulove's excellent champagne, and such erudite sneers as 'more childish valorous than manly wise' and 'one may smile and smile, and still be a villain' had rapidly progressed to, 'You are a scoundrel, sir!' and, 'Go back to your nursie before you get hurt . . .'

Several of the musicians had wagered on the outcome of the duel that had seemed in the offing, but the quarrel had been broken up before seconds could be named. January had gotten a brief glimpse of Lord Foxford as he'd stormed out of the ballroom, but saw only his opponent's back and nothing of the mortified girl.

'The fact remains,' mused January, 'that either Diogenes or young Foxford could have killed him – or either of their servants, who would have had access to the suite, or the business-manager Droudge for that matter, or anyone else staying in the hotel . . . or anyone sufficiently well dressed to get through the lobby unremarked. Despite Stuart's theory of a burglar, Derryhick clearly expected to meet someone in the suite when he returned to the hotel and clearly expected to have a quarrel with them. And whoever he did quarrel with, he *didn't* expect enough danger to make him draw his pistol before he was stabbed. There were a number of weapons in the suite—'

'What, those jeweled Indian daggers? Uncle Diogenes sent those to everyone – Patrick must have had at least five of them.' Hannibal got to his feet and proceeded, rather unsteadily, to search among the piles of books – placed carefully between the ceiling-leaks – and the shabby goods boxes that contained his few possessions. 'And what was the old boy doing in the expedition anyway? Even if Patrick wanted to saddle himself with his company – and he can be very good company, by the way – the man's the laziest thing in shoe-leather. Even his vices are passive.'

'According to Shaw, he's one of the trustees of the estate – to which young Germanicus will not succeed for eight years, or until he marries with consent of his guardians.'

Kneeling on a rafter just beyond where the floorboards ended, with only cracked lathes between himself and the gambling-room below, Hannibal paused in his search. 'And who is the other trustee?'

'Patrick Derryhick.'

Hannibal opened his mouth to say something else, then closed it and reached between the floorboards and the lathe.'What happens to Patrick's body?' he asked instead.

'It's at Quennell's. Whatever actually happened to Viscount eleven-and-a-half – and to Uncle Diogenes's son – Derryhick won't be buried in a pauper's grave.'

Hannibal had straightened up, sitting on his heels with a grimy handkerchief in one hand.

January went on: 'Officially – as a representative of the Burial Society – I'm only trying to find out which of those two gentlemen is responsible for desecrating poor Rameses's funeral and throwing his body out like a piece of trash . . . which would earn the culprit a slap on the wrist from any jury in town, and that *only* because he's a rotten-souled Englishman whom our heroic President drove back into the sea etc. etc. – it would be as much as their jobs are worth to do otherwise, with the election coming up. But the man who did that also murdered a man, rotten-souled Englishman or not—'

'Patrick would call you out for describing him as an Englishman,' put in Hannibal. He got to his feet, crossed back to the cot. '*I'd* call you out on his behalf, except that I'd have to ask you to be my second, and you wouldn't be willing to carry a challenge to yourself, would you?'

'No,' said January firmly. 'And I'm not the one who'd say he was English. Americans don't know the difference between English and Irish. But whoever it was who committed the greater crime, I won't be sorry to see him swing.'

'The boy didn't do it,' said Hannibal stubbornly. 'It's ridiculous to think he did. They'll never bring it to court – *solventur risu tabulae*.' He extended to January the handkerchief and its contents. 'Whatever information a dollar and fifty-nine cents can purchase,' he said, with grave and bitter irony, 'bring to light – and keep the change.'

'Get yourself some more medicine,' said January gently. 'Do you need me to keep it for you?'

'I seem to be doing all right lately on a few spoonfuls a day.' Hannibal looked around at the shambles of the room, and under his graying mustache a corner of his mouth hardened and turned down. 'Today was different. *So foul and fair a day I have not seen*, at least not since I gave up living with that woman who ran a flogging parlor in Venice – but not many days have been so. I'll be well, *amicus meus*. Will you be at the Countess Mazzini's tonight?' He squinted at the glaring light of the door again, the blinding yellow having mutated into slanted and violent gold.

'If I can get clear of the Swamp before the local bravos start roaming the streets.' By the sound of it, flat-boatmen, gamblers, and river-pirates had already escaped the dense heat of the Broadhorn for the moving air of the yard. Their desultory conversation gyred up to the open attic door, aimless and brutal: *we beat the crap out 'n him . . . damn yellow-bellied Injuns . . . Lost two dollars on the damn dog . . .*

'Come to supper.'

'They'll all still be there.' Hannibal sat on the edge of the cot again, like a puppet whose strings have been cut. 'Wanting to talk about it. Another time – thank you.' He repeated, '*Non omnis moriar* – I'll be all right.'

Though he flinched from the evening sunlight, Hannibal climbed down the rickety stairs with January and walked with him as far as the edge of the trees. None of the men in the yard so much as glanced at them, though the Glutton, sitting in the opening that served her dwelling as both window and door, waved to Hannibal and called out, 'You feelin' better, Professor?'

'A very riband in the cap of youth, lady!' He kissed his hand to her. 'The sight of your beauty would raise a man's spirit from the very ground.'

From the edge of the trees, January watched him walk back toward the stair and saw him intercepted by a gambler and the Broadhorn's cigar-puffing proprietress herself, and then hustled into the dark of the saloon.

SIX

By six o'clock – the hour at which Countess Leonella Mazzini opened the doors of her establishment for business – word had circulated among the whites in New Orleans about the hilarious contretemps that had befallen at a Sambo funeral that morning: 'Dropped the coffin . . . out tumbles this English feller sombody'd knifed an' switched into the box!' Whoops of laughter all around. January wouldn't have been surprised at these remarks from the customers of the Broadhorn: they'd probably have found the event equally risible had the vanished corpse been their own Pa or Uncle Ned. But the patrons of the Countess Mazzini's bordello were what passed in New Orleans as gentlemen. Men who owned the hotels, cotton presses, construction companies, and shipping lines that centered the state's wealth in the town.

Would they slap their thighs with the humor of it, he wondered, his fingers skipping through the chorus of 'Zip Coon', if it was a new-bereaved *white* family that was wondering where the body of husband, brother, son lay that night?

Do they really think we're THAT different from them?

Fed with the same food, hurt by the same weapons, subject to the same diseases? If you prick us, do we not bleed?

Or would the joke have tickled equally for a white man, provided he wasn't known to them personally – or known but not liked?

Probably, thought January with an inner sigh. *Probably*.

And most of his friends at the back of town would have laughed as hard, had the funeral been a white man's.

One thing about playing the piano at other people's entertainments for nearly two-thirds of one's life, it didn't do much for one's opinion of human nature.

The Countess Mazzini glided from one parlor to the other of the big, American-style house on Prytania Street, a beautiful Italian woman in her mid-thirties, like a full-blown rose in her tight-corseted crimson gown. She flirted with a steamboat owner here, a cotton broker there; twitted an American planter on his avuncular duties and winked at the youth he'd brought with him, a sixteen-year-old nephew from Virginia: 'What is it you fancy, *amore mio*? Pretty lambs, or a lioness with thighs of gold?' The Countess's house was one of the few brothels in town entirely staffed by white girls: pink-cheeked English belles, dreamy French brunettes. A raven-tressed Irish colleen with tourmaline eyes and a complexion like a lily of the valley, and a couple of handsome Germans, one fragile and one buxom, who worked as a team and were supposed to be sisters. January was watching the fragile one, Trinchen.

Trinchen, when not required to be shyly smiling at masculine jokes, was watching the parlor archway that led in from the hall.

It was not entirely need for money at the tail end of a very bad season that had brought January to the Countess's back door on the day after her German piano-player had broken three fingers in a street brawl. The other members of the Board of Directors of the Faubourg Tremé Free Colored Militia and Burial Society had asked January to apply for the position because word had reached them that young Martin Quennell – who, when he was not keeping the undertaker's books, was a clerk at the Mississippi and Balize Merchants' Bank – had been seen at the establishment of the French Town milliner Geneviève Jumon, buying the extremely lovely Trinchen an extremely costly hat.

A hat that no bank clerk should have been able to afford.

Ordinarily, this wouldn't have troubled anyone who didn't have their money at the Mississippi and Balize Merchants' Bank. But recently Beauvais Quennell, who for the past seven years had been the treasurer for the FTFCMBS, had, in fact, transferred the Society's funds to that bank – on the grounds that the Mississippi and Balize was more fiscally sound than the bank that had previously held them. With the Presidential election coming up, and the Bank of the United States closing its doors, even rumor of financial unsteadiness in an institution was enough to warrant a transfer. Young Quennell had spoken with authority, and the other Directors had found no reason for alarm.

But as Mohammed LePas the blacksmith said, 'There's no

dead cat out layin' in the middle of the floor, but I sure don't like the smell of the room.'

'He come in here, didn't he?' January asked the Countess softly, when uncle and nephew had retired upstairs with their choices and the cotton broker departed. In the short time he'd been employed there, he'd discovered that at this season there were frequent stretches of the evening when the parlor was empty and the unwritten rule that the piano player be blind, deaf, and oblivious to all that took place around him relaxed. He spoke in the rough English of the flatboat crews, which he found would often win the confidence of those who wouldn't trust an educated black. The Countess, who had paused beside the piano to take a quick puff on a Mexican cigarette, looked inquiring, and January elaborated. 'That English feller that was stuck in the coffin at that funeral. Mr Derryhick.'

'Mon Dieu!' Her eyes widened. 'That was Signor Derryhick? The Irishman?'

The other girls gathered around at once:

'Are ye sure?'

'How is it you know?'

'Gott in Himmel . . .'

'It wasn't Blessinghurst what kilt 'im, was it?' demanded gilt-haired Fanny. ''E 'ad the most awful row with Lord Blessinghurst—'

'Who's Lord Blessinghurst?' January's big hands vamped chords, trills, fragments of melody, so that there would never be a time when music was not audible from the street. ''Andsome bloke what always asks for Vennie?'

'Oh, him!' He mentally placed the tall Englishman as one who had been to the Countess's twice in the preceding ten days.

'He is a lord, with eight thousand a year,' Marie-Venise assured him. 'Look, he gave me these.' A toothpick finger tapped one of her earrings: paste, but quite good paste.

''E called Mr Derryhick bastard bog-lander an' Mr Derryhick drew a gun on 'im—'

'I hope His Lordship has not come to harm!'

'Where was this?' asked January, well aware that Derryhick had only been in New Orleans since Monday.

The girls looked at each other, and then at Trinchen, who shook her head. 'Martin did not say. Davis's, I think, or perhaps Herr Lafrènniére's . . . He was in two places or three last night.'

'Last night?' January's hands checked on the keys, then instantly resumed. 'This happened last night?'

The Countess stubbed her cigarette and the girls broke and scattered with a deceptively speedy languidness back to their red-plush couches and chairs, the flurry all but simultaneous with the sound of the door opening and the dusky little parlor-maid's happy greeting: 'Why, if it isn't Mr Granville!' January's fingers elided into 'Come Brothers, Sons of Jove', and he meditated, as he played, upon the person of Lord Blessinghurst . . . whom he was almost certain had been the man whom young Lord Foxford had come so close to calling out at Trulove's birthday ball.

If he hadn't seen the other Englishman's face on that occasion, he had a clear recollection of the color of his coat. That bottle-green velvet, now that he thought of it, would suit Lord Blessinghurst's complexion admirably – the man he knew from other evenings at the Countess's had hair the color of polished mahogany and emerald eyes – and he hadn't seen His Lordship wear the same coat or waistcoat, twice. The man at Trulove's party on Monday had had a deep voice, like Blessinghurst's . . .

Last night. Whether or not Derryhick had drawn a gun on Lord Blessinghurst – and he was sufficiently familiar with human nature not to trust anyone's account of so dramatic an event – it was clear that there had been a quarrel of some kind. Was Derryhick the kind of man who would get himself into TWO violent altercations in a night?

Alcohol would do it.

So would rage, and or the stress of sudden emotion.

I will kill the bastard . . .

And if Martin Quennell – who had evidently seen the confrontation – had had the opportunity to tell the lovely Trinchen about it already, it must have taken place relatively early in the evening.

January was still turning over in his mind how he would ask Martin about the confrontation – it being almost literally unthinkable for a parlor-house musician to speak to a customer, even if January hadn't been trying to remain unnoticed by that particular customer – when the young clerk himself walked in. Because the French Town and the American sector were very much separate worlds – January knew nearly everyone in the former and tended, like most Creoles, to keep his distance from anything to do with the latter – until last week he had never laid eyes on the undertaker's half-brother. This morning, when the young white man had grudgingly assisted in the carrying away of palls and plumes so that Patrick Derryhick could be laid out in the chapel, was the first time he had been in a room with him that hadn't been occupied by half a dozen chattering whores.

Martin Quennell, almost fifteen years younger than his half-brother, looked much like Beauvais Quennell would have done at that age, had the undertaker been white instead of octoroon: handsome in his way, brown curls carefully pomaded beneath a stylish high-crowned hat, with the same sharp features, the same round chin. He gave no sign of recognizing January, which was just as well and not surprising: at the undertaker's that morning had been the first time January had not been sitting on a piano-bench in his presence, and few white men looked at black men anyway unless they had to.

Certainly not with Trinchen's peach-like little breasts to ogle instead.

This morning at his half-brother's, Martin had been dressed as befitted a middle-level clerk at a small private bank: a well-worn cutaway coat that was slightly shiny at the elbows, gray-checked trousers, and a turkey-red waistcoat. Now, entering the parlor with a couple of refulgently wealthy Americans, he had attired himself to match them: one of the new frock coats in a stylish snuff-brown, trousers with a gay scarlet stripe up the side, and no fewer than four silk waistcoats layered one atop the other – two in different shades of green, one scarlet, and one gold.

January's first wife, Ayasha, whose death in Paris had precipitated his return to New Orleans four years ago, had been a dressmaker. January mentally priced the new coat, the silk of the waistcoats, the fine gloss of the beaver hat, and came up with a figure that no bank clerk had any business spending on something to put on his back.

Interesting.

The men were drunk and arguing politics with the ferocity of the semi-informed. 'Country needs a strong bank,' proclaimed their grizzle-haired leader. 'Too many shanty Irish, thinkin' they can set up as gentlemen. Too many Krauts, frogs, god-damn Freemasons, drivin' up the prices of things every way you look. What's this country comin' to, Schurtz? I ask you?'

'Confusion to 'em!' The man addressed raised the bottle of the Countess's champagne he was holding in his hand in a toast. He was tall and built flat, like a tabletop stood up on end, and had a square face with black hair that gleamed with pomade in the gaslight. Like Grizzle-Hair he wore an expensive coat and a number of gaudy waistcoats, hung across the belly with three watch chains and any number of gold and silver fobs.

Martin Quennell, who was taking some care, January observed, to keep at this man Schurtz's side – to the point of turning his face away from Trinchen's beckoning *poitrine* – brandished another bottle: 'Confusion to 'em all!'

This made the black-haired Schurtz bray with laughter, and he caught Quennell in a headlock of drunken friendliness and poured his own champagne over the smaller man's head.

For one instant, January saw in Quennell's flinch of horror, and aghast expression as he clutched at his wine-splashed silk vests, that the young man was not, in fact, as drunk as he seemed, and was perfectly well aware that he could not afford the ruin of his new clothing. But Schurtz only tightened his grip when Quennell struggled and broke into a drunken rendition of 'Little Wat Ye Wha's A-Comin'' – an anti-Jackson song from a previous election – of which January obligingly took up the tune.

'Got to christen our new partner as a good Whig!' declared Grizzle-Hair, a statement that made January – who would himself have voted Whig had he been considered a citizen in the country of his birth – cringe and wish he were a Democrat.

'Hold still, Baby,' trumpeted a fourth member of their party, a foxy little red-haired man with a diamond ring on one pinkie. 'Got to let us christen you, partner! Confusion to Jackson and Van Buren!'

'God damn Freemasons!' added Grizzle-Hair, picking up another bottle of champagne.

And Quennell – January was fascinated to note – ceased resisting, whooped, 'God damn Van Buren! God damn the

Freemasons!' and stretched out his arms, allowing the other three to pour champagne over clothing worth at least a year's salary.

Partner? Interesting.

And more interesting still, while Schurtz and Grizzle-Hair staggered, whooping with laughter, up the stairs with Fanny and Sybilla, both Foxy Red and young Mr Quennell elaborately denied any immediate interest in copulation and settled to smoke, drink, talk politics with the Countess, and keep a watchful eye on the stairs and on each other. Trinchen approached, ran an inviting hand along Quennell's arm, and was brushed away.

So it isn't just a question of staying in the running with his American friends.

'Oh, they'll come to cutting one another, by and by,' theorized the Countess, when at last the house cleared out, and January asked her what the hell was going on. 'The red-haired one – Lloyd he is called, Dominic Lloyd – he courts Schurtz's sister. So me, I think our Trinchen's sweetheart has set his sight upon the same goal. She'll bring money to the wedding bed, Miss Schurtz.'

The gas-lamps were extinguished, leaving only a prism-bedecked oil burner on the gilt marble table. Elspie the parlormaid and her brother Little J moved about in the shadows, clearing up forgotten glasses and moving the brass spittoons out on to the back porch for cleaning in the morning. Auntie Saba emerged from the back kitchen, a coffee cup full of rum for the Countess, a beer for January, and a couple of glasses of champagne for those girls who hadn't yet gone up to their rooms to sleep: actual champagne, and not the thinned apple juice and soda water that the unknowing customers paid champagne prices for the girls to drink with them.

The Countess lit a cigarette off the lamp. 'They're trying to show Schurtz how respectfully they'll treat his little sister. So they can't be seen, either of them, slavering over one of these *popottes*.' She gestured toward Sybilla and La Habañera, who were braiding each other's hair in the corner.

'He thinks they're visiting here just for the pleasure of *his* company?'

'You know *blankittes*.' All trace of Italian disappeared from the Countess's voice, and her full lips looked suddenly very

African in the glimmer of the lamp prisms. 'They know, all right, but they don't want to be reminded. Like those New Englanders who talk about how much they hate slavery but don't mind running factories to make "nigger-shoes" to sell down here, which is what makes Schurtz's family so rich.'

January turned back to the keys. Though his hands ached and his mind had the stretched, slightly fuzzy distortion of perception that comes at four in the morning, he played a little Creole lullaby his sister Dominique's nurse had sung to Minou when she was a baby: '*By an' by, by an' by, gonna lay down easy by an' by . . .*'

On his way out, he went around the back of the house and helped Elspie and Auntie Saba carry out and empty the heavy dish pan from the kitchen into the darkness at the far end of the yard, and brought them in water for the morning. It never hurt to make friends, and there was a good chance, now, that any information he could get about Martin Quennell's finances and behavior wasn't going to come from Trinchen.

In the morning – although it was in fact close to noon when he finally woke, emerging from one of the unused attic bedrooms to find the last guests from the wake helping Rose clean up downstairs – he was greeted by the information that the City Guards had arrested Viscount Foxford for murder.

SEVEN

'That's ridiculous,' said Hannibal. He looked terrible – no surprise, considering the amount of liquor he'd imbibed the previous day – but there was nothing in his person, or his hollowed dark eyes, that pointed to a resumption of drinking after January had left the Broadhorn's attic. He had shaved, bathed, and wore a clean shirt, and if his hand shook as he raised the cheap tin coffee-cup to his lips, January guessed that this was because the fiddler had been up all night. It was two o'clock now, the suffocating glare of the morning giving way to the onset of the day's inevitable thunderstorm.

'You haven't laid eyes on the boy since he was five.'

Hannibal avoided his look. 'They have nothing against him . . .'

'Aside from Derryhick's watch under his bed with blood on it?'

'Which could have been put there by anyone.'

Around them, in the dense shade of the market hall, women in bright-colored tignons stacked baskets of unsold vegetables on to handcarts, to be taken home and tossed into stews for their families. Rich voices called jests to Old Aunt Zozo at her coffee stand. A fisherman shouted with laughter at a friendly insult.

'There's something askew about this whole affair,' Hannibal said after a long silence. 'Diogenes Stuart could have signed papers to buy a cotton plantation before getting on the boat for Bengal. He'd let his own mother hang rather than get up out of his chair and cross the room to sign her pardon. The man's never had the slightest interest in the family lands – at least, from everything Patrick ever said of him – or how the Foxford money was invested, so long as he had enough to spend on Oriental manuscripts, kif and nautch-boys. Yet here he is crossing three thousand miles of the Atlantic Ocean, with old Droudge harping on him day and night about how much his way of life costs—'

'Not to mention traveling with the man he believes murdered

his son.' January rose from the rickety little table beneath the market arcade. Everyone in New Orleans, at one time or another in the day, came to this place to get some of Aunt Zozo's coffee; walking down here at the proper time for Hannibal was a good deal safer than another expedition to the Swamp.

'Good God, Uncle Diogenes wouldn't care about that. Not really. Patrick was good company, and that's what the old boy wants most: someone to play cards with him and keep him amused. But I'll tell you another thing: he wasn't at La Sirène's Thursday night, and neither, so far as I can tell, was Foxford.'

January raised his eyebrows. The Siren was well known for discretion regarding customers.

'After spending a good portion of last night going from gambling den to gambling den along Rue Royale, attempting to account for Uncle Diogenes's movements, I fetched up at La Sirène's in the small hours, far less intoxicated than I seemed to be – at least, I hope that was the impression that I gave – and claiming that the man owed me part of the money he'd won at cards at that establishment Thursday night. This immediately elicited the information that he hadn't even been on the premises Thursday, though he had been there – and apparently made quite an impression – the night before. I apologized and fell artistically down the steps on my way out . . .'

He absently rubbed a bruised shoulder. 'Someone at Lafrènniére's remembered seeing a man who looked like Patrick come in, sometime after ten. Came in, looked around, and left . . .'

'That's a good deal of trouble,' January observed gently, 'on behalf of a boy you knew as a child, and a man you haven't seen for seventeen years.'

'The boy's mother was . . . very good to me.' Hannibal turned the empty cup in his hands. 'They both were. Patrick . . .' He sighed, a sound like the rasp of a saw. 'Foxford wouldn't have done it.'

January took the cup from him and walked to the coffee stand where Aunt Zozo, in her red-striped yellow tignon, stood like a benign witch in the clouds of charcoal smoke from the fire beneath her pot. 'Has there been word, anything, of Rameses?' the *marchande* asked, and her eyes filled with pity when January shook his head. As he turned back toward the table she handed him a couple of pralines – *lagniappe*. Like Railspike, she had a soft spot for Hannibal.

'The Consul will surely have something to say—' Hannibal began, when January sat down again.

'Obviously,' January replied. 'But since he hasn't, I assume that Shaw turned up something damning.'

'Have you seen Shaw?' Hannibal glanced across the Place d'Armes, where the Cabildo's white stucco shimmered palely through the rain.

'I tried on my way here; he was out. I shall try again –' he drew from his pocket the folded note that had arrived at his house an hour ago, which was quick work considering it was the answer to one he'd penned in the small hours to be taken out to Milneburgh by his nephew on the first steam-train – 'when I've made inquiries about the part played in all this business by Lord Montague Blessinghurst.'

'Who?'

'The gentleman – I believe – who came so close to being called out by young Foxford at Trulove's ball, Monday night. And the man I suspect your friend was looking for, Thursday night.'

Hannibal looked up sharply.

'He found him, and they quarrelled – violently, according to Trinchen at the Countess's. I'm hoping that Madeleine Mayerling –' he named a former pupil, of impeccable French Creole family – 'can tell us what it was about. She was at Trulove's on Monday night, and if she didn't actually witness Blessinghurst's original altercation with Foxford, she's had almost a week to hear the details from everyone who did.'

'Trust the Creole ladies to maintain an intelligence system that the French Foreign Service would envy. Can you get to Milneburgh and back before the Countess opens her doors? The lady is strict about employees who show up late.'

For answer, January handed his friend the note:

> Saturday 8 October, 1836
> My dear Mr J,
> You must not think of trying to come out here, and perhaps missing the last train back. As Augustus informs me that you are working this summer for the notorious Countess Mazzini, in return for later information about

> EVERYONE of my acquaintance who has passed through her doors, and the disgraceful details of all that transpires in her house, I will be at home on Rue Royale this afternoon at three. I trust the summer finds you and your family well?
> Yours,
> M.M.

The downpour had lightened to fleeting squalls by the time January and Hannibal reached what had been the town-house of the Trepagier family, at the quiet end of Rue Royale. In an hour the rocks would be burning, as the saying was: the sun drawing up as steam those silver-gray lakes that lay in the streets; the air unbreathable, and ten times worse than before. The two men walked in silence, having called briefly at the Cabildo and been informed by the desk sergeant that firstly, Lieutenant Shaw was still out dealing with a bar-fight of near-riot proportions on Tchapitoulas Street near the wharves, and secondly – in irritated tones – that the British consul had no business interfering with American justice in a case when the murderer had been found to have inherited his victim's entire fortune, by the terms of the victim's will.

'I suppose I should be pleased that Aunt Elodie's fortune has returned to the family at last,' sighed Hannibal, after silently digesting this information as they walked. 'And I'm sure Patrick meant it for the best. Yet there is a time to every season under heaven, and this donation does seem to be rather unfortunately timed.'

'I wonder if the boy knew of the will.'

'I wonder if any jury will believe him if he says he didn't. Somebody in the party obviously did.'

January said, 'Hmm.'

The tall stucco town-house, dilapidated after the death of the spendthrift and abusive Arnaud Trepagier, had been recently repainted, January noted approvingly, and every window sparkled. The sale of the Trepagier plantation lands to a spur of the Milneburgh steam-train line had clearly been profitable. It had, among other things, enabled the young widow Trepagier to marry her husband's fencing master, to the gratification of everyone except the widow's disapproving aunts.

'Why this interest in the murder of a traveling Irishman?'

inquired Augustus Mayerling, emerging from the rear of the house as January and Hannibal made their way into the courtyard, past the small carriage that stood in the porte cochère. 'If there were a question of how your friend Ramilles died—'

'M'sieu Derryhick was a friend of Hannibal.' January glanced at the fiddler, who, behind a mask of persiflage, had managed to say very little about either Viscount Foxford or Patrick Derryhick on the walk from the market. 'As was the Viscount's father. The boy was arrested this morning, I understand—'

'And I understand the uncle promptly went to Mayor Prieur's office and made a complete fool of himself, demanding his nephew's release.' Mayerling paused on his way through the shaded loggia at the back of the house, raised colorless brows. 'On the grounds that he is a member of the British aristocracy – not an argument calculated to impress either a French judge, or an American one who wishes his political friends to be re-elected next month.'

They ascended the outside stairway in silence. On the upstairs gallery, Madeleine Mayerling rose to greet them, her dark beauty and ivory complexion a warm contrast to her husband's slim Teutonic pallor.

'M'sieu Janvier.' Madame Mayerling clasped January's hand, which despite the heat was properly gloved for a visit to a white lady. 'M'sieu Sefton. This concerns the quarrel at Madame Trulove's ball, you said?'

'So I believe.' At her gesture, January took one of the wooden gallery chairs. A servant emerged from the house, bearing a tray of lemonade. Another of those intricate unspoken rules, reflected January: second nature to a man of color in America, but – once he had turned back to look behind him from the freer air of Paris – a source of fascination. Just who could sit down and drink with whom? The rules shifted like a cat's cradle depending on whether he, a black man, had arrived in company with the white Hannibal; where the meeting and drinking took place; how he was dressed and whether it was winter – the social season, during which it might be *seen* that the Mayerlings would sit down and drink with a black man – or the summer, when it would be a matter of mere servant rumor. Had his skin been the lovely bronze of his mulatto mother's, instead of his slave father's *beau noir lustré*, as the dealers said, the rules would have been different still, as they would have had he not been attired in coat, vest, and gloves, or had he been a woman (dark or bright?) rather than a man.

It was not something you *could* understand, January suspected, unless you'd grown up free colored – and the son of slaves – in New Orleans.

'It might be happenstance,' he went on, his big hand wrapped lightly around the stem of his glass. 'But I don't think it is. Patrick Derryhick was last seen alive when he stormed back into the Hotel Iberville at ten thirty, Thursday evening, after a violent quarrel – I am told – with another Englishman named Lord Montague Blessinghurst.'

'Mon Dieu!' Madeleine Mayerling glanced over her shoulder at her husband. 'That was the man—'

'Indeed.' Both returned their gazes to January. The sword-master cocked his narrow, bird-like head. 'You behold us agog.'

'What happened at Trulove's?'

'Well, she knew them both.' Madeleine set her glass down, folded her hands on her sprig-muslin lap. 'That was abundantly clear.'

'Who knew them both?'

'Isobel Deschamps.'

It was January's turn to raise his brows. 'Celestine Deschamps's daughter?' Like Hannibal yesterday, he experienced a momentary flash of wonder and regret – *where ARE the snows of yesteryear?* – that the grave and sweet-faced French Creole damsel he had tutored in piano was already old enough to be causing near-duels at birthday balls in Milneburgh. Yet the autumn that he'd taken that honey-haired schoolgirl through Mozart marches and light-footed Austrian waltz-tunes, she was already bubbling with plans for her debut: *I have a fitting for my dress for the Mayor's Ball; I must go with Maman to buy gloves to go with my slippers* . . . In time the piano lessons had been discontinued, as Celestine Deschamps – just emerged from full mourning for her husband – shepherded the girl to dancing masters and corsetières in preparation for her introduction to adult society.

That was the year, January recalled, that the government of the United States had finally cleared the Red River in the north-west of the state for steamboat navigation, quintupling the value of the Deschamps plantations in Natchitoches Parish and transforming the pretty young widow and her daughters from modestly well-to-do to outright rich overnight.

Of course, it was expected that Isobel would marry well.

'She has only just returned from Paris,' went on Madame Mayerling. 'So it isn't beyond the realm of possibility that she encountered both of them there. The Viscount and Lord Montague, I mean.' Something of January's own thoughts must have snagged in her mind, for her dark brows puckered as she heard her own words.

'Not beyond the realm of *possibility*, no,' January said, answering her expression. 'But what is the *probability* that two men she knew – and knew well enough to have them fight over her – would *both* come to New Orleans during the hot season, when even the Devil is still away on vacation?'

There was a little silence, broken only by the rising thrum of cicadas in the courtyard plane-tree with the cessation of the rain, and the voice of a servant-woman in the kitchen downstairs.

'Did you see what took place?'

'Oh, yes. I was speaking with her only moments before.' A shadow of remembered anger flickered through the young woman's eyes. 'As to what happened . . . She turned her head, said, "Oh, *peste*!" and begged my pardon and tried to get out of the room. You know how crowded it was that night. Before she could reach the door, Blessinghurst stepped in front of her and took her by the hands, the way a man does who thinks he is entitled to do so. Isobel tried to get free, but he was very earnest, like a man in love . . . Only, a man who truly loves will not do such a thing to a girl at a ball, when she must either stand still and let him talk, or make a scene in public.'

'And Foxford broke in?'

Madame Mayerling nodded decisively. 'I was on my way to do so, but he was before me. He said something like, "Sir, it must have escaped your notice that this young lady was on the way from the room."' A born mimic, she captured not only the accent of Foxford's perfect public-school English, but also the stiff posture of an offended scion of the aristocracy. 'Isobel tried to pull her hands away, and Blessinghurst would not release them, and that was not at all how he acted to the other ladies that evening, young or otherwise. He made some slighting answer to the boy and tried to draw Isobel aside . . .'

She frowned again, putting events into order as if sorting out a hand of cards. 'And do you know, after that first instant Isobel did not look at young Foxford. She looked away, like this . . .'

Not the gesture of an eighteen-year-old girl embarrassed at a scene between gentlemen. It was, January thought, almost like a flinch of fear.

'She said, "Gerry, no."'

'She called him Gerry?'

'Even so. Foxford – only it was not until later that my Aunt Clothilde told me his title – put his hand on Blessinghurst's arm, and in turning to meet him Blessinghurst let Isobel go, and I got her out of the room, in spite of the crowd.' January guessed that, as a well-off young matron, Madeleine Mayerling would have far less diffidence about pushing her way to the door than a shy girl in her third season.

'In the lobby I asked her if I should fetch her mother. She was shaking all over and ashen with distress. Now, I would not put it past Celestine Deschamps to push this British Lord's addresses at her later – depending on how rich he turns out to be – but if there was a scene brewing in the ballroom she would, of course, get her out of there right away.'

'So you knew Blessinghurst is a lord?'

'Oh, yes. He'd left cards on everyone in town about a week before that, and Augustus introduced us earlier that evening. He'd had a lesson with him already at the *salle d'epée*. Everyone was saying how exquisite his manners were, and half a dozen of my aunts' friends are pursuing him for their daughters. I found him . . .' She fished momentarily for the right word. 'I found him *obsequious*, myself. But men often are when they're on the catch for heiresses.'

January nodded, recalling Martin Quennell gamely sacrificing a hundred dollars' worth of clothes to the pursuit.

'He always seems to have a great deal of money—'

'He wins a lot of that in the gambling-rooms,' remarked Augustus.

'Yes, well, so do you, *liebling*.' She reached up to touch his hand. 'It was, as I said, the only time I saw him behave in a manner less than perfectly correct.'

Hannibal spoke up. 'Did he say why he was in New Orleans at this season?'

'Traveling for his health, he said. Which, when one thinks about it, is the last thing one is likely to find in New Orleans before the first frost.' She tilted the lemonade pitcher, topping up their glasses, and offered the plate of teacakes. January took one, knowing it would be a long night at the Countess's. Hannibal shook his head.

'Would you do me a favor, Madame?' asked January, after a time of thought. 'Might I prevail on you to call on Mademoiselle Deschamps, and learn from her, if you can, why it is that she tried to flee Lord Montague on sight, and how she comes to call young Foxford by his Christian name?'

'*Prevail* upon me?' The velvety brown eyes sparkled with pleasure. 'My dear M'sieu, after what you have told me of murders and intrigues, you would have to confine me to keep me from it!'

January laughed. 'I kiss your hands and feet, Madame, with your husband's kind permission. Was Derryhick there that night, by the way? Do you know?'

Madeleine and Augustus exchanged glances, questioning and shrugging. If Monday had been the Foxford party's first evening in New Orleans, January reflected, neither would have known who Derryhick was, as they'd known Blessinghurst. And a plain 'Mister', be he ever so wealthy with mis-inherited gains, would not catch gossip's attention the way even an impoverished Viscount would. Mayerling said, 'Certainly, no one stood out among those who drew Foxford away from Lord Montague, as a traveling companion would do. The man may have been in the hotel's gambling room and heard nothing of the matter.'

'I imagine if he had been present at all,' said Hannibal, 'I would have seen him, and I didn't. And that,' he added, almost to himself, 'is probably just as well.'

EIGHT

Even in the hot season, Saturday night was the liveliest of the week at the Countess's. Little J scurried to and from the kitchen with bottles of expensive champagne for the men and glasses for the girls, adeptly switching the wine that the men had poured out for their *inamoratas pro tem* with identical glasses of apple juice, diluted with soda water to the same color. A gentlemen might think he wanted to share champagne (at three times its market value) with the girl of his choice, but January knew why the deception was necessary. 'Trust me,' he later explained to Rose, 'you don't want to see any of those girls actually drunk.'

January played, watched, and listened without seeming to, and when his banker, Hubert Granville – for whom he had done a little investigating at the beginning of summer – glanced askance at him from between the lovely Sybilla's breasts, he only beamed a greeting of wordless friendliness and went back to 'The Lad With His Sidelocks Curled'. If whorehouse etiquette forbade the piano player from recognizing any of the men who came to Countess Mazzini's to gamble, fornicate, and shout at each other about the annexation of Texas in an atmosphere of cheap patchouli and cigar smoke, in return it prevented any white man from officially taking notice of who was providing the music.

Neither Martin Quennell nor the wealthy and ill-mannered Mr Schurtz put in an appearance that night. Young Mr Foxy Red Dominic Lloyd came in late and very drunk, and proceeded to get drunker – an expensive proposition at the Countess's.

'Do I judge correctly that Mr Lloyd's courtship of Miss Schurtz's dowry has been derailed by a mere bank clerk?' January asked Hannibal later, when he emerged at the end of a very long evening to find the fiddler on the back steps, trading after-hours jokes in German with Trinchen and Nenchen.

After he had kissed both girls goodnight amid compliments and snatches of Goethe's more romantic endeavors – '*kennst du das Land, wo die Zitronen blühn*' – he untied one of Nenchen's pink-striped ribbons from around his neck and said, 'Bank clerk? According to the lovely Nenchen, Mr Quennell is an *entrepreneur* who has used his position at the Mississippi and Balize to purchase town lots out beyond Dryades Street . . . which have tripled in value since that area became part of the Second Municipality in March.'

'Using what for money, I wonder?'

'Well you may. Goodnight, goodnight, beautiful ladies,' he added, as Auntie Saba and her children came down the back steps, and Hughie-Boy – a huge hook-nosed ruffian who slept in a little room beneath the stairs – locked up the door behind them. '*Dusky like night, but night with all her stars . . .*'

'That fiddler a friend of yours, Big J?' the cook demanded, laughing. 'You better not let the Countess see him.'

'An unforgiving woman, the Countess.' Hannibal shook his head and sighed. 'And, if I may be excused for criticizing a lady in her profession, a sadly unromantic one.'

They turned right at the rear corner of the house and followed its wall toward the bluer darkness that was all that was visible of the starlit street. The fingernail moon had set early, and in this neighborhood, far out along Prytania Street, the house lots were huge and widely-spaced. For a hundred yards in any direction of the handsome pink-brick house, cypress and oak grew, as they had grown when the Houma and Choctaw had still camped on the edges of the then-walled town.

It was nearly four in the morning. Even sin slept.

Hannibal went on: 'From what Fräulein Nenchen tells me, Schurtz seems to prefer a man who can get him real estate at half the going price to the hard-working owner of a cotton press. Quennell will laugh uproariously at Schurtz's jokes into the bargain – Trinchen says she hadn't thought anyone could make a dirty story boring, but evidently that's the one talent Schurtz has – and Miss Schurtz has expressed a decided preference for young Quennell, who has presented her so far with a necklace of pearls and a Chinese shawl. I suspect either Beauvais Quennell or the Burial Society had better look to their account books. Did you find out anything further about the sinister Blessinghurst from the kitchen help?'

'Only what the girls have said of him.' January opened his hands, like a magician would to prove them empty. 'He's generous, lavish with money, and universally charming, when charm will get him what he wants. Elspie – the parlormaid – says when she refused to kiss him he took the kiss by force, and not playful force, either. He said if she told the Countess about it, he would charge Elspie with the theft of his watch, and the Countess would have her sold.'

'*Is* Elspie a slave?'

'No,' said January. 'She reported the matter privately to the Countess, and they're both pretending she didn't. The man's a good customer, and neither of them wants to upset Marie-Venise, who's one of their best "specials". When I go to the Cabildo tomorrow – today,' he amended, with resigned regret, 'this afternoon, I'll mention what we've learned about Blessinghurst to Shaw. Though by that time I suspect that whatever Viscount Foxford was really doing Thursday night, he'll have admitted it after a few hours in the Calaboso. I don't think he'll get much chiding from his uncle . . . Mr Droudge wouldn't try to blackmail him, would he? Threaten to tell his mother he'd been investigating some of Bourbon Street's gamier pleasures?'

'Lady Philippa wouldn't believe Droudge if he told her water flowed downhill. She loathes the man – at least she did when I knew her – and, considering what she put up with from the boy's father, I can't imagine there's much in the way of vice she hasn't heard of before. Droudge would tell her, of course. He's vindictive that way.' Hannibal frowned at some memory. 'But once they have a decent lawyer, and he's tracked down the girl – or boy – or multiples thereof – in question, I can't see a judge refusing bail, no matter what Patrick's will may have said.'

They had come among the large and handsome houses of the American section of town, ghostly shapes sleeping in starlight against the dark of trees. It was the hour when the wet heat briefly slacked, and wretched sleepers under pink clouds of mosquito-bar finally slid into dreams of something other than being baked alive in slow ovens. Even so, the stench of the city enfolded them: the soot of the wharves and the exhalations of a thousand privies and garbage middens. No wonder anyone who could afford to be elsewhere kept their distance from the place until frost brought an end to the tropical torture.

Anyone except Patrick Derryhick. And the young Viscount Foxford.

And, interestingly, Lord Montague Blessinghurst.

'Always provided,' said January softly, 'that the boy didn't actually do it.'

Hannibal checked his stride long enough to glance up at him – his pale face barely more than a skeletal blur in the frame of long hair and tall-crowned hat – and January thought he would have said something.

But he looked away and walked on without a word.

It was a curious fact about Americans, January had discovered, that while most American businessmen in New Orleans had not the slightest objection to fornicating themselves speechless on the Sabbath – either with their own house-slaves or with paid professionals – they were among the first to rise up in righteous wrath against any bawdy-house keeper with the temerity to maintain open hours on Sundays. The madames and whoremasters of the French Town faced no such limitation – uptown Protestants fumed that the French Creoles kept the Sabbath the way Bostonians kept the Fourth of July – but the Countess Mazzini, who shaped her business carefully to appeal to the Americans, was assiduous about closing her doors a few hours before first light on Sunday and keeping them closed until late Monday afternoon.

Thus, in addition to having his own Sunday evening to spend with Rose, January was able to meet Abishag Shaw in the brick-paved arcade in front of the Cabildo on Sunday afternoon, after what felt like far too few hours from his parting with Hannibal in the gluey blackness of Prytania Street.

'Reckon if'n your folks had any luck draggin' the bayous, I'd'a heard.' Shaw spat in the direction of a bullfrog, which was making its unoffending way from one of the puddles in the Place d'Armes to the grille of the newly paved-over gutter drain that had replaced the open trenches which had, for so many years, kept the square more or less dry.

'Heard and reported to Captain Tremouille that he can go on saving himself the trouble of assigning his own men to search?' On his way to the Cabildo, January had stopped by his sister Olympe's house and had received the news that no trace of Rameses Ramilles had yet been found.

Precisely the reason, he knew, that Patrick Derryhick's

murderer had chosen to dispose of his victim's body in the coffin of a black man he would have seen brought into the undertaker's yard.

The body of a white man would demand that the wheels of the law grind into motion.

A black man's corpse, particularly after a week or two in the river, would draw no comment.

'Captain Tremouille,' sighed the policeman, 'wouldn't take the trouble to go look for his *own* daddy's corpse, in between organizin' the First Municipality vote, an' buyin' drinks for them foreigners as have the vote, down in Marigny.' He removed his hat, scratched his long hair – the color of greasy onion-tops – caught whatever he was seeking there between dirty fingernails, and crushed it absently to death. 'You want to have a word with the Foxford boy, whilst you's here? I understand your pal Sefton put in a couple long nights oozin' around absinthe cafés an' whippin' parlors, askin' after him or Stuart—'

'Foxford is still *here*?' January's eyes widened in shock as he recollected the long, filthy, stifling room where drunkards, brawlers, pickpockets and waterfront thieves pushed and bullied among themselves for space on the bunks and floor. What the hell had the boy *done* during those four hours on Thursday night that he wouldn't admit to his lawyer?

'Has he talked to a lawyer?'

'That business manager of his went chasin' one in Mandeville yesterday. 'Course, there ain't a lawyer in this town at the moment, nor won't be till the weather breaks . . .'

January cursed. 'What about Droudge?' he asked. 'And what about Stuart? You can't say their activities are accounted for—'

'So far as Captain Tremouille is concerned,' Shaw replied drily, 'Stuart's are. A lady, name of Simone Alcidoro, come in yesterday an' confessed all off'n her own bat as how she an' Mr Stuart was up playing cribbage in her parlor till three in the mornin'.'

'Simone Alcidoro?' January was familiar with the name. 'She'd swear she was playing cribbage with Robespierre's ghost if you bought her two drinks.'

'Well, maybe somebody did.' Shaw half-turned his head as two men passed behind them, going into the Cabildo:

journalists, January recognized them, from the *Louisiana Gazette* and the *Bee*. 'For a man who spent that night playin' cribbage in a private home, Stuart was mighty quick to come up with proof of it, but you can't arrest a feller if you think he wasn't playin' cribbage with a . . . lady. I'm keepin' a eye on the both of 'em: him an' Droudge. It's all I can do.'

'Have you heard of a man named Blessinghurst?'

Shaw's gray eyes narrowed. 'British lord? Come to town 'bout ten days ago? A tad too sharp at the poker table?'

'That's the man,' said January. 'He quarreled with Derryhick the night of the murder – as far as I can place the time, immediately before Derryhick's return to the hotel at ten thirty.' As they entered the Cabildo, and crossed the big stone-floored watch room together, January recounted what Trinchen, Fanny, and Marie-Venise had had to say about His Lordship on Friday night.

'That a fact?'

'It seems to be. And also, it sounds like, after parting from the Viscount earlier that evening, Derryhick went *deliberately* searching for Blessinghurst in the gambling-parlors along Rue Royale, rather than meeting him accidentally.'

Ordinarily, the watch room was quiet on Sundays, especially at this time of year, the few members of the City Guard on duty playing dominoes, smoking on the benches set around the walls, or drawing straws for who would get the duty of whipping the slaves that owners brought in for 'correction' at two bits a stroke. Today, however, as Shaw had said, the *rentiers* and merchants of the French Town, and the landowners and sugar-brokers who held political power in the city government, were gathered in clumps by the sergeant's desk and at the foot of the stair that led up to Captain Tremouille's office, and the air was heavy with the angry buzz of their talk.

In the courtyard, the whippings hadn't started yet. There would be only two: a middle-aged man roughly dressed, like a stable-hand or a laborer, and a young woman in blue calico that was torn and dirty, as if she'd slept in it on the ground. January stood at the bottom of the stairs that led up to the cells of what was called the Calaboso – the city jail – while Shaw ascended. The prison latrine could be smelled everywhere in the court; a band of ants an inch wide streamed up the stucco to the gallery that led to the cells above. Somewhere a woman was screaming curses, muffled by the walls. Then, once more, the swift tread of Shaw's Conestoga boots on the stair.

The Viscount reached the bottom and extended his hand. 'Monsieur Janvier. Mr Shaw tells me you're here on behalf of one of my father's old friends, who knew – who knew Patrick,' he said in somewhat laborious public-school French.

The boy's godlike handsomeness had been severely marred by a black eye and a crust of blood on his nose; his linen jacket was gone and his white shirt torn, and by the sudden twitch of his shoulders and the look on his face when he scratched, he was having his first experience with the insect, as well as the human, residents of the jail.

'I am indeed,' January replied in English, to the young man's obvious relief. Foxford had, he noticed, used the polite term *vous* in addressing him, as one adult to another. Most French and Spanish creoles of the city had slipped into the habit of using *tu*, the word one used when speaking to a child, a dog . . . or a slave.

'I'm extremely grateful, of course, for your concern, sir – and for Mr Sefton's – but I assure you, there's really no need for alarm.' The haggard worry that January had seen on the young man's face yesterday had deepened; his voice was even, but there was something in the jerky motion of his hands when he folded them before him, or put them in his pockets, that betrayed how shaken he was. January's own experience with the Calaboso's common cell had been similar enough to things that had happened to him in his childhood that he hadn't had to contend with shock as well. What had the boy made of his first experience with a common latrine-bucket?

But instead of the outrage that one might expect from fortune's favorite, Foxford asked, 'Did they ever find the body of the poor man whose coffin Patrick was hidden in? My God, what a frightful thing for his family! Do you happen to know –' he turned to Shaw – 'if Mr Droudge did as I asked and sent money to the Ramilles family on my behalf?'

'If'n he ain't,' said Shaw, 'I'll sort of remind him. That's good of you, sir.'

The boy waved his words away. 'I can't think – I can't even imagine who would have done such a thing!'

'Can't you?' asked January softly, and the Viscount started, as if at the flick of a whip. 'Because that's exactly one of the questions I wanted to ask you: is there anyone who *would* have done such a thing? Who would have murdered Mr Derryhick?'

Foxford wet his split lip, ran a quick hand through his blond hair, thick and tumbling in his eyes. 'I'm afraid Mr Shaw has already been over that with me. I – I simply can't help you there. Even in London, or in Dublin, Patrick hadn't an enemy in the world—'

'Not even your uncle?'

Something in the boy's eyes shifted. He evidently had to think about that, like an inexperienced card player trying to remember what was trumps. 'I don't . . . Of course not. Are you thinking about what he said about my cousin's death . . .? You were there, weren't you, sir? In the hotel?' His eyes met January's again. 'Please don't – Uncle Diogenes knows, as well as anyone in the family, that his son's . . .' he fished visibly for a euphemism – '*shortcomings* were of Theo's own choosing. Uncle . . .' He fumbled for words. 'When someone you care for dies – even someone you know was leading a life that could only end in a stupid accident like that – it's hard not to blame. But Uncle would never . . . He was angry at Patrick, yes, but that doesn't mean he'd . . . he'd do him harm.'

He can't say it, thought January. *Can't say 'stab him and hold a pillow over his face until he suffocated to death'. It has to be just 'do him harm'*.

Grief filled the young man's eyes, and he looked away. He had what was generally called a 'frank' face, every emotion readable: *How much longer do I have to keep this up?*

Foxford went on, 'But they can't hang me for the crime because I simply didn't do it. Ask anyone who knew Patrick! He was like a father to me!' Sweat stood out on the young man's face – understandable in the heat, and yet January sensed that heat was not the only cause.

'Tell me about Lord Montague Blessinghurst, then.'

For one second there was unmasked terror in those expressive eyes. 'I don't know anyone of that name.'

January made no reply.

'I don't! Who . . . who is it?' he added with a total lack of innocence.

'He's the man Patrick Derryhick quarreled with on Thursday night,' said January gently, 'just before he returned to the hotel and his death.' The boy's eyes widened: horror and shock. 'And he's the man you called a scoundrel – and attempted to assault – at Mr Trulove's ball in Milneburgh on your first night in town. Did Derryhick know him?'

'No, of course not.'

'How do you know that,' asked Shaw mildly, his long arms folded, 'if'n you don't know who he is?'

'I – that is – I don't know who he is, but Patrick would have said . . . Patrick didn't know him.'

'An' the girl you fought over?'

'We didn't fight over a girl.'

Shaw spat. 'Then why'd you fight?'

'We didn't. I mean, I – he – he called me a – I don't remember. I was drunk,' added the boy defiantly. 'Uncle Diogenes *told* me I'd quarreled with a man but I didn't remember any of it. *Did* we fight over a girl?'

'According to witnesses,' said January, 'you quarreled – with sufficient violence as to alarm bystanders – over a young lady named Isobel Deschamps—'

'Oh,' said the Viscount quickly. 'Oh, yes – was that her name? I saw this man – this Blessinghurst, you call him – trying to force his attentions on her and I . . . Well, one doesn't simply stand by and let that sort of thing take place, does one? The man was clearly a scoundrel.'

January opened his mouth to point out that this directly contradicted his statement of three seconds previously; to ask why, since he had only been in New Orleans less than twenty-four hours at that point, the young lady had addressed him by his Christian name; to inquire what he, his uncle and their business manager were doing in a city known throughout the world as a pest hole in the summertime . . . and then closed it. The dogged wariness in the young man's eyes informed him, if the foregoing conversation had not, that he would obtain nothing but more, and clumsier, lies. Instead he said, gently, 'Your Lordship, I'm trying to help you. You say they can't hang you because you didn't do it. But if you go before a jury with the weak excuses you've given me today, I can promise you that they will.'

NINE

'Do you believe him?'

Shaw stopped in the door of the watch room, his sparse brows twitching down over his gargoyle nose. 'Do I believe him *what*? If'n I had a dollar for every lie that boy told us just now . . .'

Behind them in the courtyard came the leathery smack of a whip on meat, the girl's frantic scream. January's jaw hardened so much that he thought his teeth would break. He followed the Kentuckian into the dim rumbling confusion of the watch room again.

'Do you believe he killed Derryhick?'

Shaw sighed, and in that sigh January heard the lies of sweet maiden aunts who had murdered their brothers for the family property, of respectable French Creole society matrons who tortured slaves in their attics, of charitable gentlemen who thought nothing of raping fourteen-year-old black girls. . . .

'What is truth?' Pontius Pilate had asked: the cry from the heart of judges and policemen down through the ages.

'Believin' ain't my job,' said Shaw, after they had picked their way through the crowded chamber in a silence that January had not had the temerity to break. 'But whether or not Derryhick pulled a gun on this Blessin'hurst Lordship just before he hightailed it back to his hotel to meet his Maker, somethin' about this-all sure don't listen right to me. I'll sure look this feller up. They's only two or three hotels in town where a Lordship would put up. An' I'll look into where else Uncle Diogenes mighta been – an' this Droudge feller as well, who ain't got much better of a story than His Lordship, exceptin' that his boots was clean Friday mornin' an' there weren't no watch with blood on it under his bed . . . Any chance you can catch Quennell at the coffin shop an' ask what it was His Other Lordship said to Derryhick that got his dander up?'

'Unfortunately, not directly.' They stepped through the

Cabildo's doors into the arcade again and stood looking out across the Place d'Armes in the queer, thickening light of coming storm. 'The problem is that I'm supposed to be watching him at the Countess's for another reason entirely . . .'

'A reason that's got to do with him spendin' time at the most expensive whorehouse in town on a bank clerk's salary?'

Of course, it was Shaw's business to know who was doing what in New Orleans . . . 'A reason that's got to do with him keeping the books for the Burial Society,' January said pointedly. 'So it's best I don't draw his attention to me as a man who asks questions. I'll have to speak to the other members of the board.'

'Fair 'nuff. Consarn,' Shaw added mildly, as two youths emerged from the mouth of Rue du Levee, where that seedy waterfront thoroughfare debouched into the Place d'Armes, and pelted in the direction of the Cabildo in arm-waving panic. 'Don't folks in this town never just sit an' watch the flies?'

When Shaw strode off in the direction of the two winged Mercuries – who seized the policeman by the arms as soon as he came in grasping distance and poured out some frantic tale, pointing back in the direction from which they'd come – January considered seeking out Hannibal. But he judged that by the time he reached the Swamp – rain or no rain – the local desperadoes would be just drunk enough to be looking for trouble, and he had had, he considered, trouble sufficient unto the day.

So he returned to home, Rose, and Sunday dinner, and then an evening of sitting on the gallery of their house overlooking Rue Esplanade, watching the lightning and playing his guitar for the woman he most loved on earth.

At one point, listening to his account of the parallel events and discoveries of The Problem of the White Half-Brother and The Problem of the Deceased Irishman, Rose remarked, 'Does it occur to you that Hannibal knows a great deal more about this than he should?'

It had, but January found himself as unwilling to look in that direction as Hannibal was to consider Foxford's guilt. 'He knows the family. And he was part of Derryhick's "merry band" . . .'

'There's a difference between "knowing the family" and

being as certain as he claims to be that a boy he last encountered as a child in dresses is innocent. If, in fact, he hasn't seen the boy for seventeen years.'

January's fingers stilled on the strings. 'Did you see his face when he saw Derryhick's body? That shock was genuine. I'll take oath on it.'

'You may have to.'

He glanced sidelong at her.

'It won't have escaped Lieutenant Shaw,' she went on, 'that, for a man who's spent the past two nights making discreet enquiries in every gambling hell and brothel in town as to the whereabouts of Uncle Diogenes, Hannibal has taken good care not to come face-to-face with the Viscount himself . . . and did so even before anyone viewed the murder scene. He "absquatulated", as Shaw would put it, before the City Guard even arrived. You don't happen to know where *Hannibal* was on Thursday night, do you?'

'I don't,' said January. 'I imagine it could be found out readily enough . . . if Shaw hasn't discovered it himself already. Hannibal didn't know who the boy was on Monday night. I'll take oath on that, too. When I spoke to him Friday, after the funeral, he was simply too hung-over to lie.'

Rose's quick-flash smile disappeared as swiftly as it had come. 'You may be right about that. Still,' she said, 'there's something about his – his *certainty* – that doesn't look well.'

'I don't know whether it's certainty,' said January, 'or just wilful blindness. With luck, Lord Montague Blessinghurst will put in an appearance at the Countess's tomorrow night, and things will become a little clearer.'

That Monday night Jacob Schurtz returned to the Countess's, ebullient with champagne and eager to explain to the beautiful Sybilla, in rather fuddled detail, how Martin Van Buren's aristocratic penchant for silk dressing-gowns and golden coffee-spoons was despoiling the pockets of honest Americans – to which the Irish girl listened with a fascination that January knew would lead to hair pulling and accusations of betrayal the next time Trinchen got drunk. Trinchen spent a good deal of effort trying to edge herself into the conversation and on to the wealthy Yankee's knee, a spectacle that Martin Quennell – present also – seemed to take in good part. Quennell, January noted, had replaced his champagne-ruined attire: new-made coat, trousers, and three new waistcoats in the most stylish of embroidered silks.

Can't look shabby when you're on the town with your prospective brother-in-law.

As before, the young man restricted himself to jest and innuendo with several of the girls, and he finally settled near an elderly Pennsylvania cotton broker, to explain whether the New Orleaneans really – as the Pennsylvanian had been told – worshipped the dead.

'The Creoles don't exactly worship them,' said Quennell, his voice – and his slight accents of distaste – distancing himself from the entire French side of town. 'It's more like a work party, really . . . Only, of course, Creoles will make a picnic out of anything . . .' He shrugged fastidiously, as if his parents, his aunts and uncles, and his cousins were some kind of quaintly primitive tribe who had stolen him away from his true family in childhood, and from whom he had had the good luck to escape. 'Mostly, it's because they can't bury their dead properly here, the water-table being so high. They bury them in brick tombs, but local brick is soft and deteriorates quite quickly. You've surely seen the cemetery . . .?'

The planter shook his head, evidently as interested as he would have been about a funeral procession of gong-beating Chinese.

'It's devilish fascinating, if a trifle Gothic. They take a day to clean up the graves and make a picnic of it while they're at it. That's all.'

'Good lord. Never heard of such a thing, have you, little flower?' The cotton broker turned and stroked the knee of La Habañera, who was sitting on the arm of his chair.

'Oh, but it isn't all, señor.' The girl – who was probably young enough to be the man's granddaughter – gazed at him with doe-like brown eyes. 'It is our custom too, you understand, in Cuba and in Mexico . . . The Feast of All Saints is the day when we honor our families. The feast in the cemeteries is not only for the living – uncles, cousins, aunts, *abuelos* – but also for those who have gone on to Heaven. It is the day when we remember that we must all look out for one another in this world . . . and in the next.'

'A bit morbid, if you ask me.' Quennell waved dismissively.

'I've always preferred the American way of gathering with the family at Christmas time. More wholesome. You say you're from Philadelphia, sir? Now, *there's* a town that has some good American energy. Might I ask you what bank you deal with there? I'm in the banking business myself and looking to make a change . . .'

The two men settled into the fascinating business of discussing money, and La Habañera – completely outjockeyed – withdrew. January's hands floated lightly over the keys:

Then fill the Goblet high,
Rich with rosy wine,
On pinions lightly fly,
Th' ambrosial hours divine.

January was still turning over in his mind the possibility that Beauvais Quennell might be in partnership with his half-brother to loot the Burial Society's funds, against the greater likelihood that he had been the younger man's ignorant tool, when he bade Auntie Saba a gallant goodnight and descended the kitchen steps into the outer darkness. He'd paused indoors long enough to slather his face and neck with a preparation of Olympe's, of oil and aromatics, which helped some against the mosquitoes: big Hughie-Boy, in the kitchen to cadge a last bit of bread and pâté before locking up, asked, 'Don't it stink?' and January grinned.

'Would you bite somebody, smelled like this?'

Hughie-Boy was still trying to figure out if that was an actual question or not as January descended the backstairs and paused to let his eyes adjust to the moonless dark.

Some men carried lanterns when they walked abroad at this hour. January knew few free colored, and fewer ex-slaves, who troubled with them, except on the darkest nights. A lantern would only show you up: to the City Guards who upheld the ordinance that men of color must be indoors at sunset; to drunken gangs of keelboat ruffians who would occasionally wander this far from the waterfront looking for solitary walkers to rob; to the men who made a profession of kidnapping free blacks to sell to the new cotton lands opening in the territories. With English mills paying sky-high prices for cotton, a field hand was going for twelve hundred dollars, even in these worrisome times. And once a black man's free-papers had been torn up, no one who did not know him would believe him when he protested, 'But I'm free . . .!'

Not no more you ain't, boy.

Enough moon glimmered through the breaking clouds to show up the pattern of lights and darks that January recognized as the path around the upstream side of the house. Eight strides to the right, then fifteen straight through the muddy darkness would take him out to the skeletal blue whisper of Prytania Street. Above the roaring of the cicadas in the woods that crowded close on that side, he could still hear the voices of the girls in the house:

'Who borrowed my green ribbon?'

'You bitch, you told me that runty one wasn't no back-door man . . .'

It was the shrill bickering of those who have been helpless all their short lives, quarrelsome with after-hours champagne. Most of them weren't much older than the girls who would be returning to Rose's school within a few weeks: two at least, January guessed, were younger. Sometimes the soprano chatter, the rustle of petticoats and accusations of petty thefts touched him with a terrible pity and sadness, so similar they were to the same rustle, the same demands about ribbons and trinkets – sometimes the same giggling over secrets – traded among those girls who would so shortly be sharing the neat little attic rooms beneath his roof. Placées' daughters, or of men whose white fathers had given their mixed-race sons plantation land distant from New Orleans. Girls whose parents would rather see their daughters educated to be something other than placées in their turn.

He frowned as he moved toward the corner of the house. Something was wrong.

Frogs . . . were they not as loud as they usually were?

And no nightbirds.

He stood still. The voices of the girls dimmed from the house behind him, as the last of them sought their much-used beds. To his right, where the trees came close to the house, a *grosbec* squawked once, then fell silent.

It was foolish, and he knew that the way around the upstream side of the house was muddier and pitch-black because of the angle of what moonlight there was . . . Still, he took that way, walking softly as he'd learned to do in tiniest childhood, feeling the deep rain-puddles from the afternoon squish under his boots.

Moonlight showed him the edge of the house ahead of him. He moved into the open, to cross over Prytania Street, wondering if he was being ridiculous.

He wasn't. A shadow detached from the shadows on the downstream side of the house, and a vaguely familiar baritone called out softly, 'Is that you, Professor?'

Englishman. Customer. *Professor* or *Maestro* was the usual title Americans gave the whorehouse piano-player. The white V of a shirt front gleamed briefly against the man's moving shadow.

'It is.' At the same moment his mind registered that the man was walking toward him too fast, almost running.

Why wait in the trees?

An Englishman . . . .

January stepped back, and the man broke into a run at him. He dodged, veered, every instinct he possessed shouting at him even before the gunshot bellowed in the inky night. His attacker cursed, lunged, seized his arm – of course the bullet had gone nowhere near him – and, by his movement, January knew he had another gun in his pocket and was fumbling for it.

Does he think because I'm black I'm not going to hit a white man who just shot at me, when nobody is looking?

Evidently the Englishman did, and found out in the next split-second – probably to his astonished chagrin – how wrong he was. At six feet three inches, January had grown up used to not being challenged to fight by men his own color – and, of course, had never been permitted to lay a finger on *les blankittes* – but in Paris he had enrolled in a very popular boxing-school and had learned what was generally called 'good science'. The Englishman was only a few inches shorter than he, but bulky-strong. January hit him with sufficient force that both the man's feet left the ground, to judge by the sound his body made when it crashed down into the wet grass. It was too dark to tell whether his assailant was unconscious or merely stunned, and January didn't wait to find out.

In addition to being very strong, he was also very fast.

It wasn't by getting into fights that Compair Lapin survived his adventures.

He reached Canal Street in minutes, and only after he crossed it, to the denser shadows and street lamps of the French Town, did he slow down long enough to wonder what secret it was that Lord Montague Blessinghurst was willing to kill him in cold blood to protect.

He woke Rose and warned her of what he'd done. Some states punished a black man with death if he struck a white one, and like an idiot, he'd given Blessinghurst his name.

'Are you sure it was Blessinghurst?' She blinked short-sightedly at him in the candlelight, propped among the pillows with her brown braids tumbled over her shoulders as she groped for her spectacles. 'Both Uncle Diogenes and Mr Droudge are almost your height and—'

'Everything Diogenes Stuart owns is saturated with the smell of kif and frankincense,' he said. 'And Droudge has a nasal voice, almost shrill. And how do you know? Have you seen them?'

'*Some* of us,' said Rose pointedly, 'have classes to prepare for while certain members of the household are wallowing in sleep until noon.'

'Certain members of the household put in long hours at the bordello,' retorted January, kissing her.

'Hmm. As for Uncle Diogenes, he and I had a fascinating discussion about translating manuscripts at Landreaux's book-shop on Canal Street – not that M'sieu Stuart had the slightest idea who I was, but he was there looking at a truly astonishing Persian manuscript Landreaux had gotten. If the man wasn't boasting, he's a formidable scholar . . . even if he does smell of frankincense at thirty paces. Will the Countess back your version of the story? The man's a customer, and a wealthy one . . .'

'I know her guilty secret,' explained January, and Rose rolled her eyes. 'All I need for you to do, my nightingale, is to tell the City Guards when they come that I told you, when I got home, that I'd seen what looked like a fight and a shooting from the front porch of the Countess's late last night—'

'Your mother warned me there'd be nothing but trouble if you went to work at that place.'

'My mother has never forgiven me for refusing to pass along gossip about the customers.' He drew her to him and kissed her again, and she took off her spectacles.

Later, they descended together to the damp little storeroom beneath the house, where – behind a false wall – January had earlier in the summer made a little chamber wide enough to conceal two narrow bunks and a commode. This secret niche had been the result of several conversations back in July with a man who was organizing the New Orleans end of a network, known as the Underground Railway, to hide and assist runaway slaves. 'I didn't think,' he murmured, as Rose lay down beside him in the lower bunk, 'that I'd be the first person to try this out.'

Rose must have risen without waking him, for she was gone when he did wake, in the full hammering heat of the morning. In the kitchen, along with bread-and-butter and a cup of her excellent coffee, she provided him with the information that the City Guards had not turned up to arrest him yet. 'You couldn't have hit the man hard enough to kill him, could you?'

She sounded worried. Knowing Rose, January guessed that her concern was more that the crime might somehow be traced to him, rather than for any danger towards his immortal soul entailed in killing a man. Self-defense was self-defense, in the eyes of the Clockmaker who ran Rose's universe, but she knew January's strength.

'They'll know at the Countess's.' He'd brought to the kitchen with him a parcel made up of clean shirt and neckcloth, his good pumps, and the well-cut black suit and soberly embroidered waistcoat that comprised his professional wear. 'They should be awake by the time I get there.'

She sipped her own coffee. 'It would solve the problem if you did, of course—'

'I need to talk to him.'

'Then, since he knows it was you who hit him, we must hope he has a forgiving nature.'

January made no reply. As he wolfed down grits and eggs he was aware of her eyes on his face, yet she didn't ask, 'Why are you doing this?' They both knew why. Rose had known Hannibal for at least a year longer than January had, yet, when he'd asked her about the fiddler, she had confirmed his impression of an essential and desolate aloneness.

Patrick Derryhick, and the twelfth Viscount Foxford's father, were the only men he had ever spoken of as his friends.

As he set his empty plate and cup in the dish pan, she said, 'Be careful.'

He laid his hand to her cheek. 'I will.'

'Is there anything I can do?'

He was about to shake his head, then reconsidered. 'There is,' he said. 'Would you learn what you can about the household of Madame Celestine Deschamps? Especially, find out who her maid is, and the maid who looks after her daughter Isobel. Learn what time they go to church, and make their acquaintance.'

'If you're going to corrupt the Deschamps servants, would not some handsome young man better answer the case?' She considered the matter as she gathered the remaining dishes. 'Your nephew Gabriel is still a little young . . . Perhaps Helaine Passbon's younger brother? He's sufficiently Adonis-like . . . Or Pylade Vassage, who plays the flute so badly.'

'Too obvious. If they're young and flighty, I'll set Dominique on them.'

'First murder, now – what? Blackmail? Housebreaking?'

'I don't know.' January picked up his parcel from the table, slipped into the jacket of lightweight linen that he habitually wore, even in the hottest point of the summer, as a way of distinguishing himself from the rough-clothed working-class blacks who unloaded the steamboats at the wharves. 'But it seems to me there are an awful lot of people not telling the truth about what happened last Thursday night. And if you're looking for the way things really happened, you're more likely to get the truth from servants than from their masters.'

TEN

'Now, what would a respectable downtown Free Gentleman of Color like yourself be doin' to get on the wrong side of the City Guard?' Auntie Saba cocked her good eye at January. In the ten days he'd worked for the Countess, January had taken care never to let his English sound too polished, and had shown himself willing to help with the clean-up at the end of the night. Yet he'd been aware that the cook and her children still regarded him very much as a 'downtown nigger' – or, in the more usual parlance of the American-born, Protestant, and on the whole more African-blooded slaves owned by the Americans, a 'stuck-up downtown nigger'. The only reason the phrase hadn't been expanded to include the word 'yeller' was because, despite one white grandparent, he looked pure Wolof.

The style of his piano playing – several cuts above the general run of what was usually found in the town's bordellos – and the wide classical end of his repertoire, were a dead giveaway. He might lie with his language, but was incapable of doing so with his music.

'I didn't do nuthin',' said January gravely, and Auntie Saba grinned. 'Musta been some other Free Gentleman of Color.'

'Well, you got nuthin' to worry about, Big J. City Guards ain't come knockin'. An' if they was to do so, you was in the kitchen with us, wasn't he, babies –' her glance took in both her children as they came back with pails from the tall copper cistern in the corner of the yard – 'when the shootin' started. I'll make sure Hughie knows it, too.'

January – chopping kindling in his shirtsleeves beside the kitchen door – raised his eyebrows. 'You heard that shot, then?'

'Lordy, yes. Only reason Her Ladyship didn't was she sleeps at the back of the house.' The cook resumed her steady turning of the coffee grinder. Despite the late hour of the morning, the pink-brick house loomed silent behind them, heat radiating from the open kitchen door as if from an oven. Sensibly, Auntie Saba had built up her kitchen fire in the wide brick hearth as soon as it was light, to get the day's meals started before the heat set in, and she had moved her coffee making out under the tree in the yard where some coolness still lingered. 'After a minute or three, we went out on the gallery, but we didn't see nuthin'.'

'Not even no body,' added Little J, disappointed.

'Thank you, m'am.' January whacked another billet from the chunk in front of him. As a child he'd learned to handle an ax easily, and he'd also learned that cutting kindling was a task that would buy him favors from almost anyone. 'I appreciate it.'

Elspie's great hazel eyes widened, and Little J demanded, 'Who was it?'

January whacked another long split of wood off the billet on the chopping block. 'I don't know,' he said. 'Since I wasn't out there. But if Lord Montague comes in tonight, take a look at his jaw, see if he's got a bruise.'

'Oh dear God—' Elspie put a swift hand to her lips.

'Don't tell me you're gettin' a soft place for that cake-mouth Englishman after all,' the older woman sniffed.

'What? Nasty beast!' Elspie made a face. 'I'm just afraid I'm the one set him on you! Just talking too free . . .'

'Did you, now?' January cocked his head, spoke in his mildest voice. 'Talking to who?'

'Marie-Venise. Just talking, you know.' The girl's face showed real distress. 'Oh, I knew I shouldn't say anything about anything . . .! I just said you asked about Lord Montague, Saturday night, when I told you he kissed me like he did. He come to see her Sunday. I helped her sneak out, 'cause she don't charge him money an' she hides most of the gifts he gives her. The Countess'd snatch her bald-headed if she knew.' Elspie shook her head. 'She musta told him. I am so sorry—'

'I've had worse happen.' January straightened up. 'But if you will – all of you . . .' He looked from Auntie Saba to her children. 'Best if we don't speak of this again – not to anyone.'

Heads were shaken, and Little J crossed his heart and his fingers in mute avowal.

'I never thought he'd come after you with a gun!'

'Course you didn't,' said January. 'Why would you? I'll just have to keep one eye out behind me for awhile, that's all.' He turned the conversation to other things as he finished the kindling and stacked it by the laundry-room door. But he watched the back of the house as he worked, wondering which tightly-curtained bedroom window was that of Marie-Venise, and whether that skinny, boy-shaped French girl was watching him from it. When he donned his waistcoat and jacket to leave – depositing the little parcel of his evening clothes on a shelf in the laundry room – he was careful to depart through the woods, rather than proceed back to the French Town by way of Prytania Street.

It was nearly noon when he crossed Canal Street and regained the only portion of New Orleans, now, where he felt more or less safe. He could hear the raucous jangle of a brass band down on Rue du Levee, where the local Democrats had got up a parade in honor of Martin Van Buren's candidacy, but the colonnaded building that he sought on Rue d'Orleans was quiet. He slipped around the corner and through its garden door.

Even in the dead heat of noon, John Davis's gambling casino stirred with voices and the clink of coin. Half a dozen French doors stood open to the street, to draw in what breeze there was from the river; an equal number opened to the garden. Through them January glimpsed the establishment's regulars: French Creole gentlemen who lived in the Old Town, had cottages in Milneburgh, but preferred to come in on the steam train to meet their friends there. At one table a couple of steamboat pilots played a desultory game of cribbage, but for the most part the big, square room, with its high ceiling and crystal chandeliers, seemed half-asleep, waiting for the evening. Flies roared everywhere. John Davis himself – a Frenchman to his fingertips, despite the name of a Scots ancestor – stood near the bar that stretched across one end of the room, talking city politics with a French planter.

January positioned himself in one of the garden doorways, where he knew that in time he would catch Davis's eye. Davis saw him – there was no detail of the gaming room that the man's glance didn't touch – and gave him a slight nod, though he continued his chat with M'sieu Destrehan. It would never do for a white man to conclude a conversation with another white man and then be seen to go and speak to a black one – even a black one who'd gotten him off a murder charge a few years before. The insult would be intolerable and would possibly result in a duel. But, in time, Destrehan made his way to one of the tables to speak to another acquaintance – catching

January's eye in passing and nodding a greeting, having himself hired January on any number of occasions to play at his house – and Davis moved toward the windows.

'Ben,' said Davis with a grin as they both stepped out into the garden. 'We're starting rehearsals for Donizetti's *Elixir of Love* next month: I hope you're not intending to make your change of career permanent at this stage.' Of course, Davis had heard he was playing at the Countess's, though as a French Creole he would not, naturally, frequent an Uptown whorehouse. 'We're counting on you.'

'Oh, sir.' January wrung his hands in bogus sorrow. 'Sir, I beg your forgiveness, but it would tear me up inside to have to go back to Donizetti, after playing "Old Zip Coon" seven times a night for drunk Americans . . .'

Davis threw back his head and laughed. He had aged, January thought, and not just since the death of his wife a few years ago. The scandal and murder at the opera, the winter before last, had left its mark: on the man's lined face and in the wider streaks of white in his hair.

'What can I do for you, Ben?' He offered January a cigar – something only John Davis had the social standing to do for a black man and get away with it – and January shook his head in mute thanks.

'Just looking for information, sir.'

'You, too? I told Shaw, Friday, that Stuart fellow wasn't in here.'

'What about a gentleman named Blessinghurst? Lord Montague Blessinghurst?'

'Not him, either.'

'But there was a set-to here Thursday night?' January nodded back toward the dim cavern behind them.

'Half a dozen.'

'This one would have involved a gun and the words "bog-Irish bastard"— '

'Oh, good Lord!' The tired look vanished from Davis's eyes like dew in the sunshine, and he burst into laughter. 'Lord Montague Blessinghurst, eh? Tall fellow, good-looking, green coat?'

'That's the man.'

'That fellow, my dear Benjamin –' the impresario put a hand on his arm and drew him conspiratorially behind a pepper-tree

– 'is no Lordship, but rather a gentleman named Frank Stubbs, whom I had the ill fortune to see play Malcolm to Charles Kemble's Macbeth a few seasons ago in New York. All the ladies in the audience were swooning, God help them—'

'An *actor*?'

'Benjamin, please!' Davis recoiled in mock affront. 'Calling Frank Stubbs an actor is a slur on the whole of a noble profession! He's been on stage and been paid for it. Let's leave it at that.'

No wonder 'Lord Blessinghurst' wanted to silence me, thought January, *when he heard I was asking questions about him*. He had only to phrase the thought to discard it. Murder? There was something else. Something deeper . . . 'What's he doing in New Orleans, sir? You're sure it was he?'

'Oh, absolutely.' Davis chuckled again. 'I never mistake a voice, and his is remarkable. I'll give him that.'

As the owner of New Orleans's largest theater, and the head of her original opera company, voices were John Davis's business. And he wasn't likely to be mistaken about a man he'd seen on a stage.

'As to what he's doing in town . . . Well, I don't know the man, but by the look of things on Thursday night, I'd say he was trying to build a small amount of money into a large one.'

'You don't happen to know what the fight was about?'

'Not an inkling.' Davis shook his head again, and added, as if to himself, 'Lord Montague Blessinghurst indeed! What a name! Straight out of a three-volume novel! The good Lieutenant needs to stop taking these scoundrels at their word about who and what they say they are.'

'Did Derryhick come in with him?'

'Derryhick?' Davis frowned. 'You mean that was the gentleman whose corpse ended up . . .? Good Lord.' He stood silent for a moment, evidently putting pieces together in his mind. Rameses Ramilles had played regularly for the balls that Davis hosted in the room upstairs and for the opera; the impresario had, January knew, subscribed generously to the small trust fund that the FTFCMBS was setting up for Liselle and her children.

Davis went on, 'Stubbs was playing that night with Fitz Trulove and a couple of Americans. I was keeping an eye on the table by that time, because Stubbs – *Blessinghurst!* – was winning with suspicious steadiness. Of course, Trulove wouldn't notice if one of the other players reached over, stuck his hand in his pocket and helped himself, which is precisely what I think Stubbs was doing. But the game broke up, and Trulove and one of the Americans – Schurtz, I think his name is, just come to town this past spring and is staying out at the lake somewhere – went off to talk banking and left the other American and Stubbs to play cribbage in that corner.' He nodded in the direction of one of the smaller tables, where the regulars would go to play dominoes in the afternoon. On even a moderately busy evening, January guessed that the view of it would be frequently blocked to a man standing – as Davis was wont to do – at the wall end of the mahogany bar.

'Derryhick came in from the street and went straight to them, but I didn't think much of it, you know. My place is well enough known that if men want to meet, they often do so here.'

January nodded. It was the same with the coffee stands under the market arcade. 'So you couldn't tell if they knew each other?'

Davis shook his head. January noted again that during the whole of their conversation, the older man had been watching the room through the wide windows. He would have bet money, had he had any to spare, that Davis could have identified every man who had come in and gone out through the French doors into Rue d'Orleans, named three-quarters of them, and – like a good Creole – attached to at least two-thirds of them an account of family history, relative wealth (both actual and putative), and a catalogue of recent scandals.

'I was back by the bar talking about the election with Blodgett from the *Bee*. What a mess the Whigs are making of it, eh? Next thing I knew, I heard a chair go clattering over, where the American playing with Stubbs had sprung up and backed to the wall. The Irishman had Stubbs by the shirt collar, for all he was a hand-span shorter, and I couldn't swear it – that corner's a chasm at night – but I thought he had a gun in his other hand. I was starting over to them when the Irishman all but threw Stubbs away from him against the table, said, "The curse of Cromwell on the pair of ye's!" and went striding out into the street again. The American didn't move from where he stood, but Stubbs ran out to look after him up the street. But he was gone.'

'In what direction did Stubbs look?'

Davis thought about it for a moment, then nodded in the direction up Rue Orleans and away from the river . . . The direction of the Iberville Hotel.

'The pair of you,' January repeated. 'Did he mean the American that Stubbs – Blessinghurst – was with, sir, do you think?'

'He could have.' The entrepreneur frowned. 'I didn't have that impression, but, of course, I could be wrong. Though, now that I think of it, I'm not entirely sure the other man was an American. There was something about the way he dressed that said French Creole, but you'll seldom find a Creole keeping company with our Northern brethren.'

'Our Northern brother Schurtz has a sister with a large dowry.'

'Does he?' Davis beamed. Added to his Creole fascination for information, like most saloon and theater owners he had an appetite for gossip that would have made a maiden aunt blush. 'Does he indeed? Well, well . . . No wonder the other man hung about the way he did, waiting for Schurtz to finish his chat with Trulove. What's his name, this would-be suitor? I haven't seen him in here before, and I know most of the French Creoles.'

'Martin Quennell. He clerks for Gardiner at the Mississippi and Balize—'

'What, in those waistcoats?'

January put a finger to his lips. 'I need to ask for your discretion, if I may, sir. And so far I've found nothing,' he added, seeing Davis's bright blue eyes suddenly narrow, 'that indicates there's any question about stability of the bank. We think he's getting his money elsewhere. The bank keeps a close eye on its accounts—'

'It had better,' said Davis grimly. 'What I'm hearing about the credit market isn't good. I think the Democrats will be able to keep the lid on things until after the election, but I tell you, Benjamin, I'm moving my funds into a state bank.'

'Not having any funds to move,' replied January, 'I feel perfectly indifferent to the outcome of the contest. I shall decide for whom to vote,' he added grandly, 'by the toss of a coin.'

Davis laughed again – the idea of a black man voting for anyone being a subject of humor anywhere in the United States – and clapped January on the shoulder. 'That's the spirit!

Quennell – not Robert Quennell, of Quennell and LaRouche back before the crash of '19? Never one of the big ones, but perfectly respectable in their day. Banking must be in the blood.'

'Having a father who knows to send you to school, rather,' commented January. 'It must be galling to work as a bank clerk when you can remember better days – not to mention doing the books for the son of your father's placée. My mother tells me Quennell put Madame Corette aside – his placée, that is – when he married one of old Jules Charlevoix's daughters, but young Martin seems to have cast in his lot pretty firmly with the Americans.'

'Well, if he's planning on impressing anyone with supposed wealth and fancy waistcoats,' said Davis, with a glance back into his gambling rooms, 'he'd best not play cards with Frank Stubbs. *Â bientôt*, my dear Benjamin – I see M'sieu Soniat approaching the bar, and I promised Madame Soniat on the soul of my mother I would water any drink he attempted to buy.'

'You are a worker for the good of the world, sir.'

Davis laughed and disappeared back into the shadows of his chosen realm.

The pair of you, January reflected, as he made his way – with a certain amount of caution – back toward Rue Esplanade and, he hoped, a quiet dinner with Rose. With luck the afternoon thunderstorm, slowly grumbling its way in from the Gulf, would hold off until he reached the Countess's. The fact that Davis hadn't greeted him with, 'Good God, Benjamin, don't you know the City Guards are after you?' provided a certain amount of comfort, but still, he approached his own house almost as warily as he'd entered the casino.

The pair of you.

The Curse of Cromwell – the worst malediction an Irishman could hurl – *on the pair of you . . .*

Lord Montague Blessinghurst – or, rather, Frank Stubbs – and who else?

Someone Patrick Derryhick had expected to meet at the Hotel?

Someone, possibly, who was meeting Uncle Diogenes – or the Viscount himself – there?

Or someone else?

The Rue Esplanade lay deserted under the brazen weight of noon. January slipped around the corner, strode as inconspicuously as it was possible for a six-foot three-inch man to stride up the steps to the gallery, and ducked into the shadows of the seldom-used 'gentleman's room' – traditionally the bedroom of the master of the house, which he employed as a study. As a child, it had always puzzled him why neither he nor anyone else was permitted to step through the French doors directly into the parlor, but instead had to go through one or the other of the bedrooms on either side, but, 'Only American animals –' his mother had informed him with an explanatory slap on the ear – 'did that.'

'I take it you were able to avoid the police?' Rose appeared in the doorway from the parlor, arms filled with fresh paper, fresh ink-bottles, fresh quills.

'Were they here?'

'Not a one.' She yielded the ink bottles and quills to his grasp, and he followed her through the open archway into the dining room. 'When no one had come by noon I took the bull by the horns and went down to the Cabildo and asked Lieutenant Shaw what this rumor a market-woman had told me about you being wanted by the police was about. It was outrageous, I said, what some people don't scruple to pass along to innocent women about their husbands. I must admit the good Lieutenant regarded me askance,' she added. 'But he said no, he'd heard nothing of the kind.'

'Which doesn't mean Blessinghurst didn't storm into the Cabildo as you were leaving it,' said January thoughtfully. 'I doubt he did, though. The man's hiding something, and not just,' he added, 'that he is not Lord Montague Blessinghurst at all, but rather an actor named Frank Stubbs. What's this?' He took the note Rose handed him and identified the seals – and the handwriting – even as he spoke.

Madeleine Mayerling.

He cracked the wax, unfolded the stiff sheet:

> M'sieu J,
> A most curious circumstance: Isobel Deschamps has left Mandeville – and apparently New Orleans – and will not, her Mama tells me, be back this year.
> Yours,
> M.M.

ELEVEN

'A girl about to start her third season, leaving town before it begins?' January leaned forward in the sturdy cypress-wood chair on Madeleine Mayerling's gallery. He'd been surprised to find the lady still in New Orleans. Even here, fifteen feet above the shaded garden, the sunlight hummed with flies. 'That's unheard of.'

'It's not unheard of for a girl to *want* to leave,' remarked Madame Mayerling. Her hand, beating a steady time with a lacquered fan, seemed to operate on its own, a large deft-boned machine. 'What *is* unheard of is that her mother would let her . . . especially a mother with *another* daughter, fifteen years old, who can't be brought out until the first one is engaged.' For a few moments the only sounds were the far-off clatter of a wagon in the Rue Royale and the metallic whirr of the cicadas.

Then January asked softly, 'What's going on, Madame?'

'I don't know. But her mother wanted me out of there, when I went to call. No gossip, no queries about Aunt 'Lalie's latest attempts to force my poor cousin Marie-Alceste into marriage with that frightful Cuban planter who's been corresponding with her . . . Re-heated coffee from yesterday's grounds, it tasted like, and stale cake.'

'You shock me!' January mimed shock, and Madame Mayerling laughed.

'You don't know what you've missed, not having had a good French Creole matron try to get you out of her drawing room without violating the letter of good manners.'

January, who had nearly been crippled by a good French Creole matron who saw nothing amiss in torturing slaves – or people who in her opinion should have been slaves – only replied, 'On the contrary, Madame, good French Creole matrons have nothing on my mother when she's trying to get herself shut of a caller. She has a tone of voice that would chill lemonade in Hell. But why? Did she give a reason?'

'Half a dozen. The climate does not suit Isobel—'

'She was raised here.'

Madame Mayerling spread her hands, graceful in lace house-mitts. 'Did you imagine she was telling the truth? *She has been a little indisposed all summer*, even though I saw the girl a week ago at M'sieu Trulove's ball and she was in the bloom of health . . . until she encountered milord Blessinghurst. *In truth, she has not been the same since her return from Paris . . .*' The young woman frowned suddenly and dropped her quite-excellent imitation of Celestine Deschamps's piping voice and feathery gestures.

'Is the sister still in New Orleans?'

'Marie-Amalie,' replied Madeleine grimly. 'Yes, she is. And *she* is *not* out, much less in her third season – the point at which Mamas start writing to matchmaking cousins in other cities. If this Blessinghurst was Isobel's lover – and is, as you say, an actor – I can understand her mother wanting to get her out of the city.'

'Do you think that's what's happening? That Blessinghurst and Isobel became lovers in Paris, and young Foxford followed her here?' If it was true, a young girl in such an affair would be in an impossible situation. Neither the Deschamps family nor its web of related clans of tightly inter-wed French Creoles would permit her to marry an actor, even if she and her sister were *not* heiresses to several extremely valuable cotton plantations. And, of course, if word got back to the Stuarts of Foxford Priory that the woman sought by His Young Lordship was not virgin – whether she had consented or been forced – there was no question of *that* marriage being permitted either.

He wondered how much the young Viscount knew.

'When did she leave?'

'Friday,' said Madeleine.

'The day of the funeral,' said January. 'The day after Patrick Derryhick's quarrel with Blessinghurst – and the day after his death.'

By the time January left the Trepagier townhouse it was close to five. Only by hastening straight to the Countess's through the beginnings of the afternoon rainstorm was he able to arrive before the house was ready to open its doors, and a visit to the Cabildo – to see what Viscount Foxford would have to say to the extraordinary coincidence of the mademoiselle's departure – would have to wait. Neither Martin Quennell nor 'Sir Montague

Blessinghurst' visited the Countess's that evening. Indeed, on that hot Tuesday night only two men crossed the threshold between six and two the following morning. The Countess's firmness, tact, and temper were tested to the utmost in keeping the girls from quarreling among themselves out of boredom.

January played softly and listened, without appearing to, to the girls talk among themselves: Marie-Venise had on new earrings, sufficiently showy to arouse envy in her housemates, tears in Trinchen – which earned her a slap from the Countess – and speculation in January about where 'Lord Montague' had acquired the money needed to come to New Orleans, let alone to maintain the open-handedness necessary to convince the local planters that he was a nobleman and not a card sharp.

If Frank Stubbs did manage to marry thirteen hundred acres of cotton at thirty-seven cents a pound, the investment would be well worth a few lies or a scratched face. But where had he gotten the money to introduce himself into French society in the first place? And did he actually think that the Deschampses and their relations the Ulloas, the Verrons, the Rochers, and Duplessises – both in New Orleans and in Natchitoches Parish – would countenance such a match without checking his bona fides? This wasn't like Quennell impressing Jacob Schurtz and Jacob Schurtz alone.

Was poor Mademoiselle Deschamps that smitten?

At the close of the evening three friends of Elspie's, musicians who played the far less elegant bucket-shops on the fringe of the Swamp, appeared at the back door and walked with January back to the French Town, picking an elusive course through half-cleared lots piled with building materials and streets that were little more than muddied tracks between walls of trees. More than once they stopped to let a half-seen flash of gleaming of scales pass by and saw, in the thin moonlight, the glint of an alligator's eyes.

'You wait for us tomorrow night, friend,' cautioned the tallest of the three – Preacher – when they reached the dark house on Rue Esplanade. 'Elspie say it was her talkin' too free got this Englishman a hard-on for you, an' you knows no buckra gonna be put off just 'cause you knocked him over once. He be back with some friends. You need to watch yourself.'

* * *

Since no member of the Watch had come to the Countess's last night to discuss the temerity of black men striking white ones in defense of their own lives, the next morning January went to the Cabildo.

Shaw said, 'Maestro.' Though the watch room was more populated than its usual wont, owing to the nearness of the election, at least it wasn't crowded with constituents and prospective office-holders, and the Lieutenant had his desk back. As January crossed to it, he saw Viscount Foxford seated next to it on a broken-down cane-bottom chair, and with him, not only Shaw – looking more like a raw-boned yellow wolf than ever – and the slouched and shabby Mr Droudge, but a stout gentleman in a gray coat, shiny with wear, and a pair of much-stained checked trousers.

'My attorney, Mr Chaffinch,' said the young man in introduction, and Chaffinch looked down his bulbous, broken-veined nose at January – though he stood some eight inches shorter – and muttered in plummy Oxonian accents, 'Mmmrm – just so.'

Droudge also regarded January with fish-eyed distaste and turned back to his employer without a word. 'You were saying, My Lord?'

Foxford looked hesitant – *good manners or worry about how much I might know?* – then, with an apologetic glance at January, returned to what was plainly an account of the previous Thursday night: 'I don't know the city and haven't the slightest idea where I walked . . .'

The lawyer smelled of liquor and unclean linen from the other side of the desk. January's glance went protestingly from Shaw to the fidgeting hands and red-veined nose – *he CAN'T be the best they could do!* – and back. Now and then Chaffinch rumbled, 'Just so, just so,' or once, 'Hrmm, hrmm, quite,' but made no attempt to take notes. Nor did he find anything amiss in the inconsistencies of his client's story. Foxford, for his part, kept glancing at Droudge worriedly, as if unsure of the lawyer's competence but unwilling to press the matter for fear of getting another attorney who *would* ask him where he'd really been . . .

'Well, well. I'm sure something can be made of that,' Chaffinch said at last and started to fish in his pockets for something – probably a bottle. 'Nothing to worry about, Your Lordship. Man's innocent until proven guilty, you know, even in the United States, and quite simply they have nothing on you.'

'There,' said Droudge triumphantly. 'It's as I said.'

Only a lifetime of hard-learned lessons about what black men were and were not permitted to say to white ones closed January's mouth, but Shaw had no such compunction. 'Well, that ain't entirely true, Mr Chaffinch, this bein' Louisiana an' all. We go by the Code Napoleon hereabouts.'

'Heavens, man, don't you think I know that?' The lawyer flushed an alarming color as he heaved himself to his feet. 'I've practiced in this state longer than *you've* worn shoes, I daresay! But certain principles of justice are inalterable, sir! Just because a man cannot prove himself *alibi* means nothing.'

'Indeed,' added Droudge, folding pale, clammy hands on his knee. 'We should be a good deal more concerned if His Lordship *had* produced a detailed explanation of a simple walk on a moonless night in a strange city!' He widened a stained horror of a smile. 'They're only trying to frighten you, My Lord, into paying some outrageous sum, I daresay, once you've been in jail long enough . . .'

'I assure you,' declared Chaffinch, 'that they cannot hang Your Lordship.' He turned defiantly back to Foxford and executed a bow that made his corsets creak. 'You have nothing to fear. And you, sir –' he stabbed an accusing finger at Shaw – 'I will not have you and the Jacobin ruffians who run the City Watch attempting to intimidate His Lordship. I am not without influence in this city. I will return tomorrow, Your Lordship.' He bowed to Foxford again. 'You let me know, if these – these *Frenchmen* and their myrmidons try to trick you into a confession of being anything but a simple visitor, minding his own business.'

He glared at Shaw, as he stood, like a grubby Sancho Panza, beside the tall, stooped form of Droudge. Foxford looked as if he were about to make some protest – or maybe just put in a request that on their next visit they bring him some food – but decided against it. Shaw put his hand under the young man's arm and led him back into the yard. Quietly, January followed.

As if he read January's thoughts, the Viscount said, rather wistfully, 'Mr Droudge assures me that the man is far more reliable than he looks.'

January had to force himself not to remark that Mr Chaffinch could hardly be *less* reliable than he looked. He suspected that, besides being English, the man had been hired because he was cheap, and also available without a great deal of trouble and search.

'Besides, he's quite right. They *can't* hang me because I didn't do anything. I was nowhere near the hotel. Anyone will tell the jury that Patrick was like a father to me! More than a father . . .' His voice grew suddenly quiet, and they stopped at the foot of the steps that led up to the cells. 'I barely remember mine.' His hesitant glance made January remember that this boy was scarcely into his twenties. The age his own son might be, he thought, had he wed and settled in New Orleans rather than taken ship for Paris, that summer of 1817.

'Mr Shaw tells me your friend Mr Sefton was a friend of my father's.'

January nodded.

'Do you think – is there a chance that he might come here to see me? Mother never spoke of him,' he added. 'But then, Mother hates all Patrick's "merry band" like poison.'

'I'll ask him,' said January. 'He was badly shaken,' he added carefully, 'seeing Mr Derryhick's body that way—'

'You mean he's spent the past week getting drunk?' The boy cocked a tourmaline-blue eye at him, knowing and sad. 'Patrick . . . He understood his friends. Even poor Cousin Theo, whom I loathed, by the way . . . Well, not loathed, really. I found him pathetic and maddening. Once I beat him up, when we were both at Eton, for what he did to Mother and to Aunt Grace. But Patrick would say, "'Tis not they can't carry their liquor, Gerry. 'Tis that they can't carry the world *without* their liquor." I didn't understand at the time . . .' He shook his head. 'I should like to see Mr Sefton, if he'll come.'

'I'll ask him. I can't promise. In the meantime,' he went on gently, 'if your mother is still alive . . .'

'I don't want her worried.' The boy's face altered, grew hard. 'I'll be well.'

'You will not be well.'

Foxford turned stubbornly away.

'It would help if you would at least tell me what passed between yourself and this Blessinghurst man – whose name isn't Blessinghurst at all, by the way. He's an actor, named Stubbs.'

The boy's fair skin flushed pink, and his lips pressed tight, but he kept his face resolutely averted.

'Is he, now?' Shaw paused in his ruminative chewing. 'No wonder I couldn't find the man at any of the class hotels.' He spat at a horsefly on the wall and missed by feet.

'It doesn't matter who he is,' insisted the Viscount. 'I don't know him. I never met him before Monday night.'

'Nor Isobel Deschamps?'

'I don't know anyone by that name.'

January tilted his head a little to one side. 'Not someone you met in Paris last winter?'

The muscles hardened in the young man's jaw. 'No.' He turned to look at Shaw. 'Are we done here, Lieutenant? I should like to go back to my cell.'

And when a man prefers to be locked into an adobe hot-box with two dozen other men – unwashed, lousy, some of them lying in their own vomit in the crawling straw of the floor – over continuing a conversation, January reflected, watching Shaw lead the young man up the steps to the cells, *that doesn't augur well for future confidences*.

As he walked toward the Countess's house a few hours later his mind returned to Isobel Deschamps. Recalled the look in her gray-turquoise eyes as she concentrated on a Mozart *bourrée*, striving to be perfect not solely to please her beautiful mother, but because the music itself demanded the best she could give it. On several occasions she had asked him about Paris, and France, and what the world was like beyond the low pastel walls of New Orleans; she was the first person to whom he had spoken of Paris in those first awful months after his return. 'It sounds so beautiful,' she had said. And – because he had told her that he had left Paris only because Ayasha's death had rendered it a place of horror for him – 'It must have broken your soul to pieces to leave.'

'It did,' he had said, a little surprised to hear himself speak the words. 'But souls heal, Mamzelle.'

She'd be almost nineteen now. A startling beauty, if she'd kept the promise of her youth. Starting her third season here in New Orleans, when she could have – should have – married someone in Paris.

And she had not.

TWELVE

The uproar within the Countess's house as he reached the back steps drove all thought of Isobel Deschamps from his mind. 'Iodine,' Belgian Louise wailed when he strode into the parlor. 'She drank iodine—'

'Trinchen,' said Auntie Saba, coming down the stairs.

January bolted for the stair, and so strong was his upbringing – even after years in Paris of being able to go up any flight of stairs that he pleased – that for an instant he hesitated, wondering if he should take the backstairs . . .

To hell with it! He pounded up the hallowed treads reserved for white gentleman and found the upstairs hall crowded with girls in various stages of undress. The Countess was kneeling in shift and corset beside Trinchen's bed, forcing egg and water down the girl's throat for what was – by the look of the slop bucket – the fourth or fifth time.

'Does it hurt?' La Habañera touched January's sleeve as he pushed through the door. 'To die so – does it hurt?'

The sounds coming from the bed were horrible, but he paused long enough to say gently, 'Yes. Yes, it hurts. Even if no one finds you and tries to stop you.'

The girl swallowed and spoke in a whisper, so the Countess wouldn't hear. 'Hurt worse than to live so?'

In Carnival season January knew the girls were bulled by five and six men a night – all of them drunk. He could hear her thoughts in her voice. She was fifteen, pure Creole Spanish with a complexion like alabaster, but he knew also that when that doe-like beauty faded she'd be working places like the shacks behind the Broadhorn.

What do I say? You'll go to hell? Well, so what. She's there already – looking over the edge into the next pit down.

In one of the other rooms, two girls were howling with grief. January heard Sybilla yell, 'Mother o' God, will the lot o' ye's shut yer cake holes? Christ bleedin' Jesus, somebody get in here and lace me up!'

'Does hope hurt worse?' he asked softly in Spanish, and La Habañera nodded. 'Do you still have that?'

'*Si*.'

'Good girl.' He nodded into the room before him. 'Pray for her.'

'*Si*.'

'Damn the lot of 'em.' The Countess looked up from her task as January came in. 'If she dies it'll set the rest of 'em off.'

Nenchen was huddled up in the chair on the other side of the bed, weeping without a sound. Fanny, ever efficient with her golden hair still in curl papers, came in with another pitcher of clean water.

'How long ago did she do this?' January observed that Trinchen wore a clean shift – or one that had been clean at some recent point in the afternoon – and the laces of the corset that lay on the floor had been cut. She'd been getting ready for the evening then. Not long ago.

He knelt by the bed, laid his ear to the girl's back, listening for the wild thready hammering of her heart.

The Countess waited till he straightened up before replying. 'Nenchen thinks, not more than half an hour before she found her.'

'Do you have charcoal? Clean charcoal powder.' Fanny was sent darting off down the stairs to fetch the Countess's medicine box. 'Convulsions?'

The Countess shook her head, regarded him with a considering look in her velvet-brown eyes. 'You know a good bit about this.'

'I was trained with Gomez, the surgeon who used to practice over on Rue St Pierre. Fräulein –' he beckoned Nenchen, who raised a tear-bloated face to stare at him as if she'd never seen him before – 'can you stay by her?' Then: 'Thank you, Mamzelle,' as Fanny held out the small packet of charcoal to him. 'Would you mix that with the water, please – about three-quarters of that pitcher. Can you stay by your sister, Fräulein, and give her this water, a little at a time, all the night?' He switched back from German to French to say to the Countess, 'Sometimes we have to change what we are to get a living in this world.'

Their eyes met; she raised one plucked and painted brow. 'Is that what you think I have done . . . *Signor*?'

He paused in the act of undraping the mosquito bar from above the bed, to spread its gauzy, tent-like folds to cover both Nenchen and her unconscious sister, and laid a hand on his heart. 'I spoke only of myself . . . *Countess*. But I assume that, at some time in your life, you changed yourself from what you were – a girl like this one here, who could not fight back against what life did to her – into what you are now. I'm going to open the window, if I may, and close the door to clear some of the smell—'

'Dear God, yes!' The gaudy room reeked of iodine and vomit. 'Fanny,' she ordered – of the girls who weren't in hysterics, the English girl seemed to be the only one who wasn't getting dressed as if it were a night like other nights – 'get some pastilles burning in the hall . . .'

'Fräulein,' asked January in German, 'what happened? Did Fräulein Trinchen get word of her friend Quennell?'

Nenchen blinked up at him; she was a big buxom girl of perhaps nineteen, her blonde hair lying in a pulled ruin over her sloping white shoulders. She answered in the same language – January had never heard her use any other. 'She knew he wants to marry that American cow, Professor. It stands to reason no rich American is going to want a whore like one of us, when he can marry the sister of his business partner and have money and a house. I told her he would be back . . .' She gently stroked a sweat-matted tangle of hair away from that white, pinched face on the pillow. 'She said then, "God, yes! He'll have his fill of that whining American bitch soon." But last night she cried, when she thought I was asleep. And the night before, also.'

In the next room he could hear the Countess cursing, and then the sudden smack of a palm on flesh; the weeping ceased abruptly. 'Now you little sluts get yourselves presentable, and if I see a one of you sniveling in front of the gentlemen tonight . . .'

The short New Orleans twilight had already gone from the window when January opened it. Elspie appeared in the doorway: 'Professor? Countess says, you need to be downstairs . . .'

Of course he did. As he descended – properly via the service stair, as befitted his station – he heard the parlormaid say, in the chamber behind him, 'M'am say you can stay here with Trinchen, Fräulein.'

'*Did* she get the push from Quennell?' he asked the Countess as he shrugged into his fancy waistcoat and long-tailed coat.

The woman shrugged, her mouth full of hairpins as she twisted up her curls. 'She may have. She may have only guessed he isn't really going to take her with him when he marries the Schurtz bitch – have you seen her, by the way? Same height as that brother of hers – taller than little Martin by the span of my hand! He'll have to stand on a box to get it in her. Same horse-face.' She selected a red rose from the vase on the table – rather surprisingly, she grew them in a little garden behind the kitchen – and pinned it into her hair. 'Same *exquisite* manners. He'll be served if Schurtz does consent to the match. Who knows why whores want to end it all?'

She turned to face him, her eyes defiant, wise, and bitterly sad. 'They're always doing it. I'm just glad it wasn't on a Saturday night. Hughie!' she called over her shoulder. 'You get the gas lit . . .'

January straightened his neckcloth, glanced in the parlor mirror as Elspie moved to unlock the front door. Aside from the heavier than usual reek of incense, the parlor looked normal, Sybilla already ensconced in her usual place on the sofa where the light was best and Clemence and Marie-Venise straightening the combs in each other's hair. 'It was kind of you,' he said, 'to let her sister stay up there with her tonight.'

'Kind?' The Countess snorted. 'If she weren't up there she'd be blubbering every time anyone said a word to her. You wouldn't think it, would you? She's got herself shut of three babies that I know about, and she nearly killed another girl in her last place for stealing her stockings. As long as she's up there, I won't have to worry about the girls trying to sneak in and get at Trinchen's jewelry and money drawer. Now, for God's sake, play something. We're late opening already.'

'I am at your command, m'am.'

I am de sassy niggar, as dey call me Jim Brown.
I plays upon de Bonjo all about de town,
I hate de common niggar, I no shake dem by de ham,
O shaw, I am de leader ob de famus niggar ban,
I plays upon de fife, an I plays upon de drum,
I am de bes musian dat now or eber swum.
Lalle doodle, lalle doodle, lalle doodle laddle la,

Lalle doodle, lalle doodle, lalle doodle daddle da.

January wondered, as he played, whether the Countess would even mention Trinchen's illness to Quennell, but the matter did not arise. Neither Quennell, nor Schurtz, put in an appearance that evening, though Dominic Lloyd came in late. He didn't seem to realize that neither Nenchen nor Trinchen was present. And why should he?

January also wondered, with considerably more trepidation, whether Frank 'Lord Montague' Stubbs would arrive, and what would happen if he did. But the actor, too, seemed to have other fish to fry that night. Between choruses of 'Ching a Ching Chaw' and 'Our Old Tom Cat', January slipped periodically upstairs to check on his patient and, each time, found the German girl resting quietly. He wondered if he had done her a kindness by saving her life, or the reverse.

It was not, his confessor would tell him, for him to decide. *Only do what the laws of God direct, and leave the results to the One who sees forward and backward in time*. Still, where did one go who, at twenty, has seen the ruin of her life with a clarity that left nothing but the desire to be dead and buried with the secrets of the past?

When he descended the backstairs for the final time that night it was to find the parlor dark, Auntie Saba washing up the last of the glasses, and his three bodyguards gathered around the back-door, listening to an account of the night's excitement from Elspie and Little J. 'You downtown niggers drink American beer, Big J?' inquired the Preacher as they set off through the blackness of the woods behind the Countess's.

'I have been known to try it.' Rose, he knew, would be long asleep.

'If that Englishman waitin' for you,' pointed out the solemn Four-Eyes, 'he can just sit out a lil' longer an' get mosquito-bit a lil' more,' which made them all laugh. So January followed the others to the back room of an exceedingly shabby grocery, somewhere in the trees beyond the limits of the town proper, where the musicians who played in the seedier dives of the Swamp foregathered after hours for a final beer or glass of rum before going home.

The music at Django's was less trained than what got played after hours downtown, its rhythms far more African, reminiscent of the music at the slave dances on Congo Square on Sundays. He bought a round for his bodyguards, another for the skinny young men improvising long syncopated variations on the out of tune piano, and listened to all the gossip from the American side of town: about the Preacher's girlfriend, about Bill's mother and younger brothers, and about what the election looked like from the other side of Canal Street.

By the smell, a number of country-bred blacks, new come into town, were smoking home-grown hemp as well as highly illegal cigars in the corners, but the beer was far from bad.

He returned to his house at close to dawn and let himself quietly in to find the oil-lamp in his study burned out. Lighting a candle, he saw, tucked beneath the lamp, a note in Rose's neat, elegant handwriting:

> Per your instruction, I attended Mass this afternoon, with the intention of corrupting the Deschamps family servants. By dint of untruths concerning a non-existent but Paris-bound niece, I scraped acquaintance with Lolotte, Mme Celestine Deschamps's housekeeper. Lolotte informs me that Mlle Isobel's maid – a good, sweet girl, she says, who never caused anyone any harm – was sold earlier in the week to a dealer bound for Natchez, two days after her mistress's departure. It certainly sounds like she learned something in Paris, doesn't it?
> Pining for your love,
> R.

THIRTEEN

'My way of thinkin',' said the Preacher, when January asked him about the matter on the following night, 'is that just 'cause a dealer say he bound for Natchez, don't mean he bound for Natchez *that day*. This good maid – she bright or dark?'

'Bright, probably.' The back room of Django's was slowly emptying out; only a few candles were left on the barrels that served as tables. Up at the piano, Four-Eyes was jangling out an extremely Congo version of 'Dame Durden', while a squat, sturdy Bill circled the tune in a far-ranging improvisation, plucking rather than bowing his bull fiddle, using the deep notes almost like a lazy drum. 'We're talkin' 'bout a rich family. Creole French.' It was nearly four in the morning, but in spite of Rose's mimed horror when he'd come downstairs at close to noon the day before ('Oh, Mon Dieu! Who is this stranger whom I do not recognize, in my house?'), January's instincts told him that time with the uptown musicians, time getting to know the network of American Protestant freedmen, was time well spent.

'Bright, then.' The Preacher's long fingers ticked off points on the barrel top among the damp beer-rings. 'Trained maid, high yella, speaks French, she fetch eleven, twelve hundred dollars in Natchez. But for a fact, nobody in Natchez got that kind of money 'fore cotton harvest done in December. That girl still in town.'

'You heard anything of it? Her name's Pierrette.'

The Preacher thought, then shook his head. 'Not a private sale, I ain't. You gonna have to do this the hard way and look for her down Baronne Street.'

January had suspected as much, but the thought of searching through the dealers' offices along that thoroughfare made his flesh creep.

Going down Baronne Street – feeling the fear he knew would whisper at him as he walked along the board sidewalk past those lines of chained men and women in their stiff new calico clothing – would not, of course, be nearly as bad as being one of them. His mind turned over the scraps of information Rose had given him about her talk with the housekeeper Lolotte, while the music gyred in the smoky gloom. When his friends downtown played for themselves after hours – Mozart or Vivaldi or the popular glees and catches that came out of New York – there was often an African flavor to the rhythm. It was a way of making the music their own, like a beautiful toy. But the uptown music, far more primitive, took him back to his plantation childhood; it was not nearly as graceful, nor as technically skilled, yet there was an intensity to it that quickened the heartbeat. It was a music from a deeper part of the soul.

'Why you lookin' to find this girl?' asked the Preacher softly, and January glanced over at him, aware that he'd been silent too long.

'She knows something,' he replied. 'Saw something, heard something, that'll get a friend of mine out of trouble.'

Would I call the Viscount Foxford my friend? But Hannibal was his friend.

The Preacher picked an infinitesimally tiny speck of cigar ash from his elegant silk hat. 'Given what Madame gonna have to pay to replace Miss Pierrette, musta been a helluva somethin', to sell her off on account of it.'

The following morning, waiting for Hannibal at the coffee-stand, January found the advertisement he sought:

Irvin and Frye
TO SELL
A well-made negress: twenty-five years old, ladies' maid,
seamstress, and hairdresser, named PIERRETTE.
Speaks French and English,
reads and writes both languages, and is warranted free
of vices and diseases provided for by law. She
may be seen at our offices on Baronne Street.

January folded the thin summer newspaper, drew it through his fingers. *Musta been a helluva somethin'*.

A lovely girl of an old French family, raised poor but suddenly rich. Her widowed mother sends her to Paris with this new-found wealth . . . and with her, her trusted maid. And she meets a man.

She meets two men.

The clock on the Cathedral tower sounded one. Yesterday, at this very table, Hannibal had agreed to visit the Cabildo at noon and speak to the Viscount. Now January paid up Auntie Zozo and, resignedly, turned his steps toward the Swamp. He wasn't surprised by Hannibal's absence. Hannibal might have been aghast at Mr Droudge's decision that a cheap defense would be as good as an expensive one – 'I can't tell you how many gutters in this town I've fallen into drunk and landed on top of Harold Chaffinch!' – but at the suggestion that he go to the Cabildo himself, to try to talk Foxford into demanding someone more competent, he had balked. 'Why would he want to see me?'

'Because he knows you were Patrick's friend, as well as his father's.'

'God help the both of them.'

January had been raggedly tired then – it had been full daylight when he'd returned home after seeing Trinchen still lived, and he'd had to force himself out to seek Hannibal before returning to the Countess's once more. He'd said, 'No. God help *him*. You may be able to talk some sense into him, and that may very well save his life.'

In the end, Hannibal had promised . . . and January had deliberately set the meeting for noon, to allow himself time to go down to the Swamp and fetch him.

Why do I care? he asked himself for the hundredth time, as he circled cautiously through the murky ground near the turning basin of the canal. *The boy is nothing to me. And so far I've seen nothing to tell me that he DIDN'T actually murder the man who held on to the family money that should have been his.*

He left the shabby wooden houses behind him, the rough lots where gardens and chicken-coops straggled, and entered the fringes of the genuine swamp, which lay where the land – high along the river – sloped gradually down to the distant lake. The stink of the town grew less intense. As he walked – to keep his mind from his irritation at Hannibal – he reflected upon Isobel Deschamps.

Had she, as Laertes cautions Ophelia not to do, 'surrendered her maiden patent' to the more charming – or more insistent – of her suitors? Did she learn he was an actor before or after this happened, if it had happened at all?

She comes home – damaged in body, or only in heart?

Her maid would know.

Maids always knew something.

All the well-bred young French and Spanish Creole ladies had them. Many families – both Creole and Americans – gave their eldest daughter her first slave at the age of six or seven. Usually, a girl the same age, or a few years older: taught to fix hair, mend hems when they came down, lace corsets, scrub spots of dirt from stockings and gloves. Without them, many of those narrow-waisted, tidy-haired, spotlessly-groomed little ladies would be hard put to maintain themselves presentably.

He remembered the ladies of the Big House at Bellefleur when he was a child: his master's Spanish Creole wife, and then his master's sister, when she and her husband came to run the plantation after the wife's early death. M'am Clarice's maid had been an octoroon woman, as fair-skinned as her mistress but with African features and the curious gray-green eyes one often found among the *sang mêlées* – Serena, her name had been. January wondered what had become of her in the end.

Serena's whole life had been entwined with M'am Clarice's. As protective and caring as a sister, Serena would stay up all night waiting for her Miss to return from a ball so that she could lock away her jewelry, would get up while the sky was still black, to light the kitchen fire and roast the coffee beans so that her Miss would have a cup when *she* rose at first blush of light in the sky. She wore her mistress's cast-off clothing, combed her hair with her mistress's hand me down combs.

Ran her mistress's errands, got the curse on the same day, knew her secrets as only a sister does.

Isobel Deschamps goes to Paris.

Isobel Deschamps returns to New Orleans and flees the city within a few days of the arrival of two Englishmen who may or may not have known her in Paris . . .

Isobel Deschamps's mother sells her maid. Which was the chief difference between an actual sister and a slave.

It musta been a helluva somethin'.

* * *

He expected to find Hannibal drunk again. The fiddler had, in the past, displayed a fiendish ability to wander away and get himself fogbound at exactly those times when he was needed most. But, while still among the trees, January heard the sound of the fiddle, like an exiled angel's, weaving blithe fantasias around an Irish planxty – the kind of thing no one in New Orleans was interested in hearing. He climbed the rickety stair and found his friend sitting cross-legged on the bed in threadbare shirt and trousers, his thin body moving to the music and his eyes half shut, as if that were the one thing sufficient to keep corked the nearly-full bottle of sherry on the floor at his side.

There was no smell of liquor in the room. Hannibal had even tidied up the attic and dumped the water buckets that sat beneath the assorted leaks. Quietly, January entered, found a pair of clean socks in one goods box and, in another, a faded waistcoat of a pattern that had been the last cry of fashion in Paris seventeen years before. He threw both on the bed as the song circled to its finish, and Hannibal sat for a time in silence, as a man rests in the arms of a lover. Savoring the echo of freedom before he must return to the real world.

January wondered if he had slept at all since he'd dragged him back to consciousness here last Friday afternoon.

After a time, he asked, 'Do you fear he'll look like his father?'

Hannibal raised dark eyes, darker in circles of sleepless bruise. Head shake – slight, as if he had gone beyond the ability or desire for movement. Then he looked away. 'He was the mirror of his mother when he was five. I expect he still is.'

'Did you love her?'

'With the whole of my heart.' His gaze remained on the trees beyond the door.

A flat monotony of dull green: no mountains, no hills, no seasons to speak of. Tropical heat or tropical rain. A world where earth and water mixed, entangled in the wet heavy vegetation of the swamp.

Did Hannibal dream of Paris?

Of Oxford where he had studied – *studied what?* – before he had joined Derryhick's 'merry band' and thrown away his future to follow wine and song?

Waking in the night, did he sometimes wait to hear the bells of Oxford's spires, or those of Notre Dame as January still sometimes did?

'She came to hate me,' said Hannibal at last, and he gathered up the litter of silk scarves from the pillow beside him, in which he swaddled the violin like a mother wrapping up her child. 'As she hated Patrick. And all of us. It was hard to see it in her eyes.'

'Because he drank with you? Gambled away what money they had with you? Her husband,' he added, when Hannibal glanced back at him.

'Drank with us, gambled with us . . . God, the money we wasted, which should have gone to the upkeep and improvement of that land! *O noctes senaeque deum!* She was his cousin – well, mine as well. She'd been brought up at Foxford. She loved the land and knew better than either of us what needed to be done there. Never play cards after you've eaten opium, *amicus meus*. The sensation is amazing – you can actually smell the earth in the diamonds as they pass through your hands, and the hearts shed on to your fingers both water and blood – but the results are seldom happy. Philippa—' He broke off and looked down at his hands, folded on his drawn-up knees, as if he had never seen them before. Long hands with slender fingers: good for nothing but the making of music that could tear the heart out of one's body and set it free.

'Are you afraid he'll ask you how his father died?'

'I'm sure he's heard that from her – and Droudge – and everyone else in the family. I'm afraid he'll ask me how his father lived, and that's not a tale fit for any young man's ears.' But he drew his socks toward him and began to put them on.

'Whatever she's said about you to her son, that wasn't your name then, was it?'

The graying mustache pulled slightly to the side; a chuckle whispered in his throat. 'No,' Hannibal said. 'No, it wasn't. I suppose I'm perfectly safe.'

'Were you clean-shaven in those days?'

'As a virgin girl.' He stood, shrugged into the waistcoat, and looked around for a comb for his long hair. 'And about as experienced. And it is dishonorable of me to send you to do all the work of saving the young imbecile's life – particularly when doing so gets you shot at by disreputable actors masquerading as gentlemen. Let us go, *amicus meus – par nobile fratrum* – and see what we can achieve.'

'Another boon,' said January, as they made their way down Perdidio Street toward the center of town once again. 'Rose informs me that Celestine Deschamps sold her daughter's maid to a dealer, the moment Isobel left town. She's at Irvin and Frye's. You think you could pass yourself off as a buyer?'

'My dear Benjamin.' Hannibal drew himself up with great dignity, then skipped nimbly aside to avoid a pair of extremely drunk Kaintucks who came crashing out through the front window of the Turkey Buzzard. 'I can pass myself as anything from a street sweeper to the Archbishop of Canterbury's secretary. Fortunately, my good waistcoat is out of pawn this week. I'm sure I have something respectable-looking in here . . .'

He fished in his pocket for an elegant Morocco card-case, from which he drew a dozen or more visiting-cards, each handsomely inscribed with a name and address not his own. '*Myron Pendergast of New York City – Imports* . . . A good enough reason to be in New Orleans at this season – but what would I want a slave for? *Salve, puella*,' he added, raising his hat to Railspike as that lady strode past them through the unpaved muck. '*Ambrosiaeque comae divinum vertice odorem spiravere* . . . *Thomas Dawes of Mobile*. No occupation, but the typeface alone is as good as a bank reference.' He flicked it between his fingers like a conjuror displaying the ace of spades. 'I've even been to Mobile – briefly. An appalling town. Would you like me to tackle Martin Quennell for you?'

'Would you?' said January, much relieved. 'As Rose pointed out, I obviously can't ask Lord Montague Stubbs about his quarrel with Derryhick.'

'With the greatest pleasure in the world, *amicus meus*. One of these –' he held up Thomas Dawes of Mobile's card – 'should serve to open a conversation, which can then be led to what, exactly, His So-Called-Lordship said to Patrick that sent him slamming out of Davis's, and straight back to his hotel, in such a fury.'

'Thank you,' said January. 'The Burial Society thanks you, too, since even if I could speak to a customer, I'm not supposed to draw attention to myself at the Countess's. If it weren't for the fact that Stubbs probably could not have reached the Hotel

Iberville before Derryhick did, I'd suspect him of having something to do with the murder himself.'

'Now, you're only prejudiced because the man tried to kill you.'

January grunted. 'But whatever it is he knows – whatever his relationship is with Isobel Deschamps – I think we're going to have to have proof in hand before Lord Foxford will admit a thing.'

In this, he proved absolutely correct. 'I just walked,' said Foxford doggedly, seated before Shaw's desk in the watch room again, dirtier and more haggard than ever. 'I haven't the slightest idea where or for how long. The streets were dark, and all those little houses look the same. Everything was shut up, and I just walked.'

'You didn't meet with Isobel Deschamps?'

'I don't know her.' The young nobleman's eyes flickered to the corner of the watch room, where Shaw had retreated with a newspaper. The Kentuckian was leaning against the wall, and though there was a vigorous argument in progress at the sergeant's desk between a couple of lank-haired upriver farm-boys and a grocer, January would have bet his week's coffee money that Shaw could hear every word Foxford said.

'You didn't meet her in Paris?' Hannibal inquired, and Foxford's eyes darted side to side and then back to Shaw again before returning to Hannibal.

'No. I mean, I may have – I was in Paris last winter, and of course we must have been at many of the same balls . . . But I don't recall her. Please, gentlemen,' the young man went on, a note of desperation in his voice. 'Please don't be concerned about me. I have a lawyer, and I . . . The thought that I'd harm Patrick is grotesque. Particularly that I'd hide his body in that other poor man's coffin . . . Why would I do a thing like that? Why would anyone?'

'So that no one in your party would be accused of his murder,' said January promptly. 'So that Mr Derryhick would simply disappear, and in the fullness of time . . . What is the statute of limitations for property in Ireland, Hannibal? Seven years? Ten? In the fullness of time, Aunt Elodie's money would come to you.' 'How dare you—?' Foxford started to rise, and January replied in a steady voice:

'It's what they'll say in court, Your Lordship. That and more.'

The young man sat down again. 'I don't know any Isobel Deschamps,' he said. 'And I don't know any Lord Montague Blessinghurst or Frank Stubbs or whatever his name really is. And they cannot hang me because I didn't do anything.'

'Are you really willing,' Hannibal asked quietly, 'to have Lieutenant Shaw write to your mother to let her know you've been hanged?'

Foxford's jaw was set like iron, but January saw that the young man was close to tears. After a long time, and in a very different voice, the Viscount asked, 'Do you know my mother, sir?'

Hannibal shook his head. 'Only what your father told me of her.'

A longer silence still, in which the thwack of a whip could be heard in the courtyard behind the Cabildo, and a man's anguished scream. At last Foxford asked, 'How did he die? Mother told me – Patrick told me – he drowned while drunk. Fell from the railing of the Pont Neuf into the Seine.'

'It was a bet.' Hannibal's breath went out of him in a harsh little sigh. 'We were always making silly bets. This one was to stand on the railing of the Vert Galant – that little triangular square between the two halves of the bridge, on the nose of the island – and drink an entire bottle of cognac. I think it had something to do with that bronze statue of King Henry, which the city had replaced there only a year or two before. It was destroyed in the Revolution, you know – we were baptizing it or something. But you understand I wasn't terribly sober at the time either. I wouldn't have tried it. Patrick told Alec – your father – not to be a damned fool, I do remember that.'

'Was he drunk already?'

'Oh, God, yes. We all were. It was three in the morning – a beautiful spring night on the threshold of summer – and he stood there on the railing, pouring the brandy down his throat and weaving back and forth, and all of us afraid to breathe . . . except, of course, those who were passing bets back and forth about whether he'd fall or not. But even they were silent. Patrick was famous for doing something of the kind – balancing on the back of a chair and drinking ten glasses off the tops of the heads of the ten prettiest girls in the – er – tavern.'

'Remind me never to let you tell this story at the Countess's,' murmured January, and Hannibal grinned, a little shyly.

'I think I can still balance on the back of a chair,' he mused. 'There are some things one never forgets.' He returned his glance to Foxford. 'He claimed he could better it. He did, too. When he finished the cognac he threw the bottle to shatter on the cobblestones at the feet of King Henry's bronze horse. Then he spread out his arms in the moonlight, raised his face to the moon . . . and smiled, leaned back, and fell like that into the river. They found his body about a week later, near Rouen. Did Patrick never tell you?'

The Viscount said, 'I never asked him.'

There was silence for a time. 'Did he know, do you think, sir?' asked Foxford at length. 'What he was doing, I mean?'

Hannibal sat silent, one skeletal finger tracing the edge of the desk. Then he said, 'Who knows what you think you're doing, when you're that drunk? I know your father wasn't happy. I know he knew what he was doing to Philippa – to his wife,' he corrected himself, 'and to you, living as he did. And to his lands, for which he had . . . a great deal more feeling than most people guessed. I heard him say, more than once, that you and your mother would be better caretakers for his birthright than he was ever capable of being. He looked happy when he fell.'

Silence again. Then: 'Mother said the French police contacted Patrick, rather than her or Grandfather, when his body was found.'

'Patrick took the *diligence* down to Rouen to identify him – which they had to do by his rings, and his boots – and we all put in money to have him buried in Montmartre. Do you know it? It's a little village outside the city, among the vineyards.' The Viscount nodded. 'And then we all got punishing drunk at some brothel in memory of him, and Patrick the drunkest of all. No more than your mother would expect,' he added softly. 'But Patrick had nothing to do with making your father the way he was, whatever she's said.'

'I think—' the boy began, then closed his mouth and sat for a time, gazing out into the watch room. A couple of the City Guards had dragged in a man from the levee, bearded and indescribably filthy, twisting and picking at his urine-stained clothes with shaking hands, muttering of ants and snakes.

'What happened to his fiddle?' Foxford asked instead.

Hannibal said, 'You remember that he played?'

The Viscount nodded. 'He gave me lessons, I remember, but I was too little. And I was never any good at it.'

'I took it. It was better than my own. Did she try to keep you away from him? Your mother, I mean, from Patrick?'

'Well, she couldn't, you see.' A smile flickered on Foxford's lips, at the thought of his mother. 'By the terms of Father's will, he was my guardian, along with Uncle Diogenes, who, of course, was in India. Grandfather died when I was seven, and there was nothing Mother could do about Patrick's coming to visit. He'd never come further into the house than the drawing room, and sometimes the book room, if he had to talk to Droudge. But she'd retire to her bedroom on the days he'd be there and not emerge till he was gone. She was—'

He broke off, trying, January guessed from his expression, to explain to strangers how he could love them both, and see his mother's love through her anger at his friend. Then he shook his head again. 'I daresay he'd have kept his distance from me if I'd believed her, and wanted to stay away from him, but I didn't. She said he was like the Pied Piper of Hamlin Town. That he lured people away beneath a mountain, as the fairies used to, and they came back changed and not themselves anymore. Did he do so with you, Mr Sefton?'

Hannibal sighed. 'He did so with everyone he met.' Then his eyes changed their focus, coffee black looking into the clear green-blue of the young man across the desk. 'Don't let your mother get another letter, like the one she got from Patrick.'

Foxford looked away. 'I don't know Isobel Deschamps,' he said stubbornly. 'And I saw no one on Thursday night.'

FOURTEEN

There was no time to do more, that afternoon, toward saving the life of the young man who was doing his obstinate best not to have it saved. Shaw, who conducted them out, confirmed that no discrepancies had been found in Caius Droudge's account of a night's muffled sleep with cotton in his ears – 'Not that that means he didn't sneak out in his bedsocks an' kill a dozen men an' eat 'em, too . . .' – and that the blowzy Señora Alcidoro maintained her story of an all-night cribbage session with Uncle Diogenes.

'It's perfectly possible he was up all night – er – playing cribbage with someone else, you know,' Hannibal remarked as they emerged from the iron-strapped doors of the Cabildo. 'Another patron of La Sirène's, whose family would be horrified at his tastes and friendships. In which case we'll probably never know who—'

In the banded shadows of the arcade, January caught sight of the disreputable Mr Chaffinch – glorious in a mustard-colored coat and houndstooth trousers – approaching, with Mr Droudge shambling behind. At least this time he bore a basket of food for the prisoner in his hand; the slender rations dished up to the prisoners in the cells were beyond execrable. 'Let's hope they'll have more luck,' he muttered, turning back to Hannibal, but his friend had disappeared. Droudge didn't even glance at January as he passed.

Exasperatingly, that night at the Countess's produced no sign of either 'Sir Montague Blessinghurst' or Martin Quennell, and January had to remind himself that only a satyr would go visiting whorehouses every night of the week, and that the Countess's was far from the only such establishment in town. He found Trinchen slightly better. She had eaten a little that day, and drunk water, according to Nenchen, who was with her. A brief examination satisfied January that the girl's kidneys did not appear to be damaged, which was always the great danger with iodine poisoning.

'Has anyone sent word to Quennell?' he asked, tucking his

long wooden stethoscope back into his satchel, and Nenchen's round face seemed to darken and congeal.

'I should,' she said grimly, in the German in which he'd addressed her. 'Then when he comes here, I will take my knife and gut him so! Like a fish.' Her gesture – particularly from an Amazon close to six-foot tall – was graphic and disconcerting.

'What do you expect?' inquired the Countess, when January returned downstairs and begged the favor of leaving his medical satchel in her office for the night. 'He is a man who leaves behind him what no longer serves him, that one, like a pair of outworn gloves.'

'Many people do that, Countess,' said January. And when she glanced sharply at him across her ebony desk, to see if he'd laid any untoward emphasis on her title, he added, 'If I had not done so myself, I think I would have gone mad with grief when my wife died in Paris of the cholera.'

She sniffed. 'Bah. It is one thing, Big J, between picking yourself up and wiping the blood off your face and walking on, and another, not to speak to your mother or your cousins or your grandparents because you're afraid the Americans will say, "Weren't you the son of that banker who lost all my money for me?" Since that man was twelve years old, he has not been across Canal Street where his family lives – those who are still in this town. Not for Sunday dinner, not for the funeral of old Gran'mere Quennell, not even to be among his family in the cemetery for the Feast of All Saints.'

From the drawer of her desk she took a little flask of perfume, drew forth the stopper and touched it to her throat, her wrists, her breasts like satin mountains. Past her shoulder, among the handkerchiefs and stationery in the drawer, January saw at least a hundred dollars in gold, and a deadly-looking Prussian needle-gun. 'Only when times grew hard and he needed money, did he sink his pride to go creeping to the son of his father's mistress, that undertaker, to ask for work.'

'It seems to have served him.' January held the door for her to pass before him into the parlor. 'It sounds as if he'll have his wish and marry a woman of wealth.'

The madame stopped in the doorway, glanced up at him with wise dark eyes. 'It isn't so much that he wishes a woman of wealth, Big J,' she said. 'There are other men in this town who have sisters, who are looking to invest in town lots.

He wants the Schurtz girl because she and that brother of hers will be going back to New England. Quennell wants what he's always wanted: to get as far away from New Orleans and his family, as it is possible for him to get.'

Of January's bodyguards, only Four-Eyes appeared that night, long after the house had closed up. 'They's a hell of a fight, over to the Blackleg,' said the boy apologetically, as January stepped out of the shadows of the rear porch where he had been waiting. 'Bill got cut. Nobody knows where Preacher is or what happened to him.'

January muttered, '*Ibn al-harîm*,' which had been one of Ayasha's favorite oaths, but there wasn't much else to say. One reason why he'd never taken a job playing the saloons or bordellos before this had been precisely because of the prevalence of violence: Hannibal had more than once been beaten and robbed by patrons of the various dives he played along the levee. More frequently, January had patched up his friend's minor injuries sustained in the course of inelegant exits through windows – it was a wonder both he and his fiddle had survived this long.

Not that the Countess permitted the kind of rough and tumble in her house that lowlier proprietors permitted in theirs, of course. Hughie-Boy – and the pistol in her desk drawer – took care of that. But, as they descended the back porch steps and moved into the darkness, he reflected that with three weeks till the election, and both sides paying for as much free rum as prospective voters could drink, a major battle of some kind was probably only a matter of time.

Each night that week, the Preacher had guided them by a different route from the Countess's back door to January's own house on Rue Esplanade, sometimes by way of Django's grocery – which January still wasn't entirely certain he could find unassisted – and sometimes not. There was a sort of invisible geography to the territory beyond the town's limits that was learned by slaves and free blacks alike – whether downtown *libres* who had been free for generations or the freed slaves uptown. The oak with the crooked limb halfway along Bayou St John, the clearing, out past the turning basin, where they used to have dogfights but didn't anymore – these meant exactly the same to January as the signposts on Rue St Pierre did to the Creole French. If he was less familiar with the undeveloped lots at the back of the American section, these cautious home-goings were remedying the situation. Already, he recognized landmarks passed from different directions: a half-built house near the crossing of what he guessed to be Poydras and Jackson streets, a burned-down shack somewhere north of the Basin.

The attack didn't come until they were on Rue Esplanade itself.

They must have followed us some other night.

He heard footsteps behind them the minute he and Four-Eyes turned from Rue St Claud on to Esplanade. The moon had barely waxed from a fingernail to an orange slice; the low-built stucco houses of the back of town were uniformly dark. January glanced behind him but all he could see, even with eyes thoroughly accustomed to the darkness, were uncertain zones of black and indigo.

Maybe he hadn't really heard the strike of boots on the packed earth that was all that verged the gutters here.

But he knew he had.

He breathed, 'Shh,' and touched Four-Eyes's skinny arm. The boy stopped in his tracks, a single glint of moonlight outlining the frame of his spectacles as he turned his head.

Listening.

Nothing.

Crap.

They walked on quicker, and January thought – he wasn't sure at first – something might (or might not) have moved ahead of them. When he stopped just short of the corner of Rue Rampart he was sure of it – and it was too late. Someone was coming across the Esplanade to his left and coming fast.

Four-Eyes bolted; he was only seventeen and, January had sometimes suspected, not really officially free. January made a run for the dark passway between two houses but didn't make it. The men were on him, seeming to appear by magic out of the blackness, grabbing him by the arms, the body, the neck. He thrashed, struggled, but didn't strike out with his fists; he knew already he was outnumbered and that they were probably armed.

He clenched his thighs, brought up his hands to cover his head, braced every muscle of his belly.

Not a gun, he prayed, *Blessed Mary Ever-Virgin don't let one of them have a gun . . .*

Blows rained on his arms, his back, his thighs. He was thrown down, smashed into the corner of the nearby house, and kicked. More than one of them had canes: the crack of their weighted handles went through his bones. *If you fight back it'll only be worse . . .* He'd learned that as an adolescent, the first time a gang of white boys had cornered him.

It was something every black man learned.

He was stunned, half-conscious, when they stopped – he didn't know how long it had gone on and prayed – he couldn't tell – that there were no bones broken and that they wouldn't start again. The pain above his kidneys made him feel faint.

A man said, 'You hear me, boy?'

A kick, to make sure he was awake. The whole world smelled like blood and the sewage in which he lay.

'I hear.' French, not English. And not the voice of 'Lord Blessinghurst'.

'You mind your own business, you hear? You ask too many questions. You leave things alone.'

He whispered, 'Yes, sir.'

The sound he'd dreaded, the whispered hiss of a steel sword-cane unsheathed. He didn't dare move and wasn't sure he could have done even if he'd tried. The point dug into the side of his face. 'I didn't hear?'

Louder. 'Yes, sir.'

A gouging slash, into flesh already torn open by fists and boots.

Someone kicked him again, and then their footsteps retreated up the beaten earth of the path.

After a long time, when he was sure they were truly gone, January uncurled his body. Even lying on the ground hurt, as his flesh gorged up with blood from broken capillaries. Trying to get up was so bad that he collapsed again to his hands and knees, vomited in the gory mud. It was all he could do not to pass out in the puddles and drown.

Somehow he got to his feet, clinging to the wall beside him. Somehow he found his satchel, kicked to the side into the blackness of the passway between the houses.

Somehow he moved across Rue Rampart, reeling like a drunkard, and fell in the open gutter – and fell twice more in the block or so remaining till his home.

He called out hoarsely, 'Rose!' as he stumbled through the door into his study and collapsed, bleeding, on the floor.

He thought he might have fainted then; he wasn't sure. Pain brought him back. He lay in the darkness, hearing the muffled drone of the cicadas in the trees across the Esplanade, the scuffle of a mouse in another room and the scurrying leap of Caligula's pursuing paws. Voice thick with pain, he called, 'Rose!' again.

After a long, long time it came to him. Rose was not in the house.

Cold shock, like a cane knife slicing his flesh.

Some of them came from this direction.

No! Dear God, no!

And the door from the front gallery into his study had not been locked.

He got to his feet and to hell with the pain. Found the study table, the candle, the lucifers; staggered to the parlor where he fell to his knees. No sign of struggle, but *Rob Roy* lay face down beside the chair where she usually sat to read, and her fan lay beside it. The candles were burned far down.

NO!

The bedroom was empty, the bed untouched. The mosquito bar hung knotted back above the tester.

He lurched back toward the parlor and almost fell again. Another wave of nausea swamped him, and then panic, as he realized he hadn't the slightest idea who his attackers had been, nor where they would have taken her.

Shaw, he thought. *He'll know where to start.*

The thought of moving again made him dizzy with pain. Taking a deep breath informed him that at least one rib was cracked, maybe more.

Light. You can't catch them now. Wait till it's light. Four-Eyes had been late getting to the Countess's. Dawn wouldn't be more than an hour off.

If they wanted to kill her she'll be dead already. If they wanted to do anything else – his mind turned away in horror from specifics – *they'll have done it already.*

Whatever you can do, you can do better when it's light.

He lay down on the bed: mud, blood, and all. And passed out as if he'd been shot.

FIFTEEN

'Ben!'

Rose's voice. The sting of alcohol on his swollen face made him cry out, and he grabbed her wrist and tried to get his blood-crusted eyelids open. The smell of her soap and her hair told him it was really her.

It was daylight in the bedroom, early dawn.

Whatever you want, Blessed Mary Ever-Virgin, it's yours. I swear it. For the rest of my life.

'Rose . . .' Making his mouth move was almost as bad as being hit again.

'How badly did they hurt you?' She was already at work with her scissors, snipping off the remains of his shirt.

'I've had worse.' He had, too, before he'd reached his seventh birthday. Old Michie Fouchet on Bellefleur Plantation didn't care who he hammered when he was drunk.

It hurt like blue blazes, but he ascertained that all his teeth were still in place, and his nose hadn't been broken. On the whole he'd done a good job at protecting his head. When she helped him sit up and use the chamber-pot he saw no blood in the urine. The pain was terrible, but some of the fear retreated. 'They were waiting—'

'I know,' said Rose, with her usual cheerful calm. 'I saw one of them around midnight, across the street. This is going to sting.'

It certainly did.

'They spoke French,' said January, when he got his breath back. He took the rag, and the bowl of alcohol, from her hand, gasping as he cleaned the caked blood from the side of his face.

'I heard.' Rose shook back her hair – soft medium-brown and silky like a white woman's – which was braided down her back like a country girl's. He saw now by the silvery dawn-light – by the lamp still burning – that she wore her plainest calico skirt, the one she put on when helping with the laundry, with a sleeveless canvas bodice over her chemise, such as the market-women wore. 'The man with the sword-cane went into the Verron town house on Rue Bourbon, so I'm guessing it was Louis Verron. It looked too tall to be his father. Two of the others went into the Ulloa town house on Rue St Ann—'

'You followed them!'

Bird-wing eyebrows lifted behind the oval lenses of her spectacles. 'I wouldn't have been much use joining in the fight.'

She was perfectly correct about that, and it was certainly what he'd have ordered her to do, had he known anything beyond the immediate events. Still . . .

After a moment, she went on thoughtfully, 'The Ulloas are cousins of the Verrons – I think both families have plantations near the Mexican border, in Natchitoches Parish. And Louis Verron's father—'

'Is the cousin of Celestine Deschamps.'

'You don't think the girl actually *married* Stubbs in Paris, do you?' asked Hannibal, after some minutes of silence broken only by the rattle of occasional traffic along Rue Dauphine beside them as they walked.

'I think it's possible, yes.' January reached up, very gingerly, to touch the sticking plaster that held shut the gash on the side of his face. 'I can't think of another reason why members of her family – and the might-be groom himself – would all seek me out and tell me this isn't any of my business.'

'They do seem to be taking it very seriously. *Misce stultitiam consiliis brevem . . .*'

'Nor can I think of another reason,' he went on, 'that this girl we're looking for – Pierrette – would have returned to America with her mistress to be re-enslaved. She was free in France. Yet she came back.'

Hannibal's words broke off at that, as he took in what it meant.

'That argues a more desperate need than just a broken heart over a soured romance.'

After a time, Hannibal said, 'I don't know what it would take for me to give up my freedom . . . except, of course, I see people do it all the time. My Aunt Lavinnia's maid was devoted to her – never married, lived through Aunt Lavinnia and her family . . . She'd have given up her first-born child if Aunt Lavinnia had asked for it. And it would explain why Uncle Diogenes was invited along on the picnic.'

January nodded. 'As a trustee of the estate, he has to approve of Foxford's choice of a bride.'

'Well, he does if the boy wants to get control of his own affairs before he's thirty,' said Hannibal. 'The old Viscount tried to put a similar tether on Foxford's father – hence the hasty nuptials with Philippa, who at sixteen hadn't the experience to recognize an incipient drunkard when she saw one.' The hatred in his voice was like the sudden slash of a rusted razor. 'The business about buying a cotton plantation was obviously all my hat. Diogenes would sign whatever Droudge puts in front of him – or sends out to Bengal. You don't think that was what Blessinghurst told Patrick at Davis's, do you? That he and the girl had deceived Foxford?'

'He could have,' said January slowly. 'It would explain the family's . . . eagerness –' he gingerly touched his swollen jaw – 'to hush things up.'

'Well, an actor as a prospective brother-in-law would certainly scupper any chance the younger sister has of marrying into anything approaching respectable society – at least it would in Ireland. *Et semel emissum volat irrevocabile verbum* . . . Still, why murder you? Why not kill Stubbs?'

'That may be precisely what Verron means to do. I'm a side issue – I doubt there's a court in Louisiana that would even consider it murder, had Verron and his cousins beaten me to death and nailed my flayed hide to the Cabildo door.'

When he'd lived in Paris, he recalled, he'd spoken of such things lightly to his musician friends: something to make their grisette girlfriends squeak and shake their heads, as if he'd returned from the South Seas with accounts of native cosmetic practices.

They paused where Rue Dauphine crossed Canal Street, and like the grisettes, Hannibal inquired, 'They wouldn't even ask for an explanation?' In his best Spanish jacket and a startling ruby-red waistcoat, the fiddler looked surprisingly respectable.

'If they did, they'd get one,' replied January grimly. 'Something along the lines of "the nigger was uppity".'

'Oh, well.' Hannibal threw up his hands in a gesture of

comprehending the obvious. 'I understand everything now. Shame on you, Benjamin. *Take but degree away, untune that string; and hark, what discord follows!* Uppity – well!'

January – who had been about to lead the way across the 'neutral zone' that bordered Canal Street on both sides – stopped and made a sweeping bow to permit his white 'master' to step off the curb first. Even at this period of the year, there was a fair amount of cart traffic from the wharves at one end of the street back toward the Basin, where the canal from the lake ended. The proposal to extend the canal to the river had never materialized, but its echo remained in the huge width of the street itself – almost two hundred feet at this point – with the remains of an old drainage ditch down its center, now neatly fenced in iron chains in an attempt to appear park-like.

'What's the sister's name?'

'Marie-Amalie.' January tried to recall the younger girl, whom he knew he'd seen once or twice but could remember nothing of – except that her hair was dark, and that their mother had a tendency to dress Isobel in blue and her sister in pink. 'The mother of Isobel and Marie-Amalie Deschamps – Madame Celestine – was born Celestine Verron, her mother – Eliane Dubesc, from Sainte Domingue – having married Louis-Florizel Verron, brother to the grandfather of the gentlemen who cracked two of my ribs last night. According to my mother, Louis-Florizel was given the almost-worthless family cattle-lands up on the Red River – all of which went to Celestine when her only brother died at the age of sixteen – while the New Orleans side of the Verrons had the sugar plantations. Louis's father and uncles mismanaged and mortgaged those to the rafters. . . . I think that's how it went.'

'Trust your mother to know everything about any family downstream of Canal Street.'

'Believe me, the relationship was secondary to Maman's analysis of how the Verron and Dubesc family money was divided, with regard to Madame Celestine's ability to pay me for Isobel's piano lessons. This was just before the Red River was cleared for navigation, which reversed the original positions: the Natchitoches lands became the valuable ones, and the New Orleans Verrons the poor relations.'

'It still won't help poor Marie-Amalie get a husband,' mused

Hannibal as they turned down the street that continued on the same side of the 'neutral ground' under the name of Baronne. 'Not if the suitors' families think they'll be in danger of having to meet an actor or his family anytime they visit someone connected with the Deschampses or the Verrons. But even if Patrick returned to the Iberville and informed our young friend that Isobel had become Stubbs's wife – or, worse yet, his mistress – I still can't see that as being grounds for murder.'

'Can't you?' said January quietly, and Hannibal stopped in his tracks.

'No,' said the fiddler, his voice equally soft. 'I can't.'

'If Foxford wasn't sober?' said January. 'If Patrick wasn't sober? If Stubbs's information was that he had made Isobel his mistress and then discarded her – possibly pregnant – and Foxford said, as young men have been known to, "I don't care, I'll marry her anyway."?'

'And if Stubbs's information was that Isobel was secretly the Queen of the Cannibal Islands then I suppose Foxford could have murdered Patrick out of sheer chagrin,' retorted Hannibal.

'We're not going to get very far if you won't look at the truth.'

Hannibal faced him, suddenly very angry. 'The truth is that we don't know the truth,' he said. 'There is another explanation that we're not seeing.'

January folded his arms. 'The truth is that your love for the boy's mother is keeping you from looking at the evidence we *do* have,' he said gently. 'Foxford is twenty-two. He's been under the hand of an older man all his life, with who knows what feelings buried below the surface so far that he may not be aware of them. He's obviously so besotted with this girl that he follows her to America and drags along his trustees in the hopes he can get her to change her mind. Then that mentor, that guide, that controller comes storming into his hotel room and throws the information at him that he has proof that the girl is not only *not* what Foxford thought she was, but also that he, Patrick Derryhick, will never countenance the match—'

'You have no proof of any of this.'

'No,' said January. 'But you're the one who's going to talk to Martin Quennell and find out what was actually said. So I hope you understand that you need to ask him everything you can think of and tell me everything that he says.'

Hannibal turned without speaking and strode off along the board sidewalk, January at his heels, like a good, obedient slave.

Like every other person of African blood in New Orleans – slave or free – January avoided walking along Baronne Street when he could. It was here that most of the town's dealers in human cattle had their offices – neat square buildings of brick or wood for the most part, like any other stores in the American section, with awnings built over the plank sidewalks to protect potential customers from the brutal sun and the afternoon rains. It was here, in the fenced yards and rough-built sheds behind them, that slaves were brought in from Virginia and Maryland – where the exhaustion of the old tobacco-lands rendered so many plantations overpopulated – to be sold. With the expansion of cotton into Mississippi, Missouri, and the north of Louisiana, everyone needed slaves, and men who could be bought for three hundred dollars in the east were going for three and four times as much in New Orleans. The cane-planters were always in the market, too. Cane killed men fast.

It was early in the season for anyone to be selling, and mostly the men just sat on the benches outside the offices, sometimes talking quietly among themselves about wives, children, friends they'd grown up with – all left behind, everyone they knew – and sometimes just watching the thin traffic in the street. For the most part they were neatly dressed, in blue coats, bright with cheap dye, and shoes that probably would have been agony to walk in for more than a dozen feet. Above the shoes and below the hems of the trousers, January could see the ankle irons.

Something old – some part of him that he'd never forgotten – curled tight behind his sternum, and he felt the prickle of mingled rage and terror sweep through him like fever. Thin and jaunty, Hannibal strode ahead of him: a man who'd saved his life, a man he loved like a brother. A man who in that moment he could have struck – maybe killed – because he was white.

A girl of fourteen sprang up from one of the slave benches, darted over to Hannibal in a jingling of ankle chains. 'You buy me, Mister? I'm right smart; I can cook, and sew, and wash clothes—'

'I'm sure that you can, *acushla*.' Hannibal doffed his hat. 'But I very much fear my good wife would beat me with a broom handle, should I bring into the house a young lady as beautiful as yourself – terribly jealous, my wife, and ugly as Satan's bulldog – so I must decline.'

'I can be ugly,' she offered, and she made a horrific scowl to prove it.

Hannibal mimed terror. 'Alas, it's not to be,' he said and handed her a nickel. 'She can see through ruses like that, you see.' He moved on.

Behind them, January heard the girl's voice, addressing another passer-by. 'You buy me, Mister?'

Close your eyes, he told himself, as he had to tell himself sometimes when he worked at the Countess's and listened over his shoulder, through the music, to one of the girls chatting up a gentleman caller. *Nuthin' I love better than a Greek, Mister . . .*

Close your heart. Don't think about who those girls, those boys along this street, those men in chains would be if they could actually do even the tiniest bit of what they wanted to in this world.

You can't even vote in this country.

He took a deep breath and looked up, in time to see Hannibal stop. 'Irvin and Frye's', said the sign in the window. 'Prime Hands, Fancies.' Three men and a boy sat on the bench on one side of the door, three women – one of them great with child – on the other. Their eyes all flickered to Hannibal as he consulted the advertisement in the *Bee*, pulled Thos. Dawes's card from his waistcoat pocket, and went inside. January felt their eyes on his back as he followed.

'Have I the pleasure of addressing Mr Irvin,' inquired Hannibal of the man who rose from behind the desk in the stifling front room, 'or Mr Frye?'

No other customer. Thank God.

January folded his hands and stood to one side while Hannibal and Mr Irvin (or Mr Frye) discussed the price of slaves, the profits from Hannibal's putative cotton press in Mobile, Hannibal's equally putative wife in Mobile and her need for a smart young maid . . . *Yes*, Mrs Dawes preferred them bright, and in fact was looking for a girl who could read. *No*, Mr Dawes couldn't understand it either, wasting time teaching wenches to read, but Mrs Dawes had been to a Young Ladies Seminary in Washington and had a few notions . . .

Mr Frye (or Mr Irvin) yelled for a young man named Samson – probably a slave himself – to fetch in Estelle, Jewel, and Pierrette. 'Too old,' Hannibal said, dismissing at once the only one whose years put her out of the running to be Pierrette. 'And this one is . . .'

'Jewel, sir.'

Jewel was sixteen, thin, and fighting with everything that was in her to remain expressionless.

'Lovely,' purred Hannibal, in a startling imitation of Uncle Diogenes at his most debased. 'Lovely. Might I have the opportunity to take a more private viewing?'

'Of course, of course . . .'

Irvin (or Frye) led Hannibal and the girl to the stairs. In the stairwell, Hannibal asked about the election – was it true Daniel Webster had challenged Mr Van Buren to a fist-fight in the Capitol? Mr Irvin hadn't heard about this? Dear Lord, it was all over Mobile . . .

January stepped over to the girl left standing by the desk. 'Pierrette?'

She turned as if he'd fired a gun.

'My name is Lou. I've been asked to bring you a message.' He spoke French, though Samson – loitering just outside the rear door where a feeble breeze whispered through from the yard – probably couldn't hear them from where he stood. 'Michie Tom and I are bound up the river tomorrow; the lady who spoke to me says as how you might want a letter taken.'

The girl's eyes grew round, and January almost had to look away from the shocked hope that flooded her face. 'Who . . .?'

'I don't know her name. Feller named Ti-Jon put us together.' He named the slave – known throughout New Orleans to the enslaved – who could usually be counted on to know everybody who needed anything done. 'But she said you been sold off without your young Miss knowin' about it.'

Pierrette pressed her hands to her mouth; they were shaking. 'She didn't know,' she whispered. 'I swear she didn't know. M'am Deschamps only did it because of what happened in Paris . . .'

January cast a quick glance toward the back door, but Samson had retreated into the yard and was nowhere to be seen. Two steps took both him and the girl to the desk; she had to wipe her palms, suddenly damp with panic sweat, on her skirt before she took up Mr Irvin's pen and a sheet of paper. January stepped back, not speaking until she had done.

Miss Isobel – her handwriting staggered with her nervous trembling – *your mother has sold me off, because of what happened in Paris. Please, please help me. I was sold to traders named Irvin and Frye, on Baronne Street. The others here say we will be bound for Nashville on November 1. I think they want $700, but I will do whatever you ask, anything, scrub floors or pick cotton or anything, if you'll get Granpere Rablé to buy me. Pierrette.*

'Mamzelle'll be with her aunts in St Francisville,' said the girl, folding the letter swiftly and handing it to January. 'Ma'm Nienie Deschamps and Ma'm Heloise Grounard. It's the first house up the River Road from the landing, 'bout a mile from the town. Rosetree, it's called. There's an archway of roses out in front.'

She pressed her hands to her mouth again, struggling to gather her thoughts. The ashy pallor of her golden complexion told January that she'd probably neither eaten nor slept since the mother of her 'young Miss' had informed her that she was going to be taken to the dealer's and sold; her eyes had the bruised look of tears beyond what white girls her age had any comprehension of. She wore a pretty frock of blue-and-white print lawn, more expensive than any dealer would give to make his 'fancy' look 'smart'. She must have been taken straight out of the house in what she stood up in.

'If she's not there,' she went on after a moment, 'can you maybe get someone to take this up to Beaux Herbes plantation, outside Cloutierville, up on the Red River? Or Bayou Lente plantation, on t'other side of Cloutierville, about two miles? She sometimes goes and visits the old man there, M'sieu Rablé – Granpere Rablé, he's called all over the parish. Please,' she whispered, with another glance from the back door to the stairwell, from which Hannibal's laughter, and Mr Irvin's (or Mr Frye's), drifted unhurriedly down. 'Please. I know Granpere Rablé will buy me, if Mamzelle asks him.

Mamzelle was his poor wife's little pet, and old Granpere loves her like she was his own granddaughter.'

'I'll do what I can.' January slid the note into his pocket. The thought of journeying all the way to Nachitoches Parish – six days' travel on the low summer rivers – in pursuit of Isobel Deschamps appalled him, but he knew that, whatever else happened, its delivery was the price of what Pierrette could tell him. He made his voice indignant rather than urgent, as if the matter didn't concern him directly, when he said, 'What happened in Paris, that Mamzelle's maman would want to sell you off?'

Once the note was handed over, some of the girl's panic seemed to subside. As if, fighting to stay afloat in horizonless ocean, she'd glimpsed a plank that might be bobbing her way.

She drew a deep breath, tucked a stray curl of light mahogany-red hair back under her tignon, shook her head. 'I don't understand it,' she said. 'That Irish boy she fell in love with, that Vicomte . . . her Tante Cassandre in Paris, she asked about him and looked him up in her books, and she said, "Well, he's not so rich as some, but he'll surely do for a husband." And there was no question, he loved her like St Roche and his dog, and she him. That other Lord, that Lord Blessinghurst, she never had a glance for him, for all his roses and poetry that he sent . . . and, Mamzelle said, he'd copied the poetry out of a book.'

'Did he, now?' January murmured. 'Was he rich?'

'Lord, yes. He once gave me ten francs and promised me there was more where that came from –' she grimaced with distaste – 'if I'd tell her what a good man he was and how desperate in love with her. I gave him his ten francs back,' she added and wiped her hand on her skirt again as if at the memory. 'He tried to kiss me, too.'

'Why did you come back?' asked January. 'You didn't have to . . .'

'I wish I hadn't,' Pierrette whispered. 'If I'd known . . . But something went wrong 'twixt her and Michie Gerry – Vicomte Foxford,' she corrected herself quickly. 'Bad wrong. I don't know what it was. This was February – Mamzelle and me, we'd got there at the start of December. One evening Mamzelle came home early, before midnight, from a ball she'd been at, claiming she had a headache. But when she got up to her room she broke down crying like her heart would break. Michie Gerry came the next day, and she said how she had a headache. He begged me to take her a note, and she tore it up without reading it – that one, and the others he sent. It scared me how she'd cry. That day she told Tante Cassandre she wanted to go home, she didn't care how bad the voyage was going to be. I asked Michie Gerry what happened, and he said she'd told him she couldn't see him anymore, just like that, out of a blue sky. He asked me if she'd said anything to *me*!

'I been with other young misses,' she went on, her dark eyes filled with distress, 'and I've never seen anythin' like this. She quit eating, she didn't sleep – I know she didn't sleep because I'd sit up most of the night. She—' She broke off, twisting her hands. 'I was afraid for her,' she said softly. 'I shouldn't say this, but one night I went downstairs, and comin' back up, I found she'd got a razor from Oncl' Deschamps's room. She was just sittin' in the dark, holdin' it in her hand. I took it away from her, gentle as I could, but she was . . . strange. She got over it, a little, once we'd got on the ship, but . . .'

The girl shook her head again. 'All she'd say, when I spoke his name, was, "Don't talk about him. Don't talk about him again ever." And after all that—' Pierrette shook her head again, pressed her hand to her mouth, as if to hide from him the trembling of her lips. 'After all that, she tells her maman she has to leave *New Orleans* now. She had that look in her eye again, that empty look. It was her maman who said I was to stay here. I didn't think a thing of it at the time, but now I see—'

The street door opened. A man came in – his boots and coat and the set of his shoulders shouting *cotton planter*, of the kind just starting in the territories – and Irvin's (or Frye's) descent clattered in the stairwell. 'Good day, sir, good day – hot as blazes, ain't it? What can I do for you this fine morning . . .'

'Thank you, sir,' Pierrette whispered to January in French, and she pressed his huge hand between both of hers. 'God bless you. Get my Mamzelle that note, somehow – I know she'll get old Granpere Rablé to buy me.'

Questions unasked fought on January's lips – did she see 'Blessinghurst' the day before this ball when she'd told Foxford goodbye? Was there a time when Isobel was alone with him? Did he send her letters? But pity silenced them. He was on the track of a puzzle with a young man's life at stake, but this girl stood in terror on the brink of a precipice, waiting for the shove that would send her over. It was no time for tales of who might have said what to whom last February in Paris.

'I'll do what I can,' he promised – and meant it. *Blessed Mary Ever-Virgin, give me the strength to do what is needed.*

Hannibal came downstairs a few moments later, the girl Jewel in his wake. Pierrette went to her at once, took her hands – January heard her ask, 'You all right, *cher*?'

The younger girl whispered, 'It weren't bad. He didn't make me undress or nuthin'.'

There were planters, January knew well, who would strip women, squeeze breasts, paw genitals and – if the dealer thought it would clinch the sale – copulate with their prospective property in the name of *seein' how she'll breed*. If you didn't buy the girl it was certainly cheaper than a visit to the Countess.

The slave-dealer was still chatting cheerfully with his new customer when Hannibal moved to the door, tipping his hat as he passed.

'Not to your taste, sir? You can take Pierrette upstairs—'

'Another time.'

'Sure thing, Mr Dawes. And you think about what I said, about that boy of yours . . .' He nodded to January.

'I will indeed give the matter thought,' promised Hannibal, his hand on the doorknob. 'Until then, as the poet says, *ficossissimus esto*, Mr Frye!'

As they stepped outside, the slaves seated on either side of the door glanced at them, and January had to close his hands into fists, as if doing so would hold in the rage that swept him. If he did not, he thought, he was in danger of forgetting all about Compair Lapin, in danger of losing his temper, as Jesus had in the Temple, and storming from end to end of this street with a whip in his hand . . .

And we all know what happened to Jesus.

SIXTEEN

It would make him late to the Countess's that night – and his whole bruised body ached to lie down for the remainder of the evening – but January made it his business to visit the Cabildo. Shaw wasn't there, but the sergeant at the desk – mellowed by a tip that January couldn't well afford – led him across the back courtyard and up the brick steps to the men's cell. The *white* men's cell it was, these days, though January had occupied it himself a few years previously, before the Americans had complained about *their* drunkards and scum being obliged to share quarters with some lesser race. With any luck, within a year the new Parish Prison being built on Rue d'Orleans would be ready to receive visitors; as it was, the stink of the place made him cringe before he was halfway up the steps. At the moment the place was quiet, save for an inebriated voice extolling the necessity for a higher protective tariff and an independent national treasury. 'Somebody shut that damn Whig up,' urged a tired voice.

Foxford came to the barred judas in the door. 'Mr January! Good lord, what happened to you?'

January touched the cut flesh and sticking plaster on the side of his face. 'Isobel Deschamps's relatives cornered me on my way home last night,' he said quietly. And then, as Foxford began to stammer out some reason why this could not possibly have had anything to do with him since he had never met Isobel Deschamps, he went on, 'That isn't important now, sir. What's important is that Mademoiselle Deschamps's maid, Pierrette, has been sold to slave-dealers.'

The young man's mouth dropped open in shock, aghast: naïvety that would have been comical under any other circumstances. *Don't you understand that's one of the great virtues of slaves? That if they trouble their masters – by growing old, by standing up for better food or better treatment, by speaking for themselves – they can simply be made to disappear?*

He went on, 'Her mother did it, the moment Mademoiselle left town. They'll be taking her to Nashville to sell in cotton country, if she doesn't find a buyer here before—'

'What do they want for her?' Foxford's long-fingered hands gripped the bars, and all trace of unconcern about Isobel Deschamps was gone from his face. 'Do you know?'

'Seven or eight hundred dollars.'

'What's the dealer's name?'

'Irvin and Frye. On Baronne Street.'

'Thank you.' The grim set of the young man's jaw told January everything about his love for Mademoiselle Deschamps, which had extended to friendly affection for her maid. 'Droudge should be here in an hour with my lawyer. I'll tell him to buy her . . . That is,' Foxford stammered, suddenly recalling his former assertions, 'I'm horrified that such things should happen to the innocent—'

January held up his hand against further protestations. 'Just get her out of there,' he said quietly. 'I don't need to know anything else.'

He was starting to turn away when Foxford asked, 'Did you speak with her?'

He turned back. 'Yes, I did.'

The young man looked aside, trying to piece together something to say.

'I can't stay,' said January. 'I'll be back tomorrow, and I'll want to talk to you then.'

Foxford raised his chin. His hardened eyes, and the grim set of his mouth, told January that all he'd get for his trouble would be more lies.

'In the meantime,' said January, 'for God's sake, get that poor girl out of the dealers' hands. I don't know what's going on here, but you at least have chosen – for whatever reason – to be where you are. Pierrette's only choice was to come back to this country with her mistress from France, where Pierrette was a free woman. Don't make her suffer for that.'

He turned, and all but ran down the stairs.

The Countess's ire at January's tardiness on the busiest night of the week was mitigated somewhat when she saw the cuts on his face, the agonized stiffness with which he seated himself at the piano. 'You be all right?' she asked as he flexed his shoulders in a vain attempt to make them feel like anything other than slabs of raw pain affixed to his skeleton with red-hot nails. 'What happened?'

'Little disagreement with some of the downtown boys.' He now understood some facts about the Countess that he had not before, but those facts provided him no clue about whether she'd continue to employ him if it was known he'd angered white men who might later turn into paying customers. He removed his gloves, flexed his hands, thrummed out a long elaborate trill:

There was a country blade,
And he wooed a little maid,
Safely he conducted her home, home, home.
She was neat in ev'ry part,
And she stole away his heart,
But this pretty little deary, she was dumb, dumb, dumb.

As he played he wondered which of his bodyguards would put in an appearance that night. Or would any of them turn up at all? And if they didn't, would Louis Verron be satisfied with his promise to stop asking questions? Or would a few drinks over cards with his friends move that young man to a repeat of last night's violence, with an inevitable escalation of results?

'Hey, Mr Barton, been awhile since we've had the pleasure! Why, the girls were saying only yesterday, "Where's that big Ned Barton gone?" . . .'

The pain in his cracked ribs was like a sword driven into his side.

New York! New York!
Oh! What a charming city.
New York! New York!
Oh! What a charming city.

A razor, Pierrette had said. There were girls who'd turn to thoughts of ending their lives over a romance gone wrong, or even over a seduction, but the maidservant had seemed to be a sensible girl, and he felt inclined to trust her judgement. Whatever had passed between 'Blessinghurst' and Isobel Deschamps, it was something neither the actor nor Isobel's family wanted aired in public.

He glanced across at Marie-Venise, like a lost schoolgirl in her childish dress, whom he knew to be – in addition to an avid student of what were generally known as the Greek arts – an expert in the application and receipt of erotic pain.

A necklace of matched pearls shimmered against the white blades of her collarbone; another gift from Stubbs, in his role as Blessinghurst? Was his absence from the Countess's lately a coincidence, or had he gone into hiding from Louis Verron?

And what steps would he be willing to take to keep January from further inquiries?

Michie Gerry . . . said she'd told him she couldn't see him any more, just like that, out of a blue sky. He asked me if she'd said anything to me . . .

Don't talk about him. Don't talk about him ever again.

'Why, Mr Switters, you wicked old thing! How's the General's friends doing for votes? Yes, I read that article – what a scandal! Your Mr Webster and Mr Clay and I don't know who-all everybody else on their side had better be thankful women do not vote, because me, I would vote against every one of them! The Chair? Ah, Signor –' a tap on the pudgy arm with a black-and-crimson fan – 'I've had the girls keep it warm for you, turn and turn about, all the night . . .'

I went down to the river,
I didn't mean to stay,
But there I saw so many girls,
I couldn't get away . . .

Jacob Schurtz came in around ten, drunk and boisterous, with Martin Quennell tagging behind: new gaudy waistcoats, at least five gold fobs, stylish new hat of black silk. Champagne was ordered; Martin paid for it, laughed uproariously at Schurtz's jokes. Sybilla – the tall and supple Irish Amazon – seated herself on Schurtz's knee, self-contained and confident as a cat. You could almost see her wrap her tail around her feet.

'Captain Ryberg! Don't tell me the river's come up at last? And who's this? Well, I never – my cousin married to a man who comes from Chillicothe, Ohio . . .'

A giddy snatch of Beethoven, altered the way January had heard Four-Eyes alter popular songs, with a syncopated African rhythm – nobody was listening, after all – then blending back into 'Jump Jim Crow':

An' then I got to Orleans,
An' feel so full of fight.
They put me in the Calaboose
An' keep me there all night . . .

The reek of the incense that kept the whorehouse smells of

sweat, spilled booze, and spunk at bay – oppressive at the best of times – seemed tonight to be a poison specifically brewed to kill piano players. *Mary, Mother of God, if you can hear anything that comes from within these walls, get me home tonight in one piece . . .*

'You whining New England dog, you'd destroy this country for your goddam tariffs if it'd put money in your pocket!'

And golden-haired Fanny screamed.

His mind chasing questions about Isobel Deschamps and how best to get to St Francisville without ending up bound for Nashville in a slave-coffle himself, January whirled on the piano stool, looking for the trouble that any other night he'd have spotted before it began. A greasy-haired cotton planter lunged at the steamboat captain's Ohio friend, grabbed Fanny from off the man's lap – January suspected that Fanny, not politics, was the actual cause of the animosity – and lunged at the Northerner. The captain leaped to his friend's defense; the planter's two friends piled into the fray, and January – who knew what was expected of the house maestro on such occasions – crashed into a rousing chorus of 'Anacreon in Heaven' at the top of the instrument's iron-braced voice.

'Here, now, gentlemen, let's have none of that—' boomed Hughie's voice as the big man appeared from the kitchen, and then the ear-splitting crash of a pistol cut the din like an ax. Every man turned as the Countess tossed aside the smoking needle-gun that she'd fired into the air and produced – from God knew what hiding place – a shotgun. The ensuing silence in the room was almost deafening.

January let the piano fall silent as well. For a moment, the only sound was the clink of plaster falling from the new-made bullet hole in the ceiling.

In the stillness a man moaned in horror and agony, 'Oh, God! Oh God . . .!'

It was Martin Quennell, clutching his belly, dark blood soaking his fancy waistcoat and running out over his hands.

They carried him back to Hughie's room. Hughie strode ahead, pulling aside the rugs so that Martin's blood, and the fluid from his slashed intestines, wouldn't dribble on them. Marie-Venise found a pearl-handled penknife tossed in a corner of the parlor with a couple of handkerchiefs wadded around its hilt to keep blood off the wielder's hand, and every man in the parlor swore the knife was someone else's and produced his own knife – in several cases, two or three extras – to prove it. As January stripped Martin's shirt aside and opened his trousers, Elspie came in with two oil lamps – none of the bedrooms had gas laid on – and asked breathlessly, 'Will he live?' Raising his eyes, for a moment he met, through the doorway, Nenchen's cold green gaze. Then the big girl smiled, very slightly, with satisfaction and went up the stairs.

A little later, January heard Shaw's voice in the parlor. The Lieutenant ambled in, took one look at the wound that January was attempting to stitch shut by the light of nearly every lamp and candle in the house, and knelt beside the head of the bed. 'Who did it?' he whispered, almost in the wounded man's ear.

January had thought Quennell long past understanding anything, but the young man shook his head. 'Didn't see. Oh, God—'

Shaw glanced across at January.

'I was playing piano,' said January quietly. 'Like a good nigger, for once – and the room was pretty full.'

'He gonna live?'

Aware that Quennell could understand, though his eyes had slipped shut again, January only slightly shook his head.

The house grew quiet after that. When January went out to the kitchen to wash his hands, he saw Nenchen halfway up the stairs, sitting on a step smoking a Mexican cigarette. Their eyes met again, and she did not look away. The Countess set Elspie and Auntie Saba to cleaning up the blood. La Habañera carried in more water from the kitchen and brought up a chair beside Quennell, mopping his forehead as his fever began to climb. Philosophical, Hughie fetched pillows and blankets from the storeroom and went to sleep on the parlor floor. The rest of the girls went to bed.

At three in the morning, January heard the back door open and the murmur of the Countess's voice, speaking French. Another woman's replied, 'Ah, Didi, thank you – thank you . . .' and a moment later a woman came in, her face lined with middle age in the glow of the single lamp left burning in the parlor, but handsome still. For a moment January wondered why she was familiar, then recognized her. It was Corette Quennell, Beauvais Quennell's mother.

She went to the side of the low bed, took Martin's hand, and whispered, 'Oh, Martin. Oh, my son.'

SEVENTEEN

Beauvais Quennell was standing in the hall. When January stepped out of Hughie's room, the undertaker's eyes widened at the sight of him, and for a moment they regarded one another in silence. January started to say, 'How could he be—?' and stopped, remembering things his mother had told him when first he'd returned from France, almost four years ago. 'Was he the brother my mama said had died away at school all those years ago?'

The undertaker nodded. Looking back down the hall to the dim rectangle of the candlelit door, January saw Corette Quennell rocking to and fro, holding the hand of the young man who twitched and muttered on the bed.

In that low orange light no skin-tone looked normal, but with the mother's face bent so close above the unconscious man's, January fancied he could see, now, the traces of generations-distant Africa in Martin's features: the lie of the cheekbone, the shape of the brow. Was that why the young man had sought his pleasure at the Countess's, where there was not the slightest chance that anyone would see him next to even the fairest-skinned woman of color and note similarities?

Or had he only been desperate to put distance between himself and the blood that condemned him to a lifetime of powerlessness?

'He was her baby boy,' Quennell whispered, through a throat so tight the sound squeaked out, as if pulled through metal pincers. 'Mama's little white lamb, she called him. He was ten years old, and he wrote her that she should tell everyone he'd died. That he wasn't coming back.'

'And she did that?'

He nodded, took off his spectacles, rubbed his eyes. 'She always did what he asked.'

Half-forgotten fragments of his mother's gossip returned to him. Most of the white side of the Quennell family had left New Orleans years ago, with the death of Beauvais's father, gone upriver to Ascension Parish. He recalled vaguely his mother saying there had been white sons of the household, of whom he – and everyone else – had assumed Martin was one.

But mostly he recalled the softness in his mother's face, when she'd cuddle and sing to Dominique, the daughter of her own white protector, born when he – Benjamin – was sixteen years of age. He didn't ask, or need to, how a mother could let her child go that way. Every *placée* in New Orleans knew what a gift from God it was, to any child born able to pass for white.

The undertaker extended his hands, turned them over beneath the single gas-jet left burning in the hall, as if studying their color as he must have studied it countless times as a child, wondering why it mattered. Why it mattered so much. 'You're a doctor, Ben. How can it be, with the same mama, same daddy, he looks like a white man? I ain't that much darker.'

January looked from Quennell's face into the room to Martin's, and with the difference of the lighting between gas and flame there was no difference in color at all. The older brother's hair was a half-shade more brown than golden; the younger's eyes – shut now and bruised-looking in an ashy face – that peculiar grayish turquoise-green so common among the octoroons and musterfinos. He shook his head. 'If anybody knew that—' He hesitated. 'If anybody knew the why of it, you can be sure somebody would turn that knowledge to evil somehow.'

Quennell's eyes slid to him, caught by the thought.

Martin Quennell – only January couldn't recall whether anyone had ever said what that almost-forgotten 'dead' brother's name had been – had been sent to school in Nashville when he was very small. Most people at the back of town didn't even remember that Corette Quennell had borne her protector two sons instead of one.

He looks like a white man . . . January's mind snagged on the phrase.

LOOKS like a white man . . . He IS a white man.

He is a man, and he's white! What else do you want?

Only, of course, in Louisiana he was not. Even in Boston, were it known that one of his great-*great* grandmothers came from Africa, he would be barred from 'the best' white society . . .

And Quennell, and every other *libre* in town, thought the same.

So he only said, 'And he came back to town when your father's bank went under?'

'Father had set me up in business already,' the undertaker remembered. 'Got me apprenticed; paid for my education, same as he'd paid to send Martin to school in Nashville. Father had a stroke when the bank failed; he died soon after. It was understood that I'd take care of Martin. Only, when Martin came back, he didn't come to us. Wouldn't write, wouldn't visit. Not even on the Feast of All Saints would he come down to the cemetery and help clean up our grandpa's grave.'

Silence had settled on the house, that deep abyss between midnight and the turn of the tide. Above their heads the gas jet hissed softly, and somewhere upstairs in the darkness a girl cried out softly in her sleep. In another two hours the Cathedral bells would ring for early Mass, and the long night would be done.

'He found a family uptown – a white family, Americans – to board with; he told them he was white. He even turned Protestant.' Quennell's face twitched at the mention of that heretical faith. 'They didn't have to do with the downtown folks of course. Not many Americans do even now. He only came to us, finally, when he needed more money. I can take care of the books myself, but Maman begged me to give him something, and he wouldn't just take help for free. Please believe that,' added the undertaker. 'Please believe that, Janvier. He never stole from me.'

That you know of.

'I'd never have let Maman talk me into putting him up to look after the Society's books if I'd had the slightest doubt of him.'

January searched his face for a moment, meeting in his eyes the question: *was it the Burial Society Board of Directors that asked you to take a job here? To watch him, learn where he was getting the money he was spending?* January was afraid Quennell would ask him this out loud – and that he'd be obliged to reply – but, in the end, the undertaker did not, and the silence returned. From the tiny bedroom Corette's voice could be heard, whispering the broken thread of a lullaby:

'By an' by, by an' by, gonna lay down easy by an' by . . .'

Candlelight and sorrow erased the hue of her skin, and that of the young man on the bed, leaving only the terrible pietà of every woman who finds herself called suddenly to bury her son.

'How long?' asked Quennell at last, and January shook his head.

'Could be hours. Might be days.' He glanced along the hall to the parlor, where the Countess could be heard moving about, her skirts a silver taffeta rustle against Hughie's snores. 'She'll want him moved.'

'Of course.' Everyone had their living to make. In Quennell's voice was the echo of a thousand other madames, saloon-keepers, boarding-house owners, hotel managers: *I don't want to sound heartless, but you'll need to get him* – or her – *out of here . . .*

The first school Rose had run had not survived the death of four of her students in the yellow fever epidemic of '34.

Still neither man made a move. *My business partner*, Schurtz had called Martin, and had treated him like a dog.

Yet he had offered what Martin had always wanted. *To get as far away from New Orleans, and his family, as it is possible to get*. To outrun the slightest whisper of rumor, about what and who he was.

Wonderingly, he said, 'I can see why I never knew – I was gone for nearly sixteen years – but your brother's scheme was good, if it fooled my mother.'

Quennell laughed, a single bitter sniff. 'Not so hard. Nobody uptown knew the Quennells, so there was no chance anyone would learn Father's sons by his true wife weren't the right ages to be Martin. The white Madame wasn't about to mention it to anyone: had Noah been an American, she would have been proud to drown. The only thing anyone knew of us uptown was that Father had been a banker . . . and white. The Americans didn't find it hard to believe Martin when he said, "I want to be American and not French," instead of, "I want to be white and not black." It's done all the time.'

A sound in the parlor – a shadow against the light – drew January's eyes in that direction again, where the Countess sat beside the lamp in the parlor, her black curls taken down, a newspaper in her hands but her eyes lost in distance.

Softly, January said, 'That's true.'

At four, January returned to the tiny bedroom and found Martin Quennell's heartbeat a little stronger, his breathing the deeper rhythm of normal sleep. As he listened with a stethoscope, felt those slender wrists, he heard the Countess enter behind him and help Madame Quennell to stand. 'I think he can be moved, Madame,' he said, rising. 'Gently and carefully. As soon as it grows light—'

'No,' said Madame Quennell urgently. 'No, now. Before anyone can see.'

'Corette,' murmured the Countess. 'It's Sunday. There is time.'

The mother shook her head, impatient with this stupidity, and in her beautiful hazel eyes January saw the unreasoning single-mindedness that the grieving sometimes adopt to defend against the unthinkable. 'Not you, Didi,' she said. 'But the people at his lodging house! McPhearson's is a respectable place, a residential hotel! What are they going to think, if they see me, and Beau here, take him in—'

'Maman,' protested Quennell, 'we're taking him to the house—'

'Never!' She swung around on her son. 'What will M'sieu Schurtz say when it gets around that *we* took Martin in? They'll guess—'

'Maman, they won't guess—'

'They *will*!' she insisted. 'Beau, Beau, we cannot spoil Martin's chances! Not after all he has worked, all he has tried . . .' She gripped her elder son's lapels, almost shook him, as if the physical jolt would illuminate his mind to see things as she did. 'We have the money; we must send him a nurse, an American. Beau, *please*!'

He opened his mouth to snap at her – *Maman, he's DYING!* – and could not. With the look on his face that the Good Son must have worn during the feast for the Prodigal's return, he turned on his heel and strode down the hall and out through the kitchen to re-harness his horse.

After a few minutes, January followed, skirting the parlor and pausing there only long enough to collect ink and paper from the little secretaire in the corner, then going on to the kitchen. The smell of coffee barely masked the fug of stale smoke, incense, blood, and spilled liquor. Auntie Saba and her children wouldn't arrive until after church. He lit two or three kitchen candles and sat down to write out instructions, in English, for the American nurse, listening as he did so to the voices of the two women behind him in the hall outside the downstairs bedroom door, the soft blur of Creole French.

In time, Quennell came back in. January held up a finger, staying him on his way through; beckoned him over. 'Will you do something for me?'

The undertaker stood for a moment, looking down at him, guessing what it was going to be. But there was nothing to be said. If the other members of the board had gone so far as to place a spy in the Countess's house because Martin had been spending money he should not have had, it was clear where he had to be getting it. Quennell was an honest man. He might have looked aside from his brother's doings, rather than upset their mother, when he merely suspected that Martin dipped from time to time into the bank account of his own business.

The funds of the FTFCMBS were another matter.

'Tomorrow I'm going to bring a friend to your house,' said January. 'A white man, a lawyer.' Or a white man who happened to have a lawyer's business card in his pocket, anyway. 'I want you to write out an authorization for him to go through your brother's papers and effects. I'm pretty certain your mother won't allow me to care for Martin – she may not even permit you to visit him, or visit him herself, for fear of having someone "suspect". And we need the contents of his desk.'

'All right.'

'Get Martin to sign the authorization if you can, but I doubt he'll be able to.'

'No,' said Quennell. 'I know the look, and I see it in his face. And you're right.' He pushed up his spectacles again to rub his eyes. 'Even she won't go to him once he's back at McPhearson's.' January recognized the name of the small residential hotel on Dryades Street, almost to the city limits – as far uptown as one could get and still be able to walk to work at the Mississippi and Balize. Expensive, but of course a man who was presenting himself as an up-and-coming speculator in city lots couldn't be seen, by the wealthy, to be living in a boarding house. 'Nothing must "spoil his chances". Even now.'

'Let her have her comfort,' said January. 'In a week it will be as much a part of the past as George Washington.'

Quennell nodded. He had comforted half the bereaved of the *libres* in the French Town: husbands who had lost wives untimely, women left suddenly without the spouses of forty years. Children who had closed their parents' eyes, parents who had closed their children's. Not all of those partings had been free of bitterness. It was now his turn.

Madame Quennell was saying softly, 'Thank you, Didi. Beyond what I can say—'

'It's nothing, Corette. Truly.' The two women embraced in the cloying dark. 'I may be in the business of sin, but that doesn't mean I'm not a Christian woman. I'll send Auntie Saba to McPhearson's, as soon as it's light, to look after Martin until a regular nurse can be found. You may not find one until Monday. She's dark enough,' the Countess added, when the other woman drew in breath to protest. 'Nobody's going to think she's family. Not like if they saw you, or Beau, there. And I'll send Hughie for Pere Eugenius—'

'No!' Corette Quennell caught her hand. 'No, you can't. Martin was always . . . He says that the Protestants uptown, they know that we here are Catholics. That even that may cause someone to suspect.'

'Corette, you'd let him risk dying in sin, rather than—'

'He's not going to die!' insisted Madame Quennell. 'Don't say that! And he – Didi, you know how people are. You know how the *blankittes* are in this town. They all know – they all watch – for who might be *passe blanc* . . . You've seen how they study each other's hair and fingernails and the shapes of their noses. You've heard how they whisper, "Well, maybe *this* one is," and, "Maybe *that* one's been lying all along." Didi, think. My son has a chance to escape, this one chance. Even a whisper, and of course M'sieu Schurtz would shout it all over town rather than have the other blankittes saying that he knew all along and didn't speak . . . I can't let anything spoil all he has worked for.'

The Countess regarded her with pity in her eyes but said only, 'I understand.'

And as she called for Hughie – this woman who passed herself as Italian among American men who would hold a woman of color in contempt – January, standing in the kitchen doorway, was suddenly, and without warning, overwhelmed by the precise mental sensation of comprehension, as if he had been trying to decipher the images of a painting seen within a shuttered room, and someone had opened the window, letting in light.

Not Isobel and Stubbs – no melodramatic history of seduction and jealousy, no secret marriage or blows struck in frustrated rage – but Isobel and Foxford. *She was with him that night*. He knew it, as if he had stood, invisible, beside them and heard what the girl had told that ardent young man . . . The secret that Foxford was willing to risk death on the gallows, rather than reveal.

And he knew where the proof of his theory – of that secret – would be found.

And the thought of going there to seek it turned the blood to water in his veins.

EIGHTEEN

Hannibal said, 'I can't.'

Only the agony of two cracked ribs kept January from grabbing the fiddler by the arms and shaking him till his teeth rattled. Head throbbing with sleeplessness, body and bones a mass of pain from the events of the past thirty-six hours, he opened his mouth to shout, 'For the love of God, why not?' at him.

And closed it, the words unsaid. Understanding, from the cornered stillness in Hannibal's ashen face, that there was probably only one thing in the world that would keep his friend from undertaking the journey upriver with him to keep him – by his impersonation of a white master – from being kidnapped by slave-stealers on the way . . .

And that this was it. Whatever this was.

That he would not – and could not – abandon the son of a woman he had not seen in seventeen years.

Through the open door of the Broadhorn's attic, shouting drifted up from the yard. 'Kill 'im, you fucken buzzard! Get after him! Get after him!'

A sudden roar of voices – and, above them, the frantic, furious skrakking of enraged roosters.

Sunday in the Swamp. Had January dragged Andrew Jackson's daughter into one of the crib sheds with carnal intent, not a man would have taken his attention from the cockfight long enough to comment.

'You're sure Mademoiselle Deschamps isn't in St Francisville?' Hannibal asked, after he had waited in silence for words of anger that did not come. Under the threadbare linen of his shirt, his shoulders relaxed, and he tried to make his voice sound normal. 'That's only two days—'

'Even if she is, I still have to go to Cloutierville,' said January. 'If I don't find her, either at Beaux Herbes or Bayou Lente, I'll visit the Deschamps aunts on the way back. But I'd bet money against it, if I had any.'

'What?' Hannibal folded shut Wolff's *Prologmenum ad*

Homerum and tucked it under the pillow of his bed. He'd been sitting, half-dressed, reading it when January had climbed the ladder to his attic, and he looked like he'd actually slept some, for the first time since the funeral. 'The Countess doesn't pay you?'

'The Countess,' said January drily, 'is going to have to be forcibly restrained when she gets my note telling her I'm leaving New Orleans tomorrow morning and will be gone for twelve days. I shouldn't be much longer than that.'

Hannibal started to speak, then didn't. And what, after all, January reflected, could he say, after 'I can't'? Without a white 'master' to make a fuss if his 'slave' disappeared, there was every chance that he, January, might not come back at all from a journey into cotton country.

In New Orleans, Benjamin January was known to hundreds of men and women, white and black. Should he disappear one day – and many free black men did – he would be quickly sought, and the first place his friends would look would be in places like Irvin and Frye's. Should anyone find him there – perhaps semi-conscious and stupefied by opium – Lieutenant Shaw, or January's banker Mr Granville, or the fencing master Augustus Mayerling, or Hannibal himself, or any of a number of other white male friends, stood ready to testify in the local court that yes, Benjamin January was a free man.

In the new cotton plantations of Missouri and Mississippi, a black man who might happen to be struck over the head while walking down the street – and wake up in a slave-jail with his freedom papers missing – would learn very quickly why only white men served on juries.

The thought of leaving the French Town these days made him nervous. The thought of travel upriver – as he had traveled at the beginning of that summer, under Hannibal's protective aegis – turned him cold with dread.

Unprotected, it was unthinkable.

But understanding, as he now understood, what secret it was that Viscount Foxford was willing to let himself be hanged to protect, he knew he could not do otherwise.

At last Hannibal said again, 'I'm sorry.'

January put a hand on his thin shoulder. 'It's all right. I'll manage. Come to dinner.'

'Rose will poison me.'

'She isn't a good enough cook,' January reassured him, and Hannibal laughed shakily. 'And we won't tell her until afterwards that you're staying in town.'

Down in the yard, the shouting changed its note; the cries of, 'Gouge him!' and the shrill screams of whores – who in general took little interest in cockfights – told him that combat had progressed from the roosters to their owners.

'Two things I want you to do while I'm gone,' he went on as Hannibal got to his feet and ambled around the attic in his shirtsleeves finding his razor and shaving mug, his comb and the least threadbare of his cravats. 'Three things,' January amended. 'First: you're going to take my place at the Countess's.'

'She'll kill me,' protested Hannibal.

'What did you do?'

'Nothing! Well, nothing to speak of . . .'

'I'll write you a letter of introduction,' said January patiently, 'going bond that you will neither drink, nor engage in card games with customers, nor lay so much as a fingertip upon any of the girls. You owe me that – and I can't leave her with no one to play tomorrow night.'

'My salvation, I suppose,' sighed Hannibal. 'Though I *never* played cards with the customers. But, considerations of my safety aside, I'm not sure it will be such a good idea, as I told Martin Quennell yesterday in the lobby of the Mississippi and Balize Bank that I was Thomas Dawes of Mobile.'

'Don't worry about that,' said January. 'In that conversation, you didn't manage to bring up the subject of Stubbs's quarrel with Derryhick, did you?'

The fiddler shook his head. 'I'm to meet him tomorrow evening at Davis's. Given Trinchen's illness, I can't imagine the man would be cad enough visit the Countess's establishment— '

'Unless Jacob Schurtz took it into his head to go there,' said January, as he descended behind Hannibal down the rickety stairs. 'In which case Martin would follow – and run the risk of being gutted by Nenchen, the minute everyone's back was turned because of a fight. Which is,' he went on, as Hannibal turned, appalled, at the bottom, 'precisely what happened last night. He's dying.'

'Dear God— ' By the look on Hannibal's face, January could

tell that, in the course of his checkered career, the fiddler had seen men die of lacerated gut-wounds before.

'That's the second thing I want you to do. I'm going to take you to Beauvais Quennell's, and you're going to introduce yourself to Madame as a lawyer and get her to sign a letter authorizing you to go in and search Martin's rooms at McPhearson's Residential Hotel for the actual account books of the Burial Society.'

They crossed the yard, skirting the dirty knot of men, which had reassembled itself around the makeshift cockpit. It was noon, and it felt like the heat would continue forever, to the death of the world. There was a sort of makeshift kitchen behind the Broadhorn's gambling room, stuck into a lean-to at the end of the short side of the building's 'L'. Within, Kentucky Williams – the sleeve of her Mother Hubbard rolled up past her meaty biceps – was fishing around in a barrel of what smelled like raw alcohol mixed with tobacco. A half-empty jar of cayenne pepper, a scattering of gunpowder, and three severed and liquor-logged rattlesnake heads on the table beside her hinted trenchantly as to the composition of what she served her customers out front. She looked up with a smile like a friendly bulldog, took the cigar out of her mouth with her free hand, said, 'Hey, Hannibal; hey, Ben. Water's hot on the stove,' and went back to fishing.

While Hannibal shaved in a corner of the kitchen, January watched the proprietress of the Broadhorn add a handful of soap flakes to her wares ('If'n they don't get sick, they don't think they've had a real drink.') and reflected on the fact that, even in his worst days of illness, liquor, and opium-taking, January had never known Hannibal to be anything but as clean as it was possible to be, given the circumstances. Kate the Gouger, who ran the bathhouse in the next street, was always willing to let him use her facilities on credit, and women like Kentucky and Fat Mary, who washed their Mother Hubbards once in a summer, if that, were perfectly happy to do his laundry.

'Isn't it carrying secrecy a little far?' Hannibal asked when January had explained to him – in French – about Madame Quennell's frantic insistence on secrecy, should her younger son live. 'What will it hurt if a man or a woman of color is seen going into his rooms?'

'Everything,' said January somberly, 'if it's guessed – even *whispered* – that he's *passe blanc*. It's what you said about a girl of respectable family marrying an actor, only trebled – quadrupled. Not only would Martin lose any chance of marrying this Schurtz woman and her dowry. Schurtz – and every friend Martin made uptown – would repudiate him, because these men have their own reputations to think of. If they don't, what would *their* friends think of *them*, should it get about that one might meet a black man under their roofs without knowing it? Whatever Miss Schurtz thought of Martin, she wouldn't dare wed him if word got out, because that would put her in the position of having black in-laws. Intolerable, if you can't invite your in-laws to your house – ever – because that would oblige your other friends to associate with them . . . to recognize them socially. And with the *passe blancs* it's worse, because people you meet in their house *might* be black, only you *can't tell* . . .'

'For God's sake, Benjamin.' Hannibal straightened up from the basin, wiped his face with a clean flour sack. 'It isn't as if blacks were lepers—'

'That is exactly what we are.' January stepped over to Hannibal, wiped the back of his hand down the white sleeve of the fiddler's shirt. 'And that is exactly what they fear. To touch us, to associate with us, because doing so would result in some of our social odium smirching them.' He pointed to the place where his hand had touched. 'If you were a Southerner,' he said quietly, 'you'd be able to see the stain.'

Hannibal said nothing.

'The French are like the Spanish – they'll associate with us socially because to them it's all money and power. But the Americans have declared us to be an inferior species fit only for slavery – and so they must look for reasons to prove it's true. The *passe blancs* scare them because one cannot tell where the line should be drawn. That's why they make the women wear tignons, so even a fair-skinned woman with blue eyes can be identified as "really black", as if she'd put on light skin in a deliberate effort to defraud. They forbid the men from carrying walking sticks or smoking cigars or owning dogs – they'd forbid us to dress like white people, if they could.

'If Martin Quennell were exposed as *passe blanc*, he would

lose his job with the bank – and it's nearly impossible, these days, to get a bank job, either here or in the north. In all probability, Beauvais Quennell would lose most or all of his white customers, for being "party" to his brother's deception—' He broke off and let the anger that had risen in him as he spoke simmer away for a moment. Then he said, 'All that – and in the end it doesn't matter, because the man is dying.'

'κειτο μέγας μεγαλωστι, λελασμένος ιπποσυνάων,' Hannibal quoted softly, speaking of the Trojan warrior who had been suddenly called upon to leave his earthly concerns behind. He wiped his razor on the flour sack, folded and pocketed it. 'A situation in which we all will find ourselves one day, *amicus meus*.' They stepped outside again, no difference between the muggy heat of the yard, with its dust and stinks, and that within the building. 'And what is the third thing you need me to do?'

'Find the so-called Lord Montague Blessinghurst. I suspect that, by the time I get back, he'll be the only witness left alive who can tell us what it was he told your friend Derryhick that sent him running back to his hotel. And don't let him know he's been found.'

January made no mention of his projected journey to Natchitoches at dinner, though after he and Hannibal visited the coffin shop – where old Madame, in addition to signing the permission letter, swore them both to eternal secrecy concerning her younger son and rambled obsessively about how she would continue to guard his secret once he was safely married to Milla Schurtz and out of New Orleans – they located the Preacher at Django's grocery and arranged deck passage for January on the steamboat *Parnassus*. True to his earlier assertion, he said nothing to Rose, knowing her concern would show on her face and elicit questions from his mother and Dominique at the Sunday dinner-table.

Instead, he got his mother talking about Celestine Deschamps, one of the most beautiful young ladies in New Orleans back in the days just after the great battle there that had repulsed the hated British, back when her name had been Celestine Verron and when January's mother – nowadays the respectable widow of a *libre* upholsterer – had been among the loveliest of the ladies on 'the shady side of the street'.

The subject was easy enough to raise. Dominique, kind-hearted as always, cried out in distress at the sight of January's bruised and swollen face; their mother only sniffed with scorn at the mention of the culprits. 'I daresay Louis Verron is trying to protect that father of his from word getting around that he pays a visit to the Countess's now and again. Did you see him there, Benjamin? Making a fool of himself as usual . . .'

'Was that it?' said January innocently. 'Verron said something about forgetting who I saw there.'

'Well, and so you should. All the boys in that family are mad dogs. The New Orleans Verrons haven't more than fifteen thousand a year from sugar – Mûrier Plantation has been mismanaged since before the Spanish left. Last year they barely cleared five hundred hogsheads: hardly enough for Charles Verron to keep his mistress, let alone pay the kind of prices the Countess asks.'

Livia Levesque – sixty-three years old and as beautiful as she had been even in January's childhood – made a dismissive gesture at the mention. 'Serves the little *ratatouille* right,' she added, forgetting that local slang was beneath her these days. 'Serves that entire side of the family right. They've turned up their noses at the Beaux Herbes side of the family for years.'

'Why?' Hannibal refilled her wine glass with an expression of suitable fascination. 'Don't tell me, Belle Madame, there was a scandal!'

Had the Widow Levesque been a pheasant she would have fluffed her plumage. 'Which one of the old families in this town is without scandal? Old Granpere Verron tried to keep the peace between his sons – between the men who became grandfathers to that wolverine Louis and Isobel . . . She was a pupil of yours, wasn't she, Ben?' She turned toward January, velvety dark eyes avid for gossip. 'I've heard she left town quite suddenly – almost as suddenly as she left Paris – and that her mama sold off that girl of hers . . . What was her name?'

'I know nothing about it,' said January blandly.

Dominique opened her mouth to protest – how could a mother have simply sold off a girl's maidservant? – when Hannibal laid a deft hand on the widow's wrist and urged, 'Did one of the sons try to murder the other?'

'Murder and more.' Livia Levesque rolled the words on her tongue like a vintage cognac. 'All the fault of that girl, Eliane Dubesc, Celestine's mother. Using the youngest of the three brothers as a stepping stone to get herself close to the eldest, who was engaged already to Marie-Adelaïde Peralta. Eliane took him from his fiancée, leaving both Marie-Adelaïde and young Charlot Verron in the ditch, and ran off with Louis-Florizel – for all the good it did her. Charlot called his eldest brother to task and was shot dead for his trouble, and the middle brother – Louis Verron's grandfather Nicholas – would have taken his own revenge, had not Grandpere sent Louis-Florizel and his bride off to his Natchitoches plantation at Beaux Herbes.

'All an old tale,' she added, with an indulgent smile at Hannibal's expressions of indignation and horror. 'Whoever it was who sold you this chicken, they cheated you, Rose – even putting all those peppers into it doesn't mask the taste . . . Natchitoches Parish is where the great gentlemen of the town send the members of the family whom they don't want to have anything to do with, *cher* Hannibal, white or colored. It's up on the Red River, on the Spanish border – well, their so-called Republic of Texas now. A backwater.' Her slender shoulders lifted in scorn, and she pushed her plate a pointed inch away from herself, untouched.

'And Eliane Dubesc,' January's mother went on, 'who thought herself so clever to be marrying the Verron son who stood to inherit control of old Grandpere's sugar plantations and the house here in town, found herself wedded instead to a man in disgrace. All *he* got were the vacheries – the family cattle lands – and a few arpents of woods and swamp on the Red River, and not even a wife capable of bearing him living children. And you'll never tell me she didn't play him false, in the end.'

'*Maman!*' exclaimed Dominique, shocked.

'Don't be a schoolroom miss, Minou. That boy of theirs was nothing but a bundle of bones even before he contracted the consumption, and the other three died at once . . . and then all of a sudden, out of the blue, she produces a healthy, beautiful baby girl?'

'And that would be Celestine?' asked January softly. 'Mademoiselle Isobel's mother?'

'It would. I'm told that prig Louis-Florizel said the deaths of the other three – and the fact that the boy was a walking textbook of illnesses – was the judgement of God on Eliane, though why God would have bothered I can't imagine. But he took the boy away from her to New Orleans, leaving her alone at Beaux Herbes for all her trouble. Well, she had the last laugh on old Granpere after all. Those splendid sugar-plantations that went to the middle boy, Nicholas – Charles Verron's father . . . He had so many sons that, once the management was chopped up between them, young Louis will be lucky if he'll inherit part-interest in the house and a twentieth of what the place once brought in, provided the lawsuits of his uncles ever get settled enough to give him a sou. While the death of Eliane's rickety boy put her lovely Celestine – and the Deschampses she married into, whom Grandpere Verron never could abide – in possession of the Red River lands that have turned into pure gold.'

'Land that will go to Isobel and her sister,' remarked Rose thoughtfully.

'Hence the season in Paris – for all the good that did.' The Widow Levesque sniffed again and pushed the leaves of the salad around on her plate without tasting them. 'The land's too good to waste on the fortune-hunters that have swarmed after the girls. I'm told Charles Verron tried to get up a match between Louis and Isobel – they're only second-cousins, after all, and a French Creole would marry his own sister if it meant keeping the property in the family – and that was the reason Madame Celestine shipped her off to Deschamps's brother and sister in Paris. You don't happen to have found out, in all your enquiries, Benjamin,' she added with assumed casualness, 'why, exactly, the girl came back from Paris in such a hurry, do you?'

January shook his head, and Rose murmured, 'She seems to have spent a good deal of her life lately in flight.'

Softly, Hannibal said, 'Many people do.'

NINETEEN

The *Parnassus* departed upriver from New Orleans on Monday morning; January was part of the crew of stevedores who helped pole her from the wharf, then leaped across the widening gap of slow brown water to her deck. Even here on the water, the sun was a brass hammer, the air breathless and thick. As he coiled the ropes, set to with the other men – some of them free, some of them rented to the steamboat company by their owners – in shifting last-minute cargoes down to the holds, he was conscious of how low New Orleans looked, glimpsed above the top of the levee. No building in the French town was above three storeys in height; few in the American municipality upriver were that tall. He picked out the ostentatious brown brick and cream plaster façade of the Iberville. The pastel French and Spanish townhouses gave way entirely to the square brick structures favored by the Americans, which in their turn thinned to warehouses, cotton gins, and the reeking mazes of the Jefferson Parish cattle pens as they approached the Carrollton bend. Buzzards circled the slaughterhouses, dark on the glare of the sky. Small white cattle-egrets picked their way around the piled-up snags and mud of the batture below the levee.

Then the dark green monotony of the cane fields, as they had been in January's childhood. For his first eight years, the only world that he had known.

The engineer yelled, 'You lazy niggers get me some wood down here 'fore I comes up and asks what you all lookin' at!' and the deckhands laughed and cursed good-naturedly – Levi Sutton's bark was known up and down the river to be worse than his bite. With that began the endless, back-breaking, blistering chore of feeding the engine's fire.

As the new man on the crew, January had been put at the furnace end of the line: an inferno of shuddering darkness, suffocating heat, numbing noise – and safety. When the Preacher had introduced him to the deck boss yesterday, he'd explained, 'M' friend here goin' to see family in Cloutierville,' and Parnassus Sam had looked him over, matching up his stature and the quality of his clothing.

'For a buck your size you got prissy hands,' had been his only comment.

'I puts glycerin an' rose water on 'em, every night, to keep 'em soft.'

Sam's mouth twitched, but he kept his countenance. 'You know how to work, nigger?'

'I ain't cut cane lately, but I done it. I can sure load wood.'

'Well, that's good,' said the deck boss. ''Cause you gonna.'

If one couldn't go upriver with a white master, next best thing was to go as a member of a black crew. January knew he'd have to buy his place among them by doing his share and more of the hardest, hottest, stinkingest jobs. But he also knew it was only by showing himself willing that he'd have a chance to make it safely. Traveling deck passage – the only way a man of color could travel, on an American boat – he'd be lucky if he reached St Francisville still free.

Having worked as a slave, and grown up in the African village that was what slave quarters were, January understood the rhythms of the labor. Despite the stabbing pain in his ribs, he matched the speed of his work with that of the other men, steady-paced and unhurried. As a child he'd learned that if you got your job done quick, the master would just think up another one for you. Too spry and you'd make the other men look bad. *How come you ain't quick like Ben, Sam?* Though excessive spryness, he reflected, gritting his teeth, wasn't likely to be a problem on this voyage . . .

Too slow and you'd get a lick from the cowhide. Or, in this case, he'd just get put off the boat at the next landing.

The thought filled him with dread, but he knew at some point it would come to that. And as that first day went on – with the sticking plaster that braced his ribs beneath their bandages itching like the wrath of Satan, and every arm-load of wood like a dagger run into his side – he found himself calculating not how he could avoid being put ashore, but how long he could or should stay with the boat before striking out overland.

Louis Verron would follow him, as soon as he heard that Big J was no longer playing at the Countess's.

Verron would guess where he was bound, and why.

And would be riding hard.

Six days up, maybe four days back. *It's only days. I've lived through worse.*

There were few other boats on the river. In a week, January guessed, there'd be more. In the cotton country above Baton Rouge the first picking would be already going to the gins. Small sternwheelers like the *Parnassus,* which could navigate a low river, would be working their way up to bring it down, for those planters who considered the higher price early in the season sufficient trade-off for the more expensive transport costs. Snags, bars, tow-heads – and the occasional ruins of gutted boats – made the banks a navigational nightmare; every foot of water had to be patiently negotiated, with the voice of the pilot in his high lookout calling down warnings or shouting for the leads to be taken.

Along the banks, at almost every plantation landing, flags flew, hailing down the boat. Many places grew corn and pigs to feed their own labor force, but particularly as one got into cotton country, there were many who yielded to the temptation to put all their land into cotton. Why raise corn just to feed your field hands, when you could put the same acres under cotton at thirty-seven cents a pound and buy what came down from the prairies of Iowa and Illinois? And white folks didn't live on pork and grits. In addition to hemp sacks and baling rope, 'negro shoes' from New England and 'negro cloth' from English mills, the *Parnassus* was stocked with white flour, wines and beer, English mustard, French soap, whale oil, vinegar, beeswax candles, and the sacks of salt indispensable for preserving the winter's meat.

So the *Parnassus* hugged the banks, weaving and backing among endless, tedious snarls of submerged trees and sandbars, and January found himself listening, as if above the clatter and heave of the engines he could detect the hammer of following hooves.

Even with a day or two's head start, Louis Verron could ride straight overland. Ride like a white man, unafraid to be seen, not obliged to keep to the woods.

Working barefoot like the other men, January kept the knife that usually resided in one of his boots wrapped under the sticking plaster that braced his ribs. On his other side he kept his freedom papers and his money wrapped up in oiled silk, and two dozen matches – also in oiled silk – stitched into the waistband of his trousers. In his pocket nestled Rose's prized possession, a surveyor's magnetic compass, and in the hidden parcel of emergency food – tucked behind a strut on the lower deck – were all the notes and sketch maps he'd been able to assemble at short notice, from other members of the Burial Society, of the countryside between New Orleans and Natchitoches Parish. These were neither complete nor accurate – map-making and map-reading being skills no white man would endure in any slave or in anyone who might befriend a slave – but there were men and women in the Burial Society whose families came from the thriving community of the free colored along the Cane and Red Rivers.

He had prepared as well as he could, yet he knew that his first line of defense, his first warning of trouble, would almost certainly be the other men of the deck-crew.

The moon was waxing toward full and rose early. On a high river, the pilot would have pushed on by its light. As it was, they put in at Donaldsonville, and the deckhands and Boissier the cook went ashore to buy vegetables and milk. January stayed aboard, too exhausted – hurting too badly – to have gone ashore even if he had felt it safe to do so. When the men came back and the night got deep he lay on his bedroll in the space they'd cleared for themselves on the lowest deck, listening to the men sing in the clear blue darkness.

'*Who that comin'?*
Tall angel at the bar . . .
Who that comin'?
Tall angel at the bar . . .
Look like Gabriel—
Tall angel at the bar . . .
Look like Gabriel—
Tall angel at the bar . . .'

Swaying dark forms in the dimness, the lights of the little village glowing like jewels on blue velvet. Slow music, the call and response an echo of the songs his aunties and uncles would sing in the quarters at Bellefleur when he was tiny; nothing like the tomfool brightness of 'Old Zip Coon'.

'*If I had my way,*
Oh, Lord, Lord,
If I had my way,

If I had my way,
I would tear this building down . . .'

The next day below Claiborne Island they ran on to a submerged bar and spent five tedious hours while the pilot tried first to push the *Parnassus* through the obstruction, then tried to back her off it. Levi in the engine room cursed fit to send the entire boat to Hell, and January – sweating, aching, blistered in the hold – cursed too, knowing what those five hours of standing still in the water would cost him.

When they reached Baton Rouge an hour before dark, and the captain decided to stay on there overnight, most of the men cheered, but January went quietly to Parnassus Sam and asked if there was someone on the crew – or someone anyone knew in the town – who could describe to him the country through Avoyelles, Rapides, and Natchitoches Parishes, if for whatever reason he should suddenly find himself afoot and ashore.

Sam listened to January's request without expression, huge arms folded. 'I wondered if you had any particular reason for lookin' over your shoulder twenty-thirty times whilst we was ashore. You kill somebody?'

January shook his head. 'Playin' piano at a whorehouse uptown, I found out somethin' a gentleman there didn't figure any nigger had any business knowin'.' Which was true, as far as it went.

Sam rolled his eyes. 'You dumb bozal. Don't you know *any* time you cross their path, for no matter *how* much money nor how much you *think* you know 'em, you takin' your life in your hands?'

January sighed, knowing there was a great deal of truth in what the deck boss said. 'Guess I know that now.' For the first time, he had begun to see how dangerous a thing it was to put himself that close to the place where white men habitually got drunk and made fools of themselves with girls. Even if he hadn't been poking around for information about Martin Quennell and Sir Montague Blast-His-Eyes, it would only have been a matter of time before he'd found himself the witness to *something*.

'He comin' after you?'

January nodded.

'Gonna have friends with him?'

Almost embarrassed, he admitted, 'I think so.'

'Jesus wept.' Sam flung up his hands. 'An' you a grown man. What you doin' goin' upriver without yo' Mama, nigger? What's your man's name?'

'Verron. He'll have a couple cousins named Ulloa with him. Maybe others.'

'I'll tell the boys. I shoulda known that Preacher would push some kind of trouble off on me.' The deck boss dunked his face in the bucket of river water one of the boys had dipped up and pulled a clean shirt of checked calico from his bundle – one of the two dozen crew bundles that lay in a permanent line along the back wall of the boat's superstructure. 'He always got some damn thing up his sleeve. Shad Barrow that works over on the landin', his wife got kin in the prairie de Avoyelles –' he mispronounced it like an American – 'and can tell you how to get from the river as far as Marksville, anyway. I got a brother works at the tavern at Morganzia Point; I can tell you how to cut off them two big loops the river takes past Cat Island. You really headed to Cloutierville?'

January nodded, changing into his own better 'ashore' shirt. 'I need to speak to someone with the St John's church there. They say there's a fellow name of Roque . . .?'

'Don't know nuthin' about him, but somebody will.' Sam paused a moment, looking sharply sidelong at January, then asked, 'Those free papers of yours real?'

January held up his blistered hands. 'You think big as I am I'd have prissy hands like these if I wasn't free?'

Sam laughed. 'You got a point there, brother. Let's see if we can keep 'em that way.'

Thus it was that when January quietly left the *Parnassus* at the west-bank woodyard opposite Point Coupee, and set out afoot through the dense heat of late afternoon across the narrow neck of the Tunica Bend, he was at least armed with the most important thing a black man afoot could have: information. Had he not been certain that Louis Verron could now overtake the boat – and would undoubtedly have some story of murder or rape to account for his pursuit – nothing would have induced him to abandon its safety. Afoot, he was a stranger in a strange land and every man's potential property; in addition to his free papers, he carried a tin slave badge, a pass, and a letter – handsomely written by Hannibal in January's study after Sunday dinner – proclaiming him to be the property of Mr Augustus Mayerling of Rue Royale, New Orleans, which if worst came to worst might save his life.

Before quitting the boat he shaved the top of his head, to imitate a baldness that wouldn't be in Verron's description of him, and removed the sticking plaster from the unhealed cut on his face, lest its brightness show him up from a distance as a man carrying a wound there . . .

Yet in his heart he knew that, this far from New Orleans, his only safety lay in staying ahead of the chase.

He was in cotton country now. From the top of the low rise in the center of the Tunica neck, he could look through a break in the trees and see, all along the left bank, yellow-brown fields powdered with white, through which dark shapes waded, dragging their sacks. In less than a week, every dusty road would be heavy with wagon traffic, bearing the first of the crop to the gins and presses.

Woods and pastures rose across the river, where the plantation livestock grazed loose, pigs and cows rounded up as needed for food. From where he stood he could see that the land on his own bank of the river, downstream toward the bend, was the same. He made his way to the brown water and headed downstream now, following the convoluted loops of the river and straining his ears for the sound of hoof-beats on the road. Louis Verron would be following the identical route. There was no other. Because of the snag below Claiborne Island, there was every chance Verron was almost on his back.

So, like Compair Lapin, he ran.

He'd grown up on the river and knew he'd find the foundered remains of a boat or a raft somewhere among the snags along the bank, and he did – with a plank that could be used as a paddle. Once on the river itself the going was easier, for the double loop around Tunica Bend meant that he could travel downstream for some fifteen miles and still be heading more or less north. According to his map, somewhere ahead lay Angola Plantation and the point where he could cross the river, cross the neck of the Angola bend, and – with luck – cross again to Hog Point to put himself on the western bank. His heart was in his mouth the whole time he was on the water paddling, in full sight of the River Road along the shore, but it was also fifteen miles he didn't have to walk.

Virgin Mary, Mother of God, he prayed, as the patchy clouds drifted north from the Gulf, *draw your veil away from the face of the moon tonight. Guide me on my way.*

At least this high up there were fewer alligators.

Would Louis Verron and his cousins ride at night?

Or would their confidence that they'd catch him, still on the boat, at the Angola Ferry compound with their laziness, after a hard ride, and turn them down one of those long aisles of trees to a plantation house at its end, to beg dinner and punch and a night in a bed? Had Verron told his cousins, his henchmen, why they had to catch their prey? The reason behind the desperation of his chase?

January doubted it. It was not something a man could tell his friends and hope to have them remain his friends.

It was not something a man could tell the brothers or cousins of any woman he hoped to marry – or any man who might talk about to any man into whose family any woman of the Verrons would ever possibly wed.

He'll make up a story, thought January as he steered and paddled his light raft along the current, and the green-blue shadow of the western trees stretched out across the green-brown water before him. *Make up a reason why I must be put to death, without delay and without trial . . .*

Rape was the most usual charge. It was certainly one no young white planter's son would question.

And because the truth would not protect him – the truth that Germanicus Foxford was willing to risk being hanged himself to conceal – the only thing to do was keep moving and pray that his guess was right.

The moon rose just as he steered his raft to the left bank opposite the woodyards on Tunica Point, clear as a mirror held to silver light. In the swamps downstream he could hear coon-dogs baying as he set off across Angola Plantation's dark cotton fields to pick up the river again a mile away, trusting that, like the Children of Israel, God would somehow get him across.

TWENTY

Far down the levee, January followed the twinkling light of a single lantern; there was a half-grown boy there with a raft. 'That Marse Morgan over there, huntin'?' asked January, stepping out of the woods as casually as if he hadn't spent ten minutes cautiously circling the place to make sure the boy was actually alone.

'Nossir, that Marse Stewart an' young Dr Smith, gone huntin' with the Angola folks.' The boy relaxed as soon as he saw January wasn't a patteroller – a member of the gangs of small farmers and swamp-trappers who were paid by the local planters to ride the roads at night, making sure all slaves stayed in their villages where all slaves belonged.

'They sound like they havin' a good hunt,' remarked January, and he fished in his pocket for a silver Mexican half-reale – common coin, this close to New Orleans. 'You think you got time to pole me across to the Point?'

The boy hesitated, and January added, 'I ain't runned away or nuthin',' and showed his slave badge. 'Marse Mayerling, that's stayin' down to Sebastopol Plantation, he give me the evenin' to visit my wife in Williamsport, an' I got to get there sometime tonight an' get back as well.'

Only when they got across did January give him another couple of silver bits and say, 'You do me a favor an' not speak of this to anyone? Maybe Marse Mayerling didn't 'xactly *give* me permission –' he winked – 'but what he don' know won't hurt him.'

The boy grinned back and crossed his heart. 'You got my promise.' He pushed the raft off again into the moon-bright water. Two miles upriver at the ferry-landing, lights twinkled. There was a tavern there, and a small store, where the road in from Texas came down to the ferry.

January remembered the place from his trip upriver at the beginning of summer. Remembered sitting on the lower deck of the *Silver Moon* as it rounded Angola Point and hearing one of the other valets remark, 'You think this river's bad at low water? Lord, you should see the Red. Time was you couldn't get a rowboat up that stream, let alone one of these contraptions. You could walk across it on the snags – like a beaver dam a hundred miles upriver an' down.'

He swatted at a mosquito and wished he'd dared bring the aromatic oil Olympe made to drive the filthy creatures away. But, as long as there was the possibility that at some point he might find himself chased by dogs, it was probably better not to give them too much of a scent to go on. *Just get to high ground*, he told himself, *and you'll be fine*.

Unfortunately, in the area where the Red River flowed into the Mississippi amid a maze of bayous, swamps, shallow lakes, and cut-off oxbows, the closest high ground was Baton Rouge. January got off the road as quickly as he could, but save for a strip of cotton fields barely two hundred yards across, it was as if the countryside were a single huge mosquito-ranch. *Go bite the patterollers, why don't you?*

He moved through the cotton fields, keeping the river on his right; steered cautiously through the tufts of woods on the drier ground where the ferry-landing stood. Then he checked the compass by moonlight and turned inland, where the Texas Road branched off toward Mansura and Marksville in the place called the Prairie des Avoyelles – thin woods and round open spaces of phlox and butterfly weed. Stillness held the sleeping land, broken only by the throb of cicadas, the whine of mosquitoes, and the constant *peep-peep-peep* of frogs where the land lay low. Sometimes he would see a raccoon making its stealthy way through the cotton rows, or his brother-in-flight Compair Lapin. Once he heard the screech of a hunting owl.

When he was a child, he recalled, his mother was always telling him and Olympe to stay indoors with fall of darkness, lest they encounter mulberry witches and the Platt-Eye Devil. But there was magic in the humid darkness that no threat could overcome, and they'd wait until their parents were asleep – January seven, Olympe five and swearing if he and his friends didn't take her along she'd scream to wake *all* their parents so that no one could go. Then they'd creep out, scorning evil ghosts and patterollers alike, to run through the cane rows in the striped light of the moon . . .

It was a miracle none of them had ever got snake-bit, but

January had no recollection of any of his friends of those far-off days coming to harm. The danger was not in the woods and the night but in the Big House, with its laws and the actions of the whites. When his mother had been sold to St-Denis Janvier, and he'd freed her and they'd gone to live in that small pink cottage on Rue Burgundy, January had sorely missed the noises of the countryside at night. Many nights, in his eighth year and his ninth, he had sat on the gallery outside his little room, watching the street in the hope that somehow his father would find his way there, would take him up in his arms as he'd used to – those nights he'd come to know the deep-night sounds of New Orleans. The squeak of far cartwheels; the low, constant noise of the levees, which went on till any hour of the night; the wailing song of the scissors-grinder as he made his rounds.

It was good to hear the breathing whisper of owl wings, the voices of the nightbirds. To see Compair Lapin's jaunty white shirt-front as the wily little trickster slipped past him in the dark to steal Bouki Hyena's dinner and tup Bouki Hyena's wife.

Once he heard hooves on the road, far off in the stillness, and moved in along the cotton rows, stepping wary for fear of snakes. When the riders, whoever they were, had passed, he moved on, knowing the moon would soon be down. In the end he had to cut brush and branches in the woods at the far end of the fields and sleep in the shelter of one of the old Indian mounds that dotted that part of the country. His water bottle was empty, and he turned over in his mind schemes for getting it refilled – only a fool would drink groundwater in this stagnant, low-lying country – for about three seconds, before he crashed into profound and exhausted sleep.

The plantation bell woke him, ringing far off in the darkness. He heard the eerie wailing hollers of the field hands as they came out to the harvest in the first whispers of light. Thirst clawed him, but his first thought was to wonder if Louis Verron had gotten ahead of him in the night.

He moved on through the woods, paralleling the road with the cotton fields lying between. Farther on, he moved out, crouching between the rows, until he got near enough to the gang to call out softly to the water-boy and refill his bottle.

'You runned away?' the child asked, and January shook his head.

'I'm only goin' to see my mama, 'cross the river. Where's this place, son?'

'Injun Pipe Plantation.' The boy glanced back in the direction that the Big House lay, on the other side of the distant road. He was inches shorter than the cotton stalks all around them – January guessed his age at seven or eight. Older, he'd have been toting a sack himself. 'Marse Cribb's our marse,' he added, a little uneasily. 'I won't tell him I seen you.'

There was a stirring, away among the rows; the first outliers of the picking gang. The riding boss, with his horse and his gun, wouldn't be far behind. January whispered, 'Thank you, brother,' and, still crouching, slipped away among the rows. Later that day he heard men's voices and climbed an oak tree, heart hammering with impatience, lest they reach Natchitoches Parish ahead of him and spread word to watch out for a black runaway, six-foot three-inches tall with a wounded face: *had his way with a little German girl was staying with us, fifteen years old, she was . . .* Or whatever the story was going to be. It seemed like hours before the men, whoever they were – he never saw them, but he heard their dogs bark long after their voices had ceased – went on their way, yet by the sun it couldn't have been half an hour.

Where the bridle trace swung north to the village of Mansura he found a spring, shrunk almost to nothing with late season but moving briskly enough, in this drier woodland, to be free of scum and duckweed. He washed his face in it, after he refilled his bottle, and soaked his shirt and the filthy bandages around his ribs. The pain had settled into a dull constant, but he had given up even the occasional curse at Hannibal for not making this trip safer for him.

Louis Verron was out to do whatever he had to, to bury the reason Isobel had fled from Paris. Traveling as a white man's valet wouldn't have saved him. It would only have gotten Hannibal killed as well. Verron would have been waiting for the *Parnassus* when it docked at the ferry landing.

Better that Hannibal remain in New Orleans, to act on whatever it was *he* knew that he wasn't telling January, or anyone else, about the Stuart family. And to find 'Lord Montague Blessinghurst'.

January leaned his back against a dogwood, watched across the little clearing where he sat as a dozen lean, half-wild pigs came snuffling out of the trees, digging among the leaf mast for acorns and roots. *Rest*, he told himself, though his spirit fretted and twisted to get up, to go on . . . *I'm good for another few miles . . .*

You're not. You breathe a little, or you'll start making mistakes.

He consulted the compass, and his notes, and thought about that good-looking boy in the Cabildo cell. If what he guessed was true – if Isobel Deschamps had been with Foxford that Thursday night, and had told him why it was she couldn't wed him – then his silence, and his honor, must not be allowed to cause his death.

The only question was . . .

No. January shook the thought away. There were a half-dozen questions, and the fact that he thought he knew what was going on didn't mean that he was right. And he wouldn't know for certain until he reached Cloutierville and got into the little chapel of St John there.

Only four people could tell him the whole of the truth.

One of them – Celestine Deschamps – obviously wouldn't.

Viscount Foxford had made it clear that he would hang rather than speak.

With luck he would find Isobel at the end of his search – so certain had he been of where she had in truth gone, that he'd spent the hour or so they'd stopped in St Francisville talking to another of Parnassus Sam's acquaintances rather than going a mile and a half outside of town to Rosetree. Even had he done so, even had she been there, he suspected that she would have proved as close-mouthed as Foxford was proving, unless he could say, 'I have been to Cloutierville, and this is what I found there.'

And the fourth person . . .

January got wearily to his feet, knowing that if he lingered he'd fall asleep.

He suspected that the fourth person would tell him all the details that he now only guessed.

Mid-morning of the following day he came in sight of the river again, having cut off the wide loop it made around the Prairie des Avoyelles. There were fewer plantations here, and along the bayous and in the woods he glimpsed the old French style of cottages, huge slanting roofs covering deep galleries against the almost daily rainfall, ancient walls of mud and posts. At one of these dwellings he slipped in among the garden rows, as close as he dared, and helped himself to three yams and two eggs that he found in the hen coop, fleeing at the sudden incursion of a very small, but very noisy, yellow dog. Twice, late in the afternoon of that griddle-hot Friday, he saw parties of men riding along the river road.

He was too far off to see their faces, or their numbers, or how they were dressed, or anything about them except that they were there. And that they rode at a canter, like men with a purpose.

It could be anything, of course. There could be a slave escaped, or a brother who had shot his brother over a grasping woman. There could be a woman driven to desperate flight with her husband's money crammed in her reticule.

In his heart he knew they were hunting him.

He slept Friday night in the woods, in a shelter of cut boughs against the sudden drumming rain. He slept well, having roasted his yams and sucked the eggs and set a makeshift funnel of leaves to run rainwater into his bottle, secure in the knowledge that no matter what Louis Verron was saying he'd done – who he was supposed to have robbed or raped or murdered in their beds – nobody was going to be out hunting a fugitive in weather like this. If his directions were correct, he knew he should be getting close to Alexandria.

Noon had passed – and he had crossed the ill-kept wagon-road that had to lead into Alexandria from points south – when he became aware that men were hunting him.

As he paused in the woods to take his bearings, at the back of the cotton fields of some plantation that ran down to the river, the song of the field hands came to him distantly:

'*Hush, little baby, don't you cry,*
I done, done what you told me to do . . .
Yo' mother an' father was born to die,
I done, done what you told me to do . . .'

Then, in mid-song, the words changed, weaving themselves around a different tune:

'*Wade in the water, wade in the water, children,*
Wade in the water,

Angel's gonna trouble the water . . .'

As swiftly as he could without drawing attention to himself, January retreated into the woods, till he came to the bayou he'd passed a half an hour before. 'Wade in the water' – no matter what verses of the Bible it had been taken from – meant only one thing, when sung by the field hands: *they've got the dogs out after you, brother. Whoever you are, whyever they're after you, wade in the water, till they lose your scent.*

The bayou led back into marshy ground. It was late in the day. If he had to hide too long, January knew he ran serious risk of becoming lost in the woods when darkness fell.

Crotch-deep in the motionless black stream, fearing every second he'd feel the teeth of a three-foot gar in his leg, January waded, until he found a tree limb low enough to pull himself up on to, to climb to where he'd be hidden by the leaves. He was some distance from the bayou, hidden among the dense crown of a pecan tree, when he heard the dogs and men come cursing past along the watercourse, too far off to see.

Damn. Hannibal, he thought, clinging to the rough round strength of the bough, *you owe me . . .*

It was an old imprecation, casually spoken. It had only to cross through his mind to be dismissed: the thought that the fiddler would ever be capable of paying back anything he owed to anyone was ridiculous on the face of it. Yet he was trying, January understood. Trying to pay ancient debts – to Patrick Derryhick, to Lady Philippa Foxford – for kindnesses done in some other lifetime.

Pay me when we meet on the Other Side, old friend . . .

And if I don't want to end up on the Other Side by this time tomorrow afternoon, I'm going to have to get myself out of these woods.

TWENTY-ONE

He was twenty miles the other side of Alexandria, and thoroughly lost in the woods, when he was taken, by a couple of trappers he suspected had been trailing him for miles. The worst thing about being a black man in cotton country was that there was no such thing as a black man, slave or free, minding his own business. Every white man – and a good number of black ones as well – felt it was their business to ask who you were and what you were doing.

By the time he'd evaded the dog patrol on the road it was dark, and among the pine trees he had not dared to kindle fire even long enough to check his compass. He spent the night in exhausted sleep among the roots of a hollow tree, and through the following day he tried to work his way back to the woods that edged the cotton fields, beyond which would lie the river. Yet he had either come further south-west than he'd thought, or was on a stretch of the river where the woods came straight down to the water, or – most probably – the sketchy map he had of the territory was simply wrong. He listened for the sound of plantation bells but heard nothing, and he knew that wherever he was, he would be too far yet from Cloutierville to hear its Sabbath-bells ringing.

Toward noon he stopped long enough to eat the last fragments of bread and cheese that he'd brought from the *Parnassus*, and he re-shaved the stubble on his crown as well as he could in the stagnant water of a bayou. Since Verron would have described a clean-shaven man, he trimmed and shaped the beard that was beginning to come in, rather than remove it. Later, when he heard a dog bark distantly in the woods for the second time in an hour, he knew they were catching him up.

Climb a tree and wait until they passed? Or would delay only increase the chances of another searcher coming on his trail? Parnassus Sam's friend in Baton Rouge had described Bayou Lente Plantation as lying 'a piece' on the upriver side of Cloutierville, and he wasn't certain he could find it without knowing exactly where the town was. Moreover, he didn't know if the man he wished to speak to there would admit him, or listen to what he had to say, unless he visited the church first. He moved on, changing his direction toward where he thought the river should lie, until he found his way blocked by the dilapidated fences and straggly cornfield of a small farm. He retreated south-westwardly into the woods to give it wide berth, and heard, in the woods' stillness, shockingly close, the voice of a man.

Among the pines the underbrush wasn't thick. Movement could be seen a good distance off. He tried to slip from tree to tree, keeping an eye out for a thicket of laurel or hackberry, or an oak with branches low enough to climb on to, but moving away from where he thought the voices came from, he saw the trees thinning toward an open field of some sort – another farm? – and tried to backtrack. The day was overcast, and even this late in the afternoon – it was getting toward evening by this time – it was impossible to tell direction, and before he felt safe enough to stop and take his bearings again he saw movement away to his right among the trees.

At the same moment the dogs started barking again, off to his left. Flight wouldn't work, and he had only moments to prepare for the inevitable. Swiftly, he pulled his free papers from the dilapidated bindings around his ribs, along with the notes he'd made in St Francisville, rolled their oiled silk covering tight around them and thrust them deep under the roots of the most distinctively-shaped tree he could see, a stunted water-locust that branched so near the ground as to be shaped almost like a V. After a moment's mental struggle he added his knife to the cache and walked away from it, in the direction of the men and the dogs, his hands raised up.

Virgin Mary, Mother of God, keep me safe . . .

'There he is!'

'You stay right there, boy!'

He froze, raised his hands higher, and called out, 'Please don't loose them dogs, Marse! I ain't goin' nowhere!'

Like Compair Lapin, do whatever you need to do to survive. Show yourself to be as much a man as they are and be killed. Show that you're smarter than they and be killed. Show them *anything* except exactly what they want to see – an eye-rolling caricature of dim-witted subservience – and be killed, your death accomplishing nothing.

Like Compair Lapin, you could laugh when you were safe back in the briar patch.

His heart raced so hard that for a time he feared he wouldn't be able to keep his hands from shaking. *Let them shake. You're a poor lost nigger who's scared of dogs.*

But he knew the first few minutes would be touch and go. 'Don' hurt me, sirs – don' hurt ol' Jim!' He made his speech as rough and upriver as he could, and he used the name Hannibal had put on his faked slave pass. It took everything he could muster to simply cover his head when they surrounded him, struck him with rifle butts, knocked him to the ground. There were five of them: lean, bearded, dark men who smelled like animals. Swamp trappers, he guessed; men descended from the French and Spanish who'd first inhabited these areas and intermarried with Chickasaw girls. They knew the area and once they'd seen him, he knew he'd never have gotten away.

He tried to cover his cracked ribs and cried out in agony as a boot connected, his mind blurring as he huddled in the circle of barking dogs. Above him he heard one of the men say, 'Get that rope, Jean-Jean. We show this black bastard what we do to bucks what tamper with white girls.'

'That wasn't me, sir! That wasn't ol' Jim!' January gasped the words out and couldn't stifle another cry as the tallest of the men kicked him again. 'Please sir, please—' Not far from him on the ground was the broken remain of a deadfall hickory, half crumbled-away with age and rot. He made a move to rise, ducked another blow and threw himself as if stumbling by accident on to the harsh mess of splintery wood and bark, grinding into it the injured side of his face. When they pulled him to his feet – the wounds from Verron's beating masked with fresh blood and fresh swelling – he saw one of them did in fact have a rope, and he let his voice break with the terror he felt.

'They talkin' about that girl, an' I swear t'wasn't me! I'm Jim Blanc that belong to Marse Mayerling in New Orleans, an' I swear I'm sorry, I'm sorry I runned away!'

Virgin Mother of God, let them believe – let them believe. I'm going to God-damn kill Hannibal when I get back to New Orleans . . .

'You lyin', nigger.'

'I swear! I swear!'

The tallest hunter put the muzzle of his rifle to January's

head, but the oldest – gray and small with one wry shoulder – reached down and pulled him to his feet. January immediately raised his hands again as the hunter searched him, whispering thanks that the light was beginning to go.

'What's this?'

'That a cumpus, sir.' January ventured a timid little smile, like a child, disgusted with himself but telling himself he had to make Compair Lapin proud. 'Marse Mayerling, he say it tell him which way to go an' how to find your way aroun', but I can't make heads nor tails of it an' that's the truth. I got a pass, sir. That piece of paper, that from Marse Mayerling. I swear I meant to go home when I was s'posed to, an' I would have, 'cept for gettin' lost—'

'Shut up.' The man slapped him, open-handed, across the face, turned Hannibal's carefully-forged document over in his hands, then looked at the tin slave badge.

The tall man said again, 'He's lyin', Toco. Buck that's bulled a white girl, he'll say anythin', keep his neck out of a noose.' And the little man with the rope grinned and shook the noose in his hands, clearly enjoying the prospect of causing that much fear.

'Anyhow, he stole that cumpus thing,' The tall man mispronounced the word exactly as January had.

January shook his head desperately. 'I just borrowed the cumpus, sir, to find my way with! I sure was gonna give it back.'

'Where's your master?'

January didn't dare let the relief that washed over him show on his face. The longer you kept them talking, the likelier you were to come out safe. 'I think he musta gone on downriver by this time. He stop at Alexandria, an' wrote me a pass to see my mama, that's at Indian Pipe plantation—'

'What's her name?'

'Mammy Sally.' January gave one of the commonest names of black women. 'Please, sir, please, you write my Marse Mayering, on Rue Royale in New Orleans, an' he send me up money for me to come home. An' I swear I never run away no more.'

As he stumbled among his captors toward the bells of Cloutierville – suddenly loud in the softening Sabbath twilight – January remembered Celestine Deschamps, as he'd seen her last: a woman of striking beauty, her face alight with joy as she'd stood with her hands on Isobel's shoulders, saying, 'Her Aunt has said that she might take a season in Paris . . .'

And Isobel, almost as beautiful, lips parted and turquoise eyes bright as if she already saw the towers of that gray old city. *Tell me about Paris, M'sieu Janvier . . .*

Paris is the place where this kind of thing doesn't happen to those with African blood in their veins, Mamzelle.

Paris is the place where white young ladies of fifteen are not taught that it is perfectly appropriate to call a man their father's age 'tu' as if he were a child or a dog.

Where white boys – like the one who walked beside Toco with his rifle trained on January – *aren't told that hanging a black man on no evidence but rumor is something that white men can do without a second thought . . . Without a single consequence, either legal or moral, for taking another man's life.*

Coming into Cloutierville – a store, a church, a cotton press, a couple of warehouses, and a handful of houses ringed by dusty trees – in the last of the daylight, January breathed a prayer of thanks that they hadn't met Louis Verron and his cousins on the way. There was a certain amount of discussion among his captors about where Verron might be staying:

'Beaux Herbes?'

'No, ain't nobody there but the overseer, an' that wife of his can't cook for sour owl shit . . .'

'If he's anywhere it'll be with the Ulloas at Charette.'

And the pot-bellied storekeeper – into whose slave jail January was consigned – opined that Verron would be out at Vieudedad with his grandmother.

Toco sent tall Dago to Charette, young Landry to Vieudedad, and handed over January's 'cumpus', razor, slave badge and forged pass to the storekeeper, whose eyes hardened when they rested on him: he, too, had heard whatever foul story Verron had put about. 'Verron said the buck what did it was big like this.' He studied him narrowly in the smoky lantern-light. 'Said he'd been beat pretty recent, too.'

It was a good bet, thought January, as they locked him into the shed out back, that nobody was going to bring him dinner.

The storekeeper tied January's hands behind him, thrust him into the shed with the words, 'If I find you tampered with any of the goods in here I'll skin the hide right off your back, boy,' and locked the door; January just had time to take in the fact that the shed was in fact a storage shed for the store, and to note where the bottles of something – horse medicine, by their shape – were lined on a shelf, before the lantern was taken away, leaving him in darkness.

He called despairingly, 'No, sir! No, sir! Please, sir, you write my Marse, Marse Mayerling, on Rue Royale in New Orleans . . .' and then listened until the crunch of the man's feet on the gravel died away. The temptation was to sit down with his back to the sacks of flour for a few minutes and rest before beginning his escape, but he knew the danger he was in of falling asleep sheerly from exhaustion.

Without any idea how long it would be before Dago or Landry located Louis Verron, there was truly not a minute to linger.

Blue twilight outlined the bars of the window; the shed had clearly been used as an *ad hoc* slave jail before. They were outside the glass and looked too wide to be iron – by the shape, when he went over to see, they seemed to be stout wooden slats, nailed to the side of the shed. He turned back into the blackness, found the shelves and, with a little groping, located the bottles. When he dropped one on the brick floor, the smell told him it was definitely horse medicine, though it reminded him a good deal of the barrel in Kentucky Williams's kitchen.

Scraping and cutting at the ropes – and his fingers – with the largest piece of the broken glass, he mentally reviewed the lie of the land around the store; he didn't think the window was visible from its back gallery. The smell of horses nearby told him there was a stable as well.

Good.

His fingers, bloodied from the glass, slithered on the improvised cutting tool and he dropped it; patiently groped in the darkness of the floor.

Damn you, Hannibal . . .

Damn you, Blessinghurst, or whatever your name really is. How DARED you threaten that girl with what you threatened her . . . With what you must have threatened her . . .?

How had he found out?

January shook the thought away. *Time enough to learn that . . .*

He felt the ropes weaken and pulled his hands through, greased by the blood. He dried them carefully on his shirt, used the glass to cut the stitching on his trouser band, and drew out one of the packets of matches. He recalled seeing, lined up near the door, the big oil jars that came into Louisiana in such quantities from Spain: everyone used them, empty, for everything, from salting down pork to burying up to the neck in the ground as butter coolers, but these were still sealed. Another piece of glass, with his shirt tail wrapped around one side of it to protect his fingers, served him to scrape and chip the wax away. *Step careful – the last thing you need now is an open cut on your foot.*

Still no sound from the house. Had the storekeeper sons? A wife? This early in the evening, it was difficult to imagine that a family wouldn't come peeking around the door at one end of the kitchen, open to show the stair to the upper reaches of the house.

One match helped January locate a box of paintbrushes. He used the handle of one to break the windowglass, the brush itself to dip and paint, dip and paint oil on to the stout slats outside. In case the storekeeper came running out he daubed more oil on to the flour sacks – ready to shout: 'Oh lemme out, lemme out, somebody done throwed a fireball in through de winder!' followed by a wallop over the head the minute the door was open – then lit the oil on the window bars.

Don't let Verron come back now.

He had no idea how long it had taken him to slice through the ropes, how long it would take the hunters to locate Verron. January turned back to the greedy little rings of fire at top and bottom of each thick slat, as if staring at them would increase the rate of burn.

By the discussion of his captors with the storekeeper, this part of the country was the home territory of the Verrons – probably not only the white French side of the family that had intermarried over four generations with the Spanish both here and from Mexico, but also of the *sang mêlée* children of Verron placées. *Where the great gentlemen of the town send the members of the family whom they don't want to have anything to do with, white or colored*, his mother had said. Like sons who murder their brothers over women, or women whom one wishes one never married . . .

Or the 'vulture eggs': the children 'from the shady side of the street'. *Sang mêlée* sons were often given plantations out here, far from the legitimate families in town. Daughters – if their fathers shied from leaving them to become placées themselves – were frequently married to someone else's colored planter sons. January had always found it strange that men whose mothers or grandmothers had been slaves would think nothing of buying men and women in the markets of Baronne Street, shipping them up here, and keeping plantation discipline with the whip and the threat of sale – an opinion which always elicited from his mother a disbelieving stare. 'Good Lord, Benjamin, you can turn a sixty percent profit on a good field-hand! More, if you keep him and rent him out to build levees or work a cotton press.'

This from a woman who had known the whip and the market herself.

Would Compair Lapin, that ultimate survivor, be proud of HER?

She's free, respected, and a property owner. He probably would.

Would that wood never burn through? Dago and Landry could have walked to New Orleans and back in the time since he'd been locked in the shed . . .

At last the wood seemed eaten through – he could only assume that, with the amount of supper-cooking going on at this hour in the village, his jailer had scented nothing abnormal, especially with the breeze off the river – and he gripped each bar by the middle in turn, wrenched the mid-sections free. The window was narrow, and it was a hard scramble to writhe through – he felt like his cracked ribs were going to eviscerate his lungs and heart when he fell through on the outside – and he moved off swiftly through the darkness to the stable. The storekeeper's horse was stout and elderly and in no mood to leave her nice warm barn: January had to tie a short length of cannon fuse by a string to her rear hock, and light the fizzing, sputtering, stinking thing, in order to get her to run madly away through the trees. As well as the cannon fuse, he'd found in his jail some candles and a small firkin of raisins, a couple of handfuls of which made him feel considerably better.

With any luck at all, when Louis Verron and his cousins arrived, they'd set off looking for a horse across the fields.

January suspected that none of them would even think of checking the church.

TWENTY-TWO

And there it was.

'12 March, 1800. To Cadmus Rablé and his wife Noisette, *gens du couleur libres*, of Plantation Bayou Lente, a girl, Celestine.'

A brief check of previous parish registers turned up at least three other Rablé children – and the information that Noisette Dubesc of New Orleans, born in San Domingue in 1775, had married her husband after being first sold to him in 1794 by Louis-Florizel Verron, and then freed.

Three days later – 15 March, 1800 – was recorded the baptism of Celestine Verron, daughter of Eliane and Louis-Florizel Verron, of the Plantation Beaux Herbes in this Parish.

A faded map of the parish, tacked on the wall of the little vestry of St John's chapel, showed January that Bayou Lente lay about eight miles from Beaux Herbes plantation. An easy enough journey to carry a newborn baby girl.

With great care, January tore the page from the register and replaced the rather moldy leather-bound volume where he had found it in the shelf near the map. Soundless as a great cat, he pinched out his candle and let himself out as he had come in, through the French doors looking on to the alleyway beside the church, hoping no one would remark that the catch on the shutters had been forced with a hoof pick, abstracted from the storekeeper's stables.

A newborn baby girl.

To a woman who had lost three infants; a woman whose husband had taken her only child from her. A woman abandoned on a backwater plantation with nobody but the slaves – maybe not even a white overseer . . . A woman desperate for the comfort of a child.

'You'll never tell me she didn't play him false,' his mother had sniffed.

January wondered if Louis-Florizel Verron, haughty and self-righteous with his fragile son, ever knew *how* false his wife had played him.

It was a secret that any white man – let alone the scion of an old French Creole family who had sisters of his own to marry off into other old French Creole families – would kill to keep hidden. It had probably never occurred to Louis Verron that proof of what his Great-Aunt Eliane had done lay in the vestry of St John's church, and not simply in the dimming recollections of those who had been in the remote Red River country years before Napoleon had sold the territory to the Americans for money to finance his English wars.

As he closed up the vestry shutters, January heard a commotion of men shouting, of horses stamping and jingling their bridles, at the other end of the short village street: Louis Verron and his cousins. He guessed he would be perfectly safe if he simply retreated into the church to wait, but he didn't want to take the chance on being wrong. He crossed the church-side alley to the nearest house, dislodged a section of lattice, and crawled beneath the front porch, holding the lattice in place behind him as he listened to the tumult around the general store. A few minutes later men galloped past horseback, torch flame streaming. The assumption that January had taken the storekeeper's horse kept them from turning out dogs, and also from looking around Cloutierville itself. In truth, he was more worried about snakes under the porch than about the men riding out to hunt him.

Don't fall asleep . . .

He knew any man who had not been as tired as he now was would have debated whether anyone whose ribs, and crudely-bandaged fingers, and back, and face hurt as much as they did *could* fall asleep, but he knew he was inches from it.

It would take him two hours at least to reach Bayou Lente on foot. He'd have to follow the river, so as not to get lost without the compass. And Rose would never speak to him again if he didn't get it back.

Beaux Herbes – where Eliane Dubesc Verron had lived, sometimes with, and more often without, her aloof and guilt-riddled husband – lay in the opposite direction. That was the direction in which Verron and his men had ridden.

'Not even capable of bearing a living child,' his mother had said of Eliane. The boy nothing but a bundle of bones . . . A textbook of illnesses . . . The other three children had died at once . . .

Had she hungered for a girl, a child who would be her own to love? A healthy, beautiful child, such as her former maid-servant bore with such ease?

What did she offer Noisette, the girl who had come from Sainte Domingue with her, the girl she must have grown up with, before the revolution drove Eliane's father – who was probably Noisette's father as well – to New Orleans? Possibly money. *But what woman of color could pass up the chance to know that her daughter would become the daughter of a well-connected white family, with all that such a birth meant opening up before her?*

Celestine.

You'll never tell me she didn't play him false.

January made himself wait, telling over in his mind the first book of Pope's *Iliad*, until – when 'Jove on his couch reclined his awful head' – the last of the village's lights disappeared from upper windows, and the town lay silent beneath the white, full moon.

The plantation bell at what January earnestly hoped was in fact Bayou Lente woke him with a start. For a moment of panic, terror, nightmare, he was still back in the store shed at Cloutierville, and Louis Verron and Toco and the storekeeper and the 'boys' were coming to hang him, after first beating him to death. His body was so stiff with exhaustion, bruises, and the scrapes and gouges left by the broken stumps of the window bars, that for a time he could only lie in the far corner of the mule barn where he'd crawled an hour before moonset.

When the door opened he debated for a moment about speaking to the mule boss, then pushed himself deeper into the hay. There'd be an overseer outside.

Nobody who'd grown up on a plantation dealt with over-seers any more than they had to.

Lantern light made gold mirrors of the mules' eyes as the mule boss and his boy buckled their harnesses in place, led them out. Through the open door, January could hear the work gangs getting breakfast, and his whole body transformed into a single, silent shriek of hunger. Cotton harvest would have both gangs in the field today, and everybody else from the home place that could be spared. Bearded and caked with blood and river mud, his shirt torn to rags to bandage his fingers, January knew he'd make the worst possible impression, but he knew also that there might be very little time to speak to Cadmus Rablé and, if he was lucky, Isobel Deschamps. He'd circled the home place through the cotton fields, the fallow corn, twice last night, watching, listening for any sign that Louis Verron and his men were waiting for him here after all.

It got light. A couple of cats who'd been chasing lizards in the straw evidently heard the sounds of white folks' breakfast being carried across from the kitchen to the house, because they slipped out through cracks in the walls, and a few minutes later the two youngest mule boys came in to muck the stalls.

Feeling a little like Odysseus introducing himself to Nausicaa, January rose from the hay, and asked, 'This here Bayou Lente?'

The smaller boy flinched toward the door, but the slightly larger one grabbed him by the shirt. 'Yeah.'

'I need to speak to Michie Rablé.' January made a futile effort to knock some of the hay off what was left of his sleeves. 'And to Mademoiselle Isobel, if she's here.'

The boy nodded again. 'She here, yeah.'

Thank you, blessed Mary Ever-Virgin.

'Would you tell her, please, that M'sieu Janvier is here from New Orleans, with a message for her from Pierrette. Tell her, her mama sold Pierrette, two days after she left town.'

Both boys stared at him, shocked. The slightly larger boy protested, 'She wouldn't!'

'She did,' said January. 'And I need to speak with Mademoiselle Isobel, just as soon as it's convenient for her.'

'Tell her, Den,' ordered the larger boy, and gave the smaller a shove toward the door. And, to January, 'What the hell happen to you?'

January had not even finished washing his face in the mule trough when Cadmus Rablé crossed from the big house.

He was a big man of sixty or so, square-built, with the combination of African features and near-European coloring common in that part of the country. In his close-cropped gray hair lingered traces of the honey hue of Isobel's, but his eyes were the blue of the Gulf on a summer day. January wondered whether Celestine – and Isobel – had gotten their gray-green eyes from Noisette.

Rablé looked him up and down. 'You're never a piano teacher.'

January sighed. 'I clean up some 'fore I give lessons, M'sieu.'

Clean or dirty, the planter had used the polite address 'vous'.

January knew *libres* – his mother among them – who judged that the darker a person was, the closer they were to the despised slaves, and indeed he saw this way of looking at the world pass like the reflection of some earlier training across Cadmus Rablé's blue eyes. Then he saw, too, the man's expression shift: looking past the color, to manner and voice and the likelihood of his story. 'Come in the house.'

January looked down at his filthy clothing, his bare feet smeared with mule dung and bayou mud. 'You got to be joking, sir.'

'On the gallery, then. Den,' Rablé called to the smaller mule boy, 'you run tell Zellie to heat up a bath in the laundry – you hungry, sir?'

'Only reason I didn't eat those two boys was 'cause I was too tired to catch 'em.'

'Where'd you hear this about Pierrette?' asked Rablé, as they climbed the steps to the rear gallery of the house. Like most Creole houses it faced the river, sturdily built of timber and bousillage, like January's own in New Orleans but smaller. The rear gallery was arranged as a summer dining room, overlooking the kitchen buildings and the quarters beyond. A servant came out of the pantry with coffee and favored January's tattered clothing and bare feet with a glance of resentful contempt as he poured – *what's the likes of HIM doin' havin' coffee with Michie Rablé?* – and another crossed from the kitchen with callas and sausage.

'I spoke with her, at the offices of Irvin and Frye.' Gingerly, January washed his hands and face in the tin basin at the corner of the gallery, pulling off the filthy bandages around his fingers and hoping the scabs would hold until he finished breakfast. He suspected he made a poor enough impression without bleeding all over his host's second-best breakfast dishes. 'She begged me to come here to you, said you would buy her. Said it was inconceivable that Mademoiselle Deschamps would have known what her mother had done.'

'Of course she didn't know!' Rablé waved impatiently.

'They are like a pair of sisters. Did Pierrette say that Mademoiselle Deschamps would be here?' Wariness flickered in the cornflower eyes. 'Mademoiselle is like a granddaughter to me, you know; she and her mother both come to stay with us for a few days every time they're in—'

January shook his head. 'I know what Mademoiselle Deschamps is to you, sir,' he said softly. 'I'm here because a man in New Orleans is threatening to tell all the world.'

Cadmus Rablé, who had started out of his chair with angry words on his lips, settled back. But January could feel the anger around him still, like a bull with his head down.

'How much did she tell you about why she left New Orleans?' January asked. 'And, I presume, why she left Paris?'

'You seem to know a God-damn lot about it, for a music teacher.'

'I'm a friend of the young man who asked her to marry him,' said January. 'And who is in jail now, and facing hanging, because he refuses to admit that he knows your granddaughter, loves your granddaughter, and was with your granddaughter at the time he's supposed to have murdered a man in a New Orleans hotel room. And because I am his friend, I have come here to find out what the hell is actually going on so that I can keep him from going to the scaffold like the hero of a cheap melodrama. Oh, and by the way,' he added, as the distant drumming of hooves sounded on the avenue that led from the house to the river, 'whatever *is* going on, Louis Verron got wind of it and has been trying to kill me since a week ago Friday night.'

Rablé's eyes widened. 'You're not the buck Louis's been going around saying how he raped a French maidservant that was staying with them?'

'That would be me.'

'T'cha!' He turned his head, listening to the sound of the hooves as well. 'When Celestine told me she'd told Isobel about us – about my wife and myself, and who we really were to them – I told her then it was a mistake. No matter how many Bible oaths you take of secrecy, no matter what kind of resolve you think you've got, it's going to get out. So far I don't think she's told Marie-Amalie – who is the sweetest child in the world but has no more control of her heart than Celestine does, God bless her. Noisette – Madame

Rablé – was that way.' He shook his head, regret and tenderness turning those bright, watchful eyes suddenly soft. 'She swore when she gave up our child to Eliane . . . Well.' He shook the thought – the softness – away and listened for a moment to the sound of boots on the front gallery, the voice of a servant at the door. 'Take your bath, sir. I'll have clothes sent out. And I'll deal with this.'

TWENTY-THREE

While January was gingerly clipping what beard he could out of the scabbed mess of the left side of his face – and praying that Mademoiselle Deschamps would indeed recognize him as her piano teacher with his hair shaved back to the crown of his head – the butler who'd earlier served him coffee entered the laundry room with the information that, when he was ready, he was to go up to the house. 'Michie Louis, he sure in a state,' the man added.

'*Blankittes* mostly do get in a state, when they mistake a man's identity about what he did, and then get proved wrong,' returned January mildly.

He recalled what his mother had said about the New Orleans Verrons now being the poor side of the family, and he hoped that Isobel's mother – and Cadmus Rablé – retained enough control over them that he wouldn't have to be watching his back for the rest of his life.

And that Isobel wouldn't have to be watching hers.

As he crossed to the house from the laundry, he made enough of a detour to note that only a single horse remained under the giant tupelo trees out front. So the Ulloa boys, at least, had been sent away.

So far, so good.

Cadmus Rablé, Louis Verron, and Isobel Deschamps – grown from the pretty girl he'd known to lovely young womanhood – were seated in the parlor when January came up the back gallery steps and into the house. To the girl's startled look, January put a hand to where his hairline had been and explained, 'I shaved it back, Mamzelle, thinking the men your cousin talked to might not be looking for a bald man.'

Mademoiselle Deschamps's strained and tired face transformed into what looked like the first laughter it had seen in weeks. 'Oh, brilliant, sir!'

'Yeah, God-damn brilliant,' snapped Verron. January remembered the voice. In daylight, Verron was younger than he'd expected, in his late teens. Dark hair fell in a splash over dark blue eyes. The features, the rather delicate mouth, were refined rather than brutal, but icily cold. 'You tell anyone about my cousin?'

Rablé made a swift, slight cautionary gesture. 'You mean, other than *the letter in the bank*?' His eyes held January's, and January shook his head.

'There is no letter in any bank, sir,' he said. And, to Verron, 'No, sir. I told no one. That wasn't my intent.'

'And what was your intent, M'sieu Brilliant?'

'My intent – sir – was to secure your cousin's happiness, and your peace of mind, by helping her to marry a British gentleman of good family. She goes to live in Ireland, taking her sister with her to bring out in London when the time comes, and you no longer have to worry about who finds out what.'

'Not that no-good bastard Blessinghurst? Because I'm here to tell you, M'sieu Brilliant Goddam Piano-Player, Blessinghurst has no more intention of marrying my cousin than he has of running for Pope.'

Nearby him, January was aware of Isobel Deschamps turning her face aside and clenching her hand before her lips, but he only said, 'No, not Blessinghurst. I mean Viscount Foxford.'

'I can't,' Isobel whispered. 'That's all over.'

'Mademoiselle,' said January softly, 'please forgive me if I ask this of you bluntly, but *why* is it all over? Germanicus Stuart has put his own life in jeopardy, rather than say that he even knows you, much less that he was with you the night before you left New Orleans. Are you being blackmailed? And is it by Blessinghurst?' He spread out his bandaged fingers for her to see. 'I have risked my life to come to you and find that out.'

She drew in breath, let it out, and her clenched fist became an open palm, pressed to her mouth, as if to gag back whatever words might come out. She shed no tears, though by the look of her eyes she had shed many during the days just past. After a moment, she took her hand down and said, in a small but steady voice, 'I'm sorry for what you've gone through, M'sieu Janvier.' She called him 'vous', now, as her grandfather did, rather than 'tu'.

'Was it Blessinghurst?'

The fact that this was already known made her nod.

Louis began, 'I'll goddam kill him—'

'It wasn't like that,' said Isobel. 'It was . . .' She took another breath, and then her shoulders – slim as a half-grown fawn's in a gown that looked like she'd had it made in Paris – relaxed, and she turned in her chair to face her cousin and her grandfather.

'He did try to – to degrade me,' she said, the hesitation not coming from coyness but from the fact, January guessed, that she'd been raised as a good Creole girl, had never uttered the word 'rape' before, and didn't quite know how to speak it aloud in company. 'I bit him, and stabbed him with my hatpin . . .'

Louis turned pale as ice, but January said, 'Good girl. Did he pretend to be in love with you?'

Encouraged that the roof hadn't fallen in, she nodded. 'But it never felt real. He's very rich, so I didn't understand it.'

'He's not rich,' said January. 'He's an actor; his real name is Stubbs. Which means, I think,' he said slowly, 'that he's being *paid* by someone rich.'

Their eyes were on him: shocked, outraged, enlightened.

Louis said, 'Who the hell—?'

Isobel said, 'That's why—' and stopped herself, uncertain. January raised his brows. She glanced apologetically across at Verron. 'If you're an heiress – and I'm not a great heiress, but I know what Beaux Herbes is worth now – you get to learn what the boys are like, who just want the money. They all say the same thing: "Your eyes are like stars; your lips are like honeyed roses; I would like to carry you off to the Kingdoms of Arabia . . ." which always sounded terribly uncomfortable to me, from what I read in Tante Cassandre's geography books . . . But it's as if they've learned it from a book.' A little smile tugged at the side of her mouth, and she added, 'Sometimes you can tell which book.'

'That is no way for a well-raised girl to talk!' objected Louis angrily, and Isobel rolled her eyes.

'Honestly, Louis, you don't think girls talk amongst themselves?' She turned back to January. 'And he *didn't* sound that way, sir. But he felt . . . wrong.' She grimaced, as at a questionable back-taste. 'I can't explain. Maybe I wouldn't have noticed if I'd met him before . . . before Gerry. Le Vicomte.'

'So Blessinghurst didn't come along until after you had met Viscount Foxford.'

She nodded, suddenly shy.

'How long after?'

'Four or five weeks,' said Isobel. 'At Twelfth Night, I think . . . M'sieu le Vicomte –' she stammered a little on the words – 'had just come to Paris himself, when I arrived to stay with my Tante Cassandre.'

'And did you tell this Foxford,' demanded Louis bitterly, 'that you are a negress?'

'I am not a negress! Look at me, Louis!' she almost shouted as he jerked to his feet, paced to the open French windows that looked out toward the green rise of the levee and the river beyond. Springing up, she followed him in a soft rush of blue-and-white dimity, caught his sleeve, pulled him around to force him to face her, like the children they'd both once been together. 'Look at me! Do I look any different than I did back in September? Than I did back when we'd dance together in dancing class? Than I did when *you* asked to marry me?'

Louis struck her hand away. 'I look at you, and all I see is what Lucien Brinvilliers, and Tom Pourret, and Gautier Charrette, and all the rest of my sisters' suitors are going to say when this Blessinghurst gets to shouting it all over town that there's tar in our bloodline—'

'Your sisters are no more related to Grandpere than they are to . . . to M'sieu Janvier here—'

'And do you think,' demanded Louis, 'that is going to make one mustard-seed of difference, when the story gets around? "Where there's one, there's more," is what they'll say!'

'When *did* the story get around?' asked January. 'And how do you come into it, anyway, M'sieu Verron? Don't tell me Blessinghurst spoke to you?'

Through gritted teeth, Verron said, 'The bastard had the effrontery to write to me, demanding money to keep quiet.'

Both January and Isobel stared. Isobel whispered, 'Oh, the blackguard!'

And January, 'The idiot! Didn't he know you were likelier to kill him than pay?'

Quietly, Verron replied, 'We may trust that he will know, as soon as I return to town.'

Baffled, Isobel turned to January. 'But how did he know

about Louis? About Uncle Charles? Would he have done all this: searched my room in Paris, intercepted Gerry's mail . . . The Verrons are not that wealthy— '

'No,' said January, who had been, for the first moment, as taken aback as she. 'No, he would not. Not if he used his knowledge to break up your love affair with Foxford back in Paris. He didn't ask for money then, did he?'

The girl shook her head. 'Only that I must leave Paris and never see or speak to Gerry – M'sieu le Vicomte – again . . .'

'We may take it, then,' said January, 'that those were his original instructions. But when he got to New Orleans,' he added drily, 'I assume His Lordship couldn't resist what they call in prizefighting "a side-bet" to make a little money for himself. And when you couldn't lay hands on Blessinghurst, sir –' he had to force himself to give the coldly furious young gentleman that honorific title as he bowed to him – 'you came after me, about whom you heard . . . from Madame Deschamps, I presume?'

He nodded. 'That your wife was asking questions about Isobel, yes.'

Rose would be outraged that her inquiries had been immediately assumed to stem from him. He could just hear her: *What, cannot a woman have thoughts of her own? Is she but the pawn of her husband . . .?*

'And to answer your question, Louis,' said Isobel in a tight voice, coming back to stand between her grandfather's chair and January's, 'yes, I did tell M'sieu le Vicomte that my grandfather's *grandmother* came from Africa, with no admixture of blood in-between— '

'Do you think that makes a difference?'

'No,' said Isobel defiantly. 'It doesn't. Not to Gerry. He said, "My darling, it wouldn't matter to me if you were from Africa yourself, or from China or Siberia or the South Sea Islands." The English – Europeans – look at these matters differently, Louis— '

'Not that differently.' If he could have physically gashed her with the words, he would have.

'Maybe not *that* differently,' temporized January, 'were Mademoiselle *in fact* from Africa or China or somewhere more exotic. But as matters stand, having lived in France myself, I can attest that it would be her appearance rather than her ancestry that would cause comment, if such were the case.'

Louis sniffed.

'And you better thank God that's how they look at things in England –' Rablé jabbed a finger at the young man – 'as that's where your cousin's going to go wed – *and* Marie-Amalie – if I have anything to do with it. Was it you, told Isobel's Maman to get rid of Pierrette?'

'Of course it was.' Louis waved aside his cousin's cry of outrage. 'That's the first thing a blackmailer thinks of, is getting at the servants.'

'And I suppose that's why you got rid of that poor valet of yours, what was his name – André – the year before last?'

'May I ask, Mademoiselle Deschamps,' put in January, 'when you told Viscount Foxford of your relationship with M'sieu Rablé? In Paris, or that Thursday night in New Orleans?'

'Oh, in Paris!' said the girl. 'I would never have kept such a thing from him for so long!'

'In a letter, or face to face?'

The girl looked aside again, and color came up under the delicate pink of her complexion. 'In a letter,' she said, her voice stifled, and Louis flung up his hands in disgust. He seemed, January reflected privately, to have both knowledge and considerable sensitivity around the subject of blackmail.

Isobel winced at his gesture, but went on. 'That's how Blessinghurst knew of it. I know, because he . . . he showed me the letter. I already knew Gerry – M'sieu le Vicomte – had not received it, but I didn't think anything of it, when we realized it had gone astray.'

She pressed her hands to her mouth again, then to her cheeks, as if trying to force back the flush of shame. 'At first – when Milord Blessinghurst took me aside at a ball and told me he knew – I thought he was threatening me because he wanted to marry me himself. But no. He said I was to leave Paris, or he would see to it that everyone in Louisiana knew about what poor Grandmama had done. I asked him why – I begged him to tell me – and he only laughed and said, "Don't trouble your pretty head about it, my dear." Hateful!' She shook her head. 'Hateful. But I didn't dare tell Gerry, because there was Maman to think of, and Marie-Amalie. I thought I had put it all behind me, that I could live again . . . Then at the Truloves's ball, to see Gerry – and Blessinghurst . . .'

'Yes,' said January thoughtfully. 'Gerry and Blessinghurst.'

'I didn't know what to think. Only that I had to get out of there.' Isobel shook her head. 'It was like a nightmare. Two days – the Thursday – after the ball, Gerry waited for me outside my house in the morning. He leaped up on to the step of my carriage as it came out, said he would cling there to the window until I told him what Blessinghurst was to me. I said, he is the man who will destroy my family, if you are seen speaking with me this way.'

She folded her hands, staring out through the French doors toward the levee, struggling to keep her countenance. No boats passed on the river in this isolated season – Bayou Lente might have been the only civilization on the planet. Its limits, the boundaries of the world.

'Gerry came to the house that night. He knew Maman goes early to bed; I'd told him that in Paris. He sent up a note, and when Marie-Amalie went upstairs, I – I went across the street to talk to him, standing in a doorway. He asked what was it, that Blessinghurst had threatened? At first he didn't believe me, didn't understand how completely such talk would ruin us, for in truth one great-great-grandmother meant nothing to him! But I made him understand. We talked – hours; it was after two when at last I came in. I still had some idea that Blessinghurst wanted to marry me, for some reason – that he was playing some kind of game with me . . . But looking at what you've said, M'sieu Janvier, about him being an actor, and where would he have gotten the money to come here, of all places, and at the same time Gerry did . . .? It's someone who doesn't want me to marry Gerry, isn't it? But *why*?'

From the window, Louis growled, 'I think *that* answer's obvious.'

Don't be an ass, January was careful not to say. 'Myself, I would hesitate to proclaim any answer obvious, sir. Foxford's mail was clearly being watched *before* Blessinghurst got hold of Mademoiselle Deschamps's letter about her ancestry. We've already established that the man didn't arrive in Paris until after Viscount Foxford began trying to fix his interest with your cousin. Doesn't that sound as if someone heard that Foxford was firmly on a path that would lead to matrimony and took what steps he thought he needed to keep him off of it? Including hiring another suitor, first to turn the girl aside – which didn't work – and then to render her ineligible.

'Foxford had a friend – the Irishman Derryhick—'

'Yes,' said Isobel swiftly, 'Patrick. He was in Paris with Gerry. That Thursday night, Gerry said he'd been out with him that evening, that M'sieu Derryhick had seen how distracted he was and had asked him what was wrong. Had he spoken to me, he asked . . .'

'And Foxford told him what he knew?'

'That I was being blackmailed, yes.'

'So after Gerry left to see you,' said January softly, 'Derryhick went out to find Blessinghurst. He ran him to earth in a gambling parlor on Rue Orleans, spoke to him . . . and returned in haste and rage to the hotel where they were staying and had a violent quarrel with . . . someone. Someone who stabbed him, hid his body, and then took steps to make sure that, if the body were found, it would look as if the murder took place in Foxford's room. Swapped the sheets on Foxford's bed for new sheets unused, and put the worn ones on his own. Got rid of the bloodied rug in his own room and replaced it with the rug from Gerry's room – and, for good measure, threw his victim's blood-smeared watch under Gerry's bed.'

Rablé said quietly, 'A clever villain.'

'Clever and careful,' replied January. He glanced at Isobel, who sat rigid, taking this information in, sorting it and seeing its implications.

'And Gerry?'

'He is in the Cabildo,' said January. 'Because of the watch, and the fact that he was Derryhick's heir for a great deal of money – and because he will not say where he was. He said he would have his business manager purchase Pierrette . . .'

'To hell with M'sieu le Vicomte,' snapped Louis. 'Where's Blessinghurst? That Irish bitch I'm paying at the Countess's says he hasn't been in there in a week.'

Sybilla. The Countess would snatch her bald-headed . . .

'You can't kill him!' cried Isobel. 'Don't you understand, Louis? Whoever is behind this, whoever it is who doesn't want Gerry to marry me – is it the uncle he spoke of, M'sieu? The evil one? – Gerry is still in danger. If you kill Blessinghurst—'

'*When* I kill Blessinghurst,' returned Louis, 'he will keep his fat mouth shut, and that is all that concerns me. And you, M'sieu—' He turned savagely upon January, and Cadmus Rablé said in his quiet voice:

'M'sieu Janvier is going to return to New Orleans in perfect safety on the next steamboat, Louis. And he will remain safe. Or you will find out that there are other ways for families to be ruined. Is that understood?'

The young man stared at the old, eyes blazing, like a splendid high-couraged stallion – and about as intelligent as the average stallion, January reflected: a beautiful beast who would run himself to death in terror of flowers flickering in the wind, without asking why. But in time Louis moved his head a little, and the tension in his body changed to something else. 'I understand,' he said quietly. 'Now you understand something, M'sieu Rablé.'

He stabbed his finger at January. 'If one word, one *breath*, of this leaks to the world, about my cousin or about my family, there will be many people to suffer. But I swear to you on my father's heart, the first one will be him. And the next, his wife, and every other member of his family. And from that, M'sieu Rablé –' he turned to his host with a stiff, furious bow – 'I will not be put aside by you, or anyone.'

Turning, he stalked from the house.

They heard hooves hammer away in the direction of the levee; die into the thrumming of the cicadas in the trees.

'Well, now,' said Cadmus Rablé. 'Janvier, let's talk about what can actually be done.'

TWENTY-FOUR

True to the strict codes of conduct that governed the relationships between the light-complected *libre* planters and men of darker hue and questionable social provenance, January was given an excellent dinner on the kitchen's wide gallery, where the table was laid in summer for the house servants. January was able to steer the talk to Mamzelle Isobel and her mother without trouble, and it became clear immediately, from the talk around the table, that there wasn't the slightest suspicion anywhere in Natchitoches Parish that Isobel Deschamps was anything but the granddaughter of old M'am Noisette's white half-sister. 'And like true sisters they were, M'sieu,' the housekeeper assured January. 'They'd escaped from Sainte Domingue together, you know, at the revolution there in '91, and their poor Papa killed and M'am Noisette's mama, too.'

The sisters must have arranged things between themselves, January reflected, as soon as Noisette knew herself to be with child.

The older of the maids – a slow-moving and rather fragile woman in her fifties – handed January a bowl of greens and said, 'M'am Celestine – Mamzelle Isobel's mama – practically grew up here, with Michie Robert and Mamzelle Toucoutou and all Michie Rablé's other children. And a good thing, too, for Beaux Herbes was a sorry house in those days, and a lonely one. M'am Eliane would come here in the mornings with her little girl – how she doted on that little girl! – and not leave till dark was falling, as if this was her true home, with M'am Noisette. I felt bad for her,' she added sadly, 'for M'am Eliane had such fire in her, when first she wed.'

'It was losing her babies,' said the housekeeper. 'Poor unformed little things, not even able to live, except the boy. And once Michie Louis-Florizel got religion like he did, he kept that boy to himself.'

'Easier to blame his wife, that he shot his own brother,' said the butler quietly, 'than admit it was him that pulled the trigger.'

After supper, when January walked back across the yard in

the cooling twilight, he paused to listen to the stillness, the deep silence of the countryside, that for seven nights now he had heard chiefly as the background to imagined sounds of pursuit. Three and a half decades ago, this land of marshes and bayous that lay between the two arms of what had been, at various times, the Red River – the Old River, the Cane River, the Red's current stream – must have been a backwater indeed, and this sense of being alone on the planet a thousand times worse. For a woman used to the friends and activity of New Orleans, to be left by her husband there would have truly been exile.

'Granmere told Maman what she'd done, when she lay dying,' admitted Isobel, as she poured out coffee for herself, January, and Rablé on the big house gallery, after the servants had lit the mosquito smudges and departed. 'How Granmere Noisette had hidden her condition and went to bear the baby at Beaux Herbes. Then when Granmere Noisette died, Maman told me. I think now it would probably have been better if she hadn't,' she added, a small frown pulling at her brows.

'I'd have ridden over and put my hand over her mouth for her, if I'd known,' put in Rablé. But for his African features, he could have been any well-off cotton planter in the state. At the servants' table, January had learned that though Cadmus Rablé treated his hands well, he and his numerous progeny regarded the more African-blooded men and women they bought from neighbors or from the dealers in New Orleans as simply that: hands. You had to have slaves to run a place, and so you got them and treated them as everyone else did.

'Forgive my asking, Mamzelle,' said January, 'but were you shocked?'

Isobel nodded. The transformation of lively prettiness into true beauty appeared to extend below the skin: true and terrible sacrifice had made her thoughtful.'I was shocked, yes. But you know how it is in New Orleans, M'sieu – and here even more. One sees ladies in church, with their hair done up in tignons, and that's the only way you know that they're not French. And all my life I've grown up seeing girls – Dupres and Metoyers and Rachals, and even Granpere Rablé's granddaughters – his other granddaughters, I mean,' she added, with a slight flush – 'wearing gowns just as pretty as mine, and riding in carriages, and looking not one whit different from myself and Marie-Amalie and our Verron cousins, and being told, "Oh, no, you can't go to the same parties with them, they're gens du couleur . . ." And they looked *exactly* the same as us. Louis—'

She hesitated as she spoke her cousin's name. Then she went on, 'Sometimes – *often!* – they *do* go to Paris or London or Italy, and we hear that they've married some man in Europe, and Maman and my Verron aunts whisper about how they'd be willing to bet their best pearls that those gentlemen never knew . . . And what harm was in it?'

What harm indeed? January reflected. Even the ladies like the Countess Mazzini got more respect in the eyes of white men in their guise as Italian whores than they would have if they had the name of black ones.

The girl concluded simply, 'But I couldn't not tell M'sieu le Vicomte. I couldn't begin – what I hoped we were beginning – with a lie. Not a lie about that.'

Rablé sniffed, as if to say, 'What he don't know won't hurt him nor anyone else,' but January nodded and said, 'In my opinion, you did rightly, Mamzelle.'

'I am only sorry I did so in a letter, for that . . . that swine Blessinghurst to steal, and not face to face, as my heart first told me I ought.' She blinked quickly and rubbed her eyes, as if at smoke. 'May I come to New Orleans with you? To see him – to tell him . . .'

January shook his head. 'It's out of the question,' he said. 'I'll make sure Pierrette is purchased by Foxford and sent on here. But if, as I suspect, Foxford's Uncle Diogenes is behind this effort to keep Foxford from marrying, your appearance will do nothing but trigger the disaster that Foxford is willing for your sake to go to the scaffold to prevent.'

She bit her lip and looked aside. 'There isn't – they really do not have so much of a case against him . . . Do they, M'sieu?'

'I fear that they do, Mamzelle.' He saw the tears spring to her eyes again, glimmering in the smoky light of the cressets. 'Did Foxford ever speak of his uncle?'

'Often,' she said in a soft voice. 'He never – he always found some reason to explain or mitigate his conduct. Gerry – M'sieu le Vicomte – has no belief in the evil of men. But the things his cousin Theo would tell me—'

'*Theo* was in Paris with Foxford? Uncle Diogenes's son?'

'Oh, yes. That's who Gerry was staying with. Theo's mother

– Grace, Lady Diogenes Stuart – lives in the family town house in Paris because she refuses to go to India with her husband, or – or to live under his roof at all. Theo was drunk most of the time – or under the influence of opiates, Gerry told me – and would do and say the most outrageous things. I remember once, at a ball at the St-Glaives's, he hid in the conservatory, seized me around the waist, and said to me, "There's tainted blood in the family, my dear. You'd do well to think twice about passing it on to your sons." I didn't know whether to laugh or weep, because there are so many here in America, who would say – like Louis – that *I* have tainted blood.'

'What did he say about his father?'

The girl's face flushed, even to the tips of her ears, and she looked steadily out into the darkness for a time and shook her head. After a moment she replied in a stifled voice, 'Things no man should ever say about his own father, even if they are true. And things no man should say to a woman.'

'I beg your pardon, Mamzelle,' said January. 'I didn't mean about what Diogenes Stuart does in his – idle hours. That much I know. But did Theo say anything about what his father thought of Derryhick? Or of his cousin Foxford, for that matter?'

'Well, one couldn't really trust anything Theo said, you know.' Isobel looked back at him, her lips quirked in a sad little smile. 'Gerry – M'sieu le Vicomte – would say there was a period of about four hours, between eleven and three, when he could be relied on, sometimes . . .' She shook her head again, and her mouth tightened suddenly, as if the memory of a double-handful of winter afternoons, sitting in Tante Cassandre's parlor or riding in the park, with nothing to look forward to but happiness, had suddenly stirred to life, lacerating her inside. As she had before, Isobel took a deep breath and let it out, as if regaining her balance to go on.

'Theo said his father hated M'sieu Derryhick, on account of some aunt leaving all her money to M'sieu Derryhick instead of to the family. And sometimes he spoke of his father hating the whole family, when Madame le Vicomtesse would not agree to send him money. But Gerry said that, in fact, his uncle was too lazy to care one way or the other and hadn't been in Ireland for years. His outrage was . . . theoretical, I believe was the word Gerry used. "Uncle Diogenes is forever in a tumult over something," he said to me, after Theo had hinted at dark plots on the part of his father. "He looks to blame Aunt Elodie and Patrick and Mother and me, whenever he has to write old Droudge for an advance on his quarter's allowance, or for hush money to some pander, instead of blaming Great-Grandfather's mistresses or Grandfather's stock speculations or his own infernal laziness." It was the same, he said, with his Uncle's anger over Theo's gambling-debts and . . . and drunken sprees with women. "He is angry at Patrick," Gerry said, "because it is easier to be angry at another man than to actually come home and act the father himself."'

Rablé raised his eyebrows a little at that, and January said, 'It sounds like he is a wise young man, for his years.'

She half-smiled again at a memory. 'I think that was M'sieu Derryhick,' she said. 'For a man who was always laughing, he had great wisdom about humankind. Gerry said he was going to get Theo to write his father a letter complaining that I was a milk-and-water Miss without a word to say for myself. That that would be the quickest way to obtain his permission to our match.'

'Permission?' Rablé tilted his head. 'The boy is of age, surely?'

'Not until he turns thirty.' Isobel shook her head, her smooth forehead puckering. 'Or weds, with his trustees' consent.'

'His trustees being Uncle Diogenes and Derryhick.'

'If that's the case,' put in Rablé, 'why would this Stuart go to the trouble of hiring a man to divide Mamzelle from his nephew, when he had only to forbid the banns?'

'Probably because he could not come up with a convincing reason for wanting to retain control of the property,' said January thoughtfully. 'And again, I don't think he'd want to offend the man who, in eight years, one way or the other, was going to be in charge of sending him his quarterly allowance.'

The smell of woodsmoke from a score of cook fires drifted through the darkness, and like jewels on indigo velvet, he could see the dim flare of them between the cabins of the quarters where the women – who had been picking cotton since it grew light enough to see – now stirred stews of salt-pork and potatoes, collards and corn, to be gulped down before they slept to wake to another day's work. *Doesn't Rablé understand that the world is changing?* he thought, seeing his host turn his head at the sound of voices from the quarters. A few hours in his company had taught January that the older man was, like himself, a Frenchman, rather than an African, in his heart. *Can't he see that it's only a matter of time before the American tide overwhelms even this slow and sleepy land where libres are safe? All those fine divisions between griffe and quadroon and musterfino, which Maman's friends and the gens du couleur libre here spend so much of their time arguing about . . . Doesn't he see – don't THEY all see – that it's only a matter of time before the Americans take over completely? The Americans, who don't care how much African blood is in your veins when a single drop will allow them to sell you and make a profit, and that's all that matters?*

And his heart went out, unexpectedly, to Martin Quennell. Like Compair Lapin, doing whatever he had to do to survive in a world where no man with a provable drop of African blood in him would be allowed to vote, would be permitted to testify in court against a white man, would be considered a citizen of the country or the state he lived in.

How hard had it been to turn his back on his mother and his brother, on all his friends? To trade the comfort of the family that loved him for the rights of manhood?

To know that his home would always be the equivalent of McPhearson's Rooming House, impersonal and secret? That when his family gathered in the cemetery for the Feast of All Saints, all he would be able to do would be to jest about it with American friends?

After a time he said, 'But you're right, sir. There's something here I don't understand, facts I need to know, before I can go into a court and say, "This was the man who struck down Patrick Derryhick, and this is why." Because both of the other men who could have done the crime have stories of their whereabouts that cannot be proven false. And unless we can prove who was the true killer, and why he is so eager to prevent the Viscount's wedding, there is nothing to keep him from striking again. It's why I need to find Blessinghurst before Louis Verron does. What you've told me has helped me immeasurably, Mamzelle.' He turned his eyes to Isobel, sitting with hands folded, in the flickering light looking tired and spent. 'I haven't uncovered a single piece of treasure yet – but you've given me the map to tell me where to dig.'

'I shall pray for you, then, M'sieu Janvier,' said the girl. 'Since it seems that it is the only thing I'm able to do.'

'No,' corrected her grandfather, and a glint crossed those blue, African eyes. 'While you're waiting you can sew for your trousseau, Mamzelle –' from his pocket he drew out a piece of paper and held it out to January – 'and we'll both of us see how much help this will buy.'

January unfolded it. It was a bank draft for five hundred dollars.

TWENTY-FIVE

January remained at Bayou Lente for another day, while Cadmus Rablé sent his overseer's seventeen-year-old son over to the other side of Cloutierville, with a description of the cloven water-locust in which January's free papers were hidden and instructions to retrieve Rose's compass from the storekeeper. It was Wednesday before the *Parnassus* – laden to the top deck with the first bales of the cotton crop from the plantations upriver – was sighted, picking its way through the snags and shallows to the plantation dock.

'Damn,' said Sam, when January came aboard, 'you just lost me seven dollars and fifty cents, brother!' and they clasped hands in welcome. 'You don't look like a man gonna be haulin' wood for his passage, neither.'

'I have rented a stateroom on the upper deck,' declared January loftily, 'from which I will look down at you poor bastards laborin' and think sad thoughts.'

The men of the deck crew laughed – mostly at the jest about *any* black man being rented *any* cabin on a steamboat – and slapped his back and shoulders, and cursed about the amount of money they'd bet against his survival.

A few miles downriver, the *Parnassus* stopped at the landing by Bayou Charette to take on Louis Verron. January stepped back among the cotton bales that piled every square foot of deck. He suspected that the young man glimpsed him at some point during the voyage, but in the ensuing four days, no word passed between them. On Friday night, as the boat steamed downriver in the center of the slow, heavy current around Manchac Point, the weather turned sharply cold. It was like a long fever breaking, and the following evening, when the *Parnassus* came to dock on the levee in New Orleans, it was like coming back to another world from the one January had left two weeks ago. There were still few boats – and wouldn't be, until the December rise brought cargo prices down – but, as he crossed the Place d'Armes, January took note of well-dressed ladies on the arms of their gentlemen friends, taking the air beneath the pride-of-India trees that grew along the levee; of children dashing among the market arcades or rolling hoops across the Place's dusty expanse, shouting with delight at being back in town with their friends. Along Rue Chartres and Rue Esplanade, cafés were open again, and the melismatic wailing of the charcoal man could be heard as he went his rounds:

'*My donkey white, my coal is black,*
Buy my charcoal, ten-cent sack . . .'

Lights shone in the windows of town houses; candlelit windows stood open to the night-breeze. Voices called from carriageways and yards.

The air no longer sang with mosquitoes.

The summer heat was over at last.

January wished he had wings, so that he could spread them and fly the length of the street to where Rose would be drinking tea on the gallery, as she did at this hour of the evening . . .

And there she was, as he came up the street, rising from her chair and turning to look toward him through the descending blue twilight as if he'd shouted her name aloud, as he was shouting it in his heart.

Two of her students were with her – quiet, pretty Cosette Gardinier and a very young and very plain girl named Sabine – and January said, as he came up the steps and into Rose's arms, 'You young ladies might want to go indoors for a few minutes . . .' and the girls giggled and nudged each other and peeked back over their shoulders as they darted through the French doors into the shadows of the house, and he kissed Rose and held her close.

I'm back, I'm back. I'm alive and I'm back . . .

He barely felt the pain in his ribs, under the hard clinch of her arms around him. Didn't care when her stroking hand brushed the raw wounds on his face. *So what? Who cares? I didn't get hanged, and I didn't get shot . . .* The whole world seemed to collapse in on to those words *I'm back* – that thought – and then blossom out from them again like a world-spanning incandescent flower.

'Where's Hannibal?' he asked, after about ten minutes.

'Hannibal?'

'I want to strangle him,' explained January, 'for making me do that journey alone.'

But instead of replying she put her arms around his neck again, and for some minutes they clung together like the survivors of a shipwreck, washed up on a beach.

Then Rose said, 'He'll be at the funeral in the morning.'

'Funeral?' January paused in the act of settling into one of the wooden chairs.

Rose perched on his knee. 'They found Rameses's body yesterday, tangled in the snags that washed up on the batture below Chalmette. The girls and I –' she nodded back toward the house, where Cosette's soft voice could be heard, helping the younger student with a simple passage in Latin – 'were at Crowdie Passebon's earlier, where Liselle and the children are staying . . . Hannibal came by, on his way from the Cabildo to the Countess's.'

'The Cabildo?'

'Shaw tells me he goes there almost daily.'

'That's a change,' said January thoughtfully. 'The week before last I had to drag him—'

'He doesn't always see Gerry – Foxford,' she corrected herself with her quick smile. 'I've seen him there twice, I think – I've been taking the boy things like ginger beer, since the water they give the prisoners there comes straight out of the river . . . if not straight out of the gutter. And the food is worse. But Hannibal always asks after him.'

'He hasn't said what he's afraid is going to happen?'

Rose looked briefly surprised, then shook her head. 'You mean, other than the fact that the jail's an overcrowded pest-hole and that every good Frenchman and good American and good Irishman who gets thrown in there feels it's his right to beat up an Orangeman English landlord?'

'Yes,' said January quietly. 'Other than that. Do they have a date for the trial?'

'The fifth. Right at the start of the docket.'

'Damn.'

'Hannibal made arrangements for the girl Pierrette to stay at Mayerling's until the trial, rather than going upriver to Natchitoches Parish. Just because her testimony isn't acceptable in a court doesn't mean the judge won't hear it privately and take it into his consideration in his summing-up – Hannibal's idea, by the way, not that appalling lawyer Droudge hired.'

'So Droudge did buy the girl?'

'After being threatened with a caning from Uncle Diogenes, yes. I gather he tried to talk the dealer down, and then backed out because the price was too steep, on the grounds that they don't need testimony of any kind because the court can't condemn a man for not being able to say where he was—'

'On the night the man who left him a fortune was stabbed in the culprit's hotel room, yes.' January sighed. 'I take it nothing has been discovered that would point to either Diogenes or Droudge?'

'Well, according to Lieutenant Shaw, Captain Tremouille isn't looking. As far as he's concerned, they *have* the culprit. Uncle Diogenes – who has been making a complete pest of himself with the Mayor and City Council – is paying Mayerling the cost of the girl's board, mostly in IOUs. But, apparently, while Pierrette was staying in the servants' quarters at the Iberville, it came to light that Droudge was making arrangements to resell her at a twenty percent profit . . . Are you hungry?'

'Ravenous.'

'I've saved some table scraps for you. And there's hot water in the kitchen left over from the washing-up. The girls and I were going to walk over to Passebon's this evening. Liselle is taking it all well, I understand. I think she's glad, just to . . . to not wonder anymore. And, of course, that awful mother of hers is refusing to pay for a second funeral, which is not what poor Beauvais needs right now. He buried his brother yesterday.'

They descended the backstairs, crossed the small and crookedly-placed yard to the kitchen, where Abigail – a tiny buck-toothed woman of January's age who did daywork for half a dozen families on Rue Esplanade – dished up a bowl of leftover beans and rice, with a sausage dropped on top. The lemonade wasn't cold, but January didn't care. It was good only to be on something other than a steamboat deck and not to be worrying about who might be after him.

'So tell me,' said Rose, 'about Isobel Deschamps's shameful secret? Does she turn into a wolf at the full of the moon? Give herself to the Devil in Black Masses? Seek votes for women? Did she poison her father so she could run off with that appalling actor . . .?'

'All of them,' replied January grandly, gesturing with the sausage on a fork. 'She is a *loup-garou*, and a Satan worshipper, and a poisoner . . . and as such,' he added in a quieter voice, 'I am pledged to speak to no one of what she told me. Not even to you, my nightingale. It is nothing shameful –' Rose had turned from the boiler, frowning in concern, all jest gone from her eyes – 'but it is a secret I cannot share. She isn't married to Frank Subbs, at any rate. But there are others involved, who would suffer grievously.'

She came to him, set down the basin of hot water on the corner of the table, and he put a palm to her cheek. Looking up into her face – a face he seldom saw in terms of its color – he thought how the light milky brown of her complexion was simply a part of her beauty, like her gray-green, short-sighted eyes or the dusting of freckles over her nose. But he saw her color now, identifying her with his mother's merciless exactitude as a quadroon – a precise rung on a ladder that was of such frantic importance to every *libre* in the French Town, but that meant utterly nothing to the Americans, who saw only white or black: *can I sell her, or can I not?*

But if I start to wonder why the world is constituted as it is, it will only drive me mad.

'Now tell me about your days and the girls,' he said, 'and of all that's happened, while I've been away.'

As matters turned out, January was destined to confer with Hannibal on the subject of the son of Philippa Stuart, the Viscountess Foxford, much sooner than the following morning.

At Crowdie Passebon's modest cottage, he was told that Liselle had gone – with Rameses's mother, who had come up with her from Crown Point and was staying with Fortune Gérard the coffee seller and his wife, who was her cousin – to sit vigil beside her husband's sealed coffin in the small back parlor at Quennell's. After paying his quiet respects to her there, and expressing his sorrow to Beauvais Quennell and his wife, he returned to the Passebon's small green house on Rue Burgundy, where the wake would be held after the funeral. He had to endure the chaffing and joking and expressions of alarmed non-recognition ('Whoa, that a billiard ball

I see? Looks a little like Ben January, but January had him a full head of hair . . .') from the other members of the FTFCMBS assembled there, but Crowdie Passebon and Mohammed LePas offered him subdued thanks for arranging the delivery of the undoctored account books.

'It's bad,' admitted LePas. 'We took what funds we have left out of the Mississippi and Balize and put them into the Bank of Louisiana –' he shook his head – 'for all the good that's likely to do. Thank you, Ben.'

It was late by the time he returned home, and later still – after a more comprehensive reunion with Rose than had been possible on the front gallery earlier in the evening – before he slept, only to be wakened after an hour's sleep by the sharp rapping of knuckles on the jalousie of the French door. 'Rose!' a voice whispered outside. 'Rose, for God's sake.'

She turned over, sat up sleepily. 'What on earth . . .?'

'I have found you out at last, you wicked woman,' said January to Rose, recognizing the voice. And, padding to the French door: 'Come in through my study, Hannibal.' He scooped his shirt from the end of the bed and slithered into it as he crossed the parlor by instinct in the dark; behind him, candlelight flared briefly in the bedroom as Rose caught up her shift and wrapper. 'What is it?' he asked as he shot open the bolt of the jalousies in the study to reveal the thin black silhouette of the fiddler against the dimmest of blue starlight beyond the gallery outside. 'What's happened?'

'It's Gerry. He's ill. The note said, dying.'

'Thank God you're back,' Hannibal added as the two of them slipped from shadow to shadow along Rue Dauphine. 'And thank God you're safe—'

'No thanks to you,' returned January, with a little shove to make it clear that he didn't mean it. 'No, truly,' he added, 'I doubt you could have helped – and, in fact, I suspect Isobel would not have confided her secret in me, had anyone else been there.'

'And her secret is?'

Voices sounded on Rue des Ursulines, and the two men faded into the deeper shadows of a barred carriageway. Two weeks ago the city would have been deathly silent at this hour, but now, even at three a.m., candles burned behind the French doors of the little cottages that opened straight on to the banquette, or in the upper windows of town houses. Laughter and faint music. Shadows passed back and forth.

It was Sunday – in two hours the bells would ring for early Mass. Tomorrow night would be Halloween night, and Tuesday, the Feast of All Saints, when not only the living but the dead would gather, to say, as families were saying to one another all over town, 'I've missed you, it's good to see you again . . .'

Last year, January, Rose, and Hannibal had been in Mexico, only weeks after January and Rose had wed. Tuesday would be the first of the family feasts at which January would present his bride, when they picnicked at the cemetery. The first feast at which Rose's family – both *libre* and white – would come to find them as they cleaned the tombs, would welcome him as Rose's husband . . .

Then the whites would all go off and vote for a new President for the United States. And those with African blood in their veins would have only their families to be citizens of . . .

And some, he reflected sadly, thinking of Martin Quennell, and the beautiful Countess Mazzini, *not even that*.

Voices laughed, and the rougher jostle of talk drifted from the cafés on Rue Bourbon. The waterfront would be lively with sailors no longer worried about coming ashore to the threat of fever. January guessed that there would now be more City Guards patrolling Rue Bourbon and Rue Royale to demand of a black man what the hell he was doing, walking abroad after curfew.

Since at this hour of the morning whatever constables they might meet were just as likely to be drunk, January preferred to have the ensuing explanation take place at the Cabildo.

'Her secret,' replied January softly, 'is still a secret. It hardly seems fair that hers should be the only secret, of all of those surrounding Derryhick's death, to be turned out into the light.'

After a moment of silence, Hannibal said, '*Touché, amicus meus*.' They walked on, turned down Rue St Ann, toward the smoky lights and the dingy gambling parlors whose doors never seemed to close.

'I see you got the account books all right.'

'For all the good it's likely to do the Society,' sighed Hannibal. 'Quennell has been talking about making the money good, but by my estimate there's close to ten thousand dollars missing, and you know Schurtz won't care anything beyond the fact that the lots were turned over to him. I found Stubbs.'

'Did you?' January raised his brows.

'At least, Marie-Venise has taken to slipping away from the Countess's in the early hours of the morning – not now, I mean, but seven or eight o'clock – to arrange private appointments at a house of assignation on Terpsichore Street.'

'Who on earth would *want* her services – or *anything* along those lines – at eight in the morning?'

Hannibal spread his hands. 'Benjamin, your innocence in the ways of the world is absolutely touching. *Vivere si recte nescis, decede peritis*. She is also, according to Elspie, selling her jewelry and paying Little J to carry letters for her to the Fatted Calf Tavern on Camp Street across from the theater.'

'An accommodation address?'

'So I believe. I've taken to getting coffee there – discreetly – and have seen no evidence of the man himself.'

'I wonder if he replies.'

They crossed before the shut doors of the Cathedral and entered the Cabildo's watch room, smoky and stuffy despite the doors flung open to the chill of predawn. The night sergeant looked up in surprise and opened his mouth to protest January's presence, but Hannibal dipped in the pocket of his shabby waistcoat and handed the man a folded note. 'I only received this an hour ago,' he said, 'and it enjoins me to bring a physician as quickly as I can. Viscount Foxford is a relative of mine,' he added as the man studied the scribbled missive. 'Is he all right?'

'We have a doctor to look in . . .' The sergeant handed the note back with a touch of reproof in his voice.

'And I'm sure he's a very competent man,' replied Hannibal. 'But a very busy one, with so many to see to . . .'

'Thank God, not so many as some years.' The man crossed himself, made a sign to avert the Evil Eye, and fetched keys from his desk. 'I was afraid the boy had the cholera . . .' He shook his head. 'Three took sick like that, all at once . . . I been up two or three times to the cell, and the Negro cell also, and all's quiet for now. Still . . .'

He led the way across the yard.

The room where infirm or injured prisoners were consigned

was a tiny one, set beneath the outside stair that ascended to the main cells, and was probably once used for storage. It was opposite the courtyard privies, and the reek almost stifled the stink of vomit as the sergeant unlocked the door. 'Damn all,' commented the officer as he held his torch into the room; a few of the smaller roaches scurried indignantly for the shadows, but the big ones clustered around the two puddles of watery puke on the floor paid no heed. There were two hammocks, and a third man lay on the floor beneath one of them on a straw mattress.

Two of the sick men were sleeping. The third – the man on the floor – twisted and muttered, clutching and rubbing at his twitching legs. Sweat glistened on his face, and when January knelt beside him – he was a brutal-looking Kentuckian with half of one ear bitten off in some long-ago fight – the skin of his hands and face was not hot with fever, but clammy and cold.

'Are they voiding blood?' he asked, rising to face the sergeant again. Hannibal had gone to the hammock on the other side of the little room, stood looking down at the young Viscount's face with no expression in his own.

The sergeant nodded. 'That one on the floor – Liver-Eatin' Mike, I have heard he is called –' he pronounced the English nickname with distaste – 'said that he swallowed coals of fire. What is it, M'sieu? They have no fever. Is it catching?'

'I'm inclined to think it is food poisoning,' January said quietly. 'When did it come on?'

'Two, three o'clock this afternoon. And all three, almost at the same time. And you're right.' The man frowned, casting his mind back. 'That Mike, he's one of the worst when a man's family brings him food. He'll lie in wait and steal anything that's brought.' He shrugged, as if those who found themselves in the common cell asked for what they got.

'Gator Jack is his pal,' he added, with a nod at the man in the hammock above Liver-Eatin' Mike. 'They'll gang up and split the take. Serve 'em right, wouldn't it –' he flashed a crooked, cheerful grin – 'if the milk or the fish they brought poor M'sieu le Vicomte was bad— '

'Who brought?'

The sergeant looked at January as if he hadn't been paying attention to some earlier explanation. 'The young man's lawyer, and that sour-faced business manager, who seems to think we have servants to draw baths for every man here and maids to sweep the floor three times a day.'

Hannibal said softly, 'Droudge.'

TWENTY-SIX

'It's arsenic, isn't it?'

January felt Foxford's face, then his hands; then withdrew his stethoscope from his satchel and listened to the young man's chest. 'The symptoms are consistent, yes.' Upon Hannibal's argument that none of the three patients was in any shape to assault visitors, the sergeant had locked the cell door and gone to fetch water, encouraged by what January guessed was most of Hannibal's tip money from the Countess's that evening. He hoped the man would think to bring a lantern on his return trip as well. The torch gave shaky light at best, and it couldn't be brought close enough to a man's face to do any good.

'Will he live?'

January glanced across at his friend's dark eyes, but could read nothing in them. 'I'll know better when he comes around. The fact that Droudge brought the poison doesn't mean Uncle Diogenes didn't prepare it, you know.'

Hannibal opened his mouth, closed it, and stood for a moment in thought. Then: 'Fifty cents says it's Droudge.'

After studying him in silence for a few minutes more, January said, 'You seem awfully sure of yourself.'

'I'm awfully sure Uncle Diogenes wouldn't take time out from visiting bookshops and whipping parlors to purchase arsenic and ginger beer. He's not a greedy man. Send him his remittance – and occasional infusions of hush money to the parents of his *eromenae* – and he's happy.'

'And you think Foxford would have done that when he came into the property?'

'He has raised no objections so far.'

The cell door creaked as it opened. The sergeant had not only brought a pitcher of water and a lantern, but also a wooden stool. 'You men take care, now,' he warned, hanging the lantern on a nail on the wall and taking the torch from Hannibal's hand. 'If one of those men gets hold of that stool . . .'

January looked down at the trembling, sweating Kaintuck

on the floor, the silent man in the other hammock. Hannibal reassured the sergeant, 'I believe Dr Janvier and I can handle them.'

When the door was closed again and locked, January recounted what Isobel had told him of the events of the sixth of October, without specifying in whose house his conversation with her had taken place, or what had been the secret Blessinghurst had learned. 'The times fit,' he finished. 'Given how long it would have taken for Derryhick to find Blessinghurst.'

Hannibal whispered, 'Young fool.'

'Did he mention Gerry was staying with Theodoric Stuart in Paris when he met Mademoiselle Deschamps?'

'At the town house?'

'You know it?'

'Gods, yes. The lot of us took it over like invading Goths and turned it into Liberty Hall. I hope to God somebody whitewashed the poem I chalked on to the wall of the back drawing room. Are you thinking Theo might have written something to his father about Gerry's intention to wed?'

'I'm not thinking anything right now.' Gently, January slipped an arm under the Viscount's shoulders, eased him into a sitting position while the fiddler held the hammock steady. 'Nor do I have to, nor you either, if we can lay hands on Stubbs before Louis Verron gets to him.' The torch had provided some warmth, but the cell was bitterly cold, and none of the three patients had a blanket. The Viscount began to shiver violently and muttered a name that might have been, *Isobel*. 'My great fear is that even when we get Stubbs's side of the story – if we find out who's behind the blackmail attempt – it will do no good. Without concrete proof – proof enough to jail Diogenes . . . or Droudge, if he's your favorite – I'm afraid Foxford will let himself be hanged, rather than risk Isobel's secret becoming common knowledge.'

'Good God, what did she *do*?' Hannibal stared at him.

January returned the gaze across the Viscount's shivering body, almost marveling at his friend's obtuseness to something that had seemed so obvious to himself. And it *would* have been obvious, he realized, to anyone born and brought up in New Orleans. French and Spanish Creoles – some of the worst gossips in the known world – were forever surreptitiously studying one another's fingernails, hair, and pedigrees, and it didn't surprise January at all that Louis Verron had immediately believed Stubbs's clumsy attempt at blackmail rather than simply saying, 'It's absurd.'

For over a hundred and fifty years, the French families who had settled in New Orleans had lived side by side with those shadow offspring, those 'vulture eggs', those half-caste and quarter-caste men and women who made up the *gens du couleur libre*: neither white nor black, but something else. Everyone had heard stories of people who quietly stepped over the line when no one was looking. And everyone worried that it might happen in *their* family.

A brief gust of rage passed through him that the blood of his mother, his sisters, his friends should be regarded as a sort of taint, poisoning by contact with the smallest droplet . . .

Then he forced his mind to release the thought. *If I'm going to be angry about that then I will live in anger forever.*

'Nothing to the girl's discredit,' he said gently. 'But it will ruin her family, destroy the lives of her mother and sister . . . and may well cost her her own life, if her cousin decides killing can scotch the story. For that matter,' he added, as Hannibal's eyes widened in disbelieving shock, 'it wouldn't hurt to ask, on our way out, if Louis Verron or any of his friends paid a call on the jail around dinner time. Just to make sure.'

First light stained the sky above the courtyard when the Viscount finally rested easily enough to be left. Hannibal tucked his own shabby coat around the young man's body, despite the slim odds that he'd ever get the garment back once it was out of his sight. January did what he could for both the other men, though it was fairly clear to him that Liver-Eatin' Mike, at least, had stolen his last food from a weaker man.

'I'll get a blanket from home,' said January, when the sergeant came to let them out of the cell. His breath laid a faint mist on the dawn air. The watch room was only marginally warmer than the yard – and quiet, as public places are in the small hours of Sunday mornings. At the sergeant's desk, Lieutenant Shaw looked around from conference with the men of the night watch; he spat and signed Hannibal and January to wait.

'Boechter said as how you was here,' he said when he finally came to them beside his desk. 'The boy all right?' When January nodded, he continued, 'He sick? Or was it somethin' he et?' And the inflection in his light-timbred drawl told January that the clawing and twitching of Liver-Eatin' Mike's extremities – the burning of his throat – had not escaped him.

'I suspect,' said January grimly, 'it's something he ate. Can you keep him quarantined? Keep anyone from seeing him?'

'Can you get him a blanket?' asked Hannibal.

Shaw's pale eyes narrowed. 'He had one, beginnin' of the night. I'll see what I can do. As for keepin' him in the sick cell, Tremouille –' he nodded in the direction of the interior stair, which led up to the Captain of the Watch's office on the upper floor – 'just told me there's one of the boatmen brought in yesterday, looks to be comin' down with jail fever. I'd say your boy's safer in the main cell.'

'In spite of the fact that, if he starts refusing food, the next thing Uncle Diogenes – or Mr Droudge, as Hannibal would have it – is going to try is paying some bravo to start up a fight?'

Shaw spat again. 'He better think twic't about it. What the hell you do to your hair, Maestro? You look like my Uncle Sus after the Seminole got him.'

'Tried to sneak into a monastery.' January ran a self-conscious hand over the prickles of his makeshift tonsure. Rose would have to clip the whole head short to match. 'You think you can keep anyone from seeing Foxford for the next few days, until we lay hands on Stubbs? Tell them he really *is* sick – dying would be better . . .'

'Dyin' was what he looked to be doin' yesterday, near sundown. An' he'll need to see that lawyer of his'n, which'll be about as useful as a hanky in an artillery barrage. Trial can't be put back, neither – the whole docket's jammed from the summer. Now, I am mightily curious,' he added, turning his gaze on Hannibal, 'as to why you think the boy's business manager would be slippin' inheritance powder into his ginger beer, an' not the man who's gonna come in for all Foxford's money, an' Derryhick's, too, if'n the boy should cut his stick. What do you know about the man?'

'I know I don't like him,' replied Hannibal shortly. '*Non amo te, Sabidi, nec possum dicere* . . . He looks like a vulture, and Philippa – Lady Foxford – was of the opinion, even eighteen years ago, that his bookkeeping needed looking into: something the old Viscount would never hear of. So long as Gerry was under age, his mother was powerless to even see the ledgers. Uncle Diogenes wasn't the man to come back to County Mayo and straighten things out – not if it meant that he'd have to go through the whole tedious process of finding another man of business. I imagine he would say – as his brother the eleventh Viscount said before him – that letting Droudge "feather his nest a little" was part of the cost of doing business and cheap at the price of having a man so adept at racking the tenants out of their last shilling.'

Old anger glinted in his eyes, like a weapon drowned under decades of alcohol. Like the scorched anger that had been in his voice when he'd spoken of the man who'd broken Philippa Foxford's heart.

'An' His Lordship committin' Holy Matrimony would stick a spoke into his little wheel.'

'Yes.' Hannibal folded his shirtsleeved arms and shivered as the courtyard door was opened for the sergeant to carry up the usual slop of pulses and beans for the men in the cells. 'It would be useful to subpoena the account books for Foxford Priory and make enquiries among members of the London 'Change to see if – like our friend Martin Quennell – Caius Droudge has been investing where he should not with what he has no legal right to use, but that doesn't seem possible . . . A reason he may have included himself in the expedition to retrieve and approve of Foxford's errant bride.'

Shaw's gray glance passed from one to the other of them, as if weighing up what he suspected against what could actually be taken into court. 'You know damn-all about it,' he observed mildly at last. 'An' what you say could go just as well for Uncle Diogenes.'

'It could, yes.'

'You happen to got even one teeny-tiny spit of evidence of any of this?'

'Not one teeny-tiny spit,' said Hannibal. 'But give us time.'

'If'n I could give time,' returned Shaw with a sigh, 'to all them as needed it in this world, I'd never have no rest, for people beggin' a day here, an' a year there, to get done what they shoulda, myself included. Trial's on the fifth. That enough?'

'It's enough if we're lucky,' said January. 'But if we don't find Stubbs tonight, I suspect Louis Verron will have by Thursday.'

Rose and the girls were readying themselves for Mass when January and Hannibal returned to the house. Rose, a pagan or the next thing to it, regarded regular church attendance as part of what the parents of her pupils paid her for, and she dressed for it as if it mattered to God what worshippers wore. 'Our newest pupil, Mademoiselle Alice Truxton, is upstairs,' Rose informed him. 'She is from Mobile, and she is a Protestant. She assured us she will pray for our souls to be delivered from Papism and Hell. There should be hot water in the kitchen boiler, if you want a bath. Is the Foxford boy all right?'

'So far,' said January. 'However, the man who stole most of the food sent to him by his uncle and his business manager is dying of arsenic poison. Hannibal and I have a bet on whose idea that was,' he added, as Rose's eyes widened. 'Do you know the Fatted Calf, across from the Camp Street Theater? Do they keep open on Sundays?'

Rose frowned, but Cosette Gardinier, tucking a late bronze chrysanthemum into the folds of her simple tignon, said, 'They do, M'sieu. At least they did last winter, when Granmere told me we couldn't get ices there because it was a café for *les blankittes*.'

'When next we play for the opera at the Theater,' promised Hannibal, 'I shall go in and obtain ices for the lot of you, and I'll bring them out to the street for you to consume, to the envy of all your friends. Will you wager on the murderer, Owl-Eyed Athene?'

'Oh, Droudge,' said Rose promptly. Evidently, in her mind a man who spent half his income on manuscripts in antique Persian couldn't be all bad.

Bathed, shaved, freshly clothed, and comforted as he always was by the Mass, January made his way late that afternoon across Canal Street and down to the American Theater. He stood on the brick sidewalk for a time, looking about him as if seeking an address while he watched the shuttered front of the café.

In time the owner unlocked the street door, went back inside; a black youth of fourteen or fifteen emerged and unfolded the shutters of the French windows that formed most of the front of the building, went back inside, and came out again with a broom and a bucket of water to wash down the mud from the sidewalk. The owner came back out, demanded, 'You deaf or just stupid, boy?' and cuffed the youth on the ear.

'Reckon I's just stupid, sir.'

This got him another cuff and a shove inside. A woman emerged and took up the youth's chore of rinsing and sweeping down the bricks. When she'd finished, she retreated within, and January gave her a few minutes then crossed the street and went down the narrow passway at the side of the building and through to the yard.

As he'd hoped, she was pumping another bucket full of water. January said, 'Here, let me help you with that, m'am,' and hurried across to her; she barely came up to his shoulder and couldn't have weighed ninety pounds soaking wet.

To her smile of tired thanks, he said, 'Fact is, m'am, you can help me out, if you would.' And he produced two Spanish silver dollars from his pocket, showed them to her in his palm. 'I'm lookin' for an English feller, comes in here to pick up messages? Bit shorter than me . . .'

The smile was replaced by an odd look: a stillness, like a very angry cat getting ready to slash. 'Preston,' she said.

January slipped the coins into her hand. 'One whose whore brings him in money? Skinny girl? French?'

'That's him.' She nodded for him to follow her into the passway, where they couldn't be seen from the back door. 'You the man who's lookin' for him?' She sounded like she really hoped he was. He remembered Stubbs's attempt to kiss Elspie. 'He said the man after him was white, a Frenchman.'

January wondered if someone had told the actor, or if Louis Verron had already made an attempt and failed. 'I'm *one* of the men lookin' for him. He be in tonight?'

She nodded. 'He sent off a letter to that hotel yesterday – whining for money again, I'll bet, as if that gal of his wasn't sendin' it to him every other day.'

'The Iberville?'

'That's it.'

'You wouldn't know the name of the man who sends the messages to him, would you?' He handed her another dollar.

'It's D something,' she said. 'I know that much.' Of course, she wouldn't read. 'Somebody gonna kill him, is that why he's hidin' out?'

'Less you know,' responded January, with a finger to his lips, 'less you can tell. He got a letter from them tonight?'

She shook her head. 'But he'll be in. He's always, "Why ain't nobody send me what I need?" an', "How long they expect me to stay hangin' around this town?" Yesterday, somebody told him that Frenchman was after him, an' you'd think he was Jesus Christ about to go up on the Cross with the whole world pickin' on him an' him innocent as a newborn baby lamb. Huh.' She sniffed. 'Anythin' I can do to help you? Keep him here longer, get him out quicker? Mr Newman –' she threw a glance back at the yard behind them – 'says I got to let him ease his griefs, but I can pretend I'm sick if you need him out of here.'

From the yard, a man bellowed, 'Nina! Nina you lazy bitch—'

'Don't get yourself in trouble,' said January. 'We'll be outside.'

She smiled again, different than before. She said, 'Good,' and fleeted back around the corner of the passway to the yard.

As a man sows, reflected January, *so shall he also reap.*

Now let's just hope it isn't Louis Verron who'll be in on the harvest before tonight.

TWENTY-SEVEN

January had played at the American Theater often enough to be welcome backstage, and the information that he was there to keep an unobtrusive eye on the Fatted Calf across the street because one of its habitués had injured a young lady friend of his didn't hurt his cause. As was his habit, when a hand was needed with ropes or props for the matinee in progress, January lent a hand, and nobody blinked when Preacher or Four-Eyes or one of their many friends came to the stage door and signed to him: *nuthin' yet*.

With five hundred dollars at his disposal, January had found, invisible observation became a simple matter.

It wasn't until the bells were sounding nine o'clock in the Cathedral tower, an hour after he'd taken up the observation post himself in the alleyway between the Theater and Parnell's cotton press, that he saw a man tall enough and broad enough in the shoulder to be his quarry hurry along the brick sidewalk and duck into the doorway.

In the café window, one of the candles that stood on the tables within moved back and forth, back and forth: Hannibal's signal that it was indeed Stubbs. A few minutes later the candle was moved again: *he's coming out*.

January wondered if the expected message from his employer had arrived, and if it had contained the funds requested.

Like the late Martin Quennell, "Montague Blessinghurst" had made his home as far as he could manage from the French Town – as if he had dwelled in New Orleans just long enough to understand how seldom the haughty French and Spanish Creoles deigned to cross Canal Street. From the muted ruckus of Camp Street, where theatergoers were packing wives and daughters into carriages with mendacious promises of, 'Just going to have a chat and a smoke with Robinson here, won't be half an hour . . .' January trailed Stubbs across the tree-shrouded stillness of Lafayette Place and up Girod Street, which descended from the inexpensively modest to the baldly sordid in the space of two blocks. The remains of old cane fields were broken here and there by heaps of lumber and brick, or more frequently by slatternly constructions thrown together from dismembered flat boats. Dirty lantern-light smudged the night; men's voices cursed or laughed. Like most whites, Stubbs stayed on the unpaved streets, visible for blocks by the lantern he carried. He was easier to follow thus, January reflected, than he would have been by daylight.

Autumn wind breathed from the river; the leathery leaves of the magnolias rattled, like the wings of Halloween bats. Rameses Ramilles, at least, would have no cause tomorrow night to walk abroad. He slept among his friends at last. On Tuesday, Liselle would go with the other ladies of the FTFCMBS – Rose among them – to serve out food and lemonade to the men and children whitewashing the Society's tomb: renewing its plaster against another winter of frost, digging out the encroaching resurrection-fern from the cracks, polishing the brass till it glinted. January's mother always went, to lay out her little picnic of meat pies and jambalaya and to pay her respects to the widow of St-Denis Janvier, to his white children, and to his brother's family – with whom she was partner in a cotton press and two hotels – though she hadn't a single relative of her own in the cemetery . . .

And yet, after ten days of panic, violence, flight, and the threat of hanging, January found himself looking forward to an afternoon of physical labor, visiting friends and family, and putting up with his mother's sarcastic complaints.

And Dante probably thought the foot slopes of Mount Purgatory pretty handsome, once he crawled out of the Pit with brimstone in his hair.

The 'residential hotel' where Stubbs – or Eliot Preston, as he was apparently calling himself these days – had taken a room was one of those large, shabby dwellings in the quarter of the town that catered to the flood of Americans who came every year to New Orleans to make money from the booming markets in cotton, slaves, and gunrunning to the decaying Spanish Empire. It was considerably shabbier than McPhearson's Hotel a few streets away, where Martin Quennell had boasted his residence; the owners lived off the premises and hired a 'caretaker' to sleep in the office there in case a tenant died, went insane, or was attacked by vengeful French

Creoles in the night. January's feet squished in the mud of the trash-strewn yard as he closed the distance between himself and Stubbs, and even the night's hard chill did little to mitigate the stinks of uncleaned cowshed and chicken-run.

Stubbs whirled on the threshold, key in one hand and the lantern upraised in the other. 'Who's there?' He was unshaven and unclean, and by the pong of liquor on his clothing as January got close, not entirely sober. 'I warn you, I have a gun.' He dropped his key and fumbled in a pocket.

January stepped from the darkness, caught his wrist in an iron grip, and said, 'So do my friends out in the yard.' He nodded behind him at the abyssal darkness. 'I mean you no harm. Give me the gun, and you won't be hurt.'

Stubbs hesitated, then reached resignedly for his pocket.

'Left hand,' January reminded him.

The Englishman complied, fishing forth by its business end a long-barreled dueling-pistol of which January promptly relieved him, putting the weapon into his own pocket and opening his hand to show it empty. 'Shall we go inside?'

He turned briefly back to the darkness – which contained no one but, presumably, Hannibal, who had had instructions to follow Stubbs separately in case of evasion or accident – and made signs suggestive of telling an army of bravoes to rest upon their swords. For a man who made his living by fraud, Stubbs was a shockingly gullible subject. He gulped and stammered, 'Listen, I have money, I can get you five hundred dollars tomorrow . . .' as he tremblingly unlocked the door, and January followed him inside and up the narrow service-stair. 'I swear I was only writing what I was told to write. It wasn't my idea – they're holding my wife and children hostage . . .'

The actor's room was at the end of a hallway that reeked of greasy cooking, spit tobacco, and chamber pots. 'I beg of you, tell Mr Verron I'm leaving New Orleans tomorrow, the arrangements are all made, he need never be troubled with me again . . .' He fumbled the key in the door lock, pushed the door open, lantern held high . . .

'*You?!?*' he cried.

Oh, Christ. By his tone of voice, whoever was in there, it wasn't good.

January stepped swiftly through the door at his heels, and

in the lantern light – even at that moment added to by the yellowish gleam of a second dark-lantern uncovered – beheld the slender form of Marie-Venise, with the Countess's Prussian needle-gun in her hand.

In almost a single move, January snatched Stubbs's lantern from his hand and shoved the actor sideways into the darkness, setting the lantern down and dodging in the other direction. Marie-Venise wavered, caught by surprise. By the sound of it, Stubbs tripped over something – beyond the glimmer of the two yellow lantern beams the room was like a coal sack – and she swung the barrel in that direction, giving January the chance to lunge across the room, seize her wrist, twist the pistol from her hand, drop it, and put his hand over her mouth before she could scream 'rape' and *really* get him in trouble.

He said, 'I'm here to help you, Vennie,' thrust her aside, and dove for the door – tripping in the process over the chair that Stubbs had overset – and slammed it before Stubbs could collect himself to dive through it. 'Don't move, Stubbs,' he added, yanking the duelling pistol from his pocket, though he only had the vaguest idea of where the Englishman was. 'Mamzelle, if you would be so kind as to light some candles . . .'

He wouldn't have bet much that the French girl would side with him against her lover, but she'd evidently made her decision, because her thin, small, boyish hands appeared in the lantern beam, poking a candle into the flame. She set an assortment of mostly-burned stumps into a cheap brass candelabra on the table by the window, and the increased glow showed Stubbs scrambling to his feet and trying to get to the window beside the rumpled bed. Marie-Venise bent to scoop up the needle gun and trained it on him, her wry young face hard in the tumbled frame of dark hair. 'You stand still, *cochon*,' she said. 'You stand and tell me what you've done with my jewels.'

'My little bird –' Stubbs spread his hands, like Romeo stunned by his first sight of Juliet's beauty in Act One, Scene Five – 'you gave them to me that they might be liquidated for cash—'

'For *us*,' hissed the girl. 'Not for you to run off and leave me. To carry *us* safely to England—'

'What did this man promise you, Mamzelle?' asked January quietly.

She didn't take her eyes off Stubbs. She'd learned that much about him, anyway. 'All things – the Moon! A settlement, and a house in London. He's a rich man. Once he can get back safe to England and put his hand upon the family money there. They all have mistresses – why not me, *enfin*? But since he's decided –' she jerked her head at the portmanteau, half-packed, that lay now visible on the bed amid a tangle of folded shirts and gaudy waistcoats – 'that he'd rather go back to whatever English slut he left, I'll have back my jewels and the money I sent him—'

'My dear girl,' coaxed Stubbs. 'Such an excitable little sparrow! Of course I was preparing to leave – my enemies are closing in! I was on my way to you and—'

'How much did you lend him?' asked January.

'Fifty in cash. And all my jewels, and not just those he gave me.'

'I'll give you two hundred,' said January. 'Will you cover us, while I have a word with him?'

She moved her head just enough to glance at him, dark eyes narrowed, without taking the gun off Stubbs. 'And where's the likes of you going to get two hundred?'

'From the family of another woman he wronged,' replied January evenly. 'A woman more fortunate than yourself. I only need a word.'

She considered the likelihood of this version of events, then nodded. 'You tell him if I don't get my money he is a dead man.'

January took Stubbs's arm, led him to the corner of the room farthest from both door and window. The actor's very sweat smelled of rum. 'Who paid you?' he asked softly.

'Who paid me what?'

January's hand tightened. He didn't often exert the full strength of his grip, but he did now, and Stubbs whimpered. 'Give me the name. The name you gave to Patrick Derryhick at Davis's, the night he went back to the hotel and was killed. The name of the man who paid you to make sure Viscount Foxford would never marry Isobel Deschamps. Or, I swear to you, I will drag you straight downtown and throw you through Louis Verron's parlor window.'

'Droudge,' gasped Stubbs. 'It was Droudge.'

'Why?'

'He'd been speculating on the 'Change,' Stubbs babbled, fingers picking ineffectually at January's grip. 'Borrowing against the estate. Shocking turn-up over a load of Chinese opium that came to smash. He claimed it was his only little flier, but me, I think he'd been dipped for years, long before the old gov'nor snuffed it.'

'Where did he know you from?'

'He's my cousin. Well, he always thought Mama and I were beneath him, but he wrote to me almost a year ago in London, where I was playing Handsome Jack in *The Storm* – and being well spoken of, I might add! – and offered to pay off a few little debts of mine if I'd undertake work for him in Paris. I was to keep an eye on this American girl, intercept messages to young Foxford's lodgings – easy enough, once I'd got that Stuart boy in debt to me at the tables – find whatever I could to her discredit – and Lord, didn't I! – and generally do whatever I could to sully the prospect—'

'Including raping the girl?'

'Lord, she's a negress! I daresay I wouldn't have been—' January forced himself not to strike the man, but the effort must have showed in his face and in his grip because Stubbs amended hastily, 'That is, some quite nice people are Negroes—'

'Here's what you're going to do,' broke in January quietly. 'You're going to sit down at that table there, and you're going to write all that you've told me and sign it. Then you're coming with me to the Cabildo – my men and I will keep you safe on the way – and I'll arrange with a friend of mine there for you to be hidden until the trial. The moment the trial is over, I'll give you five hundred dollars – and don't you even *think* of trying to get more from someone else—'

Stubbs shook his head frantically. 'No, no . . .!'

'And then you'll leave the United States and never return. Not here, not to England. Understand?'

'I say,' protested Stubbs, 'I have my career to consider.'

'Shall I let Verron pay you what you asked for from him?'

'There's no need to be unkind about it. That was a miscalculation . . .'

January raised his voice a little: 'Mamzelle? Might you bring those candles to the desk, if you please?' When she'd done so and Stubbs had sat down, January dug in his jacket pocket, and handed Marie-Venise two hundred dollars in Bank of Louisiana notes. 'Thank you, Mamzelle. And don't grieve about not becoming Lord Montague's mistress back in London. He's an actor, and his name is Frank Stubbs. You'd probably have ended by supporting him.'

'I say!' Stubbs threw down his quill and turned in the chair. 'Did you have to—?'

At which point the door slammed open, four men stepped through, and Louis Verron's voice snapped, 'Kill him.'

TWENTY-EIGHT

Blessinghurst screamed in terror. Marie-Venise smote the candle branch with a blow that sent the lights clattering to the floor; January scooped the tin lantern from the desk and flung it at Verron and his cousins, and he saw the girl's slim silhouette against the window as she threw the casements open. Three shots simultaneously cracked, sounding like cannon fire in the enclosed room. January shoved Stubbs ahead of him to the window as Verron and his cousins plunged for them and tripped over the chair that had earlier felled both January and the actor. As he swung over the window sill, January heard the crack of another shot and the splintering of the window frame beside him. He dropped to the porch roof, rolled to its edge with the jumbled shapes of Marie-Venise and Blessinghurst scrambling ahead of him, and felt a burning sting as if someone had struck him on the outside of the right thigh with a red-hot metal rod.

The shock spun him around, and he fell from the edge of the porch roof, hitting the ground with stunning impact. In the pitch-black darkness of the house's shadow, he couldn't see who it was who rolled him over, pulled open his coat, and relieved him of the remainder of Cadmus Rablé's money, but by the smell it was certainly Lord Montague Blessinghurst.

By the time two men dropped from the edge of the porch roof in pursuit, 'His Lordship' was across the yard like a panicked hare and disappearing into the inky wall of nearby trees. Consciousness reeling on the edge of darkness, January heard two more pursuers thunder downstairs within the house, and with a sensation like dreaming he saw them bolt across the moonlit ground in the same direction. Gold reflections on the trees and a sudden, gritty roil of smoke informed him that at least one of the fallen candles had ignited the bedroom curtains. He hoped Verron and his boys caught Stubbs and gave him the beating of his life before shooting him dead.

Shouts in the house: new-wakened, hung-over, stricken with panic. *If, after all this, I spend the night in the Cabildo for arson . . .*

'*Amicus meus?*' Long, thin hands, surprisingly strong, rolled him over. He managed to get an arm across Hannibal's shoulder.

'*'Tis not so deep as a well, nor wide as a church door.*' He struggled to rise, knowing full well his friend would never get him to his feet unaided.

'*Quod di omen avertant*,' whispered Hannibal. 'Look what happened to the fellow who said that in the play. Can you walk?'

January pressed his hand to his leg. The muscle between his hip and his knee flashed with agony, but the wound was like a burned gash, not a hole, and no artery had been hit. 'Get me to the trees,' he panted. 'I owe you fifty cents.'

'Don't you understand?' Germanicus Stuart, Viscount Foxford, regarded his two visitors from eyes circled in smudges of darkness, and his voice barely sounded a whisper. 'Thank you – truly, thank you – for your efforts, and your concern . . . which I can't imagine how I've earned . . . but God, I wish you had let well alone. Even if evidence existed, there's no question of prosecuting Droudge. If by some miracle the jury were to accept that the sheets on the bed could have been switched by someone else – and all the rest of it – I would not even be able to discharge the man. He has a gun pointed at my heart – at the hearts of the one I love and those *she* loves.'

He made as if to reach for the tin cup of water that stood on the floor beside the makeshift cot that had replaced his hammock. Only the near certainty that the young man would be robbed, and possibly killed, while too weak to help himself had gained January's consent to leave him in the so-called 'infirmary' cell rather than returning him to the general lock-up; the Kaintuck who had been brought in with jail fever had shown no signs of either typhoid or cholera and lay propped, snoring softly, in the hammock that had previously belonged to the late Gator Jack. January, seated on the crude milking-stool that Shaw had produced from somewhere as a sort of bedside table, lifted the cup, but Foxford was able to take it from his hand and drink himself.

'It's bad enough that Patrick—' He stopped himself and looked aside.

Softly, Hannibal said, 'What happened to Patrick wasn't your fault.'

'It was, though.' The boy's hand began to shake, and the fiddler gently took the cup from him. 'I thought – I shouldn't have . . . All I knew in Paris was that she'd fled from me, gone back home. I didn't know what I'd done, or why she'd run away – God, I was a fool! I thought if I could bring Patrick, and Uncle Diogenes, here to find her, to convince her . . .'

'*Amor vincet omnia*,' murmured Hannibal. 'I know the feeling. A grand gesture didn't work for me, either.'

'Patrick suspected. I know that, now. But he was very good about pretending that we really were looking for a cotton plantation to invest in. But then when I saw Isobel with Blessinghurst – I remembered him from Paris, remembered how he'd taken her aside at a ball one night, just before she . . . she got sick and refused to see me. I thought I saw it all. The last thing I expected, when I finally spoke to her, was for her to tell me that she was being blackmailed. She said it was Blessinghurst, and that's all I knew. I didn't even tell Patrick his name – I was careful about that, for her sake, but, of course, after that party at Trulove's he guessed . . .'

'He would.' Hannibal sighed. 'He always outguessed me, anyway.'

Foxford shut his eyes, as if even the memory were a weight beyond his strength to bear. 'He got it out of me,' he whispered after a time. 'I didn't know . . . If I'd known what it was really about, I would have lied. Later that night, when she told me, I – I didn't know what to do. Because he'd tell, she said Blessinghurst would tell if anyone did anything. I think Patrick must have guessed all along that it wasn't really Blessinghurst, but someone using him as a pawn.'

'Well,' opined Hannibal, 'anyone who'd met "His Lordship" would guess after five minutes that he doesn't have the brains to conceive of anything more complicated than matching his cravat with his socks,' and the young man's face relaxed in a whispered chuckle. On the wall behind his head a line of ants crept steadily, from a crack near the floor and up to the ceiling and the cell above, glittering darkly in the thin slice of autumn light that fell through the judas. Across the tiny chamber, the boatman thrashed weakly in his hammock and called out, 'Mary . . .!' in his sleep.

After a little silence the young man went on, 'But it isn't just Marie-Amalie and their poor mother who'll be cast out, branded – exiled from everyone who has ever been their friends. That's the horror of it. It's cousins, aunts, people I've never met . . . But they're the people Isobel loves. People she was raised with, people who are a part of her life. I can't do that. Not to them, not to her. Can't . . . can't just transform them, in the eyes of everyone they know, into Africans overnight, if they must live in a world where the children of Africa are despised—'

Hannibal said, '*What?*'

For a moment he and the young man looked at one another, stunned disbelief confronting the quiet of resigned despair. Then he turned to stare at January, open-mouthed with shock. January looked aside.

'That's *it*?' demanded the fiddler. 'That's what all of this is about? Because some ancestor turns out to have been on the wrong side of the wrong blanket?'

When, after a moment, he had commanded his own anger, January returned his gaze. 'Do you doubt it?'

Hannibal drew in breath to protest, to remark, to quote some apt and cutting fragment of Latin, then closed his mouth, unable to speak. He had spent the past five years of his exile in New Orleans; January saw everything he had so casually heard passing in review behind those coffee-dark eyes. At length he said, very quietly, 'Dear God.'

'I don't want to die,' Foxford went on softly. 'I don't want—' He struggled for a moment to keep his jaw set. January wondered if the young man had ever seen a hanging – seen a man swing, legs threshing, soiling himself, for the twenty minutes or so it took to suffocate after the hoist. 'I've lain here thinking about it, thinking about what I can possibly do, and I can't – I don't know. I don't see what I can do, short of murdering Droudge, and then they'd hang me – or someone – for that. And he's . . . very careful of himself.'

'Given the number of tenants in Foxford village back home who have good reason to want to kill him,' murmured Hannibal, 'he's had plenty of practice. And he's vindictive. There was a man in Sleigh Farm . . .' He hesitated on the story, then shook his head. 'Well.'

'I remember that.' Foxford frowned. 'At least, if it's old Mr

Ghille you mean. The one whose daughter Droudge had hanged. If I brought any kind of charge against him – even if we *did* have evidence – he'd see to it that everything about M'am Celestine's true parents came out.'

'And sooner than let that happen,' said January softly, 'Isobel's cousin will kill her. And probably her mother as well. And, I have no doubt, would go to the gallows in silence, even as you propose to do, Your Lordship.'

Foxford nodded, shortly: it was not something he hadn't known before. 'I tell myself, it's as if she were – they all were – with me in a shipwreck . . . Of course, I would get them to safety, even at the cost of my own life. But then I think of Mother . . .'

January laid a hand on the wasted wrist. 'We'll think of something, Your Lordship.'

'NO!' Foxford turned his head sharply on the wad of rags that served him for a pillow. 'Sir, I beg you, don't think of anything. Don't *do* anything.' His hand closed over January's, desperate even in its weakness. 'Swear to me you won't tell Mr Shaw! My hope is gone,' he whispered. 'She could never be happy with me, knowing I'd had the smallest hand in destroying her family. Nor would I expect her to be, nor want her to pretend. Now she's safe. Her family is safe. She was only a pawn; he has no further interest in her or them. With me or without me, Droudge will go back to Britain, and if I'm lucky enough to survive that long I'll find some way of . . . of living alongside him.'

'Don't be a fool! If he ever suspected you knew, do you think he'd stick at poisoning you again? Your heir is Diogenes – do you think *he'll* care if Droudge is robbing Foxford Priory of everything but the lead in the roof tiles?'

Hannibal laid a hand on January's shoulder; shook his head when January looked up to meet his eyes. Quietly, the fiddler said, 'We won't tell Shaw. I swear it. If worst comes to worst, we can put it about that you've died, in the hopes old Droudge will drink himself to death in celebration. As Iago says, *Good wine is a good familiar creature, if it be well us'd.*'

Foxford's breath whispered out in another laugh. 'That sounds like something Patrick would say,' he said. 'With everything that's happened . . . Sometimes I think that if I get out of here, he'll be waiting for me . . . And then I remember that, whatever else happens, he won't be. I can't . . . It still doesn't seem real. That he's dead, I mean.'

Hannibal said softly, 'I know. *When once we pass, the soul returns no more . . .*'

'Patrick used to quote that portion of the *Iliad*,' said Foxford. 'When he spoke about my father . . . Achilles and Patroclus, parting for the last time:

'*Now give thy hand; for to the farther shore*
When once we pass, the soul returns no more:
When once the last funereal flames ascend,
No more shall meet Achilles and his friend;
No more our thoughts to those we loved make known;
Or quit the dearest, to converse alone.

'He didn't speak of him, but I don't think he ever stopped missing him.'

Hannibal was silent for a long time, seeing – January knew this – his friend. Not dead in the mud of the cemetery, but – wherever, whenever it had been – the last time they'd been in the same room together.

'But he went on,' said Hannibal at last. 'He lived his life regardless. Having known your father, I can say that had their positions been reversed, he would have said the same . . . and, I hope, had the strength to do the same. Though strength of spirit was, alas, not your father's leading characteristic . . .'

'No.' The young man smiled at some memory. 'Maybe not. But what I remember about him was the joy he brought to others – even to Mother; I could see it in her eyes, hear it in her voice when she spoke of him – and the music that he made.' He closed his eyes, and January thought for a time that he'd drifted off to sleep. But as he was disengaging his hand from those long, strengthless fingers they tightened, and Foxford whispered, 'Swear you won't do anything. Don't make this harder for me.'

And January said, 'I swear.'

'Thank you,' in a voice almost too faint to be heard. The boy was asleep before the guard came to let the visitors from the cell.

Hannibal was silent as they crossed the sharp noon brightness of the Cabildo yard, but when they reached the door to the watch room – and January halted to lean on the stick he'd cut, shillelagh-wise, from a hickory sapling – the fiddler asked conversationally, 'What are you doing tonight?'

'Sleeping,' January answered, 'I hope, since *someone* woke me up at two in the morning yesterday, and I haven't been back to bed since. And putting my foot up.' Under bandages and sticking plaster his leg throbbed damnably with every step, and just crossing the yard had made him feel feverish and faint. 'Bad leg or no bad leg, my mother's going to insist that I go down to the cemetery with her tomorrow for the Feast of All Saints.'

'Will you come with me now? We won't be long, and I'll hire a cab—'

'Which they won't let me ride in.'

'I'll tell the jarvey you're my servant.'

'And you'll pay for this with what?'

'I'll borrow the money from Shaw.' Incredulous, January opened his mouth to demand what the hell gave him the idea that the policeman would lend him so much as a silver bit, then closed it, seeing the strange, still darkness in the fiddler's eyes. 'I need to speak to him – and to Augustus Mayerling – and to one other respectable white man . . . Do you know any respectable white men, Benjamin? *Responsare cupidinibus, contemnere honores fortis, et in se ipso totus* . . . And then, if you would, will you come with me to speak to Beauvais Quennell and to your friend M'sieu Regnier at the Iberville?'

'What are you going to do?'

Hannibal met his gaze, quite steadily, in silence for a time. Then he said, 'The obvious.'

'I swore—'

'*You* swore,' he reminded him. 'I did nothing of the kind. It's the Feast of All Saints, Benjamin,' he added with a fleet smile. 'The night when those dead and buried come back to help the living. Just convince Regnier and Quennell to help me, and locate two white witnesses, and then go home and rest: I swear I will ask nothing of you again, neither boon nor gift nor favor, for the remainder of my life. You don't have to come.'

But January knew already that he would.

TWENTY-NINE

From Martin Quennell's small office above the back parlor of the coffin shop, where twenty-five nights ago Rameses Ramilles had first lain in his coffin, the gaslit windows of the Hotel Iberville's Blue Suite had the appearance almost of the lighted proscenium arch of a stage. The night was edged with sufficient chill that the dormer window was closed; now and then a thin Halloween wind rattled the casement and breathed like a ghost on January's neck.

'How'd you manage to get 'em to take down the curtains?' asked Shaw, leaning a bony elbow against one side of the dormer and stooping his skinny height a little, for there was room only for two chairs there, which were occupied by January and the impresario John Davis. 'You'd think Uncle Diogenes would want as much coverin' for his – uh – *cribbage games* as he could get.'

'A clumsy hotel servant tripped while carrying a chamber pot,' reported January gravely. 'M'sieu Regnier denied responsibility, refused to have the alleged culprit whipped, and in general annoyed Droudge so much that the man insisted that both windows be stripped – and Uncle Diogenes has many, many places in town where he can find congenial friends and all the curtains they need.'

'Good lord, is that the fellow?' Davis leaned forward on the sill as Droudge came into the Blue Suite's parlor. 'I daresay I'd go anywhere in town, and engage in any activity whatsoever, rather than spend an evening cooped up in a hotel suite with him!'

Shaw raised his eyebrows. 'Don't tell me he been in your place?'

'Him? Scarcely.' Davis sniffed. 'No, I had the pleasure of encountering Mr Droudge at the Exchange in the Hotel St Charles last week, buying the cheapest slaves he could find and then – I'm told by Isaiah Irvin – trying to resell them the next day for a profit to the dealers.'

On the other side of the partition that divided the attic,

January heard Beauvais Quennell's soft footstep on the floorboards, the voices of the undertaker and his wife, and caught the word 'Maman' . . .

They, too, were preparing for an afternoon in the cemetery tomorrow, to honor their family's dead.

'So he's the fellow who's supposed to have killed that Irishman, is he?' inquired the impresario, as Droudge settled himself with his ledger-book at the parlor desk. In his greenish-black coat and crape cravat of mourning, his huge grizzled head bent short-sightedly down over his book, he could have been an undertaker himself. 'You'd hardly think it to look at him.'

'Oh, there ain't much doubt. He's near to my height or Benjamin's, an' for his age he ain't no weakling. I don't 'xpect Mr Derryhick thought the man was capable of murder, much less ready to do it. But that air he's got's deceptive, quiet an' cringin' . . .'

Quiet and cringing, reflected January. And, like Compair Lapin, doing what he had to do to spare himself punishment for his thefts.

Looking at the man now, January didn't wonder that the Irishman had been off his guard. He himself well knew how the contempt of others could be used as a mask . . . and a weapon in itself.

In the gaslit parlor, Droudge raised his head.

January was conscious of Shaw's glance touching him, but didn't return it. Between his own physical pain, which had grown to a heat that seemed to envelop the whole of his body, and the exhaustion of only an hour's sleep snatched after he, Shaw, and Hannibal had finished their quest for a second witness of ancestry deemed appropriate to testify before the courts of Louisiana, he had entered a state of almost dream-like exhaustion, detached as if witnessing a tragedy he was powerless to stop.

Hannibal had said, 'The obvious,' and had parted from them on the coffin shop doorstep, walking off in the direction of the Hotel Iberville alone. *Now give thy hand* . . .

January suspected Shaw had a shrewd guess at what it was he would be called on to witness, but that he was reserving both judgement and action, having dealt with blackmailers before. One part of January's tired mind knew he should stop the proceedings – should tell Shaw of the conversation in the cell and oblige the Lieutenant to take official notice. But he found himself incapable of doing so.

Droudge got to his feet and went to the door.

That he recognized Hannibal was beyond anyone's doubt. Though his back was to his audience, the shocked jerk of his head, the lifting of his hand, was a soliloquy: his glance shot right, then left, as if searching for advice, then back at his visitor. Hannibal said something, a few words only. January reflected that the words could only have been, 'Yes, it's me.'

The two men stood for a long time in the doorway before Droudge stepped back, and with a bow so unctuous it was almost fawning, gestured him in.

Guided him to a chair and, behind his back, quietly turned the key in the lock.

Saying what?

And hearing what story from Hannibal? – who was now explaining something, earnestly and urgently gesturing with his shabbily kid-gloved hands. He'd gotten another coat from somewhere – New Orleans abounded in pawnshops – and had braided his long hair back in a neat queue, tied with Nenchen's pink striped hair-ribbon. In his old-fashioned gaudy waistcoat, January could almost see in him the worthless young sprig he'd been seventeen years ago, carousing through Restoration Paris with Patrick Derryhick's 'merry band'. January remembered Paris in those days: he had been there himself, a young assistant surgeon in the night clinic at the Hôtel Dieu. Like them, he'd come to Paris to escape the world in which he'd grown up, this flat green humid land of mosquitoes and lynch ropes. Like them – like Martin Quennell and the Countess Mazzini – he'd turned his back on his mother and his sisters and the people he'd grown up with. Odd that his path had never crossed that of those young men. But in his heart he recognized them, as if he'd heard their laughing voices – and the music of a wild violin playing down the alleyways of that ancient city. Wenchers, drunkards, spendthrifts, who'd left their responsibilities behind with their families and followed their errant hearts.

Droudge bowed several times, then raised his hand, excusing himself; disappeared through a door. Hannibal folded his hands, glanced at the bare windows, through which only darkness would be visible; idly leafed through a newspaper on the desk. While Droudge had been in the room, he'd been very much his usual self, gesturing, chatting – quoting God knew what reams of classical persiflage. Alone, the stillness returned that had been on him since he'd spoken to the Viscount at noon, in that stuffy, stinking infirmary cell beneath the stairs at the Cabildo; a stillness, in a sense, that January had seen growing in him since the day of Rameses Ramilles's funeral, when he'd seen his friend's body flung before him in the cemetery mud. Stillness, and a shadow in his eyes, as if he'd known, from that instant, that it would come to this.

Droudge came back with a decanter and two glasses on a tray. He handed one to Hannibal, raised the other as if in a toast.

Exactly as Hannibal had predicted that he would.

January lit a match, moved the flame back and forth across the dark window: back and forth, back and forth. Quietly, Shaw asked, 'Where's Mayerling's room?'

'Directly above. It's the one that woman – the maid; what was her name? – was sitting in when she heard the shouting down below on the night of the murder.'

Shaw moved his head a little to glance up at that dark window, but returned his attention at once to the Blue Suite, where Hannibal, still holding his glass as if he'd forgotten it, was explaining something else, at great length, to Droudge.

'You sure about this, Maestro? Even given that Droudge tommyhawked that Irishman – an' given he knows Sefton was Derryhick's pal – that still don't mean he'd put hisself in a false position with the trial next week. If he's the man what switched out them sheets an' set the room to look like the boy done the murder, he's smarter than that. What could Sefton know that's worth the risk?'

Droudge and Hannibal both turned their heads – Augustus Mayerling must have run down the service stair the moment he saw the signal. Like Davis and Shaw, the swordsmaster had asked no questions about the part he'd been asked to play that night: in times past, Hannibal had assisted him with keeping a secret of his own.

Droudge answered the door. The moment his back was turned, Hannibal switched the wine glasses, then settled himself back in the chair as Mayerling asked whatever question he had invented for the occasion. Droudge kept his body in the aperture of the door so that the swordsmaster was unable to see that there was another man in the parlor; snapped an irritated reply; shut the door in Mayerling's face. Then he came back to the table, raised the wine glass, and drank.

Without change of expression, Hannibal followed suite.

It was now Droudge's turn to explain at length. Gesturing with his long arms, pointing to the ledger on the table. Grave-faced, shaking his head. Hannibal nodded, put in an objection, which the business manager seemed perfectly willing to elaborate upon. Stalling for time, as Shaw had done when first he and January had encountered the traveling Englishmen in those very rooms. This Hannibal had also said he would do.

Droudge rose, walked to the window, and looked out, across at the dark coffin shop—

Calculating the location of Quennell's handcart again? Making sure the windows of the little cottage were dark?

Droudge was still standing at the window when he shuddered, exactly as if someone had knifed him in the gut, though no one stood near. He caught at the window frame, half doubled-over . . .

And looked back over his shoulder in shock at Hannibal sitting quietly at the table, the empty wine glass in his hands and nothing in his eyes. Droudge staggered, groped for the bell on the table, which Hannibal moved unhurriedly out of the way. Droudge flung out his hands, moved his head drunkenly back and forth—

'Fuck me!' said Shaw and sprang to his feet.

'Go,' said January – and, indeed, the Lieutenant was halfway to the door. Davis, on his heels, turned back as January got to his feet and staggered, catching the back of his chair as a wave of renewed agony shot through his leg. 'I'll be there in—'

Davis came back to him, offered a shoulder to lean on. He whispered, 'Dear God,' shocked horror in his voice. 'He must have been trying to poison Sefton – dear God! But why? And how did Sefton know?'

'He didn't,' lied January, as Shaw's boots clattered down the stairs. 'He knew Droudge, and he had his suspicions—'

'But for God's sake, why? Sefton's the most harmless man on the face of the earth.'

January only shook his head. As Davis was helping him toward the door, he glanced back over his shoulder, in time to see Hannibal open the desk drawer, remove an envelope, and read its contents. Then he went to the gas jet on the wall to touch a corner of that single sheet of paper to the flame, and he held it between thumb and forefinger to watch it burn.

Droudge was dead by the time January reached the hotel room.

THIRTY

Hannibal stayed sober long enough to swear an affidavit as to the events of the evening: that he'd gone to Caius Droudge's room because he had been a friend of Patrick Derryhick, recently deceased; that he'd never trusted Droudge, who had hated him on account of words that had passed between them eighteen years ago when he'd accused the man of cheating on the account books of Viscount Foxford, the father of his friend, the Honorable Alexander Stuart, whose son – the current Viscount – had come down suspiciously ill in the Cabildo after receiving food there from Droudge two days before. No, he'd had no reason to suspect that the wine was poisoned. He simply hadn't trusted anything the man had touched and had just been making sure.

Did 'just making sure' include arranging for observation by two witnesses? inquired Captain Tremouille of the City Guards, present at the questioning and not pleased at having been called from dinner with his wife's cousins back to the Cabildo to hear the details of yet another foreigner perishing in the Blue Suite of the Iberville Hotel.

'If the bastard poisoned me, I wanted to make sure he swung for it,' Hannibal replied.

The affidavit given, he disappeared, presumably – reflected January – to get drunk and remain drunk until the Viscount Foxford was tried, acquitted, married, and had left town with his bride.

January feared that the bullet graze on his leg would turn feverish and prevent him, after all, from going with his family to the cemetery on the following day. But after ten or eleven hours' sleep ('Don't expect me to fetch you your breakfast, M'sieu, since you seem perfectly willing to run about at all hours on your feet,' had said Rose), he had woken feeling much better. After examining the wound and changing the dressing, he had taken up his stick and limped the three-quarters of a mile to the cemetery, assisted by various of his neighbors who had returned to their houses in quest of trowels or lemonade or napkins or parasols forgotten earlier in the day. With the change to autumn weather the ground had dried, and wherever there was a little clear space among the tombs, families had set up their picnic blankets and opened wicker baskets. Friends and neighbors greeted him with pleasure and pointed out where his mother and Dominique could be found, and where Rose was, over near the FTFCMBS tomb in the section of the cemetery reserved to the *gens du couleur*, presiding over a basket of ginger beer.

Men climbed ladders to daub whitewash on rain-faded plaster; women set out gourds of jambalaya and 'dirty rice'. Older children dug industriously at the tufts of resurrection-fern that had sprouted between the soft bricks of the tombs; younger ones played hide-and-seek, their squeals of laughter a comfort to the dead – a reminder that life does go on. Old Auntie Zozo had brought her coffee urn; *marchandes* walked about selling flowers wrought of jet beads and wire – *immortelles* – to leave in the vases that decorated the tombs. Somewhere, someone was playing a guitar.

The summer heat was gone. With the sadness of autumn, the air held a cool freshness. It was generally around the time of this commemoration of the dead that New Orleans came back to life: the day when the different sides of families – French Creole, African Creole, Spanish Creole – met in their common task and remembered that blood is indeed thicker than the water of shed tears.

The day – as Hannibal had said – that those dead and buried were thought to come back and assist the ones they loved.

'Benjamin, *p'tit*, are you sure you should be on your feet?' Dominique rustled over to him in a delicious frou-frou of yellow batiste.

'Of course he's sure,' retorted Rose, belying the dryness of her tone by bringing up a bench for him into the shade of the Society tomb. 'He's certain, if he falls over in a faint, someone can be found to drag him home.'

He mimed a kiss at her. Serious-faced young Alice Truxton, the only one of the schoolgirls who'd remained by the little trestle table set out nearby, brought him over callas, on a bit of newspaper, and a bottle of lemonade. Rose returned his kiss with her quicksilver smile. The girl Alice still looked like she was working to avoid touching anything Catholic, but January had to grin inwardly as she stared around her at the children playing tag among the tombs, at the bright-colored tignons of the women worked up into elaborate points, at old Aunt Titine the gumbo lady, at the men singing out calls and responses from tomb to tomb as they worked.

The *libres* occupied only a corner of the St Louis Cemetery, and throughout the rest of that maze of dead-houses, the Creole French and Creole Spanish – of pure blood, though sometimes six generations removed from European soil – set out picnics of their own. The hard chill had laid much of the graveyard stink to rest, and what was left of it was masked by the smell of charcoal braziers keeping warm pots of jambalaya and plates of meat pies, and by the odors of coffee and pralines and oysters. Rose and the Widow Levesque turned with exclamations of delight to greet the sisters and brother-in-law of St-Denis Janvier, and they brought them over to say hello to January where he sat in the shade. 'All you need is a scepter and a crown, Ben,' joked one of Rose's white uncles, burlesquing a deep bow to him, and January drew himself up with kinglike mien.

'Darling!' he heard the voice of Chlöe Viellard – the white wife of Dominique's protector – and shook his head as the two women embraced. '*Please* tell me you made your wonderful beignets, *cher* . . .' Her husband's tiny octoroon daughter toddled over to grip M'am Chlöe's skirt. 'Henri's gone off to vote – for Daniel Webster of all people . . .'

It was Election Day. In-between their work of cleaning the tombs in their own section of the cemetery, the white men were coming and going, casting their votes at the Cabildo and coming back smelling of free Democratic Party rum.

'White folks,' sniffed January's mother, cocking a disapproving eye at him. 'He goes off and takes care of this *white* Lordship's troubles, but after all this, does he find the man that snatched poor Rameses Ramilles's body?'

'In fact, I did, Maman,' retorted January. 'The man committed suicide last night, and good riddance to him. So there.'

'Well,' said his mother, 'you didn't bring the man to justice, now, did you?'

January sighed. 'No, Maman.' He knew better than to try

to win any argument with his mother. 'I fear you have raised a failure for a son.'

She patted his cheek and smiled, then went back to question the white side of the family about the safest investments in the upcoming year. In time, January got to his feet, and with the aid of his stick and his nephew Gabriel, limped to the tomb of Crowdie Passebon's *libre* grandfather, where Liselle Ramilles's children were playing and Madame Glasson – still draped in deepest mourning – was telling everyone how much she had suffered in the past month. 'Far too much to even *think* about bringing my pralines, dearest, and besides I only have the strength to stay for just a moment . . .' On her knee she held a plate piled with food sufficient to feed an army.

Across the way stood the FTFCMBS tomb, where Rameses Ramilles slept in his appointed narrow bed. Liselle herself, her skirt tucked up to her knees, was on a ladder, polishing the brass flower-holders before some other musician's little resting place.

'I don't know how Liselle does it.' Liselle's mother shook her head. 'She simply does not have my sensitivity . . .'

Down another aisle, among all those close-set brick houses of mortality, January glimpsed Beauvais Quennell, quietly painting whitewash on to a modest new bench of bricks, before which his mother – in mourning almost as profound as Madame Glasson's – knelt in prayer.

Like it or not, Martin Quennell had come back to the French Town at last.

On Thursday, January's leg was well enough to allow him to limp upstairs to the courtroom on the second floor of the old Presbytery building, and sit in the gallery – blacks not being permitted to testify – to watch Germanicus Stuart, Viscount Foxford, acquitted of the crime of murdering Patrick Derryhick. Judge Canonge – hook-nosed, grim-faced, and renowned through French Louisiana for his probity – admitted the evidence of Celestine Deschamps that her daughter Isobel, and her daughter's maid, had been with His Lordship from eleven on the night of the sixth until almost two thirty in the morning.

January glanced across at Pierrette, seated a little apart from the other Deschamps house servants; at a guess, the judge had spoken to her in his office and had accepted her testimony. The state prosecutor did not inquire whether this meeting had taken place in the Deschamps parlor or in a doorway across the street, or whether Madame Deschamps had been awake at that hour. She was white, and that was what mattered.

Lieutenant Abishag Shaw of the New Orleans City Guard testified to the fact that evidence existed consistent with the murder having been done by Caius Droudge, the dead man's traveling companion, who had poisoned himself in the Hotel Iberville on the night of the thirty-first . . . large quantities of arsenic, antimony, and powdered oleander having been found in the false bottom of his strongbox.

'My God, I can't believe it!' gasped Foxford an hour later, breaking away from the congratulatory crowd outside the courtroom door to grasp January's hand. He still looked ill, and shaky on his feet, and had visibly lost at least twenty pounds. His handsome face had been stripped of the beauty of being fortune's favorite, but his eyes were radiant. An adult man's, and not a god's. 'Madame –' he bowed slightly toward Celestine Deschamps, who was deep in conversation with the British consul – 'tells me she's written Isobel . . . that Isobel will be here by the tenth . . .'

'Got to marry her out of hand, m'boy,' beamed Uncle Diogenes, clapping a hand on his nephew's broad shoulder. 'Have a dreadful journey home if you let it go till the end of the month. I'll barely be able to swallow the wedding cake myself before rushing off to catch my ship.'

'You'll be returning to India, then, sir?' inquired January politely, and the elderly diplomat nodded.

'Lord, yes. Gets into your blood, the East – though, mind you,' he added, with a glance across the hall at the slim young gentleman with oiled lovelocks who stood next to 'Jones', his stone-faced valet, 'I would not have missed the journey for worlds. Not for worlds. Gerry, dear boy, I wanted to ask you if you might possibly advance me a little on my next quarter's stipend, to ship some of the books I've bought . . .'

'I can't thank you enough, sir.' Foxford pressed January's hand again. 'You'll come to the wedding, surely? You and Mr Sefton – and, of course, your lovely wife.'

Pierrette came up then, in the company of a girl of fifteen

or so, dark-haired and rather shy in fanciful billows of ribbon and ruffles, who had to be the younger sister, Marie-Amalie. Her sea-blue eyes, and the shape of her cheekbones, were an echo of Cadmus Rablé.

'Going to be a bang-up affair,' approved Uncle Diogenes, wicked dark eyes sparkling in pouches of fat. 'Terrible shame about Derryhick, of course – and what a shocking affair that was, old Droudge popping off that way! – but, I must say, I'm glad Elodie's money came back to the family in the end. Derryhick did the right thing there. Gerry's taking him back home for burial, you know . . . as I suppose I'll go home one day, what's left of me, in a box . . . *Noctes atque dies patet atri ianua Ditis* . . . But damme, boy, you're going to have to get a new rig if you're to be wed before you've fattened up a trifle. Like a damned scarecrow. That poor girl won't know you.'

'I think, M'sieu,' smiled Marie-Amalie, 'that Isobel would know His Lordship anywhere.' Foxford smiled too, and he brushed self-consciously at the fine-cut English coat that lay so baggy on his frame – in a way, January realized, that reminded him strongly of Hannibal.

The wedding was on the twelfth of November, with Louis Verron's father giving the bride away, and Uncle Diogenes – accompanied by 'Jones' and his slender young new friend – sailed for India on the fourteenth. On the sixteenth, after the first rehearsal for *The Elixir of Love*, January went down to the now-teeming levee to see off the Viscount, the new Viscountess, her sister, the Viscount's valet Mr Reeve, and Pierrette. Looking at that radiant young woman, standing by the rail, he wondered if Isobel, Lady Foxford, would dream of Louisiana. When the strong Mississippi current carried the *York and Lancaster* downriver, toward Balize and the sea, he turned his steps inland and made his way, through streets bustling with commerce and vice, back toward the Swamp.

Enquiries discreetly pursued at the back doors of various establishments – the Broadhorn, the Rough 'n' Ready, the Blackleg, the Turkey Buzzard – eventually brought him to Kate the Gouger's bathhouse, where Kate greeted January with, 'Thank God somebody finally come for him.'

January carried Hannibal back to the Broadhorn over his shoulder and put him to bed.

When he came back the following morning, Hannibal – greenish, haggard, unshaven and comprehensively sick – greeted him with, 'Are they gone?'

'You mean Gerry and Isobel?'

Hannibal nodded. His hand trembled a little as he reached for the black bottle on the floor next to his bed – by the smell of it, his favored concoction of opium and sherry – but he closed his fist on itself and let it be.

'They're gone.' January set down Hannibal's boots – which he'd collected from Kate's on the way – and an earthenware jug of Auntie Zozo's coffee, the steam of it drifting in the attic's freezing dimness. 'Gerry asked after you – asked if you would come to the wedding.'

Hannibal breathed out a short bitter laugh. 'Wouldn't *that* be a sight to behold? Enough to send the poor girl dashing back to Natchitoches—'

January said, 'She wouldn't have to know.'

Hannibal started to reply, then didn't. Sat for a time on the crumpled and sheetless mattress, meeting January's gaze.

In time, he sighed and asked, 'When did you guess?'

'I think when you wouldn't go to Natchitoches with me,' said January. He found a couple of cups that were more or less clean, filled and handed one to his friend. 'But it didn't surprise me. I didn't know for certain until Droudge tried to poison you – something he had no reason to do, if you were just one of Patrick's old friends. The boy doesn't look like you at all.'

'No, thank God.' Hannibal sipped from his cup, then held his hand over it to warm in the steam. 'He takes after Philippa's family – the lot of them must be descended from angels . . . God knows they act as if they've got pedigrees back to Eden. I couldn't—' He fell silent again. Then, 'I'm glad Patrick looked after him.' He passed his hand across his face, as if to wipe away the mold of years, and took another gingerly sip. 'He said he would.'

'Did he arrange to identify your "body"?'

The fiddler nodded. 'As you've probably deduced, I wasn't nearly as drunk as I seemed to be when I pitched off the Pont Neuf that night. Patrick went down earlier in the day and made sure there was a boat nearby. The current's very strong there where it goes under the bridge.'

January said, 'I know.' That was where he'd thrown the trunk containing his wife's clothing – his first wife, the beautiful Ayasha – after her death of the cholera. In dreams he often stood by that rail, looking down at the moonlit water sweeping past.

'I wanted to leave her a note,' said Hannibal. 'To tell her I was sorry – to let her know how much I loved her. But, as she'd told me, my actions weren't the acts of love. Nor, I suppose, would they have been, even if I'd known any way in God's green world to stop. I knew before long she'd start hating me, and I didn't – I couldn't stand the thought of it. I don't suppose Gerry spoke to you – mentioned to you – if she had remarried?'

'It doesn't sound as if she has,' said January. 'That must have been a hideous shock for Droudge, to have you turn up on his doorstep like that.'

'Oh, yes,' agreed Hannibal softly. 'Because it meant, you see, that neither Gerry nor Uncle Diogenes had any legal control of the Foxford estate at all. That it was legally mine – still is, as a matter of fact. A terrifying thought.'

January bowed elaborately to him, and Hannibal hit him with the pillow.

'I told him I'd just returned to New Orleans from Mexico, so he didn't think I had the slightest interest in whether the Deschamps family was ruined or not. His one thought was to get me out of the way before I showed myself to Uncle Diogenes and demanded an accounting of where all that money's been bleeding away to. Cousin Stubbs was right, by the way – he always did skim, and he had ways of making money out of the tenants that my father never knew about. I think the fact that Droudge used a knife during a quarrel was only happenstance. That arsenic was in his strongbox for a reason.'

January nodded, understanding. 'And, as you pointed out to Shaw, all the evidence concerning motive was thousands of miles away.'

'More than that, there was no one – except Patrick, probably – who would even think to look for it. And me, of course.' The corner of his mouth twitched. 'Will Philippa like Miss

Isobel, do you think? Will she make a good mistress for Foxford Priory?'

'She was raised on a plantation,' said January, 'so she'll know what's entailed in running a property that size. And I should imagine that with Droudge gone – and control of the property legally in Foxford's hands – things will be easier there.'

'Not to speak of all Aunt Elodie's shekels. I always knew Philippa would be a better custodian of Foxford Priory than an opium-swilling fiddle player; I'm glad Gerry seems to have inherited that. Sometimes—' He broke off again and sat for a time gazing through the open doorway, out over the flat green monotony of the Swamp and the glitter of standing water, toward the low roofs of the town.

'He had a great deal more feeling than most people guessed,' he had said of himself, about the Foxford acres: the green and misty Irish meadows that he would never see again. In Paris, though January had sworn when he left Louisiana in 1817 that he never would come back, he had often dreamed of New Orleans, and the dreams had never been of white men with ropes, or of Presidential Elections in which he was allowed no say.

White egrets in gray river mist. The burnt-sugar smell of December fog. African drumbeats and the roar of cicadas, and men and women dancing in Congo Square.

Friends gathered together, in his mother's pink house on Rue Burgundy, with the French doors thrown open to the street in cooling twilight.

Like poor Martin Quennell, he'd been willing to walk away from it all, in order to live as a free man.

And fate had led him back.

January put a hand on his friend's shoulder. 'Get dressed,' he said. 'Wash your hair. There's a rehearsal for the opera tonight, and Davis is saving a place for you. Anyway, it's time you met the young ladies you'll be tutoring in history and Greek this winter. Will you stay to dinner? Rose has been asking after you.'

Hannibal sighed and got to his feet, pale in his ragged night-shirt like a corpse climbing forth from a dishonored grave. '*Facilis descensus Averno*,' he said, unconsciously providing the rest of the passage of Virgil that Uncle Diogenes had spoken, to reflect upon the path into Hell – and out of it again. '*Sed revocare gradum superasque evadere ad auras, hoc opus* . . .'

'*Hoc opus*,' agreed January. '*To return to the light and air*, that is indeed the work. And after the rehearsal, if Rose's young ladies can spare us, we'll go to a grocery I know somewhere upriver of Canal Street. There's music there I think you need to hear.'

AUTHOR'S NOTE

It is not the purpose of this novel to explore the origins and ramifications – political, social, and psychological – of race-based chattel slavery in the United States, nor the entangled and tragic system of prejudice and laws that made up the 'one-drop rule'. Suffice it to say that as late as 1985, a Louisiana woman was denied a passport application because she had checked 'white' on the form – having been raised to believe herself of 100% Caucasian extraction – when her birth certificate listed one of her parents as 'black', which in Louisiana at that time could mean having as little as 1/64th African ancestry. Blue-eyed blondes with characteristically African features are a commonplace in many areas of Louisiana and elsewhere in the South, and given the severe social limitations placed on blacks up through most of the Twentieth Century, it is hardly surprising that many light-complected African Americans chose to leave their communities, go North or West, and 'pass' if they could.

Common also in the records of the South are cases of children, adopted by white parents, who were later 'outed' as being of such distant and negligible African descent as to be completely indistinguishable from their adoptive families – and who lost jobs, families, and in many instances, civil rights thereby.

Similar cases existed prior to the Civil War, and the social consequences, at that time, were horrific – not the least of which being that if one of the unfortunate *passe blanc's* parents could be proved to be a slave, he or she would lose not only social position, but liberty as well. (Three of Thomas Jefferson's reputed children by the slave Sally Hemings – herself a fair-complected 'quadroon' – were said to have slipped invisibly into white society: something that was easier in the 1790s than in the 1830s.)

Moreover, to literally add insult to injury, most of the *gens du couleur libre* – the free colored of New Orleans – appear to have identified with, and sided with, the whites who had money and power, and to have distanced themselves as far as possible from the darker-skinned blacks, slave or free, who came into New Orleans with the Americans in the 1820s and '30s. This tendency did not end with the Civil War, though the genres of music purely native to America – ragtime and jazz – are a combination of the greater Classical training of 'downtown' black musicians with the stronger African musical traditions that had not been erased from the less-snobbish 'uptown' players.

In all these matters and all others, I have tried, as always, firstly to entertain.